MORAL

— A NOVEL —

FRACTURES

MORAL

— A NOVEL —

FRACTURES

R. J. WILLIAMS

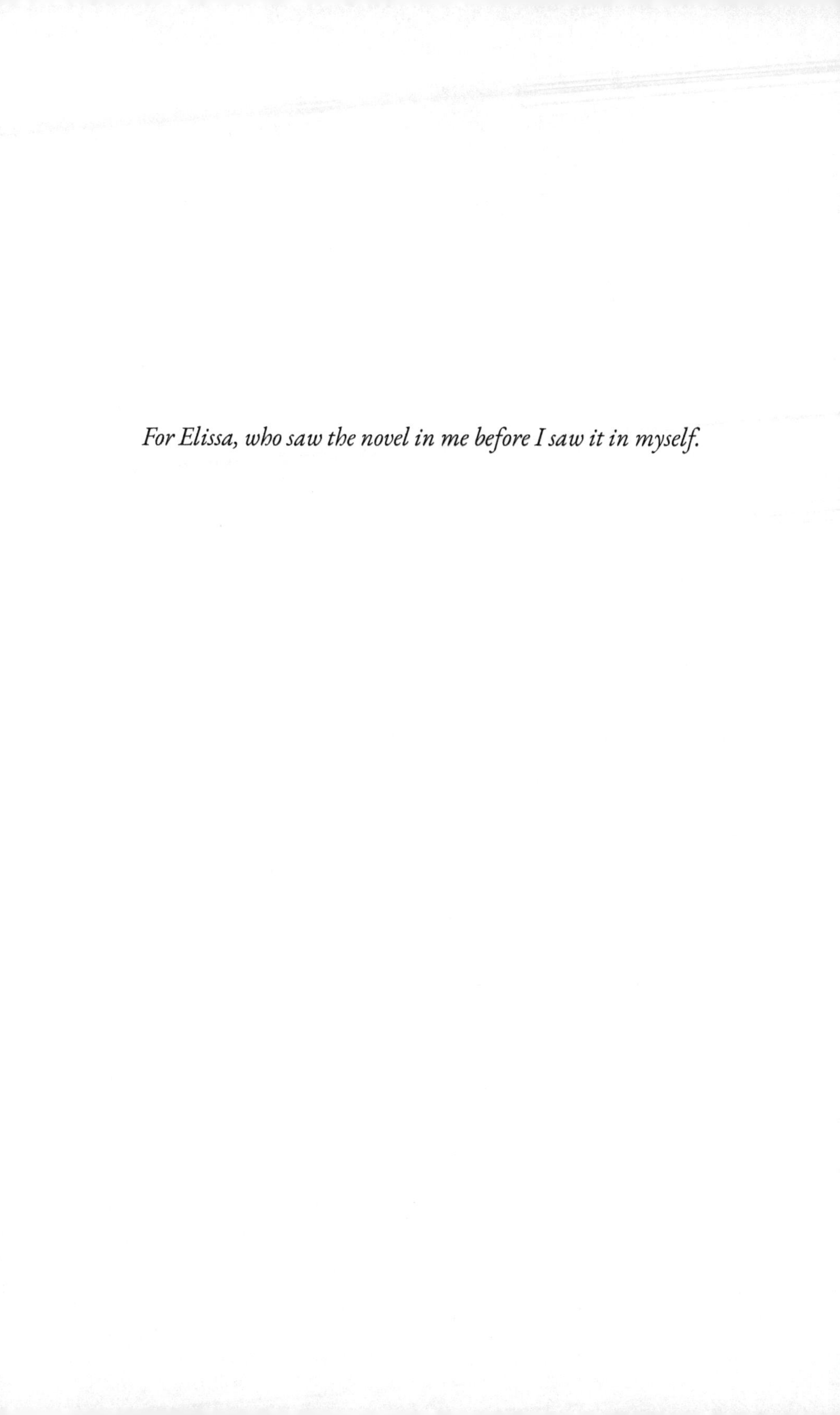

For Elissa, who saw the novel in me before I saw it in myself.

CONTENTS

PROLOGUE

Memo

To: Chief Juan Huertas
From: Roberta Macher, Commander – Professional Standards Bureau
Cc: File
Date: 21 August
Re: Detective Candidate Vincent Brown

As per department policy, a limited background investigation was conducted on the candidate mentioned above for promotion to the rank of detective.

The candidate is currently #1 in all phases of the testing process.

The candidate's HR file shows that since his hiring date, he has not used one sick day. His PTO has accumulated to a level where he has been offered to leave shifts early to use his time before it expired. The candidate has not reported any additional higher education achievements since his date of hire. He currently holds a Bachelor of Psychology degree and a Master of Philosophy in Ethics degree.

The candidate has received fourteen letters of commendation, four distinguished service awards, and one life-saving medal. The candidate was detached for six months to the state's Juvenile Crime Task Force, where he worked in the cities of Newark, Trenton, and Camden.

The candidate is a certified police instructor and teaches the Ethics block of instruction at the academy. He has also been a guest speaker at area colleges and community panel discussions on police ethics and community relations.

The candidate's peers were interviewed. They describe him as being dedicated and professional. A common reply to questions about him was that he is "by the book." Members of his current patrol squad stated the candidate is the one officer they would want to back them up if things "went sideways." They also stated the candidate would be the last cop they would want to stop a member of their family—he would write them up just as quickly as he would someone he didn't know.

The candidate's squad supervisors (both current and former) were interviewed. A universal concern they have is the candidate's inability to conform to the needs of the squad—his rigid black-and-white thinking makes him appear aloof. Although he is trusted to "be there" for the other members of his squad, his peers do not trust him enough to share personal information with him.

The candidate's personal biographical information has not changed since his date of hire.

Family members: Michael Brown (father) and Audrey Brown (sister).

As is known by command level staff of this agency, the candidate's father is the district attorney of Atlantic County. It is also widely known throughout the agency that his sister has been arrested by this department and is currently on probation. This investigation did not find any significant issues with these family members affecting his job performance.

As per policy, the candidate was not interviewed in this investigation.

Based on the totality of information collected in this investigation, it is recommended that the candidate move forward in the promotional process for the rank of detective.

Respectfully submitted,
LT B.M.

PART 1

CHAPTER 1

UNHOLY NIGHT

Anyone who has ever lived has felt this way at least once... there were a million places Vince Brown would rather be.

Even the nostalgic scent of incense couldn't mask his unease as he sat wedged between his dad and his sister in the crowded church. The polished wooden pew felt harder tonight. Maybe he wasn't supposed to feel comfortable sitting there. Maybe he didn't deserve to.

There was a time when the ritual of Christmas Eve Mass at the Rytis Eparchy of the Sea Church felt welcoming—when it steadied him from the chaos of the outside world. Believers who wore their faith on their sleeves lifted their voices in unison, joining the choir in each carol that was sung. Tonight, he felt like an imposter who wore a badge.

The confessional booth caught his peripheral vision. Last week's words of contrition weren't a sacred, solemn plea for forgiveness. They were nothing more than a rehearsed performance to please his dad. He went through the motions so he could receive communion tonight. Now he wished he had found a way to call out sick from this charade.

And then, there was Audrey, his sister.

One didn't need to be a cop to catch how she was eyeing him up and down. He very rarely saw her, and up until a little over a year ago, whenever he did see her, he was wearing a uniform.

She tucked a wayward strand of autumn-colored hair behind her ear, a nervous habit that remained from childhood. "Daddy's boy is dressed up. Kind of. Why didn't you wear one of your expensive detective suits?"

Vince had promised himself he wouldn't take the bait tonight. Not at church. Her comment forced him to remind himself of that promise. Especially now—the beginning of the Liturgy of the Eucharist. "I'm more comfortable in business casual," he answered, looking straight ahead.

"Business casual or not, couldn't you at least have worn socks?"

Michael, Vince's dad, looked down at his feet. "How many times have I told you? You have to wear socks with dress shoes. It's disrespectful. Especially tonight."

Vince's promise to himself didn't make it past Holy Communion.

"I'll start wearing socks with dress shoes when she starts wearing a bra to church. Jesus Christ, talk about being disrespectful!"

"Hey, it's the most wonderful time of the year to be perky," Audrey announced proudly. "And I'm feeling perky. Besides... I think the men in the choir like it."

"Audrey," Michael's words cut in. "That's enough. Put your sweater on."

Monsignor Augustas peered over the chalice. Their little family "talk" caught the attention of more than just the neighboring congregants. Vince looked down, drilling a hole into the back of the pew before them with his eyes. The monsignor was a well-respected and beloved priest whose larger-than-life personality matched his build. His stare from the altar made Vince more uncomfortable than when the service started.

When Vince finally summoned the courage to look up again, his eyes met the monsignor's. "Let us proclaim the mystery of faith..."

Is he talking directly to me? Vince's inner voice wondered.

The monsignor didn't change his glare at Vince as the response was given. "... Christ will come again."

Holy shit. He is talking directly to me!

On this very special day in the Church calendar, decades of religious guilt had just delivered a blessed gift of fear, wrapped in confusion, for Vince.

He looked down, his hands making tight fists. He looked up; the half-closed eyes of the dying (or dead, depending on your beliefs) Jesus hanging on the cross were filling him with shame. He looked around. The confessional booth's door signaled the betrayal he felt deep in his soul.

When it was time to go up and accept the leavened host, he made his way to the opposite side of the altar from where the monsignor was giving communion. Seeing Father Frank's smiling face and receiving communion from him would help ease his guilt. At least they could talk about it on Monday over coffee.

The older members of the congregation still whispered about how young their second-in-command priest looked. His fresh face, they say, is better suited to a college campus than their historic cathedral. But when he spoke, his quiet authority quieted their doubts.

Vince didn't remember anything said in Mass after receiving communion. He couldn't. His mind was racing in circles. The loving monsignor's looks could be, and often were, described as intimidating. *Why does he keep looking at me like that?*

When the service ended, Monsignor Augustas stood at the door, his broad frame filling the doorway. If he did a quick costume change, one would swear it was Santa himself at the door. He greeted each parishioner with a practiced warmth—the kind you come to expect of a shepherd tending his flock.

Elderly women clasped the priest's hands in both of theirs, children giggled at his grandfatherly winks, and men straightened their postures just a bit as they stood in front of him. It all reminded Vince of the time a colleague described a reporter as the kind of guy who could sell snow cones to Eskimos in the middle of winter.

The line inched forward, his dad acting as a buffer between him and Audrey. Michael Brown, the years in the DA's office had left their mark in the silver of his hair and the lines of his smile. Still seen as the most eligible bachelor in Atlantic County, the idealistic prosecutor was also a champion of mediation.

Vince made plans to turn to the side and move right past the monsignor on the way out. But his long arm and thick hand stopped Vince.

"Vincent!" The priest's voice held just a hint of genuine pleasure, like a father recognizing a prodigal son. "It is so nice to see you. And here with your family... all of you together tonight. Such a blessing, isn't it?" He clasped Vince's hand in both of his—warm and firm. But to Vince, it reminded him of a salesman's handshake when they want you to trust them.

Vince nodded. "It's nice to see you, Monsignor."

"You know, seeing young professionals like yourself at Mass..." The monsignor's eyes showed gentle humor. "I hope to see you in church more than twice a year from now on."

The statement held just enough pastoral concern to be charming. Still, something in those twinkling eyes made the collar of Vince's sweater feel tight. He forced a smile. "Merry Christmas."

"Be well, my child. May your faith be your strength. Merry Christmas."

Stepping out into the cold December air, Vince pulled the top of his coat up to his ears. He told himself the unease in his stomach was just guilt about his rare church attendance.

Behind him, he could hear the monsignor's hearty laugh, teasing Audrey about needing an extra prayer or two. This gave smiles to the line of parishioners—everyone knew of Audrey's spirited nature, and everyone knew how the monsignor's gentle guidance and compassion had given her a second chance to turn around her life.

That was the thing about Monsignor Augustas—he had a way of making everyone feel simultaneously special and somehow lacking. It was a gift, people said. A true pastor's touch.

But it was a touch that held more questions than answers for Vince.

CHAPTER 2
SIDEWAYS CONFESSIONS

Vince's breath clouded the icy air as his father's car disappeared into the night. He should go home, too. A bottle of the finest non-alcoholic wine and a woodstove that was ready to be fired up awaited him there.

Instead, he found himself staring up at the illuminated windows of the old church rectory. The monsignor had that wing of the church building converted into rooms for those trying to get back on their feet. One of those rooms was Audrey's. He'd made room for her last year as part of her promise to the court to stay out of trouble after being sentenced to probation. She was completing her twelve hundred hours of community service doing custodial work at the church.

He shouldn't go up. He hadn't been to her room since the monsignor offered it to her. But what if she could help him understand why the monsignor was staring at him at Mass? She'd been working for the church—for the monsignor—for more than a year now; maybe she could help him understand why he felt the way he did.

He rationalized that just because your sister is a train wreck doesn't mean you can't talk to her like a human one day a year. Especially on this day.

The narrow, unheated stairs held the mustiness of decades of neglect. Vince hesitated at Audrey's door, where a hand-lettered sign read "Halfway to Heaven" in flowing writing. Below it someone had scrawled "or Hell" with what looked like a ballpoint pen.

Audrey's room was exactly as he expected—organized chaos. Half-finished paintings propped against walls, sketches of horses tacked everywhere. The scent of oils and acrylics couldn't mask the underlying mustiness of the old church building. Even here, he couldn't escape that churchy smell.

"A Christmas miracle!" Her voice was a mix of sarcasm and surprise. "What's my baby brother doing here?"

Vince noticed the shadows beneath her eyes had deepened since he'd last seen her, making the striking color of her eyes seem almost too bright, too alert—like someone running on nothing but coffee and determination. "Yeah, I know. It's been a while..."

"A while? You didn't even have the decency to come to my sentencing hearing!" Her tone and volume shifted. "Maybe if you testified as a character witness, I would've gotten fewer hours. But Vince Brown had to follow department policy and not offer to testify—only if he was subpoenaed."

"Audrey, look... I don't want to rehash all that. Not tonight. Please?"

"Well, take a look around. I'm here because you—"

"You're here because you planted a device in your ex's car and recorded his conversations. Jesus Christ, you're lucky you weren't charged under the federal wiretap laws."

"Lucky?" She bit down hard on the cough drop in her mouth; the crackling sound of it bounced off the easel. "All I wanted was the truth, Vince. He was cheating on me, lying to my face, and making me feel crazy for suspecting anything... Sometimes you have to break the rules to get to the truth. What's wrong with that?"

"Wrong? I work with him. The whole fucking thing was wrong!"

"You still only see things in black and white. There's only right or wrong, good or bad for you. And ever since you became the po-po, it's either good guys or bad guys. You never grew up, did you?"

Vince walked the fourteen feet to the other side of her living accommodations. "Can we *please* not do this? I came up here hoping... hoping you could help me."

Audrey cocked her head like a dog looking at a new toy. Confused, yet ready to play. "You want *my* help? This I gotta hear."

"First, there *is* only right or wrong... And I need to know if you saw how the monsignor looked at me during Mass?"

"He was looking at everyone," she replied.

"Maybe, but he was staring me down. It freaked me out."

Audrey shrugged her shoulders and smiled. "Maybe he heard that you have doubts... that you aren't sure what to believe anymore." She looked out the one window in her room. "I mean, if I were the head priest, I'd want to know why an agnostic was taking communion at my church."

The floor seemed to move under Vince's feet. "How did you—"

"What was it again?" Her voice took on a mocking tone. "Oh right. 'Father, I'm having doubts. I'm not sure I believe anymore.'"

"That's impossible. You couldn't know that."

"Vince, priests aren't the only ones who can hear confessions." She turned back to face him.

"You were eavesdropping?" His voice dropped to a whisper. "In the confessional?"

"Oh, I hear all kinds of things." She reached for a paintbrush. "Better than Netflix, really."

"What the fuck, Audrey?" he said, standing between her and the canvas. "After what happened with Kevin's car—"

"Don't!" She returned Vince's angry tone. "Don't you dare throw that in my face. Not after you decided to abandon me when I needed you. Christ, even Dad said your testimony would have helped."

Vince leaned against the small refrigerator that stuck out into the living space. Looking at his feet didn't take away the guilt inside.

"You know what hurt most? Not that I got caught—but that my own brother couldn't bother to show up when I needed him the most."

"I followed department SOP. There's no gray area in the rules, Audrey."

"No gray area in the rules?" She pointed around the room with her brush. "Then why didn't you stop Dad from pulling strings to keep me from going to prison? Seems pretty gray to me!"

Vince turned to the painting on the easel. A chestnut roan horse. The same horse in all the paintings around her room. "Still that same damn horse." He gestured at the paintings. "What is it with you and this one specific horse? It's like you're obsessed."

"Don't change the subject."

"I'm not. I'm pointing out that you're stuck, Audrey. Stuck in the same patterns, back to making the same mistakes—"

"At least I'm not stuck in a binary world where everything has to fit in your neat little boxes." She set down her brush and smiled. "Wanna hear some juicy stuff from last week's confessions? Oh, the things people tell priests."

"This isn't a game, Audrey! These are people's private moments, their—"

"Their what...? Their sins?" She laughed hard. "The world's not as clean as you want it to be, Vince. Sometimes you have to get your hands dirty to learn the truth. Tell me you don't work with detectives who get dirty to catch the bad guys?"

"There are rules—"

"Rules?" She threw up her hands. "If rules are so important, then why do your precious rules let guilty people—like me—walk free every day? As long as your conscience stays clean, right?"

Vince turned to leave.

She followed him into the hallway. "I've got a whole list of confessions when you're ready to live in the real world and have some fun!"

The door slammed behind him. As usual, she was wrong about so many things. But her worst mistake? Thinking his conscience was clean. That was one shade of gray he'd never admit to anyone.

CHAPTER 3
DATA AND DOUBT

The winter gusts whipping off the Atlantic carried the steam from two piping hot coffee cups. As the rising sun cast its golden blanket across the deserted boardwalk, Vince sat alone at a frigid table outside Elissa's Coffee Shop, waiting.

Father Frank's shadow fell across the table. "Are you crazy? It's too friggin' cold to be out here this morning. C'mon, let's go inside and get warm."

"I thought we'd get some fresh air this morning. Isn't it you who always says there's nothing like fresh air to cure what ails you?"

Frank chuckled, pulling the zipper of his coat as high as it would go. "Sure, but I meant April through October, not when the wind chill is in the teens."

Vince's hands shivered as he held the cup, trying to absorb from it whatever warmth he could. He couldn't argue with Frank's reasoning, but this morning's coffee wasn't about reasoning. It was about getting answers. And as Vince had learned, the best way to get answers from a suspect is to make them uncomfortable.

"Nah, let's sit down and endure this together. What doesn't kill us... right?"

Frank sat on the icy metal chair, shaking his head. "Had I known this was an episode of *Survivor*, I would have dressed for it," he remarked, bringing the warm cup to his lips.

"*Survivor*?" Vince leaned forward, his cop instincts kicking in despite himself. "More like *Truth or Dare*."

Frank's eyebrows raised. "Vince, what's this all about?"

"Do you and the monsignor ever talk about parishioners?"

"That depends on the circumstances. Why –"

"Let me put it another way. Do you and he ever discuss what's said to either of you in confidence?"

Frank's reply was immediate. "Never."

"Really? Okay, then let me run this by you. I had an interesting conversation with my sister after Christmas Eve Mass."

"Audrey? How's she doing with—"

"She knew things she shouldn't know." Vince's voice quieted. "Things I only said to you in confession, *Father* Frank."

Frank's eyes widened. The coffee cup in his hands stopped halfway to his mouth. "That's not possible. Vince, are you suggesting…"

"I'm not suggesting anything, *Father*."

"Vince, I have to tell you that I'm not comfortable with this conversation. And you calling me by my title… after all these years. What's going on?"

"You tell me. I finally felt safe talking about it… bringing it up at all."

"Vince." Frank set his cup down slowly. "You can't possibly think I would—"

"What should I think? The only person I told about my doubts was you. In confession. Now suddenly Audrey knows?"

Frank stood up. "I would never violate the confessional seal. *Never*. Not even accidentally."

"Accidentally?"

"This is my life, Vince. The confessional seal isn't just about intentional disclosure of what's said." There was an edge in his voice that Vince had never heard before. "If I was careless and someone overheard me... if I even hinted at what was said—that would violate it as well. It is an absolute sacramental seal."

Vince didn't let up. If there was a crack in his friend's armor, he was going to exploit it. "That's a pretty convenient explanation."

"Convenient?" Frank's chair scraped against the wooden boards as he leaned forward. "I've known you for, what, five years now? We've shared more cups of coffee than I can count..." Frank turned his head.

Vince couldn't tell if the water in his eyes was from the wind or his accusatory words. "I've been there for your promotion, your dad's health scare... everything with Audrey. And you think I'd betray your trust? Betray my vows?" The hurt in Frank's voice was real. It was raw. Certainly not the kind of thing you could fake. "I guess I don't—"

"I'm sorry... *Frank...*" Shame filled him, right down to his soul. "I had to ask," Vince said quietly.

"No, you had to interrogate." Frank sat back down. "You don't have to be *Detective* Vince Brown every moment of your life. It's okay to just be Vince."

"Old habits, Frank... my identity... I'm sorry."

"You are so much like your dad, Vince. Driven by a deep desire to get to the truth. And I swear, looking at you... you two even look alike. No one would ever guess you were adopted."

"But you can't say the same about Audrey, can you?" Vince hoped a bit of humor would help.

"You're right there, my friend. She is definitely... well, she's Audrey. Look, let me talk to the monsignor. We'll figure out—"

"No," Vince said before downing the last drops of his coffee, which was now lukewarm. "I'll handle it."

"Vince." Frank's voice had returned to the gentle, reassuring one that always comforted him. "Whatever's going on with Audrey, whatever she thinks she knows... tell her to be careful. The confession seal exists for a reason. Some truths aren't meant to be heard."

"Oh, I thought you met my sister." Vince's laugh was genuine. Frank's wasn't. He knew Audrey too well for that.

"Same time, same place next week?" This time, Frank's smile was genuine. "But how about we make it inside... and we skip the interrogation?" His laugh let Vince know they were good.

The wind hadn't let up. It seemed to cut right through Vince's coat as he walked away. Frank hadn't betrayed him. He was nearly certain of that now.

But that left other possibilities. And somehow, the thought of his sister playing God with other people's confessions terrified him more than any crisis of faith.

CHAPTER 4
THE THRESHOLD

The detective bureau still had that new paint smell. Three months after the renovation, and Vince's desk still felt like it belonged to someone else. Someone who'd earned it. Even after almost a year up here, he still felt like an imposter.

He pulled off his coat, the chill from his coffee meeting with Frank still clinging to his suit. The other day-watch detectives barely glanced his way as they huddled in the break room getting their coffee and sharing whatever war stories "real detectives" shared.

"Detective Brown..." The unit secretary's voice carried across the bureau's open office. "Your eight-thirty is here. The Washingtons?"

Vince checked his watch. At least the kid was on time for his own intervention.

Keisha Washington filled the conference room's doorway before entering it. Her teenage son, Antoine, trailed behind; a sullen shadow of his larger-than-life mom.

Her voice greeted Vince before he could offer them seats. "Now this better be worth missing work for."

"Mrs. Washington," Vince gestured to the chairs. "Thank you for coming in."

"Honey," she said, looking right at Vince, "with this voice, I'm not Mrs. Washington. I'm always Mrs. Kitt-Goldberg. Folks describe me like if Eartha Kitt swallowed Whoopie Goldberg." As she sat, somehow, she was able to make the chair look more like a throne. "Now, what's this program y'all offering my boy instead of incarceration?"

The only thing Vince was proud of since his promotion to this pseudo-detective position was being given control over the name of the program he was charged with implementing. He decided on the "Threshold Intervention Initiative." *Threshold* evoked an image of troubled youth crossing into a new phase in their lives. *Intervention* represented the pro-active approach to addressing issues before they became worse. *Initiative* suggested to him that the program has legitimacy and purpose.

Vince sat a little taller in his chair, looking over at Antoine, who was slumped deeper into his chair. He had pulled his hood low over his eyes.

"It's called the Threshold Intervention Initiative, or T-double-I for short," Vince said, pulling out the folder he'd prepared. "Given that this is Antoine's first offense—"

"First *and* last," Keisha interjected.

"—we have some alternatives to prosecution." The words still didn't fit right with him. Number 1 on the detective's test and the last three years teaching ethics at the academy, and this was his reward? Babysitting teenage bomb-jokers?

"Alternatives?" Antoine finally woke up. And spoke up. "Like what?"

"Community service. Counseling. Weekly check-ins." Vince leaned forward. "And getting you involved with productive ways to channel your boredom instead of making stupid comments about explosives."

"Detective Brown, I tell 'em. I tell all of 'em... the whole crowd he hanging with: Idle hands are the devil's playground. And this boy's starting to act possessed with some of the decisions he making."

Vince didn't want to waste the opportunity. "This program doesn't offer exorcisms as an alternative..." Mrs. Kitt-Goldberg didn't even smile. "Ahem... But it does give teens like Antoine a chance to see there are a lot of positive things in his life, and his life has value outside a gang."

Antoine's head snapped up at the word 'gang.' *Good,* Vince thought. At least something was getting through.

"Does this sound like something you agree to, son?" The look in Keisha's eyes suggested this wasn't a question he should get wrong.

"It was a joke!" Antoine straightened his hoodie. "Everyone knew it was a joke!"

"Baby," Keisha's voice could have stripped the new paint, "the only joke here is you thinking this is funny. You better watch yourself, boy."

"This isn't a game, Antoine. We're talking terroristic threats. This could affect you for the rest of your life. You're a juvenile now, but a charge like this could seriously affect the kind of job you get, the career you choose, later in life," Vince said.

The laughter outside the room was so loud it penetrated the closed door and even got the attention of Mrs. Kitt-Goldberg. Whatever the other detectives were laughing about, he wasn't included in the joke. Maybe it was something funny about another solved case, a real case dealt with by real detectives. It was another sign he wasn't a part of the day-watch detective shift.

Vince got back to his folder and walked them through the program requirements. Keisha asked questions while Antoine retreated back into his hoodie. After he got the required signatures, Vince escorted them out.

Detective Marcus Turner from Major Crimes rounded the corner. "Mrs. Washington?" Turner's eyebrows rose. "I didn't expect to see you back so soon."

"Detective Turner." Keisha grinned and shook her head. "Neither did I. But this detective, Mr. Brown, he's got something for my son. I hope it works."

After the Washingtons left, Vince caught up with Turner in the break room. "You know Mrs. Washington?"

"Yeah, I got assigned her case last week. Extortion. When's the last time we caught a blackmail case up here?" Turner's voice had that tone—the one that said, 'real detective work.'

Before Vince could respond, Lieutenant Carmen Navarro's voice cut through the break room. "Brown! My office."

Turner's smirk followed Vince through the maze of desks to the detective bureau commander's office.

New detectives always underestimated her at first—something about her model-worthy features led them to expect a softer touch. The surprise when she cut into them with razor-sharp precision was something each of them had to experience on their own.

The lieutenant didn't look up from her paperwork as he stepped in. It reminded him of being a rookie standing at attention in roll call.

"Three T-double-I files from last week... before Christmas," she said finally, pointing to the manila folders at the edge of her desk. "They got sent back down from the captain. He wants them followed up, not closed."

"I was going to—"

"Save it." Now she looked up. "You wanted to be a detective, right? This program is your baby. I don't care how high you scored on the test or who your dad is. This program is being looked at as a potential model by the state. So do it right."

"Lieutenant, I... It's new. It's never been done before. How am I supposed to know which cases to close and which ones to follow up on?"

Lieutenant Navarro shrugged her shoulders. "Like I said, this is your baby. Do it right. Because as much as I'll have your back and go to war for you out there... in here I'll fucking lay you out if I ever get my ass chewed again by the captain for one of your fuck-ups. Got it?"

"Yes, LT." He grabbed the folders and turned to leave her office.

"Brown, this isn't the patrol division." Her tone softened ever so slightly. "We're held to a higher standard. I've read your reports—every one of them. It's probably the best report writing I've seen. You'll figure the rest out."

"I appreciate that."

Walking back to his desk, Vince felt the eyes of the other detectives on him. Turner was already sharing something with his colleagues, their laughter just quiet enough to be deniable.

He sat down, staring at the stack of folders on his desk, adding to it the three he had in his hand. Somewhere, real crimes were happening. Real detective work was being done—real cases were being solved. Instead, here he sat, processing paperwork for teenage pranksters while his colleagues worked actual cases.

His phone buzzed. A text from Audrey: "Changed your mind about those confessions yet?"

He deleted it without responding. He had enough going on right now without adding his sister's unethical and criminal ideas to the mix.

CHAPTER 5
ABSOLUTE TRUTHS

The dry-erase markers still had that chemical smell that reminded Vince of his college days. He wrote "ETHICAL DECISIONS" in bold letters across the whiteboard, then turned to face fifty-eight fresh faces in pressed uniforms. Their eagerness reminded him of himself not so long ago.

"Ethics isn't about what you *can* do," he continued the discussion, setting down the marker. "It's about what you *should* do. And in law enforcement, that line isn't just a philosophical concept—it's often the difference between life and death."

A hand shot up in the back. "But sir, what about when there isn't time to think about philosophy? When you have to make split-second decisions?"

Ever since he was a kid, Vince hated being lectured to. It continued into college, which might help explain why he majored in philosophy—it was more discussion than lecture. He swore to himself that if ever given the chance, he would never lecture anyone. Which is why his classes at the academy were always discussion-driven. And why he encouraged the recruits to feel safe in asking questions that generate discussion.

Vince smiled. They always asked this. Every class. "That's exactly why we drill these principles now. So they're second nature when you need them." He walked between the rows of desks. "By now, you've all heard the phrase, 'Better to be tried by twelve than carried by six,' right?"

Nods rippled through the room. Along the back wall, several veteran instructors shifted uncomfortably.

"Well, I'm here to tell you that's garbage thinking." Vince turned to face the class. "That mindset assumes there are only two options: kill or be killed. But our job isn't to survive at any cost—it's to protect and serve. *All* citizens. Even the ones breaking the law."

"With all due respect to the detective," Sergeant Martinez spoke up from his position by the door, "sometimes we don't have the luxury of exploring all options. Class, you'll learn that in the upcoming street survival course."

"You're right, Sergeant. Sometimes you don't. And I hope it's discussed in that street survival course." Vince acknowledged the veteran cop with a nod. He went back to addressing the class. "But if that becomes your default mindset—if you approach every situation assuming it's either them or you—then you've already failed as a public servant."

He pulled up a PowerPoint slide with Theodore Roosevelt's quote: "No man is above the law, and no man is below it; nor do we ask any man's permission when we ask him to obey it."

"When you put on that badge, you're held to a higher standard. Not because you're above the law, but because you've sworn to uphold it. There is no gray area there. No room for interpretation."

Another hand. "But what about when the bad guys don't play by the rules?"

"There are no 'bad guys.'" Vince's voice carried the weight of his master's degree in ethics. "There are people who break the law and people who don't. Our job is to deal with both groups equally, professionally, *and ethically*."

A snort from the back of the room. "Must be nice living in that black-and-white world of yours, Detective."

The comment came from Lieutenant Hayes, one of the firearms instructors. Vince had heard the whispers—how the old guard thought he was too idealistic, too rigid, too *by-the-book*.

Vince invited discussion from both recruits and fellow instructors in this block of instruction, so he went with the flow.

"It is nice, actually." He didn't miss a beat. "Because when you start seeing shades of gray, when you start making exceptions to the rules, that's when good cops turn bad. That's when we lose the public's trust."

His walk back to the whiteboard displayed all the command presence worthy of an academy instructor. The walk also masked his growing concern about the way Audrey strutted her confidence in the confessions she told him about.

Once at the board, he wrote: INTEGRITY = CONSISTENCY.

"Your integrity isn't something you can turn on and off. You can't be ethical on duty and bend the rules in your personal life. You can't justify breaking one law to uphold another."

A recruit in the third row raised her hand. "What if someone close to you—like family—is doing something wrong? Isn't there some wiggle room there? Just like professional courtesy to another police officer?"

The question hit closer to home than she could know. Vince's mind flashed to Audrey's text from earlier that morning: *Still thinking about those confessions? Lots more where that came from...*

"No wiggle room," he said, perhaps more forcefully than intended. "In fact, that's when your ethical standards matter most. When it's family, when it's personal—that's the true test of your integrity."

Lieutenant Hayes cleared his throat from the back. "Sometimes family situations aren't that simple, Detective. Wouldn't you agree that sometimes you have to bend a little to do what's right?"

Unsure whether the question was to set up Vince's answer that the lieutenant wanted the class to hear or if it was a personal one, Vince continued with his answer to the recruit. "The moment we start bending the rules for personal reasons is the moment we lose our credibility as law enforcement officers." He turned back to the board, and the words jumped at him. *INTEGRITY = CONSISTENCY*. The equation had to be congruent in his own mind, not just in black marker against a whiteboard. Audrey's message echoed in his mind.

"I think we'll end it on that note. Class dismissed," he announced, earlier than planned. "Remember—there's only one way to do this job: the right way."

As the recruits filed out, Lieutenant Hayes walked up to the front. "Nice speech, Detective. But someday you'll learn—the real world isn't as clean as your ethics textbooks."

Vince gathered his materials, Hayes' words churning in his gut. The real world. Where his sister recorded confessions for entertainment. Where absolute truth lived in shades of gray.

He checked his phone in the empty classroom. Three more texts from Audrey. He needed answers. He needed to know how she knew about his confession.

The drive to the church had never felt longer.

CHAPTER 6
PATTERNS IN GRAY

"How did you know about my confession to Frank?"

Audrey jumped, nearly knocking over her paints. "Jesus, Vince! You ever hear of knocking?"

The stairs up to Audrey's room felt steeper tonight. On the drive there from the academy, Vince felt the weight of the questions he carried, grinding his teeth every time he thought about what she'd said on Christmas Eve.

Vince pushed the door wider. "We need to talk, Audrey."

After wiping her hands on her already paint-stained jeans, she turned down the music. She steadied her painting on the easel—that same damn horse. "Well, hello to you too."

Since when did she listen to Bach? "Just answer the question."

Her eyes and smile simultaneously grew wide. "You really want to know?" Her smile became playful. "I'll do better than tell you. I'll show you."

Before he could stop her, she grabbed her iPad from the windowsill. A few taps later, a man's voice, filled with humiliation, began to play: "Bless me, Father, for I have sinned..."

His voice was stern. "Turn it off." Vince looked over her shoulder at the screen. The opened program was in a file named The Confessional. He felt his hands closing into fists. "I said turn it off!"

"Wait for it; this is a good part." She turned it up instead, talking over the confession. "See, while I was cleaning the sanctuary... you remember, part of my thousand hours of community service? I found this mini microphone mounted under the seat in the confessional. It's the same make as the one the monsignor uses at the pulpit."

The confessions continued playing. Vince's fingers dug deeper into his fists. "What is wrong with you?"

She continued to ignore his questions. "It took me less than ten minutes to figure out and match the frequency. Then I ordered the same receiver." She motioned to her window. "Look, at that side of the church."

Vince glanced out the partially closed curtains.

"It's the perfect line of sight to the confessional." She pointed to a small digital recorder on the table. "I have it on voice-activated mode. It picks up everything while I'm working. Then..." She waved the iPad in front of Vince. "Better than any podcast out there today!"

"You're recording confessions?" Each word was said with emphasis. "Do you have any idea how many laws you're breaking? You're on probation for the exact same thing, for Christ's sake." He started to collect his thoughts. "There *is* something wrong with you!"

"Oh, listen to you. Mr. By-the-Book, stuck teaching ethics to rookies and babysitting juvenile delinquents." She set down the iPad but didn't turn it off. "You know, if you'd bend those precious rules of yours once in a while, maybe you'd make it to Major Crimes before you retire."

"This isn't about my career, this is about—"

"Oh, wait... wait. Here it comes... speaking of careers." She grabbed the iPad again. "Listen to this one. You'll love it."

A woman's distinctive voice filled the room. Unmistakable. Unforgettable. Eartha Kitt swallowing Whoopi Goldberg.

Vince's blood ran cold. "Play that again."

Audrey's face twisted. "What happened to 'turn it off?'"

"Just... rewind it. Play it again."

As Keisha Washington's voice detailed the same story she'd told Detective Turner, Vince's mind raced. The extortion case. The timing. It couldn't be... or could she?

"You're blackmailing her. You're using the confessions to blackmail these people." His accusations surprised even him.

"Hey," she replied playfully, her smile reminding him of when they were kids and she knew something he didn't. "That's not a bad idea. Why didn't I think of that?"

"Think of it? There's a difference between thinking of doing it and actually doing it. You went way too far."

"Did I? It sure would make working off these community service hours more bearable." She turned to her painting—that damn horse. "I didn't—"

"Just stop." He cut her denial off, just like he was trained to do in interrogation class, holding up his hand like a cop directing traffic. "I don't want to hear any more of your lies."

"Lies? You didn't even ask me a question—all you did was accuse me. You're not a cop up here, Vince. And I'm not a suspect in your small interrogation room. Why don't you start acting like a human being—an actual person—instead of being in cop mode all the time!"

"Why don't you grow up and play by the rules?"

"The rules? There you go with the rules again." Her laugh had an edge to it. "You know what your problem is, Vince? You think wearing a badge makes you righteous. I've seen how *righteous* people operate. Maybe it's time you did, too."

"You... talking about righteousness? That's like—"

Now she cut him off. "You want rules. Here's a rule: As long as you're in my room, I'm your sister, not some scumbag you just brought in for questioning."

Vince stormed out, the stairs creaking under his angry footsteps. Behind him, Bach had been replaced by something with a harder edge. The pounding bass followed him into the cold air, almost drowning out the voice in his head that whispered, *How deep does this scheme of hers go?*

His phone buzzed. A text from work: another juvenile case needing his attention. But all he could think about was his sister. The lies. The law.

What does a cop do when they have to choose between the oath they swore to uphold and a family member who doesn't deny crossing the line?

CHAPTER 7
DEADLY FREQUENCIES

"Not now." He hit the ignore button harder than necessary.

The last person he wanted to hear from was Audrey. The last thing he wanted to see was her name on the display screen. The last thing he needed was another reminder that his black-and-white world had just acquired about fifty shades of gray.

Vince's fingers dug into the steering wheel on his way home from her room. Each streetlight that swept across his windshield flashed a trigger being pulled. But instead of a bang, all he heard was his sister's sarcasm. The recorded confessions. And blackmail?

He'd been in the detective bureau nearly a year, and now his own sister might be... He couldn't finish that thought. His mind wouldn't allow it. Not yet anyway.

Less than a minute later, a text: *Call me 911*.

He stared at the text message at the next red light. Was this another one of her games? Was she testing him? Screwing with him? But what if she really was in trouble? The light turned green. He drove another couple of blocks before putting his phone on speaker mode.

Decades of being a "righteous" brother don't switch off just because your sister's a convicted felon. He hit the green circle button.

"I knew you'd call." The smug satisfaction in her voice sent waves of nausea through him.

"Another one of your childish games. I should have known it."

"No, wait!" The playfulness in her tone was gone. "You left before the best part of the confessions played. You need to hear this."

"Audrey—"

A click interrupted him. Static. And then: "Take your time. This is a safe place."

Another voice, a man, trembling... stuttering: "I-I-I need you to know that I took no pleasure in killing him. I didn't want to kill him. I was given an assignment... it... it was more like an order. It was an order, Father. You have to believe me."

"I am listening."

"And once it was done... I dumped the body. Somewhere it would never be found. That was part of the assignment, too... If I didn't... if I didn't follow through with it, they... they would have done it to me. Father, I had no choice."

Vince's blood turned to ice water in his veins. His free hand fumbled for the mini Rubik's Cube on his keychain; the fingers of his free hand worked the different sides of it as he drove through the dark back roads to his house.

Audrey came back on the line. "Did you hear that? It's an actual murder confession!"

The cube clicked through its movements. "This is a nightmare. Do you have any idea what you've done?"

"What I've done? I just handed you your first murder case. If this doesn't get you transferred to Major Crimes, nothing will!"

"You've handed me nothing but a leaky bag of shit. That recording is illegal. It's inadmissible—it can't be used as evidence. And even worse, it's privileged communication with a priest. The Supreme Court ruled years ago—"

"Oh my God, would you listen to yourself?" The voice of the fun-loving Audrey was gone. "There's a body out there somewhere.

Someone's family is waiting for answers. Christ, you even have a confession. And you're worried about admissibility?"

"I'm worried about the law."

"The law? Someone's been murdered. What about justice?" She paused. "Unless you're not ready to finally investigate something real for once."

"I can't break the law to enforce it, Audrey. That's not how this works. There are procedures, and case laws involving evidence. It's called the fruit of the poisonous—"

"No wonder they stuck you with juvenile cases." The spotty cell service couldn't hide the disgust in her voice. "You're too much of a pussy to do real police work."

The line went dead.

Somewhere out there was a body. Somewhere out there was a killer who thought their secret was safe with a priest... a secret that was safe with God.

And here he was, with words he couldn't unhear. Evidence that could never be used in any case. Or admitted into any court.

He was a sad version of everything he thought a detective was supposed to be. A sad version of who he always wanted to be as a brother. He couldn't even figure out how to get each side of a stupid cube the same color, for Christ's sake.

Vince laughed at how he pictured himself. He was a detective who couldn't detect, a brother who couldn't protect, blindly trying to solve a puzzle that suddenly felt like a metaphor for his entire life.

He pushed his favorite band's rare live disc into his Jeep's CD player, hoping Phish could drown out what was playing in his head. But all he could hear was that trembling voice—an unknown man confessing to a murder. A man who didn't know the confessional's prayers of contrition made for better entertainment than any podcast out there today.

CHAPTER 8
THROUGH THE GLASS

"Nothing. Not a single lead."

Detective Turner set down his coffee mug. "We don't get a lot of these extortion cases. Hell, I can count on one hand the number I've investigated. And all of them were dead-ends." He kept scrolling down the computer screen on his desk. "Victims clam up, evidence disappears. You know how it goes."

"Yeah, I know." Vince did his best to keep his voice neutral. "But Mrs. Washington seems like she'd be cooperative."

Turner finally looked at Vince. "How come a juvenile liaison detective is so interested in a Major Crimes case?"

"Just poking around to see if maybe her son's behavior has anything—"

Before Vince could finish his answer, Lieutenant Navarro's voice cut across the wide-open room. "Brown. Finish what you're doing and see me in my office."

Turner's smirk and the shake of his head confirmed what Vince thought of himself as a detective on that drive home from Audrey's last week.

Carmen Navarro sat behind her desk, peering over the top of her glasses. She looked more like a librarian than a hard-ass cop. Vince had to make a conscious effort to move his eyes off the hint of cleavage behind her form-fitted blouse.

"Close the door."

Vince did. Then he waited.

"You want to tell me what's going on, or do I have to ask first?"

"I'm not sure... I don't know what you mean."

She stood up from her desk and picked up the files. "Three reports full of typos and missing demographic information. In one of them, you wrote a statement from the witness but said she was the goddamn suspect... and then you wrote that the victim gave a description *of the witness*. What the fuck is going on?"

His first lie to a superior officer came easier than expected. "Nothing." At least with her standing up, he didn't have to concentrate on not looking down her blouse. "Everything's fine."

"You're slipping. And I hear you've been poking around an extortion case."

That was the icing on the cake. Regardless of what they might think of him, he had never, and never would, betray the trust of another detective in the bureau. But someone, probably Turner, ran to the lieutenant and ratted.

"Lieutenant—"

"Cut the rank bullshit, *Vince*. We're behind closed doors." His name on her lips sounded sincere. "You're not yourself lately. You've been fucking up. That's not like you. Does this have anything to do with your sister?"

"My sister?" His mind went in all directions all at once. *How could she know? What if she doesn't know but just suspects? What has Turner told her?* "What's my sister got to do with this?" He hoped she didn't catch on to this line of true bullshit.

"Come on, Vince. I know the dynamic with you two. The whole department does. I've known Audrey since she was shoplifting lip gloss from Walgreens. And the patrol commander tells me there's a history of this kind of behavior with you whenever your sister pulls one of her asinine stunts."

He had to stop her. He had to end her fishing expedition before she hooked onto something... or before he took the bait. "I think it's just the post-holiday letdown. You know, all the stress that comes from it. Especially the family drama."

He didn't have to wait long to find out if she was buying more of his bullshit.

"Yeah, okay. But whatever drama she's stirred up, you need to compartmentalize. These reports have to be trial-ready. They won't write themselves. So get your head out of your ass and get back to the Vince Brown who earned his gold shield."

She dropped the files on her desk in front of him. A compassionate voice took over. "That's a direct order... Vince."

"I understand, LT. It won't happen anymore. You have my word."

"Your word." She studied him for a moment. "You know what I see when I look at you, Vince? I see a good cop fighting to become a great detective. Don't let whatever this is drag you down."

"It won't."

"I know it won't. And Vince?" Her voice was softer, more like a friend instead of a command-level officer. "My door's always open. Even for the DA's kid."

Vince grabbed the files and headed back to his desk. He *was* slipping. The path back to his desk was different. Unfamiliar. He'd just given his word to his boss that he was back to the old Vince Brown, who kept his word and who followed orders.

And yet...

Back at his desk, he pulled up the county database. He knew it was against policy to investigate without authorization—to do it off the books. But that trembling confession kept playing in his mind. There was a body that might never be found.

Search: "Missing persons cases in the last thirty days."

The screen filled with case numbers. He filtered them by jurisdiction, date, and circumstances. One entry caught his eye.

Name of victim: REDACTED

Date Reported: 02 December

Last Seen: Leaving fundraiser in Margate at 0027 hours.

The rest of the initial report was vague. But the last line of the supplement report was interesting: "MP is the son of the Lithuanian ambassador. Jurisdictional case closed. Turned over to FBI."

His desk phone rang. An external call.

"Detective Brown, Juvenile Unit."

Her timing was uncanny. "You sound so official." Audrey's voice was different. It was steady. She sounded like an adult.

That didn't last more than a second.

Imitating his tone, she repeated his words. "*Detective Brown.* You answer the phone so differently than when I call Dominos..."

He tried his best to keep his voice low. "Are you insane? Calling me here? Listen to me."

"No, you listen... to this."

There was static. And then: "God is merciful—"

"I'm scared, Father. I-I have another assignment." The same trembling voice from before. "An ordered hit. If... if I don't do it... they'll kill me instead."

"Who?" There was a certain tone in the voice that hinted at something.

"The county DA. District Attorney Michael Brown."

The phone nearly slipped from Vince's numb fingers. His father's name blasted into his ears like a gunshot. Out of nowhere, a high school history lesson came to mind. Hearing his father's name was like a shot heard round the world.

"Vince?" Audrey's voice returned. "Are you there? Did you hear that?"

He turned off his computer and then reached for his coat. "Don't move. Don't do anything. I'll be right there."

"Brown?" Carmen Navarro stood in her doorway. "Everything okay?"

"I'm taking a personal day," he said without looking at her.

"Vince—"

But he was already out the door, leaving behind a shutdown computer and shutdown lies. His black-and-white world had just acquired a new shade. What if gray wasn't as horrible as he once believed? It was certainly a better compromise than the alternative: the color of his father's blood if he didn't find a way to stop it.

CHAPTER 9
BREAKING POINTS

"Let me get this straight." Vince paced the full fourteen feet of Audrey's room, his mind racing faster than his feet. "Take me through it again. From the beginning."

"Really?" Audrey sat cross-legged on her bed, still holding her iPad. "You want me to explain it again? Now? After what you just heard about Dad?"

"Audrey, everything might balance on how *accidentally* you found the mic and how *inadvertently* you recorded the confessions."

"Inadvertently? Well, I can stop you there because they weren't inadvertently—"

"Audrey!" His shout surprised even him. He forced his hands down in a calming gesture, more for himself than her. "Don't. If there's any chance—any chance at all—for this to work legally, it has to be accidental or inadvertent. Just... tell me what happened."

"How I found the mic, or everything?"

"Everything." He stopped pacing and turned to face her. "And this time, don't leave anything out."

She sighed. "Fine. I was cleaning the sanctuary. I try to hit the confessional hard once a month. There's no friggin' light in there, so I have to use the light on my phone to do a good job. While I was wiping down the woodwork, I saw cobwebs under the seat. They were glowing in the dark from the light. That's when I found it."

"Found what exactly?"

"A miniature mic. Definitely professional grade. It was mounted with Velcro right under the penitent's seat." She pulled up the photo on her phone. "See? Same make as the monsignor's. You can even see the model number when I zoom in." She leaned forward. "Vince, can we please talk about—"

"Keep going." His detective training reminded him to focus on details to keep the fear at bay. "What then?"

"I was freaked out at first. I mean, come on. A bug planted in the confessional? But then I thought, why should someone else have all the fun? So, I traced the frequency and ordered a matching receiver." She stood up and pointed at her window. "Perfect line of sight. The voice-activated recorder catches everything while I'm working. But Vince, the hit on Dad—"

"So you found the mic by chance—accidentally. That we don't have a problem with." He ran his hand through his hair. "Think, Vince. Think, goddamn it." He started pacing again. "Why couldn't you have overheard the confessions? Like you were listening to an old transistor radio and they just started to play? That way, you would have inadvertently heard them."

"Nope. I found the make, model, and frequency... and ordered the equipment. Then added them to my playlist. You're not going to get past that part. So can we stop trying to figure out how to do this your way and get back to our dad?"

"When exactly was this confession recorded?"

"Oh, for fuck's sake, Vince. Really?"

He just looked at her.

"Fine. Yesterday. The guy said Dad has until some trial starts next month. You heard it."

"Yeah, I did. But if I hadn't actually heard it, maybe... Oh, Christ, I don't know."

"If Dad doesn't do what they want..." She looked into his eyes. "Vince, what are we going to do?"

He looked out her window at the side of the church, at the exterior wall of the confessional. "Why Dad? What could they want from him?"

"He's the DA. Take your pick. But that's not the point." Audrey's voice cracked. "Someone's going to kill him if we don't stop them."

"Stop them? With illegal evidence that'd get thrown out of court faster than you got thrown out of college on your second try." The words came out harsher than he intended. "Evidence that would land you in prison this time, not just probation. There is no *we* in this, Audrey."

"Jesus Christ! For once in your life, forget about the rules and do the right thing!" She stood up, blocking his view out the window, her voice raw with desperation. "This isn't some juvenile delinquent case you get to file away and forget about. This is Dad. Our dad. So, yeah, Vince, there is *we* in this. All of it!"

He stared at her. Yep, she was still a train wreck. But she was also his dad's daughter—she was his sister. The sister he promised he'd keep an eye on. Just like he took an oath to uphold the law. Just like Dad had sworn to serve justice.

Their dad's voice echoed in his memory: "Sometimes the right thing to do isn't the easy thing to do, son."

"I need to think," he said finally, heading for the door.

"Think? Someone's planning to murder Dad, and you need to think about it?"

He stopped in the doorway, not turning around. "If I do this... if I do it off the books... best case scenario, I lose my badge. Worst case, we both end up in prison and Dad still dies."

"And if you don't?"

This time he did turn. "Then I have to live with whatever happens next."

"We both will, Vince."

CHAPTER 10
PAPER TRAILS

The records room smelled like his grandfather's basement, filled with musty paper and forgotten stories. Musty paper and forgotten stories—that's what his career would be if anyone caught him doing this. Vince had checked his watch when he got in — 6:47 a.m. It was early enough to avoid questions about why a juvenile liaison detective was digging through Major Crimes' files.

He had leafed through the upcoming trial folders until he found what he was looking for—next month's docket. He pulled the first file, then the second. Nothing. One by one until he got to the middle.

Something caught his eye. A yellow Post-it with his father's handwriting: *Personal attention required—discovery*. His father's familiar handwriting, usually so confident and bold, seemed somehow different here. Desperate, maybe.

Vince grimaced. The DA never handled discovery personally. That was what assistant DAs were for.

The tab on the folder was labeled State v. Petrov. When he opened it, the cover page showed it was a counterfeit gems case. The box for *Estimated Loss* on the report was filled in: $1.2 million.

The deeper he read, the more his stomach turned. Russian-organized crime connections. Multiple jurisdictions. And his father had specifically requested to handle it himself. County district attorneys are too busy running the office to try cases themselves. He knew he didn't have to search through any more files to find what he was looking for.

Back at his desk, he was still processing what he had found when the phone on his desk beeped. An internal extension. Carmen Navarro's voice cut through his thoughts. "My office. Now."

Standing behind her desk with her coffee mug in hand, she motioned to him. "Close the door."

Vince's heart raced. He'd been called in here too many times recently for her opinion of him to be the same as when he was first promoted.

"The captain saw you in records." She set down her mug. "Care to explain why you were in the upcoming trials section?"

The lie came so easily that it scared him. Thank God he unknowingly rehearsed it at Turner's desk the day before. "The Washington kid. I was looking for connections between his mother's extortion case and his behavior issues at school."

"Really?" She leaned forward, and Vince found himself fighting not to notice how her blouse pulled slightly against her chest. "Well, that's interesting." Her voice had the edge of an experienced interrogator. "The extortion case files wouldn't be in upcoming trials."

"I... thought maybe..." His voice trailed off. It dawned on Vince that he wasn't that good of a liar after all.

"Vince." The way she said his name made him look up. "Whatever's going on... if you can't tell your lieutenant, maybe you can tell me. Let me be your friend."

"I can't." At least those words were the truth. "Not yet. Please."

She walked around her desk to perch on its edge, closer to him than strictly necessary. If she intended to make him so uncomfortable that he'd tell her what she wanted to know—the way they teach detectives to get information—it was working.

"I told you yesterday that when I saw you, I saw a good cop trying to become a great detective."

"I remember."

"You know what I see when I look at you today?"

He shook his head.

"I see a good person drowning in something he can't handle alone. And I see him too scared or too proud to ask for help."

"LT, the last thing I want is to put you in a position where—"

"Where what? Where I might have to make tough choices? That's why I get paid the big bucks, Vince. I get paid to choose between right and wrong."

"This is a little more complicated than right or wrong. It's not like it's..." He stopped himself.

"Like it's black and white?" she finished his thought, then shook her head. "You know, sometimes I have to choose between procedure and doing the right thing."

"LT... Carmen, I don't want to put you in that position. My problems are my problems."

"If all this really is family drama... like you tried to convince me..." She walked around and stood behind her desk. "If that's the case, family comes first. Up here, everyone knows that. So whatever decisions you have to make, family needs come first, Vince."

"I know family's important, but—"

Her voice was soft but firm. "Family isn't just important. Family's everything, Vince." She sat down. "Take the rest of the day off. I put you down for just half a personal day yesterday; take the other half now. Get your head straight."

"Lieutenant—"

"That's an order, Detective." But her eyes suggested it was something deeper. Like she knew something, but she didn't know what it was. "Think about what I said. About family."

He nodded. "Thank you."

"Vince?" He turned back to face his boss, who had asked to be his friend. "Whatever it is... whatever is going on. Be careful."

He couldn't look her in the eyes. *Why did she have to ask to be my friend?*

Lying... lying to her, as his friend, somehow felt like a smaller betrayal than the truth he couldn't tell her.

CHAPTER 11

ONE SQUARE MILE OF HEAVEN

The wipers were fighting a losing battle against the January rain as Vince's Jeep carried him further away from Atlantic City. Wherever he was going, he hoped this ride would help clear his mind—or at least drown out the voices of duty and family warring in his head. He hadn't planned on heading toward the Pine Barrens, but sometimes your hands know where to turn before your mind catches up.

The two-lane county road curved through dense forest, where pine needles carpeted the shoulders. His thoughts drifted between his father, Audrey, and Lieutenant Navarro's words about family. He barely noticed when the woods gave way to civilization—if you could call it that. The town looked like it had been lifted straight from one of those black-and-white TV shows his dad used to watch, the ones where problems got solved in thirty minutes and the good guys always won.

Log cabins—actual log cabins—scattered among more traditional homes, their weathered walls defying time. It was an eclectic mix of architecture and landscaping. He was so caught up in the postcard scenery that he missed the speed limit sign. And the police cruiser.

The lightbar came to life behind him. Just perfect.

He pulled over, bouncing through the potholes in the gravel shoulder. He fished for his credentials in the glove box. Then he reached for his wallet. This was a first—he'd given tickets when he was assigned to patrol but never got one.

He watched the officer's tactical approach to his window as the raindrops darkened his uniform. "License and registration, and proof of insurance, please." He was older, with the kind of face that looked more like a guidance counselor than a cop. His nameplate read "SMITH," and the gold stars on his collar marked him as the chief.

Vince handed him the registration and insurance card. But it wasn't until he opened his wallet that he felt something strange. "I'm Vince Brown. Detective Vince Brown, Atlantic City PD."

His gold badge looked up at him as if it had eyes. And those eyes had a look of disappointment.

The chief's review of his credentials in the falling rain took just a few seconds. "Well, Detective Brown, you were doing thirty-seven in a twenty-five. And..." He squinted at the registration. "This expired last month."

"I'm sorry, sir. I wasn't paying attention. And I got a lot on my mind. I'm distracted by—"

"Save it, son."

Vince prepared for the worst.

"First of all, no need to call me sir. People around here call me by my first name—Jack. If you want to be official, you can call me Chief Jack. But that's usually just a formality when I'm introduced at the monthly council meetings."

His fatherly tone and his easygoing manner brought a sense of peace that Vince hadn't felt in weeks.

"Now, about your speed. Let me guess. You were distracted by the scenery. Happens to a lot of folks who see it for the first time. We get a lot of speeders that way."

"I can see why, sir... Chief... I mean, Jack."

"One square mile of heaven, that's what the founder called it. Still true today."

Vince waited for the inevitable lecture and then for the ticket book to appear. Instead, Chief Jack handed back his documents.

"I'm not writing a fellow cop a ticket." He held up his hand when Vince started to protest. "But I can't let you drive this with an expired registration. That's not negotiable."

"I understand... Jack. Thanks." Vince pulled out his cell phone.

"If you're thinking of calling someone, you'll have better luck about a half mile up the road—the cell signal's stronger out that way."

"I'm guessing a town like this probably still has a pay phone somewhere?"

"We sure do. Glenn's Auto Repair, at the corner. But do you see that building across the street?" The chief pointed through the rain at an enormous log structure. "Biggest freestanding log cabin building in the country. The inn's got a great bar—people come from all over to escape there."

He shifted his gaze, and his finger, to an equally impressive log building just past the inn. "And that church—that's the Lakes Cathedral Church. They've got decent Wi-Fi, which is more than I can say for cell service out here in the Pines."

Vince laughed at his options. "So, it's either a drink or a prayer?"

"A detective with a sense of humor. I like that!"

Vince thought of the ethics block of instruction he teaches at the academy and the talks he gives on community relations. The chief's willingness to stand in the cold rain demonstrated how police officers are supposed to be—that they aren't better than anyone else.

"The church is always open, and the Wi-Fi is free. Why don't you go in, renew your registration online, make this thing legal, and then head home?" He leaned down, not quite sticking his head in the window. "Sometimes the best thing a cop can do is slow down. Take a breath. Let your mind catch up to whatever's chasing it."

Something in the chief's voice made Vince look closer. There was wisdom there, earned the hard way. Earned the honest way.

"Thank you, Chief. I appreciate—"

"Jack. Call me Jack." He straightened up, adjusting his rain-soaked hat. "Church's got good coffee too. Just saying."

Vince watched the chief return to his cruiser. He tucked his expired registration into his pocket, then hurried through the rain to the church. The stained-glass windows in its log walls had an inviting glow despite the gray day, like they were offering shelter from more than just the rain.

Maybe the chief was right. Maybe sometimes you needed to slow down to figure out which direction you were really heading. And maybe, just maybe, you needed to be ready to leave some things behind to move forward.

CHAPTER 12
THE HYMNAL'S PROMISE

Vince was sitting in the last pew, the Rubik's Cube twirling in his fingers, as he waited for the state's website to process his registration renewal. The cube's plastic clicks echoed in the empty space, competing with the soft patter of rain against the windows.

He found himself studying his surroundings, trying to focus on anything but the decisions weighing on his mind. While this town was like stepping into an old black-and-white TV show, the sanctuary of Lakes Cathedral Church felt like crossing into another century entirely. Small. Quaint. Picturesque.

Its preserved log walls, with bright white chinking, climbed to meet the dark wooden beams that crossed the ceiling like outstretched arms. Hanging lanterns, that looked so real Vince wondered who filled them with lamp oil every day, cast just enough warm light to create soft shadows across the altar. The colors of the stained glass windows were muted by the rainy day outside.

The wooden doors behind him creaked open, letting in a gust of wet wind along with an elderly woman with an armful of sheet music. Without warning, the papers blasted from her arms, scattering across the brick entrance like oversized confetti. Several sheets blew into the rain.

"Oh, dear." She made a futile grab at the nearest pages.

Vince was already up and at it, gathering papers from the steps before they got drenched or blew away entirely. "Let me help you with those."

"Thank you, young man." She had that special kind of smile, so genuine that it makes you want to smile back. "I'm Ginny, the organist. And you're... a visitor. We don't get many folks stopping in on days like this. How about a cup of coffee to warm you up?"

"I'm good, thank you. Just waiting on some paperwork to get finished up by the state." He lifted his phone, unsure why he thought he had to convince her. "I'm Vince," he introduced himself as he handed her the rescued music.

She saw the cube on the pew. "Ah, one of those puzzle thingamajigs. My grandkids are obsessed with them."

I've had it for years." He held it up, showing the one white side he'd managed to complete. "Can't seem to get past this point without messing everything up again."

"You know, there are plenty of tutorials online."

"I've heard. But that's like cheating—someone else giving you the solution," he replied, smiling at her surprised look. "No... I'm going to figure this out on my own." Vince looked down at the cube... one side perfect... the rest of it a mess of mixed-up pieces. "I need to figure it out myself."

"Suit yourself." She started toward the front of the church. "You remind me of our old pastor. Everything had to be his way. He wouldn't let us have bingo nights; said it was gambling. And that wasn't gonna happen on church property. Then one summer, during his sabbatical..." She turned back, with a gleam in her eyes. "Well, let's just say sometimes the rules need to bend before they break you."

"Does everyone in this town share its history?" His words didn't convey the meaning behind them. And he felt it.

Ginny's laugh belied his concern. "Only the good parts. That first bingo night saved this church. Now we have a library next door—it was an unused building we converted where people can now sit, relax, and exchange books. And there's always coffee brewing. It's all about bringing people together."

His thoughts briefly drifted to the irony of what she said. Here he was, running away from people, trying to solve his puzzle alone. And here was Ginny, showing him what happens when you bring people together—when you dare to bend the rules that hold you back.

His thought returned while she was in mid-sentence...

"... and it's those community programs—not just for our town, but for towns all around. We're now a vibrant community resource. We're flush with money and people. All because someone dared to try something different."

People around here really do like to share their history. Vince wasn't sure if that thought stayed in his head or left his mouth.

She settled onto the organ bench. "Speaking of different, want to hear what I'm practicing for Sunday?"

Before he could answer, the pipes above the organ filled with sound. The soft melody wrapped around him like a warm blanket.

"Hymn 408," she called out over the music. "What kind of voice do you have?"

"Not much of one," he shouted to the front of the church.

"If you're brave enough, feel free to follow along."

He found himself reaching for the hymnal, turning to the hymn number she called out—408. He followed along, reading the lyrics to himself. The next line hit him: "Be still, my soul, your best, your heavenly friend. Through thorny ways leads to a joyful end."

The stained glass above the altar seemed to come alive with sudden clarity. He stood so quickly the hymnal tumbled to the floor. "Thank you!"

"For what?" Ginny's fingers rested on the keys.

"You have no idea how I ended up here today, but you just helped me figure something out." He was already moving toward the door, then stopped and turned back. "Too bad you're not practicing 'Amazing Grace'—I was lost, but now I'm found. Was blind, but now…"

"That's the closing hymn," she called after him, laughter in her voice. "See? Sometimes the answer's right there in front of you. You just have to be willing to look for it differently."

The door closed behind him, but he could still hear the organ music following him into the wind and rain. He stood there, letting his jacket darken from the drops—just like Chief Jack had done. For the first time since becoming a cop, Vince didn't hate getting wet on a rainy day. There was something liberating about it, like washing away old certainties.

Maybe that was the point all along. Maybe sometimes you had to change the rules to find the right path—even if it led through thorny, wet, and uncertain ways to get there. Even if it meant getting a little lost before being found.

CHAPTER 13
PERFECT RHYTHM

The windshield wipers were finally outpacing Vince's racing thoughts as he headed back home. But something miraculous was happening, too. He had fumbled with the radio dial to play some music—noise to fill the background of his mind. He landed on a classic rock station out of Philly that had a DJ who knew and played everything Beatles-related.

Vince paid little attention to the DJ announcing the next song. Until it started to play.

The first time ever. The miracle of all miracles... his windshield wipers were keeping time with the song. The beat of George Harrison's *Got My Mind Set on You* was in perfect sync with his wipers. Since the day he turned seventeen, he had waited for this moment.

He tapped the beat on his thigh as he drove. Thrilled to experience this one in a million chance. Then he thought about the recurring lyric, the same as the song's title. His mind was set on something alright. And that something could cost him everything.

While keeping time with the song, he had been tapping his thigh. Now that the song was over, he found himself tapping the phone that he shoved in his pants pocket. He should call someone. Audrey needed to know he was ready to do something. Carmen deserved some kind of explanation. Maybe Frank might have some wisdom to offer.

No... not yet. First, he needed to figure out the plan. Plan first, then notify. That's the right way to do it.

The rain had slowed to a steady drizzle, matching his mood. Everything that had happened lately played through his mind like one of those old movies his dad watched: Audrey's recorded confessions. His lies to Carmen. Getting pulled over by a small-town police chief who saw right through him. And now, driving home from a log cabin church where a grandmotherly organist taught him more about rules and grace than all his years of wearing a badge.

Ginny's story about the church's bingo nights kept coming back to him. A congregation facing extinction until someone dared to bend the rules. Even risk breaking them. Just like Chief Jack letting him go with a warning and some wisdom instead of a ticket. Just like his boss trying to reach past rank and offer friendship.

"Be still my soul... through thorny ways leads to a joyful end."

The verse echoed in his ears. His whole life had been about avoiding thorny ways. Follow the rules. Stay in your lane. See everything in black and white because gray areas only lead to trouble. That's what made him a good cop.

But what kind of brother did that make him? What kind of son?

His father's life was at stake. The recording was illegal—that was black and white. Using it would end his career—another absolute. But letting his father die because he was too rigid to adapt? That was a shade of gray he couldn't live with.

The Rubik's Cube sat on his passenger seat, its one perfect side facing him. What if solving it wasn't about getting each side perfect one at a time? What if it was about accepting that sometimes you had to mess up one side to save the whole damn thing?

He thought about the extortion case that started all this—Keisha Washington's distinctive voice in Audrey's recordings. He thought about his father personally handling discovery in a Russian mafia case. The pieces were there, but the pattern wasn't clear to him.

And for the first time in his career, he was okay with that uncertainty. He didn't need all the answers right now. He just needed to be willing to look for them differently. It was freeing—like standing out in the rain, not caring about getting wet.

His wallet lay open on the passenger seat—he never put it back in his pocket after he was stopped. The badge in it caught the brief breakthroughs of sunlight as he merged onto the expressway. His gold shield no longer felt like a weight of responsibility. Today, it felt like a choice.

Through thorny ways...

He smiled, thinking of Chief Jack standing in the rain, his boss trying to help him find his way, and a church organist who showed him that sometimes salvation comes from breaking the rules.

It was time to see where the thorny path that stretched out before him was going to lead. He was probably going to get bloody.

CHAPTER 14
BADGE OF CHOICE

The fluorescent lights hadn't even warmed up yet when Vince caught his reflection in the dark windows of the detective bureau. Something looked wrong—jeans and a sweater instead of his usual suit and tie. But that was the point. Starting today, he wasn't going to be Detective Brown anymore.

Carmen Navarro was already at her desk, waiting for him just as he had asked when he called her last night. She looked up, her eyes catching his casual clothes. "What's going on, another personal day?"

"Not a personal day. I'm taking a leave of absence." He kept his voice firm. "Effective immediately."

She set down her coffee. "Sit."

"LT—"

"Sit down, Vince."

He did. But not on the edge like he did all the previous times she called him into her office. Instead, he sat back in it like a visitor who had asked to meet with her.

Even the chair felt different somehow, like he was already on the other side of the desk... like he was already a civilian.

"Talk to me." It wasn't an order, but a request asked with a soft voice. "Not as your supervisor. As someone who cares what happens to you. Vince, I can't help if you won't let me in."

"Just need some time, that's all."

"Bullshit. At least give me a chance. Let me decide if I can help you or not. I can't do that if you won't open up."

"I can't. I won't... not yet." He caught himself starting to open up. "Besides, like I said, I just need some time."

"I can't stop you... if that's your decision. But you know there's a process, so it won't be happening today. Your union president has to be on board, and—"

"I called him last night. He's waiting outside." He pulled folded papers from his back pocket. "And the paperwork is already filled out."

Something flickered across her face—hurt, maybe. Or disappointment. "The only thing missing on it is his signature, right?"

Vince nodded.

She picked up her phone. "Chief? I have a detective here. And his union rep. They need to see you... Yes, sir. Right away."

Vince looked at her. She wouldn't look back at him. Did he just betray the one person up here who he was sure had his back?

"Alright, let's go," she said, taking one last sip of coffee before heading out of her office.

There were no words spoken during the walk to the chief's office, which was led by Carmen in front, followed by the union president and Vince trailing behind.

Chief Huertas's face, usually readable, was statuelike. But when he locked eyes with the union president, he saw red.

"Close the door." The chief studied Vince over steepled fingers. "What's this about?" He motioned with his forefinger to the union president. "What's so important that *he's* here?"

Vince spoke up. "Personal reasons, sir. Family matters."

"We all have family matters, detective. Welcome to the world of police work." The chief scanned his office, stopping at each face. "Why. Are. We. Here?"

The union president looked at Vince. "I guess he didn't get the memo."

Carmen stepped in before all hell broke loose. "Sir, Detective Brown is requesting a leave of absence. The paperwork is completed and signed by both him and his union president."

The chief looked at the union president, who looked back with hands folded on his lap and a smile on his face. Then he looked at Vince... who wasn't smiling. "Why?"

Vince wasn't sure who he was talking to but didn't want to give his union president—who thrived on confrontations with the chief—a chance to reply. "Sir, like I said. I have some family issues I need to take care of."

"That's it? That's all you're giving us?"

Vince met his stare. "Yes, sir."

The chief picked up the LOA form Vince had dropped on his desk. He quickly scanned it and then looked up at Vince. "This kind of request is highly unusual, Detective. And rarely given except under the most extreme circumstances."

"Like family emergencies and matters like that, right?" The union president's voice cut off the chief... who was not amused.

He looked at the two of them, Vince and his union president. "You two thought of everything, didn't you?"

"I try to be thorough, Chief."

Chief Huertas didn't respond to the union president's comment. Instead, he spoke to Vince. "You understand lying on a LOA request is grounds for termination?"

"I do, sir."

"And once I sign this, you have no union representation. No protection from qualified immunity. Your pension is frozen. You're not a cop anymore, Brown... not until you complete the paperwork to come back. You're sure of this?"

"Yes, sir."

Chief Huertas signed his name, effectively making Vince Brown a civilian.

"I need your ID, your duty weapon, and your badge."

Vince placed his ID on the desk. Then his gold shield caught the morning light one last time as he laid it down. His weapon came last, carefully unloaded, the familiar weight of it leaving his hands.

Chief Huertas stood up. "You're a good cop, Brown. You've got a real future here." He shook his head. "Don't screw this up. Don't get dirty."

Vince almost laughed. Getting dirty was the whole point. But the chief didn't need to know that.

In the hallway, Carmen grabbed his arm. "Whatever you're planning... be careful, Vince."

He turned to face her. "I heard a hymn yesterday. 'Be Still My Soul.' It talks about thorny paths leading to joyful ends." He let himself smile. "I'm choosing my path, LT."

"What if it's the wrong one?"

"Then at least I chose it honestly."

He could feel her eyes on him as he walked away, each step lighter than the last. Setting down his badge had lifted a greater weight than just the metal it was made from.

The morning sun hit him as he left the building. He thought about Chief Jack standing in the rain, about Ginny at her organ showing him that sometimes you had to break the rules to save what mattered. About his father, who'd taught him that doing the right thing wasn't always the easy thing.

For the first time since becoming a cop, he walked to his car without his weapon. His fingers touched the empty spot on his belt where his badge used to ride. Maybe that hymn had it wrong. Maybe the thorny path wasn't just something you endured.

Maybe it was something you chose.

PART 2

CHAPTER 15
MESSENGER BAG

The January wind still had teeth, but at least the rain had stopped. Vince sat at their usual table inside Elissa's Coffee Shop, watching the few brave tourists stroll the boardwalk. No badge today. No gun. Just a civilian waiting for a friend.

Frank appeared through the door, messenger bag slung across his shoulder like always. "You're early."

"Old habits."

"Speaking of habits..." Frank gestured to Vince's empty cup. "My turn to buy. You got it last time."

When he returned with fresh coffee, Frank settled into his chair with the ease of a long friendship. "So. No suit today?"

"About that..." Vince started to apologize for suspecting him of breaking his vows—of breaking the confessional seal, but Frank waved it away.

"Water under the bridge." His smile was warm. And forgiving. "Or over the boardwalk, in this case."

A man approaching their table interrupted them. "Father Frank! I thought that was you."

"Another beautiful day to be alive," Frank responded with his usual warmth.

"Not just another day," the man corrected with a smile. "Another chance." He introduced himself as a motivational speaker in town for a convention.

Vince looked on with wonder at the ease with which Frank could start a conversation with anyone. Vince always stayed off to the side when he was around people he didn't know. But Frank, Father Franciscus Jakubovicius, was at ease around everyone.

As he looked on, listening to the two men speak as if they'd known each other for years, Vince was envious of the beloved priest.

Before moving on, the man looked at them both. "I believe in you."

Vince watched him disappear out the door. "Well, that was different."

"Nice man. I wonder what convention he's at." Frank sipped his coffee, seemingly unfazed by the man who was different.

"Does everyone you meet exchange life advice with you?"

"Occupational hazard." Frank's eyes squinted. "But he had a point. I do believe in you, Vince. What's going on? What did you need to talk about?"

Vince took a deep breath. "Audrey's been recording confessions."

The warmth drained from Frank's face. "What?"

"I couldn't believe it either. But I heard them..."

"Is that why you accu— ... I mean, is that why you were asking if I would violate someone's trust?"

Vince stared into his coffee, his fingers squeezing the cup. "Please don't take this away from me... Please let me apologize. I am sorry, Frank."

Frank leaned back. "I accept your apology, Vince. Unconditionally."

"That means a lot... more than you know, Frank. Thank you." Vince's shoulders relaxed for the first time since sitting down.

"But I need to ask... I need to know... how is she doing it?"

"There's a microphone in the confessional. She's been collecting the recordings like podcasts." Vince watched his friend struggle with the implications as he explained about Mrs. Washington's extortion case. The blackmailer knew what was said in the confessional, word for word.

"I'll need to report this..."

"Not yet." Vince leaned forward, lowering his voice as a couple passed their table. "Please. There's a criminal investigation now. If you report it... it'll trigger a whole lotta stuff."

Frank adjusted his collar, a habit Vince had noticed whenever his friend felt caught between duties. "And some of that stuff will come down on you?"

"Some of it." Vince watched a waitress refill cups at nearby tables before continuing. "But the majority will dump onto Audrey—it'll violate her probation. No doubt about that."

Frank changed subjects so smoothly that it took Vince a moment to notice. It was another one of Frank's gifts. "How's your father doing?"

"Why the deflection?"

"Because we've known each other too long for secrets." Frank's fingers drummed his messenger bag. "And sometimes knowing too much is dangerous."

"I didn't want to dump this on you, but I knew you would want to know."

"Now I know. It's said knowledge is power, right?"

Now Vince deflected. "Like knowing the monsignor's views on change?"

"Yeah." Frank's smile was as sad as anyone's frown. "I guess our theological... differences... are becoming more apparent."

"Hard not to see it. You're trying to build bridges while he's reinforcing walls."

"The Church is meant to be a living thing, Vince. Growing. Changing." Frank's hand rested on his bag. "It's frustrating. I admit it."

"You keep a hold on that bag like it contains nuclear codes."

"I keep a diary in here. I write about certain leadership decisions. About the church..." He met Vince's eyes. "Sometimes I write about faith. Even my own doubts."

"Careful, Frank. That sounds almost agnostic."

"Maybe that's why we understand each other, my friend." Frank stood. "Vince, talk to Audrey." His voice became serious. "Make sure she gets rid of everything... make sure she cleans her room. You know..."

Vince walked outside with him, then to the boardwalk entrance, glancing up at the security camera housings mounted on the poles. "Big Brother is everywhere."

"Everywhere indeed." Frank adjusted his bag. "Keep the faith, Vince. Whatever version you've got left."

Vince watched Frank walk back toward the church. Toward his sister's twisted idea of entertainment. Toward a confessional where people's sins had been recorded. Where a threat he couldn't ignore was still hanging in the air.

His friend's messenger bag swung gently with each step, carrying secrets of its own. Vince wondered which would prove more dangerous—the confessions Audrey had recorded or the ones Frank had written down.

CHAPTER 16
EVIDENCE AND ADRENALINE

Audrey's room door swung open with the same irritating creak it always had. Vince didn't wait for her to come to the door when he knocked. This time, his purpose made him walk in the doorway. The weight of Frank's words pressed on him, making this space feel less of a chaotic mess and more of a dangerous omen.

"My baby brother in the flesh. Again," Audrey said without looking up from her sketchbook. Her words carried their usual edge of sarcasm.

"I need the recording equipment, Audrey. All of it."

Her pencil froze on the paper. Now she looked up. "Excuse me?"

"You heard me. The recordings, the equipment... everything."

"Got a warrant, Detective Brown?" She smirked with a hint of reason beneath the joke.

"I'm not playing around." Vince moved toward her desk and spotted some of the equipment.

"Neither am I." Audrey's voice hardened. "You better have probable cause, little brother."

Since the day he was sworn into the department, Vince never took evidence without probable cause. Her words cut into him. He felt naked. No gun, no ID... no badge. He wasn't a cop right now, but she didn't know that.

Vince reached for a USB drive, and Audrey lunged to grab it first. For a moment, they stood frozen in a moment of sibling rivalry turned serious.

"This isn't my idea; it's Frank's."

Audrey's grip on the drive loosened slightly. "Father Frank? Why?"

"Because it's not safe for you to have this stuff anymore." Vince softened his voice. "He's worried about you, Audrey... I guess we both are."

"Oh, now you're worried?" She released the drive but crossed her arms. "Mr. By-the-Book is suddenly okay with destroying evidence?"

"This isn't about—"

"The monsignor's dirty, Vince." The words burst out of her. Out of nowhere. Like she had been waiting for the right time. "You might not know how dirty, but he *is* dirty. And I think you'll find out a lot more if you grow a set of balls and listen to the recordings."

Vince didn't respond to her comment. A comment that rang true in his heart... *If I can find the balls to listen to them.*

Audrey used her phone to follow Vince around the room, acting like a news reporter narrating his moves. "Right now, we're live in the room of Audrey Brown while Atlantic City Police Detective Vince Brown confiscates his first USB—"

"You better not be recording this." His look was stern, yet sincere. "I'm serious, Audrey."

"Father Frank really believes I'd be in danger with them here?"

"He does. Which is exactly why you can't keep any of this here." Vince continued gathering the equipment, shoving it under his hoodie. "I'll handle it."

"Handle it how? Vince Brown isn't going to conduct an off-the-books investigation, is he?" Her laugh was harsh. "Isn't that against department policy?"

Vince paused, his hand on another drive. "You let me worry about that."

Vince looked out her small window that looked out to the side of the church. The side where the confessional was located. *What the fuck am I getting myself into?*

Audrey broke the silence with another one of her unfiltered comments. "They're going to kill Dad, aren't they?"

The question hung in the air between them. Or was it a statement disguised as a question?

"I won't let that happen." He meant it to sound confident, but it came out more like a prayer.

When he finally had everything concealed under his hoodie, he headed for the door. "Just... stay out of it from now on, okay?"

"Like hell," Audrey muttered, but Vince was already in the hallway.

The January air hit him like a slap as he stepped outside. He'd made it three steps before a familiar voice froze him in place.

"Vincent! What a pleasant surprise!" The monsignor stood by his car, his cassock rippling in the wind.

Without his badge and gun, Vince felt every inch the imposter. "Monsignor." He forced a smile. "Just visiting my sister."

"Ah, working on that relationship?" The older man's eyes were shrewd. "Your father would be pleased."

"Trying to." Vince held onto whatever he could through the pockets of his hoodie, squeezing it all tight against his lower ribs, praying nothing would fall out.

"You should join us for Mass more often." The monsignor's smile didn't part his lips the way a genuine smile would. "Remember, my son, faith is a mystery. Faith can unlock many doors."

"I'll keep that in mind."

They parted ways, and Vince didn't breathe until he reached his Jeep. His hands were shaking as he started the engine. Is this what it felt like to be undercover? This constant dance of truth and lies, never knowing if your next word might be the one that gives you away?

He didn't want to wait any longer than he had to, but the engine in his old Jeep demanded a few minutes to get warm. The shivering he felt—his hands shaking, his legs feeling weird… wasn't from being cold or even being scared. The adrenaline that coursed through his body rebounded back to his brain. And it felt good, like a feeling of being high.

This was a rush!

Without looking down, Vince felt the outline of crucial evidence through his hoodie and wondered about the mystery of faith. He wondered how much faith he would need in himself to pull this whole thing off.

CHAPTER 17
THREE COPIES

The morning sun filtered through pine trees, casting long shadows across Vince's front yard. His small rancher sat back from the narrow country road, more cabin than house really, with weathered cedar siding that blended into the surrounding woods. Behind the house, the gentle sound of a small river provided a constant backdrop to his thoughts.

Vince sat at his kitchen table, staring at the USB drives laid out before him. Each one represented a piece of evidence that could bring down a murderer—or get someone killed. His laptop hummed as he began the systematic process of transferring the recordings.

"One copy isn't enough," he muttered to himself, reaching for a fresh USB drive. Years of collecting evidence had taught him the value of redundancy. He created a covert email account and uploaded the files, then backed everything up to a secure cloud service. Three copies. Three insurance policies if this were to go south.

The day crawled by as Vince planned his next moves. He chose dusk because there would be fewer people out, yet still be enough light to see. His reflective winter cycling jacket felt heavy with the equipment from Audrey's room as he zipped it up. The new USB drive, placed in an envelope, went into a separate pocket, away from the others. Something about keeping it isolated felt right, like isolating the truth.

Before leaving, he locked Audrey's original USB drives in his bedroom gun safe. He laughed out loud at the irony of it—protecting evidence that was gained by breaking every protocol he'd ever followed—starting on a path that was against every ethical point he'd ever taught.

For the first time in his life, Vince was playing a game he didn't know the rules of. And the rules he had lived by suddenly seemed all wrong. He counted on the hour-long bike ride to clear his head.

The causeway bridge stretched before him as he pedaled his bike through the growing darkness. One by one, he pulled pieces of recording equipment from his jacket and dropped them into the water below. Each splash felt like a step further from the clear lines of right and wrong that had always been his trusted companion.

Jayne Westwood's law office was his final stop. The lights were still on—she'd always worked late, even back when she was with the public defender's office. He made his way to her desk. Here familiar red reading glasses were perched low on her nose.

She looked up, surprised. "Vince? What brings you to these parts?"

He placed an envelope on her desk, along with a crisp ten-dollar bill. "Congratulations. You're now my attorney."

"I'm what?" She picked up the ten. "What is this?"

"Retainer fee." He nodded toward the envelope. "Don't open that unless something happens to me."

Jayne stood up, concern printed on her face. "Vince, what's going on? Are you in trouble?"

"The less you know, the better." He turned to leave, then paused. "Just... secure it. Keep it safe."

"At least tell me—"

"Thanks, Jayne." He was already walking out, leaving her concern behind.

The ride home was easier, his jacket lighter without the equipment. But the weight of what he had just done weighed on his shoulders like an unfamiliar burden. The thought of what he was about to do…

It was completely dark now, and Vince forgot to turn on the bike's light. He'd never done that before. He never rode at night without first turning on the light that was mounted to the handlebars. He wouldn't even leave his driveway without it on. And yet, now… now he was breaking the law: "Every bicycle ridden at night shall have a front headlamp visible from at least 600 feet away. Every rider shall ensure that it be illuminated between the hours of dusk to dawn."

Vince knew this law by heart. And like all the other laws on the books, he followed it to a T. Part of him, feeling reckless from what he had just done, wanted to ride the rest of the way home without turning it on. *There are hardly any cars on the road now. What could it hurt?*

The black-and-white world of right and wrong was bleeding into shades of gray, and for the first time in his life, Vince was torn by it. Downshifting a few gears to climb an incline, he remembered how difficult this stretch could be in a higher gear. Just like in life, sometimes we have to lose a few gears to make the ride easier.

He'd risk it. He'd run with scissors. He'd throw caution to the wind. It would feel good!

Nope. He couldn't do it. Vince reached down and flicked the switch that turned on the light for the rest of the ride.

Back home, he locked his bike in the garage and sat on his back deck. The river's constant flow seemed louder now, or maybe he was just more aware of it. It's said that you can't step into the same river twice. The flowing water is already downstream by the time you take that second step—into different water.

What if this game he's just gotten himself into is like that? What if it keeps moving and he can't stop it? Who is he going to be when he steps into this river again? The former him carried downstream to an inevitable conclusion he can't see.

Three copies of the evidence. Three chances to save his father. Three steps away from the man he used to be.

The methodical detective in him had covered every angle. Now it was time to see if the son in him could finish what he'd started.

CHAPTER 18
SPREADSHEET TRUTHS

The USB drive felt heavier than its small size warranted as Vince plugged it into his laptop. His own voice emerged from the speakers first—his confession to Father Frank the week before Christmas Eve Mass. He quickly hit pause, not ready to relive that moment. Not ready to hear himself confiding in a man who might have betrayed not just him, but everyone who trusted him.

Keisha Washington's voice came next. The same acts she committed that she told Detective Turner about in his report, word for word. Word for word—exactly what she had confessed to Father Frank. Vince's stomach churned. The evidence was pointing somewhere he didn't want to look.

Hours passed as Vince cataloged each recording. He focused on the confessions to Father Frank, delivered in English, heavy with guilt and hope for absolution. There were other confessions in what sounded like Russian, all from male voices, given to the monsignor. But those weren't the ones giving Vince agita. It was the pattern he couldn't ignore, and he worried other confessions were being used for extortion... confessions that had been made to Father Frank.

"It can't be you," Vince muttered, opening Excel to start a new spreadsheet. "There has to be another explanation." But his training wouldn't let him look away from where the evidence led, even if it led to his best friend.

Columns for date, time, and notable details grew as he worked. The dates and times remained frustratingly blank—Audrey had set the recording device to voice-activated mode. Smart for saving memory, useless for establishing a timeline.

"Always see the big picture," Vince reminded himself, his voice fading in the quiet room. It was how he was taught to approach every case—step back, see the patterns, then dive into details. But this time, the patterns were showing him something he didn't want to see.

Then he found it. The confession about a murder. It was followed later by the same voice speaking of being ordered to kill his father. Vince played both recordings again and again until his ears rang, searching for any identifying detail—an accent, a speech pattern, background noise. Nothing except a growing suspicion he wished he didn't have.

He rubbed his tired eyes. If he were still on the job, he could take these recordings to Major Crimes and let their detectives listen. Someone might recognize the voice. But he wasn't *Detective* Vince Brown anymore, just Vince Brown. A private citizen conducting an unauthorized investigation that, if done poorly, could get people killed. At the very least, it could get him fired.

His phone sat on the desk, Audrey's contact open, ready to hit "Call." Maybe she had noticed something he missed. Maybe she heard these men coming or going or caught a glimpse of them. Maybe she could tell him something, anything, that would point to someone other than Father Frank.

Vince stared at the spreadsheet, its neat rows and columns a stark contrast to the messy reality they represented. The big picture was there, hidden in the data. He just had to figure out how to see it before it was too late... and before he lost his faith in the one person he trusted most.

CHAPTER 19

SHARED FREQUENCIES

Audrey's vacuum cleaner hummed in the empty sanctuary. She liked cleaning when no one else was around—it gave her time to think, to notice things others missed. Like the way sunlight hits the stained-glass windows at a slightly different angle each day, or how the wooden pews creak when the heat kicked on.

She spotted Vince the moment the old church doors slammed shut behind him. She started to wave him over, but his subtle headshake stopped her. Even from this distance, the look on his face was easy to read.

"What's wrong?" she asked, meeting him halfway up the aisle.

He quickly scanned the perimeter. "Not here."

He saw that Audrey sensed concern in his voice. "Vince, what's—"

He cut her off. "Your room."

Vince followed her to her room, where he pulled out his phone and an adapter. "Just listen," he said, plugging in a USB drive.

The first recording filled her small room—a man confessing to a murder. Then another confession, the same voice talking about their father. Audrey's fingers twisted in her lap, another habit from childhood she'd never broken.

"It's the same person, right?" Vince asked.

"Obviously." She rolled her eyes. "So, what?"

"All the confessions are in English except for some that are in another language," Vince said, looking at her for some kind of answer.

"I think you missed something."

"What do you mean?"

"Play them again." She leaned forward, her face intent. "Listen to who's taking those confessions."

Vince frowned but did as she asked. His expression shifted, listening to them once more. "That's... that's not Frank."

"The monsignor," Audrey said confidently. "You were so focused on the voice of the guy confessing to the murder that you didn't even notice who was hearing the confessions. Not only are those Russian-sounding confessions to the monsignor so are the two from the hitman." A small smile came to her lips. "Some detective you are."

Their bickering continued over the recordings playing on Vince's phone.

"Vince, shut up!"

"No, you shut up!"

"Vince, I'm serious. Shut the fuck up and play that last recording again."

He went back to the beginning of the recording.

"Turn up the volume," she ordered.

Two men speaking in a foreign language, possibly Russian. One was unmistakably the monsignor. Audrey looked at Vince, as if for a reaction. "Do you hear it?" she asked.

"Hear what? All I hear is the monsignor talking to some guy in Russian."

"The other guy, Vince... his voice...doesn't that sound like..." She looked into Vince's eyes.

He was staring down at his phone.

"Vince, I'd swear that's... I mean, it sounds like..."

Vince's face went pale. "Dad."

Audrey barely got out the words, "Jesus Christ, Vince."

Vince saw she was looking at him. He didn't know what to do. What to say. He stood speechless, frozen in place. He hadn't blinked his eyes since hearing his dad's voice.

"Vince? Vince... Vince! Are you okay?"

He didn't look up. He rubbed his temples. "What have I gotten myself into?"

"What have *we* gotten *ourselves* into?" she corrected.

"No." His voice was stern. "You're not involved in this. You can't be. You're on probation, Audrey. These recordings alone could send you to prison."

"Oh please." She stood up, pacing the small room. "You think you can handle this on your own? Your biggest cases involve keeping kids from smoking behind the gym. You're in way over your head."

Vince finally looked up. "I can handle it."

"Right. I suppose you'll just hand everything over to Lieutenant Luscious and let her sort it out."

"Who?"

"You know who I'm talking about. Your boss, Lieutenant Navarro?" Audrey grinned. "Come on, you'd have to be blind or gay not to see she's the hottest cop on the Jersey shore."

"That's...she's attractive..." Vince sputtered. "But department policy prohibits—"

"Department policy?" Audrey laughed. "You're conducting an off-the-books investigation right now! What happened to Mr. Ethics, huh?"

"This isn't an off-the-books investigation..." His voice trailed off.

"So, this is on the up-and-up. Who you partnered with?"

"It's not like that." Vince hesitated. He looked down and away from her. "I took a leave of absence," he finally admitted. "So technically, I'm not violating any policies."

"You what?" Then her face softened, and she chuckled. "Not violating policies, but fuck... what about breaking the law?"

"None of this would have happened if you didn't record those damn confessions."

"Yeah, and if I didn't, we wouldn't know about the plan to kill Dad."

Vince shook his head. "I'm gonna get dirty on this one, Audrey."

"Well, well. Look who's finally willing to see some gray in his black-and-white world."

"Gray? I'm hoping it doesn't turn blood-red."

Audrey stood at one of the paintings hanging on the wall. "I never noticed something until right now, Vince. The reds I put into all my paintings... If that gray does turn to blood-red, promise me it won't be your blood."

"I promise I'll be careful... I'll watch my six." He hadn't seen that look in her eyes since they were teenagers. "But I'd be lying if I told you I wasn't scared."

Audrey let out a breath, shaking her head slowly. "Who are you, and what have you done with my by-the-book brother?"

"I don't know about either of those," he answered.

Audrey stepped forward and did something she hadn't done in over twelve years. She hugged her baby brother. Her embrace brought back memories of high school, of the sister who shared laughs with him, who was there for him before everything went wrong.

"You promised to be careful," she whispered into his shoulder. "Please."

When he pulled away, he saw something new in her eyes—understanding. Maybe they both just took a step toward growing into the people they were meant to be.

CHAPTER 20

WINTER CONFESSIONS

The January wind cut through Vince's jacket as he scanned the boardwalk for what felt like the hundredth time. The paranoia was new—this constant feeling of being watched. Is this what it's like for undercover cops? Always looking over their shoulder, never sure who to trust?

The last three days were like this—a feeling, a sense. His gut telling him something. Maybe it was listening with Audrey to his dad's voice in the recordings. That was certainly the reason he needed to talk to his friend.

"We need to talk outside," Vince told Frank, who looked at him like he'd lost his mind.

"Again? Vince, it's freezing. The wind chill's in the teens."

"Please, Frank. Let's get them to go."

Frank nodded yes. But everything else about him said no.

The coffee shop's warmth quickly faded. They found a corner between two shops where the wind wasn't quite as brutal. Steam rose from their coffee cups, immediately taken away by the wind.

"What's going on?" Frank asked, pulling up the collar of his coat.

Vince looked around, then up. Security cameras appeared to be mounted to streetlights at every corner. Even on the boardwalk. He paused, taking in the fleeting warmth his cup provided to his hands. "If you heard something horrible in a confession..." he began. "Something that could get someone killed. What would you do?"

Frank's face grew serious. "I'm guessing this isn't a hypothetical question."

Vince's head shake was barely perceptible.

"Vince, like you, I've taken an oath to be a part of the organization I serve. My oath is that of fidelity, and it includes the vow of the sacramental seal. This is part of the canonical law..."

"In English, Frank..."

Frank's headshake was more pronounced than Vince's. "It means I cannot, and will not, violate the seal of confession. I told you that. I can never reveal anything said in confession."

"Even if it was about someone you care about?"

"Unfortunately, yes, Vince." Frank's voice was gentle but firm.

Vince pulled out his phone, his fingers trembling. He told himself it was from the cold, but a deeper part knew it was from nerves. "Just listen." He logged into his cloud account and played the murder confession.

Frank rubbed his eyes. "Vince... How did you get this?"

Vince's reply was quick. After all, he'd prepared for it on his way there. "Remember all that stuff with Audrey recording confessions?" Vince watched Frank's reaction carefully. "Do you recognize the voice?"

"No, but..." Frank frowned. "That's the monsignor taking the confession."

"Listen to this one." Vince played the second recording—the threat against his father.

Frank's stunned silence spoke volumes.

"Say something, Frank!"

"You don't understand," Frank began. "It's more complicated than I could ever explain. More complicated than I even know."

"This whole thing is complicated, Frank. I'm just trying to find some answers. If you can't give me answers, at least give me leads. Tell me where I need to look."

Now Frank was looking around. Looking behind Vince, making sure they were alone. "You must know that the monsignor... he's done so much good. The food bank, the children's parties, getting the school up and running again—"

"Don't defend him!"

Frank ignored Vince's admonition. "But consider this—didn't Jesus himself hang out with sinners?" Frank spoke lower. "Some parishes... they look down on how the monsignor associates with certain people."

"What people?"

Frank hesitated. "There are rumored to be members of the Russian mafia who come to church. They... they have a unique relationship with him." His eyes lowered to the cold pavement beneath them. "I can tell you this: that voice in the recording? It sounds like one of them."

"And you're okay with this?"

"Vince, stop looking into this. Let the authorities handle it. Give it to the Feds. Give the burden of this to someone else."

"Burden?" Vince's voice cracked. "While they kill my dad? You're just going to stand by and do nothing?"

Frank shifted his feet to turn his back to the gusting wind. "I've taken a solemn oath, Vince. I've promised to—"

"I took an oath, too, Frank! But I'm also a decent human, and I can't sit back and do nothing. Do you have any idea what I'm risking?"

Frank stayed silent.

"I'm risking my job... my career in law enforcement. God knows I'm probably risking my own safety. All I'm asking is for you to meet me halfway. You can trust me, you know that."

"Vince, I trust you with my life. *You* know that. And I am not about to suggest that the oath I took holds more weight than the one you took. But I cannot violate the vows I've taken. And I cannot apologize for that, Vince. Not even to you."

Vince breathed in deep. The cold air stung his lungs. "I'm risking everything. You're risking nothing. I guess I thought I knew you better..."

"That's not fair, Vince!" Frank clutched his messenger bag closer. "I will not break my vows. But... I can tell you what I've seen." He leaned closer. "Every couple of weeks, the same group of men comes for confession. It's like... like he's holding court in there. Six months ago, he implemented an online confession schedule. He's suddenly very into technology, especially cryptocurrency donations."

"Frank, what kind of—"

"Hey guys!" Audrey's voice cut through the wind. "What's going on?"

Vince's stomach dropped. "Audrey..."

"Are you telling him about the recordings?" She turned to Father Frank. "The ones in the foreign language?"

"Audrey, stop—"

"I think they're Russian," Vince cut in, trying to salvage the situation.

Frank asked to listen to another snippet. "That's not Russian. They're speaking Lithuanian."

"Interesting," Audrey replied with widened eyes. "Well, I gotta get my steps in before it gets any colder." As she turned to leave, she dropped another one of her leaky bags of crap on them. "Oh, and Father Frank? Make sure you tell Vince about the monsignor's 'special blessings' on the homeless girls."

She walked away, leaving silence in her wake. Frank's hand tightened on his messenger bag—a detail that didn't escape Vince's attention.

A sharp bark cut through his thoughts—it was more a distressed cry than a bark. The cries sounded like how Vince felt—distressed, desperate, cold.

Through the swirling wind, Vince spotted a medium-sized dog, maybe a Lab mix, tied to a bench. Its leash was tangled around its neck. He ran over, carefully freeing the frightened animal. A note attached to its collar read: "Please give this dog a good home. I can't take care of her."

When Vince looked back, Frank was gone. He had always been there for Vince. Except now, when he needed him the most.

The dog looked up at Vince, her sad eyes speaking a language his heart understood.

The local vet, a friend of Vince, confirmed the dog wasn't micro-chipped. "She's perfect for you," she said as the dog nuzzled Vince's hand. "Sometimes the best companions find us when we need them most."

Vince scratched behind the dog's ears, wondering what he would name her... and how many more surprises this investigation would bring. At least now he wouldn't face them alone.

CHAPTER 21
SACRED GROUND

Vince found Frank exactly where he knew he would be—visiting the graves of parishioners after Divine Liturgy, like he did every Friday. The Orthodox church cemetery was five miles inland from the city, its treelined setting a stark contrast to the dirty buildings and crime that made up the neighborhood around the church.

Vince stood at the gates, taking in the acres of three-barred crosses rising from snow-dusted graves that stretched out in front of him. The bare trees created a montage of skeletal shadows across the frozen ground. How many times had they stood here together, Vince the detective and Frank the priest, watching families lay their loved ones to rest?

Today was different. Today, Vince wasn't here for support; he was here for answers. He approached his friend, who had his back to him.

"Running away yesterday?" Vince's voice broke the sacred silence. "That was chickenshit, Frank. That's not like you."

Frank didn't turn around. "Sometimes running away and stepping back are the same thing, Vince." His head dropped to the hand that was holding his messenger bag. "But I knew you'd find me."

"Yeah? How's that?"

"Because you're like a dog with a bone when you want answers."
Now Frank did turn, slowly—his face wearing a look of worry. "And because this is where we've always had some of our hardest conversations."

"Harder than yesterday's?"

"Yesterday's conversation wasn't hard, Vince... it was impossible. It was impossible for me to be a part of the conversation you wanted. Of the conversation you *needed*."

"Bullshit." Vince kicked at the hard ground. "It wasn't a choice between hard and impossible, it was between what you would or wouldn't do. And you chose to run away from a hard conversation."

"A hard conversation involves opening up, sharing pain... being vulnerable," Frank replied.

"You want to talk about being vulnerable... friend? Do you have any idea the vulnerability I—"

Frank cut him off. "What you asked of me yesterday was impossible. It was something I could not do, no more than I had the power to make that dog stop barking. It wasn't a matter of whether I wanted to or didn't want to. I couldn't... no matter how hard I would have tried. It was simply impossible."

"Impossible? Is that your truth in this?"

Frank made the sign of the cross in his religious tradition, right to left. He paused, looking down at a grave marker with Cyrillic script. "Yes, it is, Vince, and I've been carrying around my truth for months." He patted the messenger bag. "Right here in my *dienyas*."

"Your what?"

"My journal. Dienyas—it's Lithuanian." Frank's breath created a cloud in the cold air. "There are things in here... things I'm not sure I can tell anyone. Not even my best friend."

Vince's anger softened slightly. "Try me."

Frank walked to a nearby bench, brushing off the snow before sitting. "You know how many crises of faith I've helped others through, Vince? Now I'm having my own. Some days..." he swallowed hard. "Some days I'm not sure what I believe anymore."

"Frank—"

"That's not all." Frank squeezed the bag's strap. "I've struggled with my identity, my... orientation. Not that it matters with my vow of celibacy, but if anyone read this..." He gestured to the journal. "It would bring shame not just to me, but to the church."

Vince sat beside him. "How would your personal struggles shame the church?"

"Because they're not just personal anymore." Frank's voice dropped. "The monsignor... he uses the confessional for private meetings with certain men. Russian mafia. He believes anything said in there can't be used against him. That's why he created the confession schedule, so these men know when to come to him instead of me."

"What kind of meetings?"

"Business meetings disguised as confessions. He even insisted on telling me about the cryptocurrency donations in the confessional." Frank shook his head. "He's so ultra-conservative he's medieval. The role of women in the Church... he believes, like children, they should be seen and not heard."

"He sounds like an asshole!"

"Think of him the next time you say, 'holy shit'... it'll be the most accurate truism ever spoken."

Vince once shared with a group of new officers what he heard in a resiliency seminar: "Trust grows when truth is shared in safe spaces." The shared truth that Monsignor Augustas is an asshole was enough for both men to share a laugh.

Frank took a moment to wipe tears from his eyes. "I haven't laughed like that in a while. I guess I needed it."

"I think we both did," Vince replied, wiping his eyes as well.

The laughter faded, leaving behind the kind of silence that comes before a confession.

Frank looked off into the distance, his expression growing serious. "You know what's not funny, though? The way he treats people's guilt like currency. If he could, he'd bring back paying for indulgences. The worse the sin, the more you pay for forgiveness." He lowered his voice. "I have a feeling he's already making parishioners pay... somehow."

Vince rolled his eyes in disgust. *How bad could her sin have been for Keisha Washington to be blackmailed by him?* "And Audrey's comment about 'special blessings?'"

Frank brought his hand up over his mouth. Vince had seen this behavior many times when questioning suspects—when they reluctantly told the truth but subconsciously wanted to stop it. "The homeless shelter in the basement...some of the women... I suspect he..." the devoted priest couldn't finish the sentence.

"Jesus Christ, Frank."

"I've tried to see good in him. But my journal..." Frank pulled out a leather-bound book. "It documents everything. Including his connection to someone in Lithuania. A figure they call the Rook. *Bokstas* in Lithuanian. No one's sure if this person even exists, but the monsignor both fears and reveres them."

"Who is it, this Rook figure?"

"A shadow. A whisper. Someone with connections throughout the Baltic States and Russia. And by connections..." Frank looked around the cemetery, as if concerned the dead might be listening. "I mean the worst kind possible."

"What else do you know about this Rook person?"

"Only that they're to be feared. The monsignor mentions the Rook often, always with a mixture of awe and terror." Frank stood, shaking snow from his backside. "Vince, whatever you're planning... whatever you think you can do... be careful. The Rook isn't someone to be played with."

Vince stared at the headstones surrounding them, thinking of what they represented—the death of someone who's remembered by loved ones. Right now, he felt caught between the memory of his dying self and the future of a loved one who unknowingly needs his help.

"Your journal holds evidence that's different than what I have, Frank. What's in your journal can be used for probable cause. It can be admissible in legal proceedings."

Frank clutched the bag tighter. "Knowing what's in here... it changes things. Changes people."

"I'm already changed." Vince stood, ignoring the snow that clung to his pants. "The question is, are you with me?"

The wind whipped through the cemetery, carrying with it the burden of Frank's silence.

Finally, he nodded. "God help us both."

CHAPTER 22

LOST IN TRANSLATION

Vince stared at his phone. Google Translate wasn't cutting it. The Lithuanian voices came through tinny and fast—too fast for the app to catch more than fragments. He slowed the playback, but still only caught about two out of every three words.

"There has to be a better way," he said to Echo, who was lying in her bed in the corner of the room. He swiped the screen to the app store, reading reviews on the best translation software. It was a paid version, but the price would be worth it. The premium version of the app he found worked flawlessly, letting him re-record cleaner English versions of each conversation.

What he heard made his blood run cold.

"The week's haul..." "The church's cut..." Each conversation began with mock reverence—"May you confess all sins worthy of forgiveness"—followed by barely concealed laughter. Some of the men even threw in sarcastic "Father forgive me" openings.

The pieces started falling into place. Money flowing to the Refuge of Divine Mercy Church in Lithuania. The Russian mafia's satisfaction with their arrangement. But what turned Vince's stomach was the monsignor's bragging about his side hustle—blackmailing parishioners who'd confessed to Father Frank, demanding payment in untraceable cryptocurrency. The same kind Keisha Washington had mentioned.

"Stupid, naive Americans," the monsignor's voice was filled with contempt.

Vince's finger hovered over the next recording—his father's voice. He needed air. Now.

The January cold hit his face as he stepped outside, but the relief was short-lived. A dark SUV turned into his long driveway—unmistakably the chief's vehicle. Vince's heart stopped. His dining room table was covered in recording equipment and translation logs.

Chief Huertas emerged from the driver's side. Then, his boss, Carmen Navarro, got out of the passenger door. She wouldn't look him in the eyes.

"Thought we'd check on you," the chief said, extending his hand. Vince hoped the chief wouldn't feel his trembling.

"I'm okay," he managed. "Just getting some air. Family stuff."

Carmen's expression was unreadable. He couldn't tell if it was supportive or if it was a threat.

"How about some coffee?" The chief smiled. "After that mind-numbing domestic violence lecture at the academy..."

"We saw your dad there," Carmen cut in. "He was presenting to all the command staff personnel in the county."

The chief cleared his throat. "He seemed surprised about your leave of absence. Sure, the DA shouldn't be aware of every leave of absence in the county, but when that DA has a son in one of the departments, you'd think he would know about it."

"Well... like I said, it's family... and I—"

"So," the chief cut right through his words, "I thought we'd swing by and see how you were doing."

The four or five seconds of silence that followed felt like four or five hours.

"Well…" The chief's smile widened. "Are you going to invite us in or do we need a warrant?" He chuckled. Carmen managed a forced laugh, but her eyes stayed sharp.

"Love to," Vince said, forcing a laugh of his own. "Let me get my dog first. I have to get her contained, or she'll jump all over you. We're still working on her manners."

He hurried inside, scooping armfuls of recording equipment and spreadsheets into a magazine rack.

"What's her name?" the chief called.

Vince dropped the last handful into the rack. "Echo!"

"Echo?" The chief accepted Vince's invitation to go inside. Carmen was right behind him. "Interesting name."

"Down, girl," Vince snapped, pulling her off his chief's chest. "Sorry about that. Like I said, we're still working on manners."

"Don't yell at her, Vince. I like dogs with some spirit in them." The chief patted her on the head. "She's a good girl. Why 'Echo?'"

Vince launched into an explanation about her name. Pythagoras, the number five, the age of his childhood surgery, the letter E. He brought up anything to keep them from looking too closely at the corner rack.

But Carmen saw the magazine rack, recording equipment, and ledgers hanging out. She subtly positioned herself between the chief and the evidence, drawing his attention away.

"When can we expect you back, Vince?" the chief asked. "Any medical reports we should know about? You know the department's liable if you're not fit for duty—physically or psychologically."

"I'm fine," Vince insisted. "Just need some time."

"Look at that," the chief said looking at his watch, "we don't have time for coffee after all. Checking in on my men like this isn't something I normally do. But this is a little unusual—authorizing a leave of absence with no real reason given for it. Think of this as an unannounced locker inspection. How do you think you did, Detective?"

Vince's words came out of nowhere. "I think I passed with flying colors, Chief!"

Chief Huertas gave a final look around the room, one last inspection before they left. He seemed to look right past everything in the magazine rack. "You remember the one thing I told you… the one thing I tell every officer when they get hired? The one thing I won't tolerate?"

"That was more than seven years ago, Chief." The next sentence would be a lie. "I'm not sure I recall what—"

"I told you the importance of honesty. The one thing I will not tolerate is lying. I'm glad you're a man of integrity, Vince. Don't let this leave of absence change that."

Vince nodded and they left soon after. But Carmen stayed a few steps behind. "You better fucking call me tonight," she breathed through clenched teeth.

Audrey might have been right when she said his boss was the hottest cop on the Jersey Shore. But today, Lieutenant Carmen Navarro was as cold as ice.

Either his body was numb or he had become immune to it, but he didn't feel the icy wind as he watched the chief's car pull out of his driveway. Maybe the relief and thrill of not being caught created a warmth inside him that insulated the outside of him.

Back inside, Vince spread everything out again and put on headphones. His father's voice filled his ears, speaking Lithuanian to the monsignor. The translation cut into his soul.

"You betrayed your word to the organization, Mykolas." The monsignor's voice was stern. "They've forgiven you too many times now. There must be a price."

Mykolas. "Michael" in Lithuanian. "How deep is he in this?" Vince asked himself.

Then came the "game show" options—three doors. Michael could choose his punishment. He could choose what's behind door number one: his own life. What's behind door number two: Audrey's life. Or what's behind door number three: Vince's life.

The truth about the orphanage came out. How his father had made a deal with the Russian mafia to save Vince and Audrey. How seriously the organization took a man's word. How many times they'd overlooked his failure to follow through with what he was supposed to do.

But not this time. They weren't going to overlook his disobedience this time. This time, they were serious.

The final exchange caught Vince's attention. The monsignor was asking about the Rook, mentioning strange messages, wondering if they were being played with. Asking Vince's dad if he had heard from this mysterious figure.

Vince removed the headphones, his mind racing. The truth about his adoption was bad enough.

But Lieutenant Navarro's warning, his father's predicament, this mysterious Rook figure...

He looked at Echo curled up in her bed. At least one of them would sleep tonight.

CHAPTER 23

OPENING GAMBIT

Vince was up before dawn. Echo's gentle snoring was the only sound in the house. The recordings had played in his head all night—his father's voice speaking Lithuanian, the monsignor's corruption and his threats, the mystery of the Rook. Each time he tried to put the pieces together, something inside him flung the board into the air, and the puzzle went flying.

In his sleepless night, something had formed in the darkness. Something grew inside him—rage.

He'd spent his whole career playing by the rules while men like Augustas twisted faith into a weapon. No more. Vince wasn't just angry—he was ready.

So many things that he thought were right were wrong. What was supposed to be up was down. Those who were believed to be righteous were evil. Vince had interviewed enough addicts to be familiar with the phrase, "My world is spinning out of control." But he never imagined it would ever be his world that was spinning like that.

The only thing stopping him from taking a baseball bat to everything in sight was the feeling of Echo's cold nose against his arm. He was so angry; she was so gentle. He was filled with rage; she was demonstrating compassion.

His world was spinning out of control. Echo was grounding him. He at least owed it to her to promise not to do anything foolishly impulsive.

Some promises are hard to keep...

The church office door crashed open. "We need to talk!"

Monsignor Augustas looked up calmly from his desk. His carefully maintained appearance, with his clean-shaven head, spoke of wealth and reminded Vince of a banker who enjoyed counting his money. "Vincent. What a pleasant surprise." His voice held a fake welcoming tone. "What brings you here so early?"

"I know what you're doing. I know you're into a lot of crooked shit. I'm going to prove it. And when I do, I'm going to nail you to the wall."

"Now, son—"

"Don't call me son," Vince snapped. "You're not my father!"

"Ah, but do you know who is?" Augustas's smile exposed his evil heart. "Wouldn't you like to know your real father, Vincent?"

"What I know is that I'm going to Vilnius. And when I come back, I'll have enough dirt to bury you."

"Americans," Augustas sighed. "Always taking the path of least resistance. That path won't lead where you need to go."

"Your days as a priest are numbered. I'll confirm everything in Lithuania. And when I'm sure—"

"Is that so?" The smile vanished. "Now listen to me, Detective, I don't know where you've gotten these absurd ideas about me. But it seems obvious you don't have the slightest clue who you are dealing with. Now, my advice to you is to back down while you can."

"Oh, I know exactly who I'm dealing with. And I'm not backing down... In fact, when I find the Rook..."

"What was that?" As if he wasn't sure he heard what Vince said. "Did you say, 'the Rook?'"

Vince didn't respond. He stood, looking daggers into the monsignor's eyes.

Augustas's hand slammed the desk. "I asked you a question, goddamn it!"

After a brief moment, he stood and composed himself. "I mean, I wasn't sure what you said, Vincent. Please forgive my blasphemous outburst."

"Hit a nerve, did I?"

For the first time, real fear flashed in his eyes. "Vincent, there are mysteries that none of us fully understand. Yet some mysteries are understood by those who have earned the right to discern them through devotion and elevation to certain callings." Augustas adjusted the expensive nameplate on his desk, the one that read *Monsignor Augustas* in bold lettering. "I will suggest again that you back down from mysteries you do not understand."

Vince glanced over at the chessboard set up on the coffee table. "Looks like you enjoy playing games. I might not know all the rules of the game you're playing. But mark my words, when I get back from Lithuania, that board is going to look a lot different than it does now." Vince leaned across his desk. "I'm going to take you down, you sick fuck."

The monsignor's voice switched back to being loud and stern. "You are nothing but a pawn in this game, Vincent. A pawn that is a mere inconvenience. There is no evidence you could ever produce to prove your wild claims. And you *will* get sacrificed if you try to play against the real masters of this game."

"Isn't that piece in the corner called a rook?"

"Get out," he yelled. "Get out of my office!"

Vince left, but not before catching the tremor in Augustas's hands. He'd found the monster's weakness—now he just had to follow it to Lithuania.

Driving home, he had to adjust himself in the seat to get comfortable. Maybe the set of balls Audrey told him he had to grow had started.

CHAPTER 24

PLAN B

The Belt Parkway stretched endlessly ahead as Vince began his drive home from Kennedy airport. His suspended passport was on the passenger's seat, thrown there when he got back into his car at long-term parking. *How could I be so stupid!*

He'd practically gift-wrapped his plans for Augustas. "You have no idea who you're dealing with," Augustas had warned. Now Vince knew exactly what he meant. *If he could pull this off, what else could he do?* That was the question he asked himself for the next two and a half hours.

Vince walked through his front door long after dark. Echo greeted him with her usual enthusiasm. "I'm back sooner than expected, aren't I? But don't worry, girl. There's always Plan B."

It would have been more believable if Vince already had one in mind.

Before he started on a new plan, he had to cancel an important part of the first one. Vince called his sister. "Hey, it's me. Listen, I'm back home... Yeah, look, I don't have time to explain. I just wanted to let you know that you don't have to stop over to take care of her... I can't right now. I'll let you know when I come up with something... Me, too."

Reading didn't help, nor did watching TV. Even meditating didn't work. Vince had to face a hard truth—he wasn't going to sleep tonight. His mind raced with possibilities, each one more desperate than the last.

Sometime between 5 a.m. and first light, an idea formed—the kind of idea that would have horrified the old Vince. But the old Vince was gone, replaced by someone willing to not just bend the rules but break them if needed to accomplish a mission.

If people could be smuggled into the country, wouldn't it stand to reason that a person could be smuggled out?

The Golden Lotus Massage Parlor didn't open for business until noon, plenty of time for him to do what he had to do—get in and out before the first customer could ID him. With his old patrolman badge tucked in his pocket and holding his portable radio as a prop, the back door kicked open. The frightened owner bought the ruse and gave him a name.

That name led to the boardwalk, to a T-shirt kiosk run by an ex-Port Authority cop whose human trafficking conviction was overturned on a procedural technicality. The negotiation was tense, but money talks. The guy demanded ten grand—up front. Then more for each person along the way.

"Make sure to get a burner phone. Pay for it with cash," the man told him. "No credit cards; leave them home. And set up a Western Union account. Load it with as much as you have."

Vince said he understood. That was only partially true. He wanted this to get started immediately. The guy told him it could take as long as a week to get everything in place. "You'll get a text—it'll be nothing but a time and location. Be ready; they won't wait for you."

On the way home, Vince made careful withdrawals from his accounts—all under ten thousand dollars to avoid IRS flags. He wasn't robbing each bank he visited, but the guilty feeling in the pit of his stomach made him feel like a criminal, nonetheless.

Then came the hard part. "Hey, it's me again... New plan... I don't know when it will start... The day you don't get a text from me will be the day. Come over to take care of her, just like before. But this time my phone and credit cards will be on the dining room table... Would you just listen! The screen will be unlocked. Use it to call for pizzas and other takeout. Pay for it with the credit cards."

Vince looked down at Echo, snuggled in her bed so peacefully. He envied her. How he wished he could be that carefree. Instead, he had to face the truth of what he had just done—he had betrayed the badge. His badge, the one he held up in the air after kicking in the door.

"I don't know, maybe a week or so... I can't. Just trust me, okay? Yes... I am really doing this... because I have to."

The next two days dragged by. He made sure his backpack had everything he would need. Vince was bored but determined to make this happen. Passing the time by trying to solve the Rubik's Cube only made him more frustrated.

Finally a text—*Atlantic Packing Marina. Monday. 6 a.m.*

Vince got down on the floor with Echo, wondering when he'd see her again. The wooden floor that supported his weight was a hard contrast to the soft, plush bed she was in. The scene represented an ideal question for him to consider: the soft Vince versus the hardened Vince.

The old Vince would never take this risk. But the old Vince didn't have a father marked for death.

If the monsignor thought a suspended passport would stop him, he didn't know who he was dealing with either.

CHAPTER 25

SIX HOURS OUT

The fishing trawler F/V Marek's captain's words hit Vince harder than the waves. "Six hours minimum. Strong northerly wind."

"Six hours?" Vince's stomach lurched. "I thought—"

"We're going out to sea, not up the Intracoastal. Fishin' boats fish in the ocean." The captain's tone made it clear this wasn't negotiable. "Plus, compensation for losing a day's catch."

Vince checked his backpack. There was enough cash, that was for sure. He remembered everything he thought he'd need for his time in Lithuania. Except for one item: motion sickness pills.

By sunrise, he had nothing left to vomit over the side. The icy spray had numbed half his face, but the dry heaves continued until they finally reached the Metedeconk River. The smoother ride was of no use to his digestive system, and the forty-five-minute ride up the river to the dock was excruciating.

The walk to the small airport would test his resolve. Dehydrated and dizzy, Vince stumbled into a Walgreens on his way there. Leaving with Dramamine and electrolyte drinks gave him a glimmer of hope. It would turn out to be too little, too late.

"You look like shit."

The voice belonged to a woman in her mid-twenties, standing outside a hangar at the small airport.

"I'm waiting for someone," Vince managed between sips of the lemon-flavored drink he bought fifteen minutes earlier.

"You're waiting for me." Her smile was disturbingly cheerful. "You ready to go flying?"

She looked more like a party girl than a pilot. In fact, she looked nothing like a pilot. "You're the... I mean, you're the person who's going to fly me to—"

"Just got my license last month." She started walking toward the tarmac. "You coming?"

Vince followed, doing mental math. "How long have you... how many hours do you have?"

"Eighty-two. Got them cheap too." She looked over her shoulder at Vince, who was doing his best to keep up with her. "Sleeping with the flight school owner has its perks."

Vince didn't know how to reply to that, so he replied with what he thought was a valid question. "So you think you're qualified to fly a plane all the way up to Nantucket?"

"Nope, not at all..."

Vince looked up and down the tarmac. No planes in sight.

"I have no idea how to fly a plane," she said, pointing with a playful smirk.

Vince's knees went weak. "That's a helicopter."

"Safer than planes. Stop being a pussy and get in."

The pre-flight briefing didn't help. "Don't touch the stick between your legs, the lever by your left hand, or the pedals. And we might hit some weather from that nor'easter."

Less than an hour into the flight, Vince was emptying his duffle bag to use as a makeshift airsickness container. But they made it to Nantucket.

The next leg promised to be better—a real plane with a real pilot, a pilot with thousands of hours of flight time. Until that pilot mentioned flying below radar, dodging ice storms, and his sketchy past, which included a stint running drugs from Colombia.

Vince fought the double dose of Dramamine, determined to stay awake. But thirty minutes out over the Atlantic, his mind was as dark as the moonless sky around him.

Three and a half hours later, he woke to unfamiliar runway lights and his pilot's voice. "Welcome to Halifax. Well, not Halifax proper. We can't risk Stanfield Airport. You've got four hours to make your cargo flight. Better start walking."

Alone in the frigid night, he was exhausted, bordering on dehydration. At least the dry heaving had stopped. Vince pulled out his burner phone. No apps, no GPS, no options. He stared at the keypad, then dialed 4-1-1, praying Canadians still believed in directory assistance.

"Halifax operator assistance, how may I help you?" Vince almost laughed with relief. At least something in Canada was familiar. He was connected with Yellow Cab of Halifax. An unusual pick-up location meant he better have a believable answer.

The story came easily. "Bachelor party gone wrong. Guys thought it'd be funny to drive off when I was taking a leak. Got an early flight out of Stanfield."

Forty-five minutes later, huddled under an airport outbuilding's overhang, he saw headlights. The cabbie was suspicious. Who wouldn't be, picking up a stranger at this hour? Vince made sure this version was the same as when he spoke with the cab company.

The heat in the cab was heaven. So much comfort that Vince wished he could spend more time in the back seat. But at 2:30 a.m., they reached the main terminal. Vince paid cash, earning a raised eyebrow from the driver.

The airport map on the pole showed what he needed—the service road that led to an airport overlook. Vince did some quick math: a two-mile runway with a quarter-mile clearance at each end. That equaled at least a three-mile walk. With just a few hours of sleep in more than twenty-four hours, his judgment was sketchy, but he had no choice.

He kept the airport fence to his left, counting hangars. One wrong turn cost him ten precious minutes. At 3:18, exhaustion made the darkness feel alive.

Headlights in the distance sent him into the woods. The vehicle passed, but something rustled in the underbrush—breaking twigs, strange cries. His mind fabricated bears stalking him... before remembering they'd be hibernating. But the sounds followed him, growing more intense with his pace.

At 3:56 a.m. the wooden sign appeared: "Airport overlook parking." It was nothing more than an icy, muddy field, no bigger than a convenience store lot. The animal sounds stopped. They were replaced by the rumble of an SUV. Its lights were off.

The driver's thick accent was unmistakenly Scottish. "Get in." After a short drive to a nearby golf course, they switched to a box truck. Vince got a company shirt, cap, and a new identity. He was now a cargo handler trainee.

The security guard at the airport's rear gate knew the driver by name. Finally, something was going smoothly.

The hangar's lit doorway led to three pilots and the blessed sight of freshly brewed coffee. They even had a shower. If he could get washed and get some caffeine in him, he would feel almost human again. They told him there was plenty of hot water and to take all the time he wanted.

After his shower and hot coffee, Vince learned his new cover—he was the broker's rep for a DC-10 being sold to Polish firefighting services. These ferry pilots were legitimately flying it to Warsaw, where it would be gutted and retrofitted for its new purpose.

"Built in the '70s," one pilot mentioned casually. Another joked it hadn't flown in more than a decade. They both told him to read up on the specs of the DC-10 from a three-ring binder on the table... just in case he was asked about it when they landed.

The warmth he got from the shower was replaced with cold fear. Vince's stomach turned. "But at least I'll be asleep if anything happens," he told himself.

Vince nearly cried when he saw the interior of the plane – completely stripped except for a small jump seat next to one of the side doors. A jump seat at a fixed ninety-degree angle. So much for sleeping.

"I hope you brought a warm jacket," one of the pilots yelled from the cockpit. "Most of the insulation's been removed to make it lighter and cheaper to retrofit. Let me know if you need a set of earbuds when we get to altitude, it can get pretty noisy up there."

Great—cold, loud, and no way to recline to sleep. Vince had heard of no-frill flights that depart and arrive at Atlantic City International, but this was taking that idea to a whole new level.

The eight-hour flight to Warsaw was exactly as advertised… with a lot of bumpy turbulence thrown in—just for fun.

At least getting through customs was easy. His passport passed customs inspections just as the pilots told him it would—they only checked the expiration date. By 10:06 Warsaw time, he was studying bus schedules to Vilnius.

The last bus for Lithuania's capital would leave in a little more than an hour. He found a cushioned chair in the layover lounge and worked on his cover. He pulled out the journal he purchased just for this trip and crafted his story in the way of entries: Russian mafia threats, fear for his family, a mysterious meeting arranged by the monsignor.

The bus pulled up at 11:30. Eight hours to Vilnius. At least he could finally sleep.

CHAPTER 26
PARALLEL LINES

Tuesday 4:15 p.m.—Atlantic City Police Department
(Tuesday 11:15 p.m.—Lithuania)

Carmen Navarro's heels clicked down the hallway to the chief's office. The sound of each step a sign of her growing unease. Through the glass, she saw Chief Huertas wasn't alone. Sitting across from him was Vince's dad—Michael Brown.

Of all the detectives under her supervision, only one had a dad who was the county district attorney—Detective Vince Brown.

Perfect.

"Close the door, Lieutenant." Chief Huertas's voice had that edge she'd learned to dread. "The DA's received some interesting information about your detective."

Michael Brown cleared his throat. "I received an anonymous tip earlier today. Vince was denied boarding a flight at JFK last week. He was trying to get to Lithuania." His command presence as a prosecutor shifted to a concerned parent. "His passport's been revoked."

As shocked as she was to hear it, Carmen kept her face neutral. "First I'm hearing of it."

"Is it?" The chief leaned forward.

Michael Brown stood. "I should go. Keep me informed?" The question seemed directed more at Carmen than the chief.

After the DA left, Chief Huertas dropped his professional facade. "Is this really the first you're hearing of it, Lieutenant? Because if I find out one of my officers has gone rogue..."

"Sir—"

"I'll have his badge."

"I'm telling you... I know nothing of this."

"If I find out you did, I'll have your badge, too." He stepped around his desk. "Now... I want data warrants. Phone, financials, maybe even his house."

Carmen's phone vibrated in her purse. She reached for it instinctively.

"Are you serious right now?" The chief's face contorted. "Put that damn thing away!"

Her fingers fumbled, nearly dropping it. She held it awkwardly, too rattled to return it to her purse.

"Sir, we need probable cause for warrants. He is on a leave of absence. He is free to travel wherever he wants to go." She tugged on the seam of her business suit jacket. "There's case law —"

"Spare me your legal expertise, Counselor. You haven't even taken the bar exam."

"With all due respect—"

"No, *not* with all due respect, Lieutenant, this is a direct order. I want a warrant on my desk by tonight."

Carmen straightened. "I won't violate the law, sir. Even suspecting Vince of something doesn't override his rights."

"Vince? It's 'Vince,' not 'Detective'? What kind of unit are you running where you refer to your subordinates by first name?"

"It is just the two of us in here. We're not in public. I see every one of my detectives as a person first. Then a cop."

"Your detectives? They're not your detectives. They're the city's detectives. They're the department's detectives... they are *my* detectives. You got that?"

Her eye roll was uncontrollable. So was her response. "Whatever."

"That's insubordination!" The chief's voice dropped dangerously low. "Think carefully about your next words. They could end your career."

"I have rights, too, Chief. They include due process and a hearing."

"That would take time, wouldn't it?" Huertas looked at the clock on the wall. "I'll give you some time to think about this... to follow through with my direct order. Monday morning." He jabbed his finger at her. "That's your deadline. Use the next week to consider your future here."

"My future..."

Huertas's smile was cold. "Or maybe we should discuss your fitness for duty? Are you still taking the antidepressants you self-reported when you completed your medical file last year?"

Carmen's jaw tightened.

"And that ankle... is it still bothering you from the training accident? Looks like you're favoring it."

"I'm fine."

"Are you? Because a psychological evaluation or a physical might say otherwise. If you were to fail either one..." He shrugged. "You're done. No badge, no hearing, no recourse."

Carmen stood, her phone still clutched in her hand like a shield. "Will that be all, sir?"

"Monday morning, Lieutenant. Don't let me down."

She left without being dismissed, her heels clicking a defiant rhythm down the hall.

CHAPTER 27

NIGHT RIDERS

Tuesday 11:30 p.m.—Warsaw Bus Station, Poland
(Tuesday 4:30 p.m.—Atlantic City)

Two passenger vans emptied their contents—fifteen impossibly tall men and four handlers, all carrying gym bags and reeking of alcohol. Their loud Lithuanian voices echoed through the terminal, the same harsh consonants Vince remembered from the recordings.

"You American?" One giant pointed at Vince's cowboy hat—his attempt at a different identity suddenly felt amateur compared to these professionals.

"Yes." No point lying. The hat ruse failed. It was a dead giveaway. He counted on something he'd picked up from watching narcs work—include a kernel of truth, they always said. "I'm from Florida. I have relatives here. I guess you could say I'm looking for family roots."

They bought it. The basketball players adopted him. Through alcohol-soaked grins, they rambled on how they just won an international championship tournament. They're heading home, back to Vilnius. Their flight was grounded due to an approaching storm. This was the last bus to Vilnius for days—until the storm let up. The roads to Vilnius are very dangerous to drive in the snow. They hoped to get into town before the worst of the storm hit.

They had bottles to share. Vince politely declined.

They insisted. Vince resisted the temptation. But he thought about how a good swig would take the edge off. How it used to take away his pain and his worry... until he'd wake up the next day feeling like crap.

Instead of a drink, Vince decided to try something he hadn't done in years. He prayed. He prayed they'd pass out quickly into whatever seat where they landed. The more he prayed, the louder they got. Some kind of team fight song threatened to split his skull. More than one coach tried to control their behavior. Whatever they were drinking from their gym bags was stronger than the coach's resolve.

By 2 a.m., they were all unconscious. Silence finally descended. Vince pressed the side of his head against the cold window. Another attempt at prayer: Please God, take this headache away. Only he and the driver were awake as the bus rolled through thickening snow. At 3:30, his mind finally surrendered to sleep.

A nudge woke him. "You're in Vilnius."

Vince blinked at his watch: 12:31. Impossible. They were supposed to arrive at 7:20. He looked out the window. Daylight filtered through the bus station's overhang. Beyond it, heavy snow was falling.

"Time?" he asked one of the players, who just stared blankly.

The driver spoke English and apologized for their late arrival. "Not easy drive in snow."

Vince pointed to his watch, confused. The driver smiled. "Did you change time in Warsaw? Is 7:30, not 12:30."

As Vince adjusted his watch, fragments of a dream tugged at him. In the few hours of restless sleep, he had a dream so vivid that he could have sworn it was real. He'd had dreams like that maybe twice before, where reality and sleep blurred completely.

Carmen... Now that he was awake, he wondered what she was doing—it was just past midnight back home. Something about that thought felt important, but his exhaustion took his mind in a different direction.

Welcome to Lithuania.

CHAPTER 28
TRAIL CAMERA

Tuesday 9:45 p.m.—Atlantic City
(Wednesday 4:45 a.m.—Lithuania)

She needed to get her thoughts together. Carmen sat in her unmarked car, the engine off. The deserted business parking lot was three blocks from the station. Yet she felt miles away from the department. The trail camera rested in its case on the passenger seat. This type of department property was never signed out this late at night.

"What the hell am I doing?"

Professional Standards should be handling this. Or the DA's Special Investigations Unit. Instead, here she was, about to conduct surveillance on of her own detectives. The chief's threats from yesterday were still fresh in her mind. But this was less about saving her career than it was about Vince.

She looked around her—an empty parking lot on an empty street. The property log would show that she signed out the camera tomorrow morning. She should care more about that.

Each passing car on the twenty-minute drive to Vince's made her pulse jump. She drove by slowly on the first pass. His house sat back from the two-lane road. It was dark except for a dim light in the living room and the front porch light. She drove slow enough to see Echo's shadow pass by a window—at least someone was taking care of her.

Carmen pulled onto a dirt road across the street, killing her lights as her car came to a stop. The winter-bare trees offered little cover. Anyone driving by would spot her car. She started to come up with reasons why a lieutenant was out here alone at night.

But if she could find out who he was communicating with—who was coming and going from his house—before Huertas did, she'd be able to confront Vince and get to the bottom of it without search warrant affidavits being filed. Maybe she'd be saving both their careers in the process.

Her hands grabbed the camera and her flashlight while her conscience wrestled with duty. This wasn't just career suicide—it was betraying procedure, everything she'd built her reputation on.

Why does it feel like I have to do this for him?

The beam of headlights sent her diving behind a tree. The car passed slowly. She convinced herself it was someone checking their phone. But her heart still pounded away. Two full minutes passed before she moved again.

The tree she chose was perfect—a clear view of Vince's driveway and sturdy enough to hold the camera. Her fingers fumbled with the straps in the cold. The camera had to be high enough to avoid snowplows and angled just right to catch license plates.

A branch snapped behind her. Carmen spun, her hand instinctively going to her belt holster. A deep sigh of relief—it was just a deer, its eyes reflecting her light before it bounded away.

She finished securing the camera, then checked the angle one last time. Tomorrow night she'd be back to download whatever it caught. The chief wanted answers? Fine. But they'd be her answers, not his.

Walking back to her car, Carmen remembered the last time she'd broken procedure. It was during her days in the academy, covering for a fellow recruit who'd screwed up badly. After that almost got her kicked out, she swore never again.

Nonetheless, here she was going against policy for someone who never violated a policy or broke a rule... a detective who was, as his colleagues called him, squeaky clean.

"Some rules are worth breaking," she muttered, starting the car. She just hoped she was breaking them for the right reasons.

CHAPTER 29

MORNING STAR

*Wednesday 7:40 a.m.—Kaunas, Lithuania
(Wednesday 12:40 a.m.—Atlantic City)*

The cabbie's words crushed Vince's plans. "That church isn't in Vilnius. It's two hours away, near the Russian border."

"But it's called the Refuge of Divine Mercy Church *of Vilnius*," Vince protested, showing him the name he'd written down.

"Ah." The driver pulled up a map on his phone. "It is in Vilnius Eparchy—the diocese. Not in Vilnius city." He studied the route. "I cannot take you that far, but I know a place in Kaunas. It's a historic city." He pointed to a small dot on the map. "A good hostel. It is halfway there. Fewer questions in a hostel than a hotel."

Fewer questions sounded perfect. Vince hadn't dared make any reservations for any part of this trip. He couldn't risk leaving an electronic trail. The cabbie called ahead for him. An hour later he was at the Forest Camping Hostel and was introduced to Justina, the owner.

"Forty dollars for a private room, with a shared bath," she said. "Tea in the morning for you and this nice kitchen to cook in."

Justina's level of hospitality included escorting Vince to his room. Once she left, he headed straight for the shower. Vince let scalding water wash away travel grime while his brain tried to process everything. The old clock radio on the nightstand read 9:49 when he decided to lay down "just for a moment."

He woke disoriented. The clock radio read 2:45 p.m. Five hours were lost to exhaustion.

Vince wasn't sure where to go for something to eat—where to have his first real meal in two days. Justina's restaurant recommendation led him to Olde Town Pizzeria. The pizza was surprisingly good, and the owner's English was even better.

"Half of Lithuania speaks English," she told him. "What brings you here?"

"It's personal. I'm kind of using Kaunas as a home base" he replied. *Keep it vague,* he reminded himself. "Looking for a church. Thought it was near Vilnius. Turns out it's—"

"Then you must see Aušrinės Katedra," she insists. "The Cathedral of Morning Star. It's the most beautiful church in Lithuania."

Vince thanked her for the tourist information and the complimentary coffee and tiramisu.

The cathedral's dome pierced the winter twilight. Vince hadn't voluntarily entered a church since... he couldn't remember when. If it weren't for Father Frank, he'd probably never step foot in a church. But this one drew him in—ancient stone, stained glass, carved ceilings reaching toward the sky. There was a time in his life when he would have seen them reaching toward heaven.

"American?" A priest in black approached, switching smoothly to English. "I am Father Petras, the parish vicar."

Something in his gentle manner made Vince drop his guard. He mentioned wanting to visit the Refuge of Divine Mercy Church. Vince watched Father Petras's expression change.

"Why there?" Concern replaced the vicar's initial welcoming voice.

Vince gave his cover story—visiting an old orphanage, adoption records, family tree research. He used "Vince Michaels" again, his father's first name becoming more natural each time he used it as his last name.

"What do you know of the monsignor there?" Father Petras asked.

"Just that he might have answers. I'm hoping he can tell me things about the orphanage."

Father Petras's body language checked off every red flag mark Vince had learned in interview training. When Vince called him on it, the priest gently squeezed his shoulder. "Just be careful."

He walked to the altar, knelt briefly, and then blessed Vince with the sign of the cross. "May the peace and the love and the fellowship of God the Father, God the Son, and God the Holy Spirit be with you. Now and forever. Amen. Safe travels, my son."

The word "son" triggered something. Vince smiled at the great contrast between how it had enraged him when Augustas used it yet brought a reassuring comfort from this humble priest.

Father Petras disappeared through a side door, leaving Vince both unsettled and reassured. His reaction confirmed one thing—he was definitely on the right track.

CHAPTER 30

MIDNIGHT CONFIDENTIAL

Wednesday 11 p.m.—Atlantic City
(Thursday 6 a.m.—Lithuania)

Her car sat on the same dirt road across from his house, but this time she pulled to the end—completely out of sight from any passing cars. Carmen stood just in from the roadway, using a large pine tree to cover. Her breath in the icy air was the only visible sign of her presence.

The trail cam footage from the past 24 hours showed nothing regarding Vince—his car never moved, and there was no sign of him anywhere near or in his house. But there was one person who visited six times. Audrey.

The first thing the trail cam picked up was her pulling into the driveway last night, at this same time—11:02 p.m. Carmen looked down at her watch, 11:04. Right on cue. Audrey's Volkswagen pulled into the driveway.

Time to roll the dice.

Carmen followed on foot, then waited until Audrey was fumbling with her keys before sneaking up behind her. "It's a little late for a dog walk, isn't it?"

Audrey didn't even flinch. "Jesus, you're as bad as my brother with the dramatic entrances."

Carmen stayed right behind her when she opened the door. Echo's tail thumping against the wall kept a steady rhythm.

"Oh, please, won't you come in?" Audrey said sarcastically as Carmen made her way into the dining room."

"We need to talk."

Audrey's words caught Carmen off guard. "About Vince trying to get to Lithuania?"

"How do you know about—"

"Yeah, the chief and Dad talked. Dad told me. I wouldn't be surprised if the whole precinct knows by now."

"Audrey, this is serious. Do you know where he is?"

"Knowing my brother, he's trying to find a way to get to Lithuania." Her smile was pure mischief. "You going to ask me anything else?"

Carmen spotted his phone on the counter. "What else do you know?"

"Everything. The monsignor's shitty side. The recordings... Want to hear them?"

"Audrey—"

"Oh right, you're a good cop. By the book." Her tone shifted. "But Vince always said you were a cop's cop. That you had your detectives' backs."

"I'd like to think I do..."

"Then investigate the monsignor's background. If the recordings are just a part of what he's into, the Feds will have something on him. Use your cop computer to compare notes with the big boys."

Carmen pressed her fingers to her temples. "It's not that simple. One database search triggers a notification, and every federal agency gets flagged. The chief's looking for a reason—"

"So use someone else's computer."

"That's not how it works. Intelligence files are locked down. Any inquiry gets logged, a report is generated. I can't risk it."

"You can't risk it? I'm risking my freedom for Vince."

"Audrey, listen..."

"No, you listen!" Audrey's ditzy persona was transformed into a determined advocate. "The worst that happens to you is you lose your job. Do you want to trade that with me? Prison? 'Cause that's what I'm risking."

"It's more than what's at risk for me. If the wrong people find out about this, Vince's career is over. Whatever we do... I mean, whatever I do, can't come from any of my login IDs."

"Then call in a favor." Audrey's intensity reminded Carmen of Vince. "Someone must owe you. FBI? DEA?"

Carmen's mind went to Kristen, her academy roommate. She's now with the FBI. They still texted regularly. Kristen had taken the Bureau's offer their last week of academy training—straight to Quantico.

"Maybe." Carmen chose her words carefully. "I know someone. But this stays between us."

"Of course." Audrey's grin returned. "I'm great with secrets. Just ask Vince."

The irony of Audrey's statement wasn't lost on Carmen. Audrey promised Vince not to tell anyone what she knew. But the only way Carmen could help him was because of the information Audrey just gave her.

Carmen watched Echo curl up in her bed, oblivious to the plans being formed around her. "Your brother better appreciate this."

"He will," Audrey replied, reaching down to stroke Echo's neck. "Once we figure out where he is and then get his ass home safe."

CHAPTER 31
SMOKE SIGNALS

Thursday 10:20 a.m.—Sakiai District, Lithuania
(Thursday 3:20 a.m.—Atlantic City)

Vince spent the hour-long bus ride planning his moves. All of them centered on getting to Monsignor Dominykas Klastūnas.

He stretched his arms in the air on the near-empty bus. It's amazing what a good night's sleep can do. Especially when it's the first full night's sleep in three days.

The bus terminal in Sakiai District looked nothing like the transit hubs Vince knew from home. This wasn't even a real city—just a cluster of villages where Russian seemed to compete with Lithuanian on the streets.

"The Refuge of Divine Mercy Church?" he asked everyone who passed.

Blank stares until finally in broken English: "Fifteen minutes' walk." The man made a phone call as he walked away, speaking rapid Lithuanian.

The church complex sprawled across a hillside, knee-high stone walls enclosing perhaps twenty acres of weathered buildings. Vince stood outside the walls, studying the layout, trying to guess which entrance to try.

The stench of cigarette smoke hit him. He turned to see where it was coming from and saw it immediately. An old woman, probably homeless, stood a few yards behind him. Her hand holding a lit cigarette. Her face was a map of wrinkles under her wool scarf.

"Kas tu eso?" she asked repeatedly, her voice lifting at the end like a question.

"I am American," Vince tried, speaking slowly.

"American," she echoed, then: "Kas tu eso?"

Not knowing what to say, he went back to basics. "My name is Vince."

"Ah, Vincentas." Her smile revealed knowledge behind the simple exchange. Only his father had ever called him that, explaining it was his Lithuanian name.

She took a final drag from her unfiltered cigarette, holding it between thumb and forefinger like a joint, then motioned for him to follow. The reek of stale smoke trailed behind her as Vince was led to a side door where a nun answered her knocking.

After a brief exchange that Vince didn't try to understand, both women motioned for Vince to come in. He looked around the large room, his thoughts interrupted by the old woman's cough that rattled her entire body. Between wheezing breaths, she watched Vince with an unsettling familiarity.

"Welcome, Vincentas." The nun introduced herself as Sister Lina. "How long have you been looking for a child?"

The question blindsided him. She didn't give him time to respond. Instead, she led him on a whirlwind tour—a gymnasium full of wary children, dormitories segregated by gender, and the one-room schoolhouse connected to the main church by a covered walkway.

Most of the tour was spent in the schoolhouse. "The best teachers," Sister Lina proclaimed proudly.

Vince couldn't suppress a cynical chuckle. Best teachers? Three miles from the Russian border in the middle of nowhere?

The laugh felt good—he felt more like himself. But with that familiar sensation came the loneliness he'd struggled with even back home. He briefly wondered about home, four thousand miles away. What time was it there? What were they doing—his dad, Audrey, Frank, Lieutenant Navarro?

"We should talk in my office," Sister Lina suggested.

"Ma'am... I mean, Sister. I think there's a misunderstanding. I'm not here to adopt... I'm not looking for a child."

"Then what brings you to our church?" Her face was no longer cordial. Her smile was replaced with suspicion.

"I'm looking for Monsignor Dominykas Klastūnas. Am I at the right church?"

Her stare could have frozen hell. "No one sees the monsignor without first learning about our work."

"Okay, I've learned about your work. Now can I see the monsignor?" "The monsignor is a very busy man." Vince wouldn't have believed it if he hadn't seen it himself—her stare became even more intense. "Tell me the purpose of your visit, and I will check his calendar for next week."

A brief memory of his teenage years came to mind. He had friends who attended Catholic high schools, and they told him that nuns don't take any crap. *Is this what Catholic school is like?* "Ma'am, I don't have... I may not be able to wait that long. Please, I need to see Monsignor Klastūnas."

"Perhaps if you had made an appointment." She headed toward the main church building without checking to see if he was following.

In the courtyard, the old woman stood smoking, watching. When their eyes met, she gave a slight nod before flicking her cigarette into the wind and disappearing among the buildings.

CHAPTER 32
EPHPHATHA!

Thursday 5:55 a.m.—Atlantic City
(Thursday 12:55 p.m.—Lithuania)

The laptop hummed to life in the maintenance room. Like everything else the monsignor touched, the security system was just for show. He'd bragged about the state grant in press releases while the recording equipment gathered dust. He'd made the company reps install the software on this shared laptop, not wanting them near his office computer. Then he lost interest once the publicity died down.

Child safety meant nothing compared to his moment in the spotlight.

Audrey typed "Ephphatha!" into the login screen and smiled. The monsignor's pride in his "clever" password spilled out of his mouth to too many people. The Aramaic word meaning, "be opened," would be his undoing.

The surveillance system's interface blinked to life. Dormant since installation, updates were needed. Finally.

The monsignor had been so proud of his state security grant, showing off the cameras to the community while never actually monitoring them. She doubted he even knew how to operate the recording software. She would be the first to take advantage of the technology.

One camera covered the parking lot. It was set to record only on movement. That would make this easier—she wouldn't have to go second by second. She breathed a sigh of relief when the program menu showed that the last forty-five days of footage were automatically archived.

As Audrey downloaded the data to her last USB drive, a shadow moved outside the maintenance room window.

Fight replaced flight. She inched toward the figure instead of away. The faint parking lot lights barely reached the telephone pole on the street. The pre-dawn quiet was broken by a stepladder folding with a metallic click.

"Hey!"

"Audrey?" Carmen's voice. Relief mixed with wariness.

"What the hell are you doing?"

"Shh. Keep it down. What are *you* doing?" Carmen countered.

Audrey glanced up at the telephone pole, at a plain black box poorly disguised as cable equipment. "Surveillance camera?"

"Don't—"

Audrey pulled out the USB drive. "You can take yours down. Everything we need is right here."

"What do you mean it's in there?"

Audrey pointed to the roof of the school. "The footage from that surveillance camera on the corner of the building. That camera captures everything in the parking lot for the last forty-five days. Now I have it."

"Jesus Christ, Audrey." Carmen's voice dropped. "That's unauthorized computer access. It's a third-degree crime. And you're on probation."

Reality hit. Her brother's boss or not, this lieutenant could end her.

"Audrey, relax. I'm not going to report this to your PO," Carmen said quickly. "But if anyone finds out that I knew…" She let the implications hang in the early morning frost.

"The monsignor's probably already told his guys to lay low," Audrey reasoned. "Your camera's not going to catch anything now. Let me handle the footage. That way you're clean."

"And how exactly will you get me the plate numbers?"

"I'll figure something out."

Carmen studied her for a long moment. "Fine. When you do, text me. But Audrey... if the monsignor's half as dangerous as we think, Vince's life might depend on you keeping quiet. And I'd guess that our asses are now on the line as well. Got it?"

"Got it." She smiled. "Trust me."

"That's what worries me," Carmen said as she folded her ladder.

Audrey squeezed the USB drive, recognizing the look in Carmen's eyes. It was the same look Vince got whenever Audrey's impulses threatened to blow up in their faces.

As Carmen drove away, Audrey recalled a Bible verse often told by Father Frank. In the cold parking lot of his church, Audrey realized what it meant to walk by faith alone. Trust better work both ways—they had just handed each other loaded guns.

CHAPTER 33
COLD RECEPTION

Thursday 2:30 p.m.—Sakiai District, Lithuania
(Thursday 7:30 a.m.—Atlantic City)

Rather than take the hour bus ride back to Kaunas, Vince decided to stay in the village area. The fried bread with cheese in a rundown luncheonette in a nearby village had given Vince time to think, but not to cool his determination. He walked back to the Refuge of Divine Mercy Church, this time heading straight for the main entrance. No more playing by Sister Lina's rules.

The sanctuary doors were locked. Of course they were.

A novice nun crossing the courtyard spotted him. "Orphanage office—"

"No." Vince's voice carried more edge than he intended. "I need to see Monsignor Klastūnas... Now."

She scurried away, but minutes later, Sister Lina emerged from a side door. The midday sun had burned away the morning's chill, but Vince felt colder than ever under Sister Lina's icy stare. Her earlier patience was replaced with frustration. "I thought I made myself clear, Vincentas."

"Crystal. But this isn't about adoption. It never was. And I think you knew that."

"The monsignor is very busy—"

"Cut the act." The words felt foreign in Vince's mouth. Back home, he'd never speak to a nun this way. But back home, he wasn't desperate. "We both know you're his gatekeeper."

"Gatekeeper? Americans have interesting ways of describing people. There is no gatekeeper here, Vincentas. Just me—Mother Superior of this church and the monsignor's confidant."

"Fine. Tell him someone from Rytis Eparchy is here."

Sister Lina's guise slipped for just a moment. "Atlantic City?"

"Smart woman." Vince stepped closer. "Now, about that appointment."

"The monsignor sees no one without proper scheduling." Her voice dropped. "Especially Americans who don't know their place."

"My place?" Vince barked a laugh. "Lady, you have no idea—"

"No idea? I have more than an idea… Detective Brown." Her smile was venomous. "The monsignor has many friends. Some in immigration."

Vince's stomach dropped. She knew. But what did she know?

What did she mean by "monsignor?" Was it the monsignor here or Monsignor Augustas? And what about "immigration?" Was she referring to immigration here being aware of his presence in the country, or back home where his passport was rejected?

"Come back next week." Sister Lina turned to leave. "Perhaps by then, you'll remember proper respect."

"Next week?" Vince watched her disappear inside. "Respect goes both ways, Sister."

In the distance, he caught a glimpse of the old woman watching, another cigarette glowing between her fingers.

CHAPTER 34

TAXI DANCE

Thursday 2:45 p.m.—Sakiai District, Lithuania
(Thursday 7:45 a.m.—Atlantic City)

The wind cut through Vince's jacket as he started the walk back to the bus stop. He was curious about the taxi slowing beside him. Then the window rolled down, and he became suspicious. How many cabs drive around with their top light off, then pull alongside a foreigner and roll down their window?

In broken English, the driver offered Vince a ride—if he was going to the bus station. He said Vince could share the fare with another passenger headed that way.

Why would a stranger offer to share a cab ride with him? And how would they know where he was going?

"Uh, I don't know..."

A gust of wind hit his face and stung his reddened ears. Fifteen more minutes of walking in this icy wind or a five-minute ride in a cab with a stranger? The next gust of wind took his breath away. The warmth of the cab lured him right in.

The cigarette smell hit him before he even closed the door. It was her. The old woman from the church sat in the back seat, that same unsettling half-smile on her face.

"Well, the journey continues," Vince muttered.

"Tavo kelione tik prasideda, Vincentas," ("*Your journey is just beginning, Vince,*") she replied.

Vince stared at her.

"Praeitis ir ateitis susidurs taip, kaip negalejote jsivaizduoti." ("*The past and future are about to collide in ways you could not have imagined.*")

Vince caught his name in the stream of Lithuanian. He noticed the driver's curious glance in the rearview mirror. "What did she say?"

The driver's eyes met the old woman's in the mirror before returning to the road. "I... I am not sure."

The stench of stale smoke made Vince's head pound. Then she turned to him again: "Ar tiki likimu, Vincentas? Kartais musu keliaa parenkami mums gerokai anksciau, nei tai suzinome." ("*Do you believe in fate, Vince? Sometimes our paths are chosen for us long before we know it.*")

Her smile softened. "Po visu siu metu gabalai pagaliau stoja i savo vietas." ("*After all these years, the pieces are finally falling into place.*")

At the bus stop, she paid the full fare with crumpled bills before Vince could protest. When he asked the driver about her words, the man hesitated.

"Something about your journey just beginning. She asked if you believe in fate." He sorted the wrinkled cash. "She said pieces are falling into place."

"Between the church and now her, I have to admit, I'm a little creeped out," Vince said.

"What this means—creeped out?"

"It means eerie. A little scared."

"Ah...afraid. Understand." The driver pointed across the street. "Good pub there. Good place to become not scared until the bus comes. Best kepta duona in the district."

Two mugs of Svyturys Nealkoholinis and a plate of fried bread later, Vince let the cold air clear his head. He watched the villagers hurry past, each with their own destination, their own story—just like the boardwalk back home. But here, someone seemed to know his story better than he did.

On the bus, sleep toyed with him. His last conscious thought was of the old woman's knowing smile and all the mysteries it held.

My journey is just beginning...

Do I believe in fate...

The pieces are falling into place...

CHAPTER 35
DOWNLOADING

Thursday 11:35 a.m.—Atlantic City
(Thursday 6:35 p.m.—Lithuania)

Audrey's hands shook as she plugged the USB drive into her iPad. Nothing. *File Format Error* flashed on her screen. *Nothing worth doing is ever easy.* Vince's words, not hers. Vince said it was a quote by someone famous, but she never paid attention to who he was talking about.

Here she was, trying to help him, and she kept hitting a wall of error messages.

A quick internet search showed that only paid programs could open the surveillance footage. She couldn't use her nonexistent credit cards—past financial mistakes saw to that. Vince's card was sitting idly at his house, tempting her. But using it would only put him in more danger.

There was no other choice. It was back to the laptop at the church.

The maintenance room felt different now. It was later in the day. The sun was up... it should have felt warmer. Somehow, it was colder. Her only chance was to gain access to the administrative functions.

What the hell, give it a shot. The monsignor's one and only password—"Ephphatha!" No sooner did she enter the password than the screen jumped to life—she was in the admin settings where the surveillance system could be accessed. His arrogance in that clever Aramaic word said so much about who he was.

The USB began collecting the data. The progress bar moved slowly.

The door creaked behind her.

"Ah, Audrey." His voice brought fear to many of the homeless girls in the shelter. But the way she described it in group was different—it turned the blood in her veins into red-hot lava.

"Monsignor…"

"I didn't expect anyone here."

She turned, positioning herself to shield the laptop. "Just checking next month's schedule. I know how you want everything perfect if we have special guests."

He prowled the room's perimeter while she pivoted, keeping the screen hidden. "I can't think of any special guests next month. We're still in January."

"Well, with Christmas done, I wanted to make sure all the supplies were stocked just in case we get an unexpected VIP." Her throat tightened as he moved closer. "I wouldn't want you disappointed if we were caught off guard."

"Oh, Audrey. You've never disappointed me." His eyes held memories that made her stomach clench. "If my memory serves me correctly, some of your talents are unforgettable."

The urge to vomit warred with the desire to wrap her hands around his throat. Instead, she did what she'd learned long ago—she smiled through the bile rising in her throat. Her fingers fumbled behind her back for the USB drive.

"You seem… tense." He was another step closer.

Add a kernel of truth to the lie. "Worried about Vince," she managed. "You don't know him like I do. The stress at his work… He internalizes everything."

"Yes... Vince." The monsignor's voice softened to a familiar, dangerous tone. "He did seem... how should I put this? Different... lately. I hope that stress doesn't lead to unwise decisions."

Unwise decisions... If he only knew.

The progress bar was nearing completion when he turned toward the door. "Don't forget, my child." He continued through the doorway without bothering to turn around. "I am concerned for both your well-being. His... and yours."

"Thank you, Monsignor." The words tasted like hot ash.

Finally—*Download complete.*

In her room, Audrey's hands still trembled. But not from fear—from rage. She'd survived him once. She'd survive him again. And this time, she had evidence that would help take him down.

CHAPTER 36

THE PASSENGER

Friday 10:20 a.m.—Sakiai District, Lithuania
(Friday 3:20 a.m.—Atlantic City)

The bus's air brakes hissed as Vince settled into a window seat, his journal open on his lap. He needed his cover story to be airtight, written as if each entry happened in real time.

"Is seat taken?"

He looked up to rows of empty seats before finding the source of the question. His stomach dropped. "No, but—"

"Good. I will keep you company on way to Sakiai District." The old woman from the church slid in beside him—but something was definitely different... she spoke English.

The cigarette smell hit him as she settled in. "Good morning, Vincentas. How did you sleep?"

"Okay, I guess." The words came out forced.

She coughed deeply. "It is important to get rest when traveling so far from home. Time difference affects energy on person. You want to keep all energy you have."

"Who the hell are you?"

"In time, Vincentas. Everything revealed in time." She studied him with an unsettling familiarity. You are going back to Divine Mercy, yes?

"The Refuge of Divine Mercy?"

"Here it is called Divine Mercy only. No Refuge..."

"Fine. Yes, I am going back to *Divine Mercy*." His tone of those last two words mocked her broken English. He shifted away from her stench. "But you already knew that."

"What I know is complex. You are not ready to learn everything, Vincentas. Person must walk before they run... you just beginning to crawl."

"What the fuck is going on here?" He half rose from his seat. "Who are you and what do you want?"

"Ah, Vincentas, so quick to anger. Very unlike your father. Do not let fear of unknown cloud judgment. I am here to help."

"I don't need help. I need answers."

"If we do not learn from answers we receive, what value is new knowledge? No, Vincentas. You are here to learn. You must learn. Questions to answers you seek will give knowledge you need..." She paused meaningfully. "To take down Augustas."

His jaw went slack. "What the fuck?"

She laughed, a surprisingly warm laugh. "That saying is universal in any language. What fuck, for sure!"

Vince studied her up and down. "Who are you?" This time he was sincere, and the question came out softer.

"There is freedom in being underestimated, Vincentas. Being seen as just another babushka on bus has advantages."

"More riddles. More bullshit." His voice rose. "Should I beg? Is that what you want?"

"No. Brown family is too proud to beg. You... too smart to give up." She leaned closer. "Tell me, Vincentas, why do you go to Divine Mercy? What do you hope—" A coughing fit cut her off.

When she recovered, Vince answered carefully, "I need to find a connection between two churches."

"What kind of connection?"

"That's all you get, old woman." He paused. "I mean, you are a woman, right? That's what people call you?"

Her laugh filled the bus. "Yes, people call me woman...sometimes. I am called other names, Vincentas. But you want to know if you can trust me, correct?"

"That'd be a start."

She ticked off points on her gnarled fingers. "You are in foreign country. Do not speak language. Know no one here. No one knows you are here. Left United States in secret. You try not to raise suspicions. Is this true so far?"

Vince turned away like a guilty child. His right to remain silent had never felt more appealing.

"Oh, Vincentas. Being police detective you are naturally suspicious, yes? Learn to trust no one. Survival depends on it. Every good policeman skeptical, become cynical. Becomes...how you say in America, part of DNA?"

He met her gaze but stayed silent, using his interrogation technique of creating tension through silence.

"As policeman, you learn advantage of being in control. Now you are not in control, are you, Vincentas? This makes you uncomfortable, yes?"

"Listen, lady." He leaned in close. "Maybe I wasn't careful enough. Maybe you know things. But now that I'm here, I've got work to do. When I'm done, maybe we can have coffee... become friends. Maybe then we'll finish whatever game this is. Until then, leave me alone."

"Now that is determination and... how do you say... feistitude that will help you succeed."

"Feistitude? Did you just try to use 'feisty' as a noun?"

"Yes. Feistiful? Feistment?"

"It's feistiness. And that's the wrong use entirely."

"There." She smiled, revealing surprisingly even teeth. "You correct my English, Vincentas. Yet moments ago, you were ready to dismiss me as babushka who cannot speak. Shows how quick we judge, yes?"

Vince slumped against the window. "Fine. You made your point."

"No point made yet, Vincentas. Point is still coming." She lit another cigarette. "You come to Lithuania searching for truth about Augustas. But truth about Augustas connected to many truths—about church, about your father, about you."

His head snapped up. "My father? That's the second time you mentioned my father. What do you—"

"In time, Vincentas." She waved smoke away from his face – a surprisingly considerate gesture. "First, you tell me: what makes detective decide to break many laws to come here? It is more than professional curiosity."

"He's going to kill my father."

She nodded slowly. "Now we reach truth, Vincentas. But still question remains—why do you think answers are in Lithuania?"

"Because that's where everything started. The monsignor, the Russian mafia, the—" Vince caught himself. "Why am I telling you this?"

"Because you know I already know. Question is how do I know?" Another rattling cough shook her body. "Was because I was there from start? Was because I watch it all unfold, year after year? Maybe because I was unable to stop it... Until now."

"Okay, but I still don't know who you are." To his surprise, Vince's voice held no judgment, only wonder.

"I am person who can help you save your father. Or..." She shrugged. "... I am crazy old woman who smells like cigarettes. You must decide which one, Vincentas."

"And if I decide to trust you?"

"Then you learn sometimes most dangerous move is most important move. In chess, most dangerous move is one opponent never sees coming." She smiled that unnervingly knowing smile. "Bishops believe they are playing against pawns. Pawns have use, but pawn is expendable. And rook... rook is piece that—"

"So, by trusting you," he cut her off. "Are you saying there is danger in trusting you?"

"Vincentas, you ask questions for answers. You must question answers so you can learn."

The bus slowed for a curve, and Vince used the moment to study her. Behind the smell of stale smoke and her apparent age, something sharp lurked in her eyes. Something that had seen too much. Her gray hair was dull, but her eyes were sharp and knowing.

"If—and that's a big if—I believe you can help... what's the catch?"

"Catch is simple, Vincentas. You must trust me. Must follow my lead, even when path seems wrong. You must learn to think like Augustas to beat Augustas." She stubbed out her cigarette. "And hardest of all... you must accept truth you find may hurt more than lies you live with now."

"That's a lot to ask from someone who won't even tell me her name."

"Names have power, Vincentas. When time is right, you will know."

After that, she fell silent, closing her eyes as if their conversation had exhausted her. But Vince noticed how her fingers remained alert on her lap, how her head tilted slightly toward any sound from the aisle. Even when resting with her eyes shut, she was aware of everything.

Vince's mind raced for the remainder of the ride. Who was this woman who seemed to know everything about him? Why did she care about taking down Augustas? And why did he have the unsettling feeling that she was testing him somehow?

The bus began to slow as they approached the Sakiai District stop. Her eyes snapped open as if triggered by an internal alarm. She turned to him with that knowing smile.

"Now we begin, Vincentas."

"*We?*"

CHAPTER 37

ANONYMOUS TIPS

Friday 4:15 a.m.—Atlantic City
(Friday 11:15 a.m.—Lithuania)

Audrey's alarm pierced the darkness. Perfect timing—too late for mid-watch detectives lingering over paperwork, too early for day-shift arriving with coffee. The anonymous tipline would be empty, waiting.

Her night of reviewing surveillance footage had yielded a tidy list of license plates, dates, and times. Cars that brought mysterious men to confess their sins—or conduct their business—with the monsignor.

Vince's voice echoed in her memory: "The first thing Carmen does every morning is check the overnight tips. AG's orders, they're totally untraceable. Builds community trust that way." For once, his endless explanations of police procedure might actually help.

Audrey looked at her phone. 4:20 a.m. She called the tipline, her heart pounding despite knowing the call couldn't be traced.

"December second, eleven-thirteen a.m. New Jersey plate L-L-S-two-two-zero. Yellow Chevy SUV. Two men." Her voice stayed steady as she worked through the list. "December eighth, one-forty-nine p.m. New Jersey plate one-one-eight-G-E-Y. Blue Mercedes. One man."

She hung up immediately after reading off the last plate number. Staring at her ceiling in the dark, sleep felt impossible. Where was Vince right now? Had she helped him or made things worse? The questions circled like vultures.

She looked at her phone again. 6 a.m. Time for Audrey to try her hand at being a detective.

Someone as good-looking as Carmen Navarro—her hair, her make-up, her outfits—would need at least an hour to get ready. The lieu-tenant's work ethic was legendary—first to arrive, last to leave. That would play into both their favors—she'd listen to the tipline before the first detective arrived.

Audrey hit dial.

"Make sure to check the tipline when you get in."

"Audrey? Is this—"

"Yes. Just check the tipline first thing. Goodbye."

She ended the call before Carmen could say anything or ask any questions. Give the lieutenant an out about where the information came from. Sometimes the best way to protect someone is to give them plausible deniability.

Now all she could do was wait. And worry. And hope she hadn't just made everything worse.

CHAPTER 38
LESSONS IN TRUST

Friday 11:30 a.m.—Sakiai District, Lithuania
(Friday 4:30 a.m.—Atlantic City)

The winter air hit them as they stepped off the bus.

"Now we begin, Vincentas."

"*We...* I don't believe this," Vince mumbled, but loud enough for her to hear.

Her smile widened. "You have only begun not believing things, Vincentas."

Vince pushed his bare hands into his lined pockets. He watched the bus pull away, leaving him here with this stranger who, as he told the cab driver yesterday, was creeping him out.

"Come, Vincentas. We start at Divine Mercy, yes? We talk. You can ask anything you wish on walk there."

"Fine. How about, who are you, and how the hell do you know so much about me?"

"Good questions, Vincentas. But why not tell me who you think I am? Will help stimulate thinking brain—part of brain that solves problems. You need that part working best very soon."

"So again, no direct answer?"

"I did answer. You were not ready to hear what I said." She lit another cigarette. "You must learn to play game if you want to survive, Vincentas."

"I'm not here to play games!"

"Vincentas, who do you think I am?"

His answer was swift and sharp. "A crazy homeless lady who's gonna die from lung cancer, based on your smoking and that cough."

"You are direct, Vincentas. This trait from home or police work?"

The question caught him off guard. No one had ever called him direct before. His mind wandered to interrogation training—the tilted chairs, the psychological pressure, the careful invasion of space. Was that what she was doing to him? Squeezing him like a suspect until his truth leaked out?

Shame washed over him. "Ma'am... I'm sorry for what I just said."

She chuckled. "There is no need, Vincentas. In anger and frustration, you answer question. I *am* going to die from lung cancer." Her eyes met his. "When I am gone, my secrets go with me. Everything I know, gone forever. This is why you must learn to trust me. Without learning from experience, what good are answers?"

"I understand. But, still, I am sorry. You don't know me but it was out of character. It's not how I was—"

"It is not how you were raised," she said, finishing Vince's sentence for him. "Yes, I know... it is not how you or your sister were raised."

Vince didn't acknowledge or respond to her statement. Instead, he allowed the cold wind to hit him in the face, taking it as a form of self-punishment for the way he talked to her.

"Vincentas, we have much to talk about. We will not get to see Monsignor Klastūnas, but we still must go to Divine Mercy."

"Why? Is he that powerful or so important that only a select few get to meet him?"

"No, not important. But smart. Very smart. Smarter than Augustas. This is why he can use Augustas for his purposes. Augustas is too, how you say... naive?"

"What do you mean he's been able to use Augustas? How do you know about Monsignor Augustas?"

"More questions, Vincentas. You want answers to questions you ask instead of learning what you need to know."

"How am I supposed to learn if I don't get answers to my questions?" Vince demanded.

She did not acknowledge his question, and they walked in silence until they reached the old stone wall of the Refuge of Divine Mercy Church. The orphanage building stood to one side, the building Sister Lina gave him a tour of yesterday.

"You learn by paying attention, Vincentas. And by listening. Let us start here. Here is where you begin to learn, Vincentas."

"But I thought you said I wouldn't be able to talk with the monsignor?"

"We are not here to talk to the monsignor, Vincentas. We are here to begin learning."

"Learning about what?" Vince begged.

"Learning about you, Vincentas. This is day one of that learning. And this is location number one of that learning."

"What does a church in the middle of nowhere have to do with me?"

"This more than church, Vincentas. Look at orphanage. It is open more than thirty years."

Something shifted in Vince's chest. "Is this... is this where I was adopted?"

"Yes, Vincentas. Where your father adopted you and Audrey."

The weight of history pressed down on him, making each breath feel sacred. He searched desperately for any memory, any fragment that might connect present-day Vince to the toddler who once lived here. Nothing came, but something deeper stirred... a soul-deep recognition that transcended memory.

The old woman's voice softened. "Take time, Vincentas. Take all time you need."

Vince had heard the phrase "hallowed ground" before but never understood it until now. Here, in this cold, dreary landscape four thousand miles from home, the core of who he was began to reveal itself.

"Pizza?" she asked suddenly, lighting another cigarette. "Good pizza place few blocks away."

Vince nodded, still lost in the magnitude of the moment. His beginning—their beginning— was here. Everything he thought he knew about himself shifted, realigning around this new center of gravity.

CHAPTER 39
MORNING ROUTINE

Friday 6:45 a.m.—Atlantic City
(Friday 1:45 p.m.—Lithuania)

Carmen hurried into the detective bureau. Her hair was still damp from her rushed shower. The tipline machine was more important than her makeup today.

She hit play, scribbling dates, times, plate numbers, and the number of men in the car. The message was erased before the ink of the last license plate scribbled in her notebook dried. The notebook went straight into her locked desk drawer.

Coffee first. This morning could appear no different than any other morning. Maintaining normalcy mattered. Her day-watch detectives were used to a fresh pot of coffee brewing when they arrived each morning.

She'd just filled the reservoir with water when a voice behind her made her jump.

"Hey, LT, what brings you in so early?"

Marcus Turner. She hadn't noticed his desk light on. Stupid mistake. "Oh, Marcus... you startled me. I couldn't sleep," she managed. "What about you? How come you're in so early?"

"I picked up Nancy's birthday cake from Meister's. Her favorite— bee sting."

Carmen forced a laugh. "Nancy... You boys better behave. You know how she is about her age. No candles on it, right? Or do I have to make that a direct order?" This time her laugh was genuine.

"Come on, LT. Let us have some fun. We promise not to print out her driver's license from DMV and frame it this year." Detective Turner's grin was a combination of mischief and loving affection."

"You want to mess with her, do it at your own risk, Detective." Her smile matched his. "Just remember, the unit secretary can make your job. Or make your job... miserable."

"So, no fart machines like we did with the captain, either?"

"Sometimes I feel like I'm babysitting instead of supervising. It's a good thing you guys know how to get results," she said, turning to walk away.

Then she froze. She had to know. "Hey, when did you get in?"

"A few minutes before you. Heard you play the tipline message. It sounded like gibberish. You want me to run it down?"

Her stomach tightened. "Thanks, but I've got it. How's the Washington extortion case?"

"Dead end. ISP traces to Austria. They used encrypted proxy servers. Probably going to close it in thirty days."

"Keep me posted on that one, Marcus." Her request had little to do with what it would mean for the solve rate in the bureau as much as it did for a solid lead on the monsignor. "We don't get a lot of blackmail cases. If we can track this one down, it would send a message to the minority communities that they aren't forgotten." She turned to go.

"Sure. LT? You okay?"

"Why?"

Marcus shifted uncomfortably. "Never seen you without... I mean, your hair and makeup..."

She stared him down, then softened. "Relax, Marcus. Thanks for caring about professionalism." She tussled her hair. "I was a little preoccupied when I got dressed. I better go check myself in the bathroom so I look presentable the rest of the day. Now, let's go catch some bad guys."

In her office, Carmen ran the plates through DMV. She wrote everything by hand—no printing, no trace. Every database query left breadcrumbs in Trenton. She'd learned that when a rookie ran the governor's name out of boredom.

She would wait to check criminal histories. Too many searches at once would raise flags. For now, the intelligence files would have to do. They detail names, associates, and suspected activities—all enough to start building a picture.

The handwritten notes went into her small purse, buried in her larger bag. One step at a time. One breadcrumb at a time. She searched her soul for assurance that these weren't the kind that would lead back to her.

CHAPTER 40

THE REAL STORY

Friday 1:15 p.m.—Sakiai District, Lithuania
(Friday 6:15 a.m.—Atlantic City)

The "few blocks away walk" the woman promised turned into a ten-minute trek in thirty-mile-per-hour winds. Frigid gusts made conversation impossible. Vince kept his fists balled in his jacket pockets, conserving what little warmth he could.

Marijos Autentiska Picerija appeared around the corner, its sign featuring a classic Neapolitan pizza. Inside, the owner greeted the old woman with a kiss, calling her by name—it sounded like "Evelyn." Vince filed that away. The old woman called her Maria.

They settled in the far corner, Vince facing the door—cop habits. His companion noticed.

"Vincentas, do all police officers choose farthest table, to face door. Or only good ones?"

"It becomes instinct," Vince admitted.

She placed her cigarettes on the table. *Oh, dear God, please don't smoke in here*, Vince said to himself.

"So police have predictable habits?" She reached for her cigarettes.

"Is it habit or addiction?" Vince countered.

"Ah, Vincentas, now you are starting to learn game. Answering questions with questions that make person look inside."

"So, do I get a gold star?" Vince asked with a laugh.

"You want gold star, or do you want more answers that help you learn, Vincentas?" the woman answered with a condescending tone.

"Another question, even a joking one, is answered with a question from you. I can't win, can I?"

"I am not your opponent, Vincentas. Your opponent is—"

"My opponent is myself... yeah, I know."

"Maybe, Vincentas. But you have another opponent who is more dangerous than you could ever be. He must be stopped. And you, Vincentas, are one who must stop him."

Vince focused his eyes on hers. "The monsignor?"

"Augustas is evil, Vincentas. You know that, yes?"

Vince thought about all he had learned from Frank and Audrey about the monsignor. Evil was the most fitting word he could think of.

Their verbal sparring led Vince to play his card. "What about you, Evelyn? Are you evil like the monsignor?"

Her eyes widened. "Vincentas..."

"I heard the lady call you by it when we walked in. Not only do cops have a habit of sitting in the farthest corner of a restaurant, but the good ones also have a habit of paying attention. And I was paying attention when we walked in."

"Okay, Vincentas. Let us not play any more games with my name. I will tell you my name is not Evelyn."

"Bullshit. Your face gave it away as soon as I said it. Chalk one up for Vince for paying attention."

"Not Evelyn. Evelina." She met his gaze. "It is my birth name. Means 'strength to live' in Lithuanian. My name became more meaning as my life went on."

"So, I got it right. I just mispronounced it. Still, chalk one up for Vince."

"Vincentas, earlier you said you thought I was crazy homeless woman. Did you think that because of the way I am dressed? Was it because of how I look?"

"Well, *Evelina*," Vince said, leaning into her given name so as to parrot the woman's cadence, "As a cop, I'm a trained observer, and from my experience, what I observe when I see you is someone who looks homeless. I'm still adding up all the votes in my head on whether or not you're crazy."

"If I looked different than I am now dressed, would you think different of me, Vincentas?"

"Without question," Vince shot back immediately.

"So, Vincentas, you judge people by how they look? You see only outside to make assumptions?"

Vince paused, knowing he had been drawn right into a trap he laid for himself. How many times had he lectured police recruits about not judging someone by how they look? How many times has he prided himself on not being a judgmental prick like so many other guys he works with who are quick to judge anyone who doesn't look like them?

"Evelina, I'm sorry. I've been an asshole. Please, believe me, this isn't who I really am. It's no excuse, but I'm really out of my element here and I'm trying to figure things out. Please accept my apology."

"Oh, Vincentas, there is no need for apologize. But if you feel better by me accepting your apology, I do accept it."

They both shared a smile that spoke louder than any words could do justice to.

Even the lines on her face warmed. "Vincentas, what would you like to know about me?"

Vince shrugged his shoulders, as if answering her questions with a question of his own.

She smiled back as she revealed her past. She had no family, she was from a small village in the area, and for seven years she was known as Sister Evelina at Divine Mercy.

"You... you were a nun?" Vince thought about the way he talked to her and all the f-bombs he had dropped since they met. "Holy fuck. I mean... I mean, holy cow. I mean... I mean, I'm sorry, Sister, please forgive me."

Evelina tried, but couldn't hold back her laughter, "Holy fuck is just, how do you say—is just half of it, Vincentas."

Between that laugh and the time the pizza arrived at the table, Evelina—formerly known as the old smelly homeless lady—explained to Vince how she was a nun at the orphanage at the Refuge of Divine Mercy Church when Augustas arrived there as a new priest. He arrived in 1997, about five years after Evelina received her first assignment there at the orphanage.

She went on to describe the relationship between Augustas and Monsignor Klastūnas and how they became Vory v Zakone—thieves in law—with the Russian mafia. "Augustas never wanted priesthood," she continued. "He needed hiding place from authorities. Was part of Vilnius Brigade—threats, kidnapping, murder. When gang leader was arrested, he fled to Russia."

She detailed the Russian mafia's scheme with trafficked children, "recycling" them between orphanages, exploiting desperate American couples. "In 1990s, Russian adoptions were big business. Wherever there is money, there is Russian mafia."

She laid it out for him. "Americans with money came to Russia to adopt children. Orphanages in Kaliningrad, near border with Lithuania grew. It was safer for Americans to fly into Vilnius than drive over border to Kaliningrad. It had become customary for Americans who just adopted child to pay their way out of Russia."

She checked in with Vince. "Are you paying attention, Vincentas?"

He nodded. She continued to lay out the recycling scheme.

Russian mafia set up ambush points on road leading out of Kaliningrad. Parents with newly adopted children were stopped and threatened at gunpoint. The mafia roughed up the parents and then took all their money. The thugs then took the child and told the parents to keep driving into Lithuania.

The parents, frightened for their lives, drove into Lithuania, where they were met by the "courageous and compassionate" Augustas, who took them to Divine Mercy, put them up, and worked with them to get back to the United States. He even offered to try to get their child back.

Meanwhile, the Russian mafia returned the child to the orphanage in Kaliningrad, and the process started all over again. This continued until the child was old enough to understand what was going on and then was legitimately adopted out.

Vince's blood boiled.

The orphanage at Divine Mercy was filled with these children, as well as children from human trafficking rings also run by the mafia. It was Augustas who described this scheme as "child recycling."

Vince pounded his fist on the table. "That motherfucker!"

"I had suspicions," Evelina said, "but was not confirmed until 1999—"

Vince dropped his slice to the plate when she mentioned the year, just as the pizza shop's bell above the front door clanged. Two officers entered. Policija.

"Vincentas, have you enjoyed pizza?"

"Yes, it's good. Do you want another piece?"

"We must leave. But not too soon. Grobuonis see everything."

"But I want to hear about what happened in 1999."

"Not now, Vincentas." She and Maria nodded in unison.

Maria distracted the officers while they slipped out. In an alley two blocks away, Evelina produced a key fob. A pristine BMW X5 chirped to life.

"Come, Vincentas, we must leave."

"What the—" Vince froze.

"Because I look like this means I cannot drive nice car?" Her weathered face cracked a smile. "Are you coming, or taking chances with grobuonis?"

"The what?"

"Predators, Vincentas. Vultures. Always circling, always watching."

Inside the luxury car, reeking of stale smoke, reality hit him. He was running from the police. Detective Vince Brown, for the first time, was on the wrong side of his black-and-white world.

His mind drifted to high school. When he refused to lie for Audrey about the party. Because he didn't do what she asked—what she begged—him to do, she lost her scholarship. He wouldn't cover for her. He wouldn't lie. Their relationship never recovered.

He had already lost the relationship with his sister for being so rigid. He couldn't risk losing his father for the same reason.

"First time for everything, yes?" Evelina said, reading his thoughts.

Vince stared at the gray countryside. His wholesome world was now in the rearview mirror. To save his father, he'd have to learn to accept these shades of gray.

"So," he asked, "where are we going?"

CHAPTER 41
INTERRUPTED SIGNALS

Friday 11:35 a.m.—Atlantic City
(Friday 6:35 p.m.—Lithuania)

Carmen methodically searched each name from her DMV list in the department's intelligence database. The pattern emerged quickly—street-level shakedowns and extortion threats. Known associates linked them all, either directly or through intermediaries.

Most reports tagged them as "suspected low-level organized crime." One caught her eye: "CI states connection to Russian mafia." A patrol officer's note from last year. His confidential informant claimed one of the monsignor's visitors had mob ties.

Unreliable without proven CI history, but still...

The lieutenant spun her chair to face the window. Through the gray winter sky, her mind drifted to her AWOL detective—Vince Brown. How deep was his father tangled in this, if organized crime really was at the heart of it all?

Her phone buzzed. The contact read "PITA."

"Audrey, I told you to call me only in—"

"I know." She cut her off. "This isn't... but did you get the info? Run the plates? You deleted the message, right?"

"Audrey, look—"

"Oh, please don't tell me you didn't get it. I left a message early this morning. What? You're not going to look them up? Okay, you can't. Is that what it is?"

"Jesus Christ, would you shut up and listen!" she said through clenched teeth.

"Alright, I'm listening. I promise I won't interrupt. Just tell me what you found."

"Audrey, would you calm the fuck down and listen. Jesus Christ, you can be annoying."

"Sorry, I'm just worried about Vince. And Dad. And now you... I mean, you are going to—"

"Shut. The. Fuck. Up." Carmen pinched the bridge of her nose. "Are you on meds?"

"Yes, actually. But I'm shutting up now."

Carmen explained about deleting the message and confirming the registrations. She kept quiet about the intelligence files. Audrey didn't need to know that yet.

"Is that it?"

"That's as far as I've gotten. Audrey, remember, I shouldn't even be doing this. I could get fired. Or worse."

"I know, LT... that's what Vince always calls you—LT. That's a sign of affection, right?"

Carmen deflected. "My whole unit calls me that."

"I guess you're as respected as Vince says."

"Audrey, I'll let you know if I find anything else that'll help. But this little investigation of ours has to—"

A familiar voice from her doorway cut her off: "Who's Audrey?"

CHAPTER 42

BEHIND THE WHEEL

Friday 2:35 p.m.—Kaliningrad Region, Russia
(Friday 7:35 a.m.—Atlantic City)

"Vincentas," Evelina noticed his discomfort, "crack window for fresh air."

The stench of stale cigarettes permeated the BMW's cabin, each breath driving spikes through Vince's sinuses. His head throbbed in time with the luxury SUV's motion as Evelina navigated unfamiliar roads. The nausea began, as it always did, when he sat in the passenger's seat instead of driving the car. It got worse with each turn.

The bitter wind from the open window stung his ear, offering no relief. "I always do the driving back home," he managed through short breaths.

"Do you like to drive, Vincentas?" The question surprised him.

If they were back home, Vince would jump at the opportunity. But here, in a foreign country, with no identification—in a car worth at least a hundred thousand dollars next to a woman he doesn't know. "I can't. No license, no idea where we are, and..." he gestured at the expensive interior. "This car?"

Evelina pulled the car to the side of the gravel road. "Vincentas, you will drive to make yourself feel better. You will be fine. It is promise."

"What about the gro-bon-a-whatever you called them, the police we saw back in the pizza shop?"

Evelina grinned. "You mean, grobuonis, Vincentas? You do not worry; police only come here if there is problem. Police wait to be called here."

After adjusting the seat and the steering wheel, Vince took his time making sure the mirrors were right where he wanted them before pulling back on the road. The feel of the leather steering wheel felt uncomfortable in his hands, as did the plush leather seats that warmed his rear end. The ride was the complete opposite of his Jeep back home.

"Vincentas, do you still not believe this is my car?"

"It's your car now. I'm just not convinced that you didn't steal it!"

"Vincentas, even woman who looks homeless has money. Maybe much money. Money, but no family. What should happen with money once I die?"

Before Vince could respond, she tensed. "Grobuonis!"

Through the windshield, a police van approached on the narrow road. "What should I do?" Panic filled his voice.

"Pull little to side, not too far. Make them drive into ditch on other side covered by snow." Her voice held strong. "And Vincentas? Lower your window when we pass."

"Are you insane? The tint will hide us—"

"Trust me, Vincentas. I always have plan."

His heart hammering in his chest, Vince eased the BMW toward the road's edge, leaving not quite enough room for the van. As they drew even, he lowered his window. Evelina reached across him, her middle finger extended toward the startled officers. Then she shouted something in Lithuanian that made their eyes widen.

"Fuuck!" Vince let out a sigh of resignation.

"There is no time for that now, Vincentas," she said, laughing. "Gun it!"

The BMW's engine roared as Vince accelerated. In the rearview mirror, he watched the van's rear end tilt skyward as it slid into the hidden ditch.

"Jesus Christ," he muttered. "I just ran police off the road."

He looked over at Evelina, who was taking another deep drag on that putrid cigarette. She directed him through a series of turns until they reached a gated facility.

"No." Vince dug his fingers into the steering wheel, refusing to turn off the ignition. "No way."

Vince didn't need to understand the words on the signs written in both Lithuanian and Russian to know this was a border crossing.

"Sometimes to understand present, we must visit past. Even if past is painful. Or dangerous."

"I appreciate learning about the orphanage, but this? This is Russia."

"You are safer with me in Russia than alone in Lithuania without papers." She opened the door and flicked her cigarette into the air. "What do you choose?"

Vince swore he heard distant sirens. His decision was made for him.

Minutes later, they approached the guard station on foot. To Vince's amazement, the guards embraced Evelina like old friends. They crossed a bridge spanning the shallow Šešupė river.

"Dobro pozhalovat' domoy, Vinsent," Evelina announced.

"What?"

"Welcome home, Vincentas."

The words hit him like a physical blow. "Home? What do you mean?"

"The border between what is true and what you have believed your whole life is as thin as the one we just crossed, Vincentas," Evelina said.

"What are you talking about?" Vince demanded.

"Some truths cannot be unlearned. Vincentas." They walked a gravel road into deepening woods. "You must prepare yourself."

The woods opened to a clearing, and Evelina began her story. December 1999. A couple arriving to adopt a brother and sister at an orphanage in Kaliningrad. Private adoption, all fees paid. They left the orphanage with their new children, heading for this very border.

"They had no way of knowing about Russian mafia scheme," Evelina continued. "New gang member wanted to impress them. He opened fire into car when he should not."

Vince bit his lip imagining the scene.

"Wife was in back seat. Threw herself over children." Evelina's voice softened. "This mother died protecting her children."

"What kind of animals...?"

"Vincentas, father had no choice but to obey orders from mafia—drive to Lithuania or same thing happen to him. And children be stolen from him. He watched his wife dragged from car and left on side of road. He drove fast to save his two new children... they were covered in their mother's blood, Vincentas."

Vince looked around the clearing and noticed the quietness in the air. If he hadn't known better, he would have thought he was in the pine barrens of southern New Jersey.

"Augustas was waiting... as he always did, on Lithuania side of border. He took father and children to Divine Mercy. Made them feel special."

"Wait... the father took a brother and sister to Divine Mercy? In 1999?"

"Your mother, Vincentas. Maureen died protecting you and Audrey."

He doubled over, retching onto the frozen ground. Steam rose from the puddle as cold sweat dripped down his face. His ears rang with a high-pitched whine.

Vince stripped off his jacket and sweatshirt, letting the bitter wind cool his overheated skin. His mind raced with images—his father's face, old wedding photos of a beautiful woman with the softest eyes he'd ever known. Maureen. Mom.

What would she look like now? Who would she have become? Could she have healed the rift between him and Audrey that his rigid morality had created?

"I had a mother?"

Evelina paused, as if to allow Vince's own words to be absorbed in his heart. "Yes, Vincentas. She was your mother. If only for a short time, you and your sister had mother."

Vince slowly shut his eyes. "How short a time, Evelina?"

"Vincentas, you deserve truth. No matter how much hurt it causes. You are owed truth." Evelina hesitated, mustering the strength even a woman with her life's experiences would need to answer Vince truthfully. "Just a few minutes, Vincentas. Maureen was your mom for just a few minutes."

A few minutes... What Vince wouldn't give to have a few minutes with her now.

"Your pain comes from information you were not prepared to hear, Vincentas," Evelina said gently. "But you deserve truth. Audrey deserves truth. Your father protected you from it, and now his life is in danger."

"Why? Why is his life in danger now?"

"Because he made deal with Russian mafia. He accepted deal from them, Vincentas."

Vince brought his hands to his head. "What kind of deal?"

"Augustas put on mask of kind and brave priest. He told your father he would do what was possible for body of his wife... for Maureen's body to be brought to Lithuania. Michael wanted proper burial in America for his wife."

"For my mom..."

"Yes, Vincentas. Proper burial for your mom. Russian mafia left her on side of road for scavengers. Augustas made your father believe he put pressure on them to give back Maureen's body. But Russian mafia had own idea. They would only let her body go if Michael agreed to help them when he got back to United States. To do favors for them."

Vince's hands became clenched fists without any conscious thought.

Evelina continued. "Vincentas, Russian mafia told Augustas that if Michael did not agree to deal, they would take you and Audrey back to orphanage there. And he would never see Maureen again. If your father did not agree to do what he was asked, you and Audrey would have..." She couldn't finish her sentence.

"And my mom... and Maureen?"

"She would have been left for scavengers. Your father could not know at time what Russian mafia wanted. Your father only wanted to take you and Audrey to safety in America. And give proper burial for his wife."

"But why is my dad in danger now?"

"Because he has stopped doing favors for Russian mafia in Atlantic City. They have warned him in past, Vincentas. They are serious this time."

"Where did all this happen? I need to see it for myself!"

"You are standing here, Vincentas. This is clearing where ambush happened."

Vince dropped his head back, closing his eyes. "This whole thing is a dream, right?" He pleaded with the gray sky. "I just... I just want to go back to before—"

"Before you learned Augustas is not who he appears? Before you learned of danger your father is in?"

"How do you know all this, Evelina?"

"I was young nun when Augustas arrived. He abused sisters, demonstrated power in many ways. We feared him—not respect-fear, but experience-fear." She shifted on the icy road. "After Y2K fears started, I left order. I have made it life mission to expose truth about Augustas. All truth."

"But how?" Vince pressed.

"I give information to people who need it. They think I am just pawn. They do not know what I really am."

"What, like a double agent?"

Instead of laughing, she stared across the clearing. "You are part of truth too, Vincentas."

"What?"

"In orphanage, one sister cared for you and Audrey. Fed you. Changed diapers. Read stories. Took Audrey to pet horses in field."

Vince's breath caught. "Horses?"

Evelina pulled an amber necklace from beneath her coat. "One special horse. Lithuanian Heavy Draught. Beautiful chestnut roan named Gintaras—means Amber, like this stone. Most gentle horse in field. Audrey would pet for hours. Horse understood her in way I did not understand."

Vince saw his sister's paintings in his mind—always the same damn horse, the same field. A memory her conscious mind couldn't grasp but her soul remembered.

"Vincentas…"

He looked at Evelina. Were they tears in her eyes? "You? You were the nun who took care of us?"

"I rocked you both to sleep. Every night… You were so scared." Evelina's voice cracked. "Now you know truth. Whole truth."

"So help you God," Vince whispered into his hands.

"What God?" Bitterness filled her mouth. "What God allows such evil against children? What God lets men like Augustas wear collar?"

"I don't know that God either," Vince admitted.

"This is why I have no faith anymore. As you say, it is complicated."

"But you were a nun."

"Simple, Vincentas. I have no fucks left to give." She gestured at his shivering body. "Put on clothes. We walk little further."

As they moved deeper into the woods, Vince's mind struggled to process everything. His mother's sacrifice. His father's decades of silence. Evelina's role in his earliest days. The horse that haunted Audrey's art.

The truth hurt worse than any lie, but at least now he understood. The black-and-white world he'd lived in had shattered here in this gray Russian afternoon. But maybe that's what he needed to save his father—

to finally see all the shades between right and wrong, good and evil, truth and lies.

"Ready to continue, Vincentas?" Evelina asked.

He nodded, pulling on his sweatshirt. Whatever came next, at least now he knew where his story really began. On this road, in this clearing, where love and sacrifice and evil had collided to shape the man he had become.

CHAPTER 43

INTERNAL THEATER

Friday 4:45 p.m.—Atlantic City
(Friday 11:45 p.m.—Lithuania)

Carmen checked her watch. Friday afternoon, she should be heading home. Instead, she paced outside Chief Huertas's office, summoned by his text.

The secretary directed her not to his office but to the conference room. Inside, her stomach dropped. Chief Huertas, the deputy chief, the city attorney, and Lieutenant Roberta Macher from Internal Affairs—the one who snuck up in her doorway earlier and asked, "Who's Audrey?"

Roberta—"Bobbie"—Macher. AKA: "LT Bowel Movement." She earned her nickname in the department because of the way she signed her memos: LT B.M. Her reputation as LT Bowel Movement became cemented by the way she left a stench of destroyed careers in her wake.

A digital recorder sat on the table, red light glowing.

"Lieutenant Carmen Navarro," LT Bowel Movement began, "this interview concerns IA case twenty-five dash zero-zero-six. Charges include improper initiation of criminal investigation, unauthorized use of

NCIC and DMV systems, interference with an ongoing investigation, and failure to supervise... specifically, Detective Vincent Brown."

Carmen's mind raced. How much had Macher overheard earlier? What did they know about Vince?

After reading Garrity and Miranda warnings—both of which Carmen had to sign—Macher's predatory smile emerged. This was her chance to take down another officer.

But Carmen stood, straightening her jacket. "Interesting that the department's only two female command officers are now adversaries. Makes me wonder about the real agenda."

The best defense is a good offense is a phrase Carmen Navarro heard several times playing sports when she was younger. Now she had to put that advice into practice. At the very least, she needed to buy some time before this investigation gained any momentum.

She pulled out her cell phone, holding it deliberately. "Everything's recorded these days, isn't it, Chief? Phones can capture conversations without anyone noticing."

Chief Huertas shifted in his seat and went on his own offensive. "You're goddamn right, Lieutenant."

"Yes, I am right, Chief." Now holding her phone up above the table, with its face up like she was going to read a text message or email from it. "Someone could be using one of these to record a conversation without the other person noticing, couldn't they? I mean, as long as the person recording the conversation didn't make it look obvious."

She then turned to LT Bowel Movement. "Lieutenant Macher, you know what the department policy says about following illegal orders from superiors, correct?"

"Yes, Lieutenant," Macher answered through gritted teeth.

"And I'm sure you know the policy about recording conversations..." Carmen held her phone higher. "A personal device can record any conversation, as long as the officer remains present."

Carmen was on the offensive for sure. Now it was time to go all in.

Chief Huertas's eyes widened as she continued.

"Hypothetically, if a subordinate... say, a lieutenant... recorded a superior giving an illegal order."

His fists slammed the table. "We're done for today. Lieutenant Navarro can consult her union rep and attorney."

In her frozen car later, Carmen gripped the steering wheel. Her gamble had worked—for now. The chief didn't know she hadn't actually recorded his illegal order about the warrants. But how long before he retaliated?

Through the defrosting windshield, she read the sign above the entrance: Integrity. Accountability. Respect.

She laughed bitterly at the hypocrisy, then checked her rearview mirror. The "Reserved for Detective Bureau Commander" sign reflected back. She wondered how much longer it would be hers.

CHAPTER 44

SACRED RUINS

Friday 3:10 p.m.—Kaliningrad Region, Russia
(Friday 8:10 a.m.—Atlantic City)

Standing before the crumbling ruins, Vince felt another chill despite his restored layers of clothing.

"This," Evelina said softly, "is where your life started, Vincentas."

Graffiti marked the stone walls of the abandoned Russian orphanage. Gang tags on sacred ground. "The irony," Vince whispered to himself. "A dead building where my life started."

"Irony can take something bad and make good, Vincentas."

"This place that once symbolized life… a sacred gift that was shared with my parents by an unknown person is now a hangout for thugs who use spray paint to mark their territory. I guess this is what humble beginnings is all about."

"Humble beginnings," Evelina agreed. "But look what you have accomplished, Vincentas. And what you must still do."

"Augustas?"

"Yes. You are chosen one to stop him."

"Chosen by who?"

"By me." She lit another cigarette. "I have waited more than twenty years, Vincentas. Waited for you to become who you are. Now time has come for Arabian checkmate."

Vince shuffled so he was upwind from the foul smell. "More riddles."

"No riddles, Vincentas… Take one final look. See where you started. Use imagination to see what once was. Then come with me. We must go now."

Evelina turned and began a slow walk down the road from where they came. "Vincentas, now you know your beginnings. You must know your opponent better. You must focus now only on opponent. Let me remind you story of Augustas," her voice hardened. "Are you listening, Vincentas?"

Vince hurried to catch up to her from the ruins of the orphanage. "Yeah, I'm listening."

"Good. Now pay attention to details, Vincentas. Before priesthood, he was member of Vilnius Brigade. When police closed in, he fled to seminary, changed name. At Divine Mercy, he met Dominykas. Together they worked with Russian mafia, selling children through orphanages."

Her words came faster now, like poison being purged. "Americans would adopt, then be ambushed on way to airport. Until young gangster shot your mother."

Vince flinched at the memory he never had.

"Augustas arranged everything—your adoption, death certificate of Maureen claiming food poisoning instead of bullets. Made your father agree to help Russian mafia in America. When Divine Mercy learned of his abuse of nuns, Augustas was sent to America—to church in Atlantic City. Pattern never changed—abuse of power, money laundering through church, cryptocurrency deals with Dominykas."

Vince stepped in front of her. "You didn't tell me this was going to be a laundry list of evidence. Should I be writing this down?"

"Do not write anything, Vincentas. Pay attention and remember."

A violent coughing fit. Vince steadied her shoulder as she pressed a handkerchief to her mouth.

"I am alright now, Vincentas. No one can expect to live forever. Timer is clicking on this match. You must be ready in America for next move."

"I'm still not sure I understand..."

"Pay attention and focus, Vincentas," she said, walking at a quicker pace. "Cryptocurrency used by Augustas and Dominykas is called Monero. It is only cryptocurrency that cannot be traced. Do you understand, Vincentas?"

"Monero... Yeah, I understand."

"Augustas announced church in Atlantic City accepts Monero cryptocurrency for donations. He uses in blackmail of people who confess sins—confessions to him are recorded. People trust monsignor of church... their sins recorded for him to threaten them. He is evil man, Vincentas."

"Yeah, I know that, Evelina. So why are you—"

"Augustas is evil to young girls," she continued, ignoring his question. "He continues his abuse of girls in America—in basement of church. Just like to sisters at Divine Mercy. They must play chess against him. If they lose, must pay by doing sex act on Augustas. It is what he did at Divine Mercy to sisters. In shelter of church in Atlantic City, if girls refuse to play game, he throws them out of shelter. Sisters at Divine Mercy did not have that choice."

When she stopped walking to catch her breath, Vince had to find out. "The chess games," he said when she recovered. "With the women in the shelter. And at Divine Mercy...here. Did he... to you when you were a nun?" Vince scrunched his eyes in frustration. Some questions are too personal to ask. Some answers that are no one's business. He couldn't take it back... he wished he had more constraint.

"Yes." Her voice held no emotion. She stared at the ground. "He believes he is chess master. But he only plays those who do not know game. That was once me. No longer."

The rage that was building inside finally exploded in his words. "As soon as I get home, I'm going to put a case together against that son of a bitch!"

"What case, Vincentas? Everything learned started from recording of confessions. Those recordings are illegal in United States, yes?"

Vince mouthed the word *fuck*, as though he had forgotten how all this began. *Audrey. Why is it always something with her?* Vince asked himself. "Yes, Evelina, they're illegal."

"And you cannot use anything illegal to start investigation, yes? You call it fruit from poisonous tree?"

"You know, for an old homeless lady, you sure do know a lot about the United States."

"Vincentas, remember what you have learned—things are not always as they appear."

A gentle snow started to fall, creating a faint, pure white blanket in the forest around them. "I can't use any of this... fruit of the poisonous tree."

Her smile was sharp. "In America, yes. But Lithuania has no such doctrine."

They neared the bridge back to Lithuania. "How will you know what happens when I return home?"

"I knew what you did before coming here. Why would that change?" She paused. "Speaking of home, Vincentas, you have plan?"

Vince explained his idea for getting back without papers.

"Good plan," she nodded. "Let me help make it great plan."

CHAPTER 45
THE STAGE IS SET

Friday 9:15 p.m.—Vilnius, Lithuania
(Friday 2:15 p.m.—Atlantic City)

Back at the hostel, Vince changed into his original travel clothes—the same sweatpants and sweatshirt he'd worn to the marina. If anyone checked security footage in Atlantic City, the clothes would match.

"I am going home," he told Justina when she questioned his packed bag.

On his jog to the bus stop, he dropped his backpack into a bonfire burning in a metal barrel. The Friday night bus to Vilnius was surprisingly full—party crowds. For the hour ride, he drilled Evelina's information into his memory. He followed her directions not to write anything down. Instead, acronyms gave meaning to what he learned from her.

The walking route Evelina gave him led him across the Liubartas Bridge. Halfway across it, he dismantled his burner phone, scattering the battery, SIM card, and shell into the Neris River below. Now he was truly untraceable—a potential John Doe if he were to be discovered now. The mile walk to the Old Town's party district kept his mind focused on the next phase.

The neon bar sign appeared exactly where Evelina had described. In the back lot, Vince checked his watch—10:35 p.m. "Shit!" He quickly adjusted it back seven hours to match Atlantic City time. The folded paper in his pocket would be crucial if—

The first blow caught his lower back, driving the air from his lungs and dropping him to the gravel. His jujitsu training kicked in as he fought back with his legs. Through the pain, he remembered one final task. With the last bit of strength he had left, he reached into his pocket for the small vial he asked Audrey to get him before he left.

He downed its contents, gagging at the taste, just as a hood was pulled over his face. Zip ties bit into his wrists. Something heavy struck his shoulder—the crack of breaking bone followed by searing pain. His clavicle.

A blow across his chest shattered his ribs. Each breath became agony. They tossed him onto cold metal—the floor of a van. Someone's weight pinned him down.

"Stay calm, American, and you will live," a voice ordered in a heavy accent.

The hood trapped his CO2, each labored breath harder than the last. His broken ribs screamed. The kidney blow throbbed with a pain he never imagined was possible.

The inside of the van fell silent. Then—smack! Something connected with his face. Blood ran warm down his cheek, and filled his mouth. The high-pitched ringing in his right ear pierced the quiet.

"Vincentas, be still and let people finish their work. Do not move head."

Evelina? Is Evelina here?

"You fucking bitch!" he moaned through his swollen jaw and blood-filled mouth.

"Trust me, Vincentas. This is part of plan. Remember when I asked you to trust me? You must trust me, Vincentas."

Strong hands gripped his head. Through the slit they cut in the hood, a bright light shined down on him. Then cold liquid splashed his neck. A rough cloth scrubbed. More liquid. Then the stinging pricks of needles, a line of fire from below his ear to the middle of his throat.

"Evelina, are you still here? I'm scared," Vince said while spitting blood out of his mouth.

"Yes, Vincentas, I am here. Be calm and stay still. This is almost over."

"*What* is almost over, Evelina?"

"This part of plan, Vincentas. This part of plan is almost over."

"But we never talked about anything like…" Words became harder to say. "What the fuck was that?" Vince asked.

"That was numbing medication," Evelina explained softly. "Trust in bigger plan, Vincentas. All will be okay."

Vince wanted to believe her, but every neuron in his brain was screaming for him to fight back.

As if she was reading his mind, Evelina reassured him. "Do not listen to those voices, Vincentas. You must force thoughts to take you to goals. Do not let fears take you away from goals."

For the first time since meeting her, Vince finally was able to interpret one of Evelina's mixed-up sayings. He was sure she was trying to quote Nelson Mandela, who said we should align our choices with our hopes, not our fears.

Well, at least she did her best, Vince said to himself above the ringing in his ear. He couldn't believe that in this predicament, he found a way to laugh at something.

The pressure came next—like at the dentist, but on his neck. Vince wondered if he'd been cut in all the commotion but didn't feel it because of the intense pain elsewhere in his body.

"It is done," someone announced.

Vince didn't know a lot about emergency sutures, but this seemed to take too little time to complete. If it was completed properly. "At least you cleansed it before sewing me up. Thanks for that, I guess."

"You have not been sewn up, Vincentas," Evelina said. "You have been cut wide open."

The van lurched into motion. Vince rolled helplessly with each turn, blood pooling in the hollow of his throat, then splashing out of his mouth.

The GHB from the vial began to take hold.

"Vincentas," Evelina's voice seemed far away. "Repeat after me. 'I was attacked by Bratva. Russian mafia tried to kill me.'"

"I was killed by the Russian mafia," he slurred, euphoria setting in. "Man, those guys are tough…"

As consciousness faded, he felt something pressed into his pocket—Evelina's amber necklace. "This was very special gift to me, Vincentas. Someday you will meet someone special," her voice floated through the haze. "Give them this."

The van stopped.

If he were conscious, he would have felt them remove the hood and dump his body at the curb.

He would have heard the M-80 firecracker explode over the embassy fence, followed by the van's tires screeching away into the night.

CHAPTER 46
EMERGENCY PROTOCOLS

Saturday 7:40 a.m.—Vilnius, Lithuania
(Saturday 12:40 a.m.—Atlantic City)

Medical scrubs came into focus through Vince's blurred vision. His head pounded with each blink as he tried to make sense of the bright room. A massive man in a suit stood to the side—built like a bodybuilder but with government credentials hanging on his lanyard.

"Where am I?" The words barely audible through his dry throat.

"You are in hospital in Vilnius," answered a tall nurse in accented English. "Can you tell us what happened?"

His mind was a blank canvas with only fragments painted in—packing his room, the bus ride, tossing things in the river. Everything else was darkness. "Venice?"

"No, Vilnius, Lithuania." The nurse's smile was gentle. "My name is Ieva. I am your nurse. You are in Vilnius University Hospital trauma ICU. Do you know how you got here?"

Before she could continue her evaluation, the baritone voice cut through the room. "Can I talk to him now?"

"Not yet, sir." Her voice was stern. "We still have protocols to follow."

She asked Vince who he was. He responded with his real name. The large man's nod caught Vince's attention.

Then she asked about the date. Vince had practiced how to answer that question since he left the docks in Atlantic City. His answer was intentionally wrong by a week. The next question was the day of the week. "Tuesday... maybe Wednesday?" Her concerned glance at the suit didn't escape his notice.

"Can you tell me what hurts the most right now?"

Vince didn't need any time to think about an answer to this question, "My head, ma'am. My head is pounding and there is a loud ringing in my left ear."

"That is because you have suffered a concussion. You are lucky that there is no bleeding in your brain. You are very lucky, sir."

The large man stepped forward. "I'm Terrance Coleman, the senior special agent with Homeland Security's Eastern European branch. I'm here on the ambassador's orders."

"Sir, you have to wait while—"

"I can't tell ya a lot," his voice boomed. "But I can tell ya this is a matter of national security. And I'm gonna interview him."

"Homeland Security?" Vince was confused. "Why—"

Agent Coleman ignored Nurse Ieva's threats to call security and began speaking to Vince.

"We ran your prints through AFIS. Got matches from your coaching certification, academy training, and ACPD hire. When the Lithuanian ambassador makes calls, things move quick in D.C."

"That fast?"

"Getting your beat-up, bleeding ass dumped at the U.S. Embassy gates with an explosion tends to expedite things." Coleman produced a note, holding it where Vince could see. The Cyrillic letters meant nothing to his concussed brain.

"What am I looking at?"

"It's Russian." Coleman read it in perfect pronunciation before switching to English: "The American is no longer needed. Take back your trash. Send greetings from Atlantic City."

"You speak Russian?"

Coleman's grin was wide. "When Homeland finds out you can speak Russian, they send you to Eastern Europe. A Black man, looking like this, speaking Russian—I know, right?"

Vince started to apologize, but Coleman waved it off. "Man, I love catching people off guard with it. Let's me overhear all kinds of interesting conversations."

His expression turned serious. "Look, someone's hornet's nest got kicked. You were drugged—there's GHB in your system. That's why ya can't remember. We're getting ya out."

Vince gave very few valuable clues to Agent Coleman during the ensuing interview. Then, on cue, two DSS agents appeared. Over Nurse Ieva's protests, they released his bed's brakes and wheeled him through a maze of corridors to an elevator.

Agent Coleman walked beside the bed. Everything was happening at lightning speed now. Vince was confused, not knowing who the men were or where they were taking him.

"My job was to get information from you. Here's my card if you think of anything else. Their job is to protect your ass. They protect diplomats all over the world; they know what they're doing. My job is done, Detective. Theirs is continuing."

"Continuing?" Vince asked.

The "doctor" holding the elevator turned out to be another agent who produced keys to the roof access.

The winter wind hit as they pushed him toward the waiting helicopter. A man in an olive drab flight suit helped him aboard.

"Logan Coyle," he introduced himself through the headset. "Air Force PJ."

"PJ?"

"Fucking civilian." Logan shook his head. "Pararescueman. And before you ask, no, not like an Army medic. See this patch, asshole?" he said, pointing to his chest. "It says USAF. I'd throw you out this door if you suggested that again."

"Oh, so you're from the Air Force."

"I'm not *from* anything, dickwad. I'm *in* the United States Air Force. And the United States Air Force assigned me to this bullshit ambulance attendant job for a year."

"Bullshit job? Then what's your role in all this?"

"Keep you alive till we land. Wherever that is. It's above my pay grade to know more." His tone switched to resentment. "Stuck on diplomatic taxi service when I should be with my unit. Nine more months of this shit."

As they flew northwest, Vince's headache intensified.

"That headache coming back?" Logan asked, his skill of paying attention to details obvious to Vince.

"Yeah, it's getting bad."

Logan noticed his discomfort and checked his charts.

"Toradol," he decided, meticulously cleaning the IV port. Vince watched him count each alcohol swab stroke aloud.

"Pretty fastidious for a glorified ambulance attendant."

"I told you I'll throw you out this fucking door!"

Logan injected the Toradol into the IV port. "Only one right way to do things," he said without looking up. "When people think they can change black and white to gray, that's when problems start. But do I get credit? Nope. Just reassignment for having an attitude problem. Can you believe that? Me... an attitude problem?"

Vince saw himself reflected in Logan's words. Had his own rigid thinking affected his relationships the same way? Was this why he worked alone, reporting directly to Carmen instead of through normal channels?

The medication kicked in as Logan reached for his bag. To Vince's amazement, he pulled out a Rubik's Cube. "Still trying to figure this little fucker out," Logan admitted while twisting it. I can get one side, but then everything else goes to hell."

"Are you shitting me?" Vince laughed despite the pain in his ribs. "I carry a small one everywhere. Can't get past one side either."

Logan checked the property report. "Yep—one multi-colored cube, one watch, and one charm necklace."

The necklace. Vince's hand went instinctively to his empty pocket. Something about amber... Baltic gold... the memory slipped away like smoke.

"So what's your story?" Logan asked. "Another embassy brat who pissed off the wrong people at a club?"

"Not exactly." Vince hesitated. "You said you have clearance?"

"Highest levels. Can't talk about half the shit I've seen. But this assignment..." He made a face.

"The Russian mafia grabbed me. They took me to Lithuania. At least that's what they think happened. From what they told me in the hospital, I'm lucky to be alive. And... the GHB wasn't recreational."

Logan's demeanor shifted instantly from irritated to alert professional. "No shit? So this is an actual mission."

"Yeah, I guess it is."

"Tell me everything." The Rubik's Cube lay to the side, forgotten, as Logan listened intently to what Vince could remember.

"Man," he said when Vince finished. "And here I thought this was another diplomatic babysitting gig."

Vince noticed the PJ patch on Logan's shoulder: "THAT OTHERS MAY LIVE."

"We're a lot alike," he realized aloud.

Logan didn't look up from the notes he was scribbling on the chart. "How's that?"

"Black-and-white thinkers learning there are grays. And both trying to save lives, just... different ways."

Logan considered Vince's words. "Maybe. But I still say there's only one right way to do things."

"What about your cube?"

"Shit." Logan picked it up again. "Okay, maybe some problems have multiple solutions."

Vince smiled, thinking of his own cube back home. Home. He had work to do when he got there—and people to protect. The thought gave him clarity he hadn't felt since waking up. But with that clarity came concern.

"You good?" Logan asked.

"Yeah. Just realized sometimes you have to make your own right way."

"Now you sound like my commanding officer." Logan checked his watch. "Two hours to the transfer point. Try to rest. Something tells me you've got a long road ahead."

Vince closed his eyes, letting the whine of rotors wash over him. The necklace toyed with his memory—a gift given? A promise made? Like the hours he'd lost, it all remained just out of reach.

For now, he had to trust that the right path would become clear. After all, he had learned from the best... a chain-smoking chess master who'd taught him that sometimes the winning move isn't the obvious one.

CHAPTER 47
FEDERAL VISITORS

Saturday 5:07 a.m.—Atlantic City
(Saturday 12:07 p.m.—Lithuania)

Car doors slammed in the church alley. Audrey peered through her window to see suited men exiting glossy black SUVs. Her heart raced—they had to be law enforcement.

Did they find out about the computer files? Is this about Lieutenant Navarro?

She looked at her phone—Vince had once told her raids are conducted in the early morning hours. She crept to her door, hearing radio chatter: "Rear exit secure... No sign of movement."

For twenty tense minutes, Audrey listened to fragments of communication. Something about "Nighthawk-one" and "Garden State Parkway route." Her hands trembled as she calculated escape options—the fifteen-foot drop to pavement ruled out the window.

At 5:30, soft knocks. "Audrey, it is Monsignor. These gentlemen are with the FBI."

She opened the door to find Augustas and two agents. "It's alright, child..." His use of "child" meant he was performing for them.

"Your brother's been injured, but he's okay," one agent explained. "We believe he was kidnapped. He's being transported home from Lithuania."

"Lithuania?" The word hit like a punch. "How did he—"

"That's what we're investigating. Right now, we need to get you to safety. Pack what you can carry."

The drive to Newark took ninety minutes, during which Audrey kept silently repeating, *Thank God he's okay.*

CHAPTER 48
ALTITUDE REVELATIONS

Saturday 12 noon—Šiauliai Airport, Lithuania
(Saturday 5:00 a.m.—Atlantic City)

It felt like they were descending.

"Are we going down?"

"Never say 'going down' in a helicopter unless it's literally going down," Logan scolded when Vince asked. "But yeah, final approach. Hold on a sec."

Logan reached for a switch that was on the wire of his headset. He adjusted it and Vince could see his lips move but couldn't hear anything. A couple of seconds later, Logan adjusted the switch, and Vince could once again hear him. "Pilot says we'll be on the ground in a couple of minutes."

"Then what?" Vince asked.

"Beats me," Logan replied. "I'm just here for the ride. I take orders and don't question them. I'm sure we'll find out soon enough what's next."

Through the window, Vince spotted rows of aircraft with unfamiliar insignias. "U.S. base?"

"Not our planes," Logan said, studying the markings. "We're probably still in Lithuania. We'll find out together."

Vince didn't know whether to be concerned or comforted by Logan's carefree attitude. The skids at the bottom of the helicopter touched down on a remote part of the airport. A Lithuanian officer met them, his double-cross patch confirming their location. The Unimog transport delighted Logan more than the surrounding military jets.

"Can you believe this?" he exclaimed. "We get bounced around in junk, and they get a Mercedes!"

Security screening was quick but thorough. Vince shivered standing on the tarmac in his hospital gown until a deafening whine drew his attention. A gleaming white jet taxied toward them, its engines mounted near the T-tail giving it a distinctly luxurious profile. No identifying numbers marked its pristine fuselage—just a thin gold stripe from nose to tail.

The man who conducted the security screening opened the side door of the plane, which folded out in one smooth motion. "She's all fueled up just for you, Mr. Brown. Have a safe trip home."

"Can I ask you one question?"

"Sure, what is it?"

Vince looked around the airfield. "Where are we?"

"This is Šiauliai Airport."

"Siau... what?" Vince asked, giving up on attempting the proper pronunciation.

"You are at a military base that is also used as a passenger airport. Or you can look at it as a passenger airport used by the Lithuanian military."

"So, we *are* still in Lithuania," Vince said, as if he was asking to confirm where Logan already told him.

A British pilot emerged. "Hello, Vince. I'm Damien. You'll have company in the cabin—another U.S. citizen's already aboard." His British accent surprised Vince. "Nothing to worry about, mate," Damien grinned. "We'll fly the tits off her. Get you home by supper."

Vince looked at Logan. Logan shrugged his shoulders. "Definitely not our military. Probably a State Department pilot. From what I hear, they're pretty good."

"Good enough to get us back to the States in one piece?" Vince asked.

Damien spoke up before Logan could respond, "Even in the U.K. we know our east from our west. We just say things the proper way. Now stop being like a Cock Knocker and let's get the wheels up."

Logan and Damien traded good-natured military branch insults as they boarded. Inside, plush leather seating stretched the cabin's length. Vince set his eyes on the sofa—the perfect place to lie down and sleep.

A federal air marshal greeted them, pointing to fresh clothes laid out on one of the chairs. "The State Department got you something to wear instead of that gown," he explained.

Another man had his back turned and seemed occupied in the galley as Vince passed by him.

For as small as it was, in both width and height, this bathroom was nicer than most of the men's rooms he'd been in. Vince splashed water on his bearded face. He managed the sweatpants one-handed, one leg at a time. The pain was worse when he tried draping the shirt over his injured shoulder.

He let himself smile through the pain. Oh, how good it would feel to be sleeping in fresh clothes for the eight-hour ride home.

CHAPTER 49
HIGH-ALTITUDE REVELATIONS

Saturday 13:20 Zulu time—flight level 500

"Hello, Vince." The voice froze him in the lavatory doorway. "You look like you've been through hell, son."

Vince stood in stunned disbelief.

"Dad?" Vince stared at Michael Brown, the beloved district attorney of Atlantic County. Their last encounter had been at Christmas Eve Mass, where at least some things still made sense. Now he faced a father he thought he knew, carrying the weight of everything he'd learned.

"What... how?"

Vince stepped toward the lavatory door, tempted to go inside and lock the door behind him.

"I'm here to take you home." His father's face crumpled. "This is all my fault. I never imagined they'd go this far, that they'd hurt you like this."

"Who's 'they?'"

"I've made terrible mistakes, son. Mistakes that put you in danger."

It clicked. His father thought the Russian mafia had kidnapped him. The last person Vince expected to convince was serving up the perfect cover story. He tested the waters. "I can't believe you would risk my life—or Audrey's."

"I promise I'll explain everything if you'll let me," Michael said, his tone heavy with decades of guilt. "But right now we need to get you home safely."

"Home?" Vince met his father's eyes. "Is that where we're going, or is this another lie?"

"You must have questions. Lots of questions... questions you might not want answered."

"Just one. Who are you?"

Michael nodded slowly. "That might be the question you don't want answered. For now, let's start with where I am—I'm here for you. Can that be our foundation?"

Vince spread his belongings across the sofa, leaving no room for his father. Michael took a seat across the aisle, head bowed. The jet engines' whir filled their silence as they climbed to cruising altitude.

"I'm sorry, son."

Logan, who was charged with the continued caring of Vince until he got home, busied himself with medical supplies up front, giving father and son space.

"Vince, you said you wanted the truth, and I told you I would lay out everything for you. Son, I have nothing to hide from you. Not anymore."

Leaning in on the edge of his seat, he continued. "I don't expect you to understand this, or even believe it, but everything I did—all the crap I got myself caught up in—was because of my love for you and Audrey." Michael took out a handkerchief to wipe his eyes. "Since the first day I held you and Audrey, my life has been centered on my love for both of you."

Vince remained silent. Partly for emphasis, but mainly because he had never heard his dad speak with such passion about him or Audrey. And because he had never heard his dad speak like this, Vince had also never remembered feeling this way before. "I'm listening, Dad."

"I made a deal with the Russian mafia," Michael said. "It was more like extortion, Vince. They used you and Audrey as currency."

"What do you mean?"

"My wife—my soulmate—was just murdered. Her blood was on all of us." Michael's hands trembled. "I'd lost the only woman I ever loved. I couldn't lose you and Audrey too. They would have taken you back to that orphanage if I didn't agree."

Michael stood and turned away from Vince. Tears flowed down his cheeks. "They would have left Maureen's body to be eaten by scavengers in those woods…"

"Why not go to the FBI once we were home?"

"Because when we got home, a man was waiting with an envelope." Michael put away his handkerchief. "Photos of the shipping crate that contained Maureen's body. Detailed threats about what they'd do to all of us if I didn't cooperate. Do you understand what I'm telling you?"

"Yeah, Dad. I think so."

"The death certificate said food poisoning—listeria. But she died protecting you both." Michael wiped his eyes. "They made it clear: either I helped them, or they'd make me watch them torture you and Audrey before killing you. Or force you to watch them kill me."

"Motherfuckers," Vince whispered.

Hours passed. Vince tried to sleep but couldn't. His father stared out the window at the Atlantic passing below. Logan brought water and checked Vince's vitals periodically, his presence a buffer between father and son.

"Your CI told you about me, didn't he?" Michael asked suddenly. "That's why you started looking into Augustas."

Vince's nondenial was like a carefully constructed lie. "How did you know?"

"An anonymous call to my office about your passport being suspended. Then the chief told me about your leave of absence." Michael leaned forward. "Why didn't you come to me?"

"I needed time to get my head straight." The lie didn't sit well in his gut. "Then I woke up in a hospital in Lithuania."

"Bullshit." Michael's prosecutor voice emerged. "First the leave, then denied boarding, then kidnapped and beaten. You're leaving out everything in between."

"Dad—"

"No more lies, Vince. Not from me, not from you. I need to know something, and I need you to be completely honest with me."

"Complete honesty... go ahead."

"Vince, who else knows about what your CI told you?"

"No one, Dad. This whole thing has been off the books..."

"You? An off-the-books investigation?"

"You asked me to be completely honest," Vince deadpanned.

"Vince, I need you to promise me... this is really important. Is there any chance that anyone else knows about this?"

"Dad... Jesus Christ. You can ask me the same questions in different ways, and the answer will always be the same. No one knows but me." Vince wondered if he oversold it.

Michael looked at him, eyeing him like he was a defendant on trial. "It's just that there are things you don't... I need to be sure, that's all, Vince."

Logan appeared with his medical bag. "Time to check that IV and recheck your vitals, Vince." His timing couldn't have been better.

When Logan finished what he had to do, Vince looked over at his dad. "You asked me to be completely honest with you, and I was. Can I ask you a question?"

"Absolutely."

"How serious are they about killing you if you don't help them this time?"

"As serious as I've ever seen them."

Vince forced a smile. "Dad, you look tired. Close your eyes and get some rest before we land."

The silence of Vince's mind was filled with the roar of the engines. Vince had never been in a private, multi-million-dollar jet before. Reflecting on the events that brought him onboard this aircraft, he breathed in as deeply as his broken ribs would allow.

How did it get to this point? A juvenile officer assigned to create diversion programs for kids was now immersed in a world of fraud, extortion, and murder. And lies.

Was he a hypocrite? A man with a master's degree in ethics. A man who taught ethics at the police academy, who preached the importance of character and honesty to his teenage charges, who was flying in a luxury government jet... for all the wrong reasons.

Or were they the right reasons to fix the wrongs of evil men?

There but for the grace of God go I... How many times had Vince heard this at meetings? How many times has he said it? He hadn't thought about God, truly thought about God, since he stopped believing in a vengeful God years ago. But here he was, looking at his reflection, pondering these words that spurred compassion and empathy more than judgment and condemnation.

Was this God's grace?

In the past, in the days when the old Vince would self-medicate his guilt and fear, he would have been half shot in the ass by now. But in this moment, that old itch was gone. Replaced with a knowing feeling that justice was going to be swift.

As they began their descent, Logan proudly predicted their approach to McGuire Air Force Base. But as they were just above the runway, the plane accelerated and climbed. A series of sharp maneuvers had Vince and his dad gripping their armrests.

Diplomatic security measures often include a ruse on where the plane is landing. In this case, last-minute orders diverted the plane to Lakehurst Naval Air Station about ten miles away.

Once they landed, a U.S. marshal boarded the plane to escort them into witness protection. Michael's legal expertise emerged as he argued against detention without a warrant.

"Do you want me to start citing case law?" Michael asked. "U.S. versus Bacon? Feingold? The second circuit appeals in Awadallah?"

"Sir, I'm not here to debate—"

"This isn't a debate. Are you really willing to risk a civil rights lawsuit? Let's focus on getting my son home."

The deputy retreated to make calls. Vince looked on in awe at the way his dad handled the marshal. Logan used the moment to remove Vince's IV.

"Dad, where'd you pull all that BS from? Those case laws... that was great thinking!" Vince said as he watched the deputy move out of sight.

"It wasn't BS, Vince. I've been looking at them for the past couple of weeks. I have an upcoming case... an important case that I'm prepping," Michael said matter-of-factly. "We got information where we might have to use federal case law that allows a material witness to be detained if they refuse to honor a subpoena. I all but have the case laws memorized."

Vince couldn't help but wonder if that case was the case Evelina told him about. The case Vince looked into weeks ago. The case that involved fake jewelry and counterfeit gems. The case that has put his dad's life in jeopardy.

"Here," Logan said, pressing his Rubik's Cube into Vince's hand. "Maybe you'll have better luck than me."

Vince turned it over, finding the Air Force Pararescue insignia engraved on the completed blue side. "Thanks, Logan. I'll let you know when I get the other five sides done."

"You pussy," Logan laughed, patting his back gently. "Get off our plane. And Vince... good luck."

Walking to the waiting SUV, Vince clutched the cube. He thought about everything he'd learned—his mother's murder, his father's decades of silence, the price of refusing to cooperate with the Russian mafia. His black-and-white world was in shattered pieces, scattered before him into shards of gray—so sharp that everyone he knew was at risk of being cut by their edges.

But one truth remained clear—he had to stop Augustas before the Russian mafia's deadline expired.

His father's life depended on it. The cube's blue side caught the sun, reminding him of Logan's patch: THAT OTHERS MAY LIVE.

CHAPTER 50
SAFE HARBOR

Saturday 2:05 p.m.—Lakehurst Naval Air Station, New Jersey

Like Audrey earlier that morning, Vince and Michael found themselves in the back of a government SUV with armed men in suits up front. For Audrey, those men were FBI agents. For Vince and his dad, they were deputy U.S. marshals.

After a brief exchange with one of the marshals, Michael settled back in his seat. "We're going to Atlantic City," he told Vince. "Just temporarily, until they clear our homes."

"The church," the deputy up front confirmed, checking his phone. "We're heading to a Byzantine church in A.C."

Vince took in a deep breath, then closed his eyes in disbelief.

Michael started to speak, then stopped. Then, "Wait. We're going to a church? What church?"

"Hold on a minute," said the deputy in the passenger seat. "We got the address plugged into the GPS, but let me find the name in the text message."

Vince looked at his dad in silence as they both waited for the name of the church to be revealed.

"Rytis Eparchy of the Sea. Ry...tis. Ep-archy? Is that how you pronounce it?"

Michael's eyes grew wide. "Yes, deputy. That is the correct pronunciation."

"An Agent Gwynne suggested it. She said you had a good relationship with the monsignor there, Mr. Brown."

Vince stared at his father, who was rubbing his hands together nervously. "Agent Gwynne?" Vince whispered. "I thought you ended that?"

"I did," Michael mouthed silently.

The drive down the Garden State Parkway passed in tense silence. Vince formulized different plans on how he would handle seeing Augustas. Should he fake it? Or should he let his real feelings show and punch the motherfucker in his face?

Maybe something in between.

Familiar landmarks appeared—the train trestle, the convention center. Angst and worry replaced the calm and relief he had felt when they landed. Vince glanced at his father, who stared ahead in an almost trancelike state.

"Dad, are you okay?"

"Yes, Vince. I am okay," his dad answered, still looking straight ahead in a gaze. "Maybe for the first time in a while, I feel okay."

"Then listen to me," Vince said softly. "I know you don't know everything about what's going on with me, and I sure don't know what's happening with you. But I need you to trust me."

Michael's face didn't change.

"Dad, I need you to promise me that you will trust me and give me some time." Vince went for broke. "I know the clock is ticking, Dad."

Michael blinked down hard and turned to his son. "What do you mean, you know the clock is ticking, Vince?"

"Dad, please. Please trust me and give me some time. Promise me that you won't do anything until I let you know that I've tried everything I can. Dad, please promise me that you will trust me."

"Vince, it's so far over your head..."

"Give me this one chance to repay you for everything you've done for me and Audrey—you brought us to safety. Let me repay you for that."

"Vince, you don't understand... you have no idea wha—"

"Yes, I do, Dad. I do understand," Vince said.

He touched his dad's forearm in a way a loving child touches their parent's arm, but in a way that was foreign to him... until now. Vince spoke softly, yet confidently. "Dad, I know we don't say it that often, if ever at all, but you need to know that I love you..."

Tears filled Michael's eyes, and he made no effort to wipe the flow of them from his cheeks.

"I love you, Dad, and I know Audrey does, too," Vince said. "Well," he continued, "in a way that only she can." Vince shared a deep belly laugh with his dad. "And if you let me, I'll show you that you've done a hell of a job raising me. I can prove to you that I can not only serve and protect the people I've been sworn to take care of, but I can serve and protect my family as well."

"Vince, you should know that I..." Michael let his words fade into nothingness.

"Save it, Dad," Vince said, squeezing tighter on his dad's muscular arm. "Just promise me you'll let me do what I need to do. If I fail, we go down together."

"Vince, I think you're in way over your head... but so am I. I give you my word, son."

Vince let go of his dad's arm and sat back in his seat. "Dad, forget about everything we discussed on the plane. Just act as if the last week never happened. And I'll let you know what you need to know... when you need to know it."

"Oh, so now I'm you and you're Logan, the Air Force's number one PJ medic," Michael said with a smile.

Vince again thought of the patch on Logan's shoulder: THAT OTHERS MAY LIVE. "Yeah, Dad. Something like that."

The SUV pulled into the rear parking lot of the church. FBI agents opened the rear doors and escorted Vince and his dad into the church's fellowship hall.

Vince spotted Augustas immediately. He approached from behind, taking control of the interaction. "Monsignor, thank you for offering this sanctuary," he overemoted. "How can we ever thank you?"

Augustas's face was filled with confusion before his practiced smile appeared. "Vincentas is home!" He embraced Vince gently, whispering, "Bravo. At most, you've captured a pawn. I hope you are prepared for the sacrifices ahead in this very real game."

Augustas's parting "accidental" elbow to Vince's injured arm sent its own message.

Vince fought the urge to punch the motherfucker in his face, glad he had pre-planned this scenario on the way here even if it didn't turn out the way he had hoped. The advantage Vince thought he had was gone. At best, it was now a level playing field between detective and cleric.

Vince turned to look for his dad but was interrupted by Agent Gwynne. "Let's talk privately in the food pantry office."

Their interview had just begun when...

"Where is he? Where the fuck is he?"

Audrey burst in, crushing Vince in a hug that sent pain shooting through his ribs. "Vince, what the hell happened to you?" she demanded, oblivious to his discomfort. "They said you were kidnapped by the Russian mafia."

"They?"

"The FBI," came her reply. "They snuck into my room this morning and took me to their headquarters. They tried to question me for hours. The dumbasses. They're all assholes, Vince. They tried, but I didn't say a word. They—"

"Audrey," Vince said forcefully, trying desperately to get her to stop talking.

"Vince, let me finish—they even threatened me. They told me I better be honest with them. But don't worry, Vince, I didn't say anything."

Vince nodded in the direction of Agent Gwynne. "Audrey," he said, taking in a deep breath, "this is Agent Gwynne from the FBI."

"Oh... well, you could have told me that sooner."

Shaking her head, Agent Gwynne left the room laughing.

Vince winced in pain as Audrey grabbed him by the shoulders, once again ignoring his injuries. "Echo's fine. But you have no idea all I've done for you, little brother."

"What do you mean?"

"I know you said it was too dangerous for me to get involved. So I had a pro help me," Audrey said with a laugh.

"What the—"

"Carmen and I got all the information on the license plates, and she has a list of names of the people who visited the monsignor."

Vince threw his good arm up in the air. "What do you mean, you and Carmen?"

CHAPTER 51
AFTER HOURS

Saturday 4:30 p.m.—Atlantic City

The hot water pelted Vince's weary body, washing away the stale air of his travels. He exhaled sighs of relief and inhaled feelings of bliss. His smile from Echo's warm welcome home stayed with him in the shower.

The drive from the church had been so thankfully quiet, Agent Gwynne respecting his need for solitude. Now, finally, he could just be.

His old towel brought a flood of memories. He paused before grabbing it, the water that covered him pulling heat from his naked body. Vince felt a shiver run through him—from the chill and from the memories this towel held. Vince remembered the first time he used this towel.

Purchased the night before entering treatment years ago, it had become a symbol of his recovery journey. He bought it to wash away the shame the night before he entered treatment. The fabric, now soft from years of use, reminded him of his resilience—especially this past week away from his support system.

He thought about the stresses he faced and how he had done so with the strength often discussed in meetings.

The bathroom mirror revealed the full extent of his injuries—the bruising, the swelling. As he examined the bandage on his neck, now soaked despite Logan's warning to keep it dry, a sound from inside the house caught his attention. Echo barked.

Echo kept barking—excitedly, joyfully.

"Hold on, girl, I'll be right there." Wrapping the towel around his waist. "What have you gotten into now?"

Opening the bathroom door, he froze.

The last person in the world he'd expect to be there. Carmen stood in his hallway. "You want to know what I've gotten myself into now?"

As their eyes met, Vince felt the consequences of every decision that had led him here—to this unexpected crossroads. The towel, a shield of vulnerability and a symbol of past struggles, suddenly felt inadequate in Carmen's sight.

Vince caught her looking at his body instead of his eyes. He waited for her eyes to travel up to his face. "I've gotten into your house because you didn't lock the fucking door, Vince!" she shouted at him. "How could you be so careless... so stupid, after what you've just been through?" she demanded.

"LT, I must have forgot," Vince said, trying his best to hide the smirk on his face... and the growing bulge behind the towel.

"Forgot?" Carmen said, starting to tear into him like an overprotective friend would. Or the way a caring, compassionate boss might show tough love to one of their favorite charges.

"Boss, *look*," Vince said, unaware of the subtle suggestion. "I forgot. Hell, I even forgot to take the bandage off my neck before I got into the shower. So—"

"Vince," Carmen cut in, "I'm not here as your boss." She crossed her arms in front of her. "I'm here as a friend... and I want to help. Audrey filled me in on everything."

"Audrey filled you in?" He walked around her, looking out his window, still wearing only the damp towel around his waist. "I can't fucking believe it. I told her not to tell anyone. Why am I not surprised?"

"Vince... Why didn't you tell me?"

Vince turned to face her. He looked down at the towel in front of him.

Maybe it was the surprise of seeing her in his house. Maybe it was the excitement and danger of learning he had left his front door unlocked. Perhaps it was her angry yet caring tone. Whatever was causing it, suddenly it was obvious there was a part of Vince that was happy to see her.

And a part of him that was proud of his accomplishment. So, he didn't try to hide it. "Tell you?" Vince said. "If I told you, you would have had to make a choice. And that wouldn't be fair to you."

"How many times have we been in the thick of it?" Her expression softened. "We've worked too closely not to have each other's backs."

Vince sighed, running his good hand through his damp hair. "I know. I just... I didn't want to put you in that position. This whole situation is a mess."

"Speaking of messes," Carmen said, looking around the hallway. "You look like you could use some rest. And maybe," she added with a smile, "some clothes."

After changing into sweats, Vince found Carmen perched on the edge of his small couch, holding a folder.

"Your sister did some good detective work."

"I knew I couldn't trust her."

Carmen leaned forward, her elbows on her knees, her chin in her hands. "You can, Vince. And maybe you should consider thanking her instead of being pissed at her."

"Why's that?" he asked.

"Because now I'm here. Not as your lieutenant, but as someone who cares about you... I want to help, Vince."

Vince felt a warmth in his chest. *What did she mean by that?* "I appreciate it, LT... Carmen... More than you know."

"Well," she said, reaching into her bag. "I hope you'll appreciate this too."

"Appreciate what?" Vince asked

She pulled out a folder. "Audrey got into the church's surveillance computer system. She made a list of the license plates of the cars that pulled in where men got out to see the monsignor."

Vince's eyes widened. "She didn't..."

Carmen smiled, "Yes, she did. And she gave me the list. Vince, your sister risked everything for you. Like I said, I think you should be thanking her."

"Is that the list?" he asked, pointing to the folder.

"Well," Carmen said teasingly, "it *is* a list."

"Carmen, c'mon, is it the list of tags?" Vince begged.

"It is... and more," Carmen said, a mix of mischief and determination in her eyes.

Standing in front of her, he was now more aware of himself than just a few minutes ago when his naked body was concealed by just a towel. "Let me see it."

Carmen playfully pulled the folder up over her shoulder. "Oh, now you want to see the fruits of your sister's labor. A minute ago, you were ready to tear her head off."

"I said you were right... full credit to you," Vince said, smiling. "Now, what's in the folder?"

Carmen stood up, took a couple of steps, then turned to him. "Vince, what if I told you that this isn't just a list of license plates?" she asked, opening the folder in front of her. "What if I told you that it's a compilation of registered owners, their names, addresses, and criminal histories on all of them?"

Vince's eyes widened, "You didn't!"

Carmen smiled. "I did. I ran them through the DMV database."

Vince stared at her, a cocktail of emotions swirling inside him—gratitude, admiration, and something else he wasn't quite ready to name. "Carmen, I... this is..." he stammered.

She stepped forward so she was standing in front of him. "This is us having each other's backs, Vince. This is us doing the right thing, even when it's not easy."

His heart pounded inside his chest. He ignored the pain from ribs that were broken less than two days earlier. Inches from one another, their eyes locked.

PART 3

CHAPTER 52
DAWN'S CLARITY

Vince stirred, his eyes adjusting to the soft morning light filtering through the bedroom window. As he turned to Carmen, he was struck by a detail he'd never noticed before.

"Your eyes," he murmured, his voice still rough with sleep. "They're gray."

Carmen smiled, a playful glint in those newly discovered eyes. "Well, what do you know? Vince Brown has actually embraced the gray."

Vince paused, his expression softening. "I haven't just embraced it. I see the beauty in it..." He trailed off, his gaze intensifying. "I see the true beauty in it now."

As they lay there, the familiar strains of "Chalk Dust Torture" filled the room. Carmen propped herself up on one elbow, her brow furrowed. "Isn't this the same song that was playing when I arrived last night?"

Vince nodded, a small smile playing on his lips. "Yeah, it's 'Chalk Dust Torture' by Phish. Best song they play live."

Carmen raised an eyebrow. "You're full of surprises, Detective Brown. I never pegged you for a Phish fan."

Vince's smile merged with a soft chuckle. "There's a lot about me that might surprise you, Carmen. A lot I'm still figuring out myself."

Vince got out of bed, ignoring his nakedness—and perhaps proud of his toned, muscular physique. He walked to the window and turned the tilt wand to open the blinds fully. His thumb and forefinger separated the two slats at his eye level to make them wider.

"What's going on in that head of yours, Brown?" Carmen asked.

Still looking out the window, Vince said, "Just thinking... about everything. This case, my sister, my dad... us."

Carmen's reply was soft but firm. "Vince, you don't have to carry all this on your own. Whether you like it or not, I'm in this now. We both have a lot to lose if the shit hits the fan with this thing we've gotten ourselves into."

Vince turned to face her, his naked body with all its bruises and flaws, exposing both the physical and emotional vulnerability most men try to hide. But he felt safe with her.

Being vulnerable... what Vince once thought was a weakness, he was now beginning to see as a strength. And he made no effort to hide it in front of Carmen. She made him feel that safe.

"Carmen, have I screwed things up for you? I mean, what we just did, has this put your career in jeopardy?"

"What do you mean, 'put my career in jeopardy?'"

"You know," Vince replied. "What we did .... us... last night. It's against department policy. And I'm afraid I—"

Carmen started to laugh. "Vince, do you mean the policy that says a subordinate can't screw his boss, or the policy that says a boss can't screw her subordinate?"

Vince drew his hands to his face and buried his eyes. "Cute, Lieutenant. Very cute. But you know what I mean. It's bad enough my career is probably in the shitter." He gently rubbed his sore shoulder. "I'd feel horrible if I caused yours to be, too."

Carmen found one of Vince's sweatshirts lying on his dresser to wear as she walked toward Vince, adjusting the warm top around her waist. "Vince, if my career is in jeopardy, it's not because we made love last night."

"What do you mean?" Vince asked.

"Do you want to know what I was doing this time yesterday afternoon?"

"Yeah, if it's important, I guess I do," Vince said.

"Well, it's *hard* talking to you this way," Carmen joked, motioning to Vince's unclothed body.

"Why don't we get dressed, and I'll tell you over a cup of coffee that you're going to make me."

Vince looked down and scanned the area of his body Carmen was referring to. "Just like last night, you're pretty sure of yourself, Navarro."

"It's my job, Detective. Now, get dressed while I use your bathroom, and I'll see you in the kitchen."

Carmen walked into the kitchen wearing Vince's sweatshirt... and a pair of his boxers. "I found these in your dresser. They're comfy," she said, taking a seat at the table.

"I'm glad you like them. I'm not sure if I'm supposed to say they look better on you than me," Vince said with a grin.

"Well, I don't care how they look. I wasn't about to sit on your chair with my bare ass," Carmen said.

Over cups of coffee, Carmen laid out what happened with LT Bowel Movement and the chief in his conference room yesterday. Vince remained quiet for most of it, not interrupting her—he wanted to hear everything before responding. Or, in this case, reacting... to what he heard.

Vince recalled the times his dad spoke highly of the chief, calling him a friend. Was his dad's judgment of Chief Huertas wrong, or had his dad been lying to Vince about the chief's character all this time?

After he was sure Carmen had stopped talking, and after a long pause of quiet, Vince spoke up. "Carmen, I had no idea the chief was a prick. I knew he was demanding, but I always thought it was him demanding the best out of his department."

Carmen set her cup down on the table. "Oh, he wants the best out of the department. *And* he's also a prick!"

"I guess we both had an interesting past couple of days," Vince said.

"Interesting? If this past week was interesting, I'd hate to see stressed out and treacherous," Carmen joked.

Vince stood up from the table. "I have to put Echo out. Why don't you listen to some music while we're out back?"

"Umm, okay, where's your CD player?" Carmen asked.

"CD player, "Vince said through a broad grin. "Are you serious? You do know this is the twenty-first century, right? We'd have to go sit in my Jeep to listen to a CD."

"Funny," Carmen shot back.

"Just ask Alexa to play my playlist," Vince said, walking briskly toward the back door where Echo was waiting.

"What do I do, just yell it out into the air?" Carmen said.

"Never mind, I'll do it... Alexa, play my favorite playlist," Vince said loudly toward the middle of the room. "I'll be right back."

A few seconds later, the music played through a speaker sitting on the counter.

When Vince and Echo returned, Carmen was looking through the dining room hutch. "Do you have a search warrant, Lieutenant?"

"Nope. Don't need one. I have verbal consent," Carmen said seductively. "At least I did last night."

Vince stood in the doorway, shaking his head.

"Nah, I'm just trying to get an idea of what makes Vince Brown tick," Carmen continued. "And I can promise you, any evidence I uncover *will* be used against you."

Vince ignored the ruse and began shaking his head to the beat of the music that played through the speaker.

"'Chalk Dust Torture' again?" Carmen asked. "What is it about this song?"

"I don't know," Vince said, questioning himself as much as he was answering Carmen. "I guess it's because it's about struggling with life's challenges, feeling trapped but finding a way to push through. It's always resonated with me—ever since the first time I heard it."

"Sounds fitting..." Carmen said, adding a dramatic pause. "Life's been throwing a lot of chalk dust at you lately."

Vince walked to Carmen and held her in his arms. "Alexa, stop," he yelled at the speaker. Then, looking into Carmen's eyes as if searching for comfort *and* confirmation, "Maybe it's time I stop seeing it as some kind of torture and start seeing it as a challenge to overcome."

"Vince, you see my eyes? You see the color of them? Seeing the world in shades of gray doesn't mean losing your sense of right and wrong. It means things are more complex than they seem."

Vince squeezed her tightly. "I know. It's just... it's hard to change. But this past week... everything happening... I think I've found not just a reason, but a just cause that's forcing me to see things differently."

Carmen nodded.

Vince continued. "Like the beauty I'm looking at right now. I think I'm seeing things again for the first time. If that makes sense."

A tear rolled down Carmen's cheek. "You're stronger than you think, Vince. And you've got people who believe in you."

"And who are counting on me, right?" Vince added. "People who are counting on me. My dad... God, I don't know what I'd do if something happened to him. And now that Audrey's done exactly what I asked her *not* to do, I have to make sure she's safe. Even Frank... he knows what the monsignor has been doing... or at least he suspects it. What would they do to him if he came forward with what he knows?"

The buzz of Vince's phone interrupted the moment. He picked it up and read the message, his expression hardening.

"What is it?" Carmen asked in a concerned tone.

Vince held up the phone so Carmen could read the screen. "It's from a private number. It says, 'Back off. We're watching.' What the fuck, Carmen... who's watching me?"

"Vince, does it matter who's watching you? They want you to back down. We'll be careful... but we won't back down."

"I'm not going to back down—" Vince said with determination, before abruptly stopping his sentence.

"Talk to me, Vince."

"It's just… I've always believed in the law—the societal need for law and order. Right and wrong… black or white. But now, with everything that's happened, I'm questioning everything—even my own father. How could he think so highly of the chief if he's such a fucking prick?"

"Vince, we'll figure this out together. I'm in it with you. You're not alone," Carmen said, placing a comforting hand on Vince's muscular bicep. "Questioning is good, Vince. You know that."

Vince looked down at her hand on his arm. "I know that *now*," he said. "I can't… I don't understand it myself. But I feel like the Vince Brown I've always been is… dying. And I'm not sure who I'll be when this is all over."

Vince's gaze went from Carmen's hand to the hutch Carmen had been searching just minutes earlier. He spotted the mixed-up colors of one of his Rubik's Cubes that he left there weeks ago. For years, he had not been able to solve the cube, getting just one side finished but never progressing any further.

There has to be a way to solve it, he heard himself whisper inside his head.

Vince walked to the hutch and picked up the cube. "Could it be that it's not about getting one side perfect, but about first seeing how all the sides interact?" Vince asked.

Carmen moved to him and guided the cube back down to the hutch. "I think you're onto something, Detective Brown."

Vince looked back into her eyes. "Carmen, I don't know if I can figure out how to navigate this gray area. I might not ever be able to navigate it. But I will solve it. I promise you that."

"That makes us a great team, Vince," Carmen said.

"What do you mean?"

"You work on solving it. I'll help you navigate your way there."

CHAPTER 53

SAFE SPACE

Vince parked his Jeep outside the Atlantic City Community Center, the winter wind biting at his face as he stepped out. The community center was a few blocks from the diner on Tennessee Avenue, and this would be the perfect location to park his car so it wasn't seen at the diner, and he would be able to see the exhibit the students had worked on for months.

The sound of laughter and music drifted from the open doors, a stark contrast to the grim thoughts that had been occupying his mind all day. As he approached the entrance, a commotion caught his attention. A group of adults was huddled around a teenager with brightly colored hair, their voices carrying on the wind.

"Here comes the '*It!*'" one man sneered. "I bet the *shim* would like to join the talent show," came a comment from a woman next to him.

Vince's jaw clenched. He'd started this program to give kids a safe space, and he'd be damned if he'd let anyone ruin that. Without hesitation, he changed course, heading straight for the group.

"Is there a problem here?" he asked, his voice calm but authoritative.

The adults in the group had a collective look of surprise. The teen-agers with them looked ashamed and turned their faces away from the beloved detective, who was a regular at their school.

"Umm…" one adult stammered.

Another spoke up, looking at the teenager who was outwardly composed but with eyes betraying hurt, "No problem here. Right?"

The teenager didn't lift their head from the cold sidewalk below.

Vince knew each student in the group by name. And they knew that he knew them. Although he was a regular fixture at the school, Vince wasn't employed by the school. This gave him more latitude than a teacher, an administrator, or a counselor could in the way he spoke to students to get through to them.

"We'll talk later this week," he said to them in a voice they each recognized as a sign this detective wasn't messing around. "Why don't you go inside and see if you can find something that's your favorite? I'll be looking forward to hearing what all of you have to say about what you like in the exhibit."

The students shifted their eyes back and forth to each other.

"Go ahead," Vince told them, "Get inside… now."

Now it was just Vince, the teenager who now had a flicker of relief in their eyes, and the adults who had been hurling insults. Vince stood next to the teenager and, with a caring tone yet strong voice, said, "Quinn, it's great to see you. How have you been since we last talked?"

The teen's shoulders relaxed. "Hi, Detective Brown. I've been good."

Vince changed his focus to the adults, sure that they heard the teen refer to him as detective. Without moving his look at the adults, he continued to talk to the teen. "Quinn, I know how much you've been looking forward to this. I bet your painting is the best inside those doors," he said, pointing to the entrance.

Quinn's face became flushed with pride.

"Someone who creates something from their heart," Vince said, tapping gently at his chest, "and then has the courage to be vulnerable by displaying it in an exhibit shows just how strong you are. I'm proud of ya, kid!"

Quinn smiled wide and then looked at the adults, who were no longer making eye contact with them.

"Thanks, Detective Brown... for everything. But especially for believing in me."

"I do believe in you, Quinn," Vince said with a warm smile. "You know, Quinn, you are going to meet people who aren't as strong as you, who don't have the courage you have. They'll act tough when they feel superior to you. But as soon as the playing field is evened, they'll tuck their tails between their legs and stand there like a puppy who's just been caught doing something it knows it shouldn't have done."

Quinn smiled. And shared that smile with every adult who had been tormenting them before Vince arrived.

"Quinn, remember what I told you about character and integrity. Character is doing what's right even when you know nobody is watching. Sometimes, you run across people who have no character... or integrity. These are the kind of people who take a dog for a walk. When the dog takes a shit, they first look around to see if anyone is looking. If they know someone is looking, they'll pick it up—they'll only pick up that pile of shit if they know they're being watched. But if no one is watching, they'll leave it there and walk away," Vince said, looking at the adults.

Quinn nodded.

"They know they've done wrong. But they don't care because they have no character. They have no integrity. Do you understand?"

Quinn's smile grew even bigger. "I sure do."

Vince smiled back. "Why don't you head inside? I can't wait to see your painting."

Quinn walked into the center. Vince stood, looking at the adults who said nothing.

Vince kept his posture strong—as strong as it could be with broken ribs that were healing and sutures in his neck. Maybe it was the appearance of someone who was wounded coming to the aid of someone who was vulnerable. Maybe it was something different. Whatever it was, Vince didn't have to say another word for each of the adults to walk away in shame.

As Vince entered the community center, a teenage girl with a guitar case slung over her shoulder beamed at him. "Detective Brown! You made it!"

"Wouldn't miss it for the world, Sarah," Vince replied, returning her smile. "How's that new song coming along?"

Sarah's eyes lit up. "Great! I can't wait for you to hear it. It's so much better than what I played at last year's exhibition."

Vince felt a warmth in his chest, a reminder of why he'd fought so hard to keep this program running. "I'm sure it'll be amazing. Break a leg up there."

Sarah motioned to a few adult couples who were across the foyer talking with each other. A man and woman walked to Sarah and Vince. "Mom and Dad, this is him. This is Detective Brown from school."

"We've heard a lot about you, Detective," said the woman.

"The man reached out his hand to shake Vince's. "Thank you for being there for the kids. With everything you hear on the news, it's nice to know someone is there for our kids. We appreciate you, sir."

There wasn't a flash of light. There wasn't a light bulb illuminating in his head. It was more subtle, yet felt so direct. His words came easy and honestly. "It's the best gig in the department," Vince said, returning the handshake. "And it's students like Sarah who make it worthwhile."

"We're proud of her," the dad replied. "We hope to see you inside." Turning to his wife, he said, "We better get in and find our seats, hon. It's nice to meet you, Detective. And again, thank you."

Vince walked further into the center, greeting students and parents alike. He then saw a familiar face. Antoine Washington—the student who joked about a bomb being in the school. He was holding up a wooden serving tray, showing it to other students.

"Well, what have we got here, Mr. Washington?" Vince asked in a kidding manner.

"Detective B! Check out what I made in woodshop!" Antoine replied. "You was right. I needed to get interested in sump'n, and woodshop was it. What ya think?" Antoine asked, handing the tray to Vince.

Vince bobbed it up and down, checking its weight in his hands. "Sturdy. Well constructed. And look at this," he said, pointing to the edge of the tray, "You included some intricate notches to give it character. This is really nice, Antoine. I'm proud of you, young man."

"Thanks. I can't wait to bring it home for my momma to see. She said she gonna use it for Easter when everyone come over for supper."

"Make sure I get an invitation to that dinner, Antoine. I want to see this put to good use," Vince said, handing the tray back to Antoine.

As Vince walked away from the students who were with Antoine, he overheard Antoine say to them, "See, I told ya he was cool."

Vince laughed out loud and turned around at the group. "Keep doing the right thing... all of you."

Vince looked at his watch, his smile fading slightly. He'd promised himself he would only stay for an hour before heading to the diner for surveillance. The warmth he felt from interacting with the kids was slowly replaced by uneasy anxiety about the case.

He pulled out his phone, hoping to see a message from Carmen. Nothing. His stomach tightened. Was she having second thoughts? Or worse, had something happened to her?

Vince shook his head, trying to dispel the worry. He needed to focus. If he was right about the monsignor and the TAC, these kids needed him and so did his father, and many more people he didn't even know.

As he put his phone back in his pocket, Sarah approached again. Her eyes filled with excitement. "Detective Brown, I'm up next! You are staying to watch, aren't you?"

Vince felt his chest constrict. He wanted nothing more than to support Sarah, to see the fruits of her hard work. But every minute he spent here was a minute lost in the much-needed surveillance of the Lithuanian American club.

"I..." Vince started, his voice catching. He cleared his throat and forced a smile. "Of course, Sarah. I wouldn't miss it."

As Sarah beamed and rushed off to prepare, Vince's smile fell. He clenched his fists, torn by the weight of his conflicting responsibilities bearing down on him. How could he balance being there for these kids with the urgent need to gather evidence at the club? And where the hell was Carmen?

He made his way to the auditorium, his mind racing. He'd watch Sarah's performance, then make his excuses and leave. It wasn't ideal, but it was the best compromise he could manage. As he took his seat, he couldn't shake the feeling that time was running out—for the case, for his father, and maybe even for whatever had kindled between him and Carmen.

Vince concentrated his best on Sarah's performance. He wanted to be completely present for her. Sitting in front of her parents, he wanted them to see that he was fully present for her. *Be where your feet are* was something he heard in resiliency training and what he taught to recruits at the academy. It was time to practice what he preached.

Sarah's performance was nothing short of amazing. At least in the eyes of her favorite detective.

Vince felt the emotions that she created with the strings of her guitar. For a teenager, her song was more traditional than what Vince imagined she would write or sing. Sarah's song was so beautiful that it earned her a standing ovation.

The ovation was the ideal time for Vince to leave. As the ovation was coming to a close, Vince pulled out his phone and looked at it as if he had just received a text. Turning to make sure her parents saw what he did, he asked them to tell Sarah she was great and to apologize to her that he had to leave for an emergency. Sarah's mom told Vince they understood and asked him to be careful.

Vince pushed his hands into his jacket pockets as he stepped out the doors and walked into the parking lot. The two-block walk to the diner would take less than five minutes. Vince checked his phone five times during the walk to see if he had missed a text from Carmen. The distant sound of multiple police car sirens broke the silence of his walk. Vince couldn't help but wonder, even fantasize, where they were going and what kind of call they were responding to. What would they find when they got there?

While civilians are warned not to walk down dark, unlit streets, Vince ignored the broken streetlights on his way to the diner. Even though this wasn't his beat when he was in the patrol division, he had no concern for his safety. While it wasn't the nicest part of the city, it also wasn't the worst part.

The water vapor of every exhaled breath was visible whenever he walked past the few working streetlights. One of the row houses he passed still had its Christmas lights lit. The diner's neon sign equaled the same warm invitation that those Christmas lights offered, but with a guarantee of hot coffee inside. Vince saw the sign when he turned the corner onto Tennessee Avenue. The Lithuanian American club was across the street from the diner.

The Lithuanian American club is where the department's intel files said the men who visited the monsignor hung out. The detective bureau's investigative reports identified these men as members of the Tennessee Avenue Crew—the TAC is the moniker its members proudly gave themselves. Carmen shared this information and more with Vince two nights ago. Now it was up to Vince to corroborate all of it. This would be needed to make a conspiracy case against all of them... including the monsignor.

As Vince approached the club, he saw groups of men milling around outside smoking cigars. He could also see cars parked up and down the street. He planned to sit in the diner, grab a window booth, and enjoy a couple of cups of coffee while documenting the men who came and went and what cars they drove.

The layout of the streets in this part of the city meant Tennessee Avenue acted as a wind tunnel this time of year. Vince was looking forward to the warmth of the diner as much as a cup of that coffee. His ears would definitely thank him for thawing out from the walk.

Vince's trained eyes took stock of the street, taking note of the cars so he could check them off a list he had in his pocket. Then he saw it. The monsignor's Cadillac Escalade. It was parked right in front of the club entrance. *Ha, gotcha*, Vince murmured under his breath. Vince recognized this vehicle immediately. He'd seen it in the church parking lot countless times. He'd seen the monsignor get into and out of it often.

Seeing his big white Caddy parked at the club, Vince knew he got him dead to rights. He'd nail the son of a bitch... but good.

Vince asked for a window booth at the rear of the dining room. Although he wasn't technically a cop at this moment, the cop inside him still needed to sit at the back of the room facing the door. The hostess escorted him to the middle of the dining room.

"Unfortunately, this is the only window booth not taken, and the table is broken. You can sit over here in the booth across from it," the hostess said, pointing to a two-person booth opposite the window booth with the broken table.

Vince would rather be at the very rear of the room, but he was willing to sacrifice a tactical edge for the sake of seeing the club entrance across the street. Vince pointed to the booth he needed. "I'll be real careful. I'm only going to have a cup of coffee anyway. And I promise," he added with flirty eyes, "my tip will reflect my appreciation for this."

Vince began to slide into the booth when the hostess stopped him. "Sir, no one can sit here. Our insurance won't allow it. Please have a seat here," she said, pointing to the two-person booth. "Or do you want your coffee to go?"

Vince glanced around and noticed that it was nearly full, with all the window booths taken. He tried to look out the window where the hostess wanted to seat him. All he saw was the reflection of the ceiling lights in the panes of glass. "If I sit here, will I be able to get the next window booth when it becomes available?" he asked the hostess.

"Sure, hon," she answered sarcastically. "I'll seat you at a booth where four people would be ordering dinners so you can order a four-dollar cup of coffee and leave my girl a dollar tip."

"I was just trying to—"

"So, you want me to get that coffee to go, right?"

"Fine," Vince said with a loud exhale. "I'll take this booth."

A plastic-coated menu was dropped on the table in front of Vince as he was placing his phone and pocket notebook on the table.

Vince was settling into his booth, frustrated by the reflection of the lights on the window across from him, when his hand ran across the poorly mended tear in the vinyl seat. He hoped the sticky residue on his hand was from the glue used to repair it and not from a spilled food product... or worse.

He lifted his head to scan the diner. Suddenly, Vince froze. Although his back was to Vince, there was no mistaking his profile. The familiar silhouette—the large build, the broad shoulders that rose above the seatback, the balding head.

Vince's heart raced.

There, in the last window booth at the rear of the diner, sat the monsignor. Vince noticed his head turning to casually look out the window as he sipped a cup of coffee. Vince clenched his fists in his lap and bit down hard on his bottom lip. *What the fuck is he doing in here?* Vince asked no one but his inner self.

Suddenly, the monsignor's deep voice cut through the diner's ambient din. It was clear and calm, without even turning around. "Vincentas, in chess it is crucial to anticipate your opponent's next move. Why don't you join me for a cup of coffee, and we can discuss the game?" the monsignor said, tapping his iPad screen's online game. He gestured to the empty seat across from him. "No one should sit alone on this kind of cold, bitter evening."

Vince's mind was reeling. *How did he know I was here?* And, more importantly, *What kind of game was he referring to?*

He fought a feeling of rage when the monsignor called him Vincentas. The way the prick said it either demonstrated he didn't know its Lithuanian meaning or the prick knew it and was mocking him for what he was named.

Ever since his dad told him the meaning of his name when he was young, Vince has worried that he'd never be able to live up to his dad's expectations of it. Now, sitting within a few feet of someone truly evil, Vince felt that worry and doubt grow deeper.

Vince caught a glimpse of himself as he pushed himself up from the booth. Through the glaring reflection, Vince saw an unfocused image of the person he was. But it served as a clear message for Vince to consider—he was no longer who he was... but not yet who he was becoming.

If Vince was to ever stand a chance of living up to his name, it was now. Not at this time in his life, not this year, not this month or this week. Not even this day. It was now, right now, that he would start to become a *winner over evil*.

"Monsignor," Vince said, walking confidently to the monsignor's booth. "Monsignor Augustas Zukauskus, before my very eyes," he continued. Then, leaning into his face, "Or should I say, Monsignor Augustas *Paulauska*?"

Augustas recoiled hearing his true last name—the name Vince learned from Evelina when she told him everything she knew about Augustas. That included Augustas entering a seminary with an alias for a last name. For the last couple of decades, he lived in America, where everyone knew him as Augustas Zukauskus, the beloved pastor of Rytis Eparchy of the Sea Church in Atlantic City.

Vince wasn't about to let this interruption of Augustas's pattern of thought be wasted. Augustas was visibly shocked, and Vince needed to take advantage of it. "I don't know what kind of game you want to discuss," he said with eyes burrowing into Augustas's gaping stare. "But

I'm not playing a game. I'm exposing a fraud... and I'm going to win over evil, you fucking psycho."

Vince got the attention of the hostess who, along with everyone who was close enough to hear his dressing down of the monsignor, was looking at him. "I *will* have that coffee to go, ma'am," he said, making his way to the cash register.

Although he never turned around to confirm it, Vince imagined the look on the monsignor's face had to be one of shock. Taking his coffee to-go out the door, Vince pulled up the collar of his jacket and looked for a place to observe the action at the club.

In the short time he was in the diner, the howling wind seemed to have increased in intensity. Vince held the Styrofoam cup in front of his face. He breathed in the steam from the opening in the lid. It did nothing to warm him, but the aroma was a nice contrast to the cold, salty air that stung his nostrils. Grimacing against a fierce gust, Vince hunched his shoulders and scanned the street for a vantage point that would give him concealment.

A small vacant lot next to the diner was in the shadow of the glow from the diner and the streetlight in front of it. This would give Vince the concealment he needed. His arms were stiff against his sides, holding the coffee in front of him in both hands. He stopped wearing the sling for his fractured collarbone that morning, and his collarbone was telling him it was not happy he had made that choice.

Vince leaned against the outside of the diner, shivering against its cold brick exterior for the next three and a half hours. He made notes on his cell phone, carefully hiding the screen so the light of it didn't attract attention. Although Vince was able to ignore the urge to check his text messages, he wasn't able to ignore the pain in his shoulder and chest. Nor could he stop wondering how the monsignor knew so much about his moves.

Vince took particular note of the monsignor's parked SUV—it hadn't moved in the time he was standing there. More than once, Vince found himself turning quickly behind him to see if the prick was there.

To avoid running into him again, Vince walked away from the diner and away from the direction of where he parked his car. After he was sure he was far enough away where he wouldn't be seen by anyone at the club, or the monsignor, Vince pulled out his phone and checked his messages.

He pulled it out at the next corner. Then again two corners later. And again, and again until he was back in the community center parking lot, with the same result—nothing from Carmen.

CHAPTER 54
CONFESSIONAL TRUTHS

The confessional's old wooden door muffled the sounds of the empty church beyond, but it did little to dampen the tension between the two men inside. Father Frank shifted uncomfortably on the hard wooden bench. His cassock suddenly felt too tight around his neck. While he had seen many men summoned into the confessional by him in the past, this was the first time Frank was called here to meet with him.

On the other side of the grille, Monsignor Augustas Zukauskus—no, *Paulauska*—leaned closer, his large silhouette barely visible in the dim light. "Bless me, Father, for I... am about to sin," the monsignor's voice dripped with sarcasm. The irony of their positions—Frank as the confessor and the monsignor as the penitent—was not lost on either of them.

"Tell me, Francis, what is your definition of loyalty?"

Frank's hands trembled slightly as he clasped his prayer beads in his lap, keenly aware of the sacred space defiled in this unholy inquisition. "I'm not sure what you mean, Monsignor," Frank replied, trying his best to keep his voice steady.

A low chuckle came from the other side of the grille. "Well then, let me ask you this. Do you believe I have the best interests of the church in mind when I make difficult decisions?"

"Monsignor, I have no reason to doubt any of your decisions," Frank replied, as an Army private might answer a general. "I believe all who have been called into the priesthood have the best interests of the church in mind... at all times."

"You are not answering my question, Francis. Why won't you directly answer what I have asked you? Must I repeat myself?"

Clutching his beads even tighter, "No, sir, absolutely not," Frank said. "But I do have some questions of my own, if you will indulge me. I find this very uncomfortable. Why are we having a discussion here?"

"First, he won't answer my questions, and now he insults my intelligence," the monsignor said with disgust. "I looked in the mirror just before I entered this confessional, and I know I didn't see *Asshole* written across my forehead. Do you understand me, Francis?"

"Monsignor, I meant nothing by—"

"You meant everything by it," the monsignor cut him off, his voice now sharp. "Fine, we will do it this way. Father Franciscus Jakubovicius, under your Oath of Fidelity, what exactly have you been discussing with your... friend, Detective Brown?"

Like many others, Frank knew that whenever he called someone by their proper Lithuanian name, the monsignor meant business. The addition of the Oath of Fidelity in this threat was something new to Frank. He was torn between honoring his oath to the church or honoring his friend. "I'm not sure what you mean, Monsignor. Vince and I have talked about many things. He's been going through a difficult time lately."

"A difficult time?" came a strong reply. "Not too difficult to be digging in places where he doesn't belong!"

Frank felt a chill run down his spine. The monsignor's words pressed in on him from all sides of the cramped confessional. *How much does the monsignor know about Vince? How much does the monsignor think Vince knows about him? And how much does the monsignor think I'm responsible for what Vince knows?*

These questions bounced around inside Frank's head the way a steel ball ricochets inside a pinball machine in a boardwalk arcade.

"You are well aware, Francis," the monsignor continued, in a venomous conversational way, "there are passages in the Bible that speak of righteous violence. God Himself has condoned, even commanded, the taking of lives for His greater purpose."

Frank worried the sound he made when he swallowed would be heard by the monsignor. His throat now dry, "I'm aware of those passages, yes. But surely—"

"Surely nothing," the monsignor barked. "In His infinite wisdom, God has shown us that sometimes... sometimes sacrifices must be made. And here, in this sacred space, you and I can speak freely of such divine mandates, can't we?"

As hard as he tried, there was no saliva left in Frank's mouth to swallow.

The wooden high-backed chair on the other side of the grille creaked as it always does when the confessor shifts his weight. "It would be a shame if someone were to become a pawn in this divine game, wouldn't it? Someone who, perhaps, has been asking the wrong questions?"

The implication was clear, and he was now certain the monsignor could hear his heart pounding inside his chest. The most Frank could get out was, "The best interests of the church at all times... right?"

"Maybe it would be in *everyone's* best interests if you were to tell your friend this," the monsignor said, his voice as calm as it was stern. "In addition to saving souls, Father, it would be an opportunity for you to save a life."

The small door behind the grille slid shut with a soft thud. Frank—*Father Frank*—remained frozen in place, the monsignor's words playing over and over in his mind. Frank closed his eyes in the silence of this dimly lit stall, focusing on the hand squeezing the beads.

The monsignor's stern voice, the uncertainty, the feeling in his hands. It all brought him back in time...

Twelve-year-old Franciscus sat on the porch swing of his grandfather's house, the warm summer breeze carrying the aroma of his grandmother's kugelis from the kitchen.

It was so vivid, as if it happened just yesterday...

His grandfather, Senelis Antanas, sat beside him, his weathered hands holding an old, creased black-and-white photograph.

"Who are they, Senelis?" Franciscus asked, pointing at the group of grim-faced men in the picture.

Senelis Antanas exhaled deeply. "These were my friends back in Lithuania, before we came to America. Good men, they were. All of them." His voice lowered. "But not all of them stayed good."

Young Franciscus leaned in, intrigued by the old photo. "What happened?"

His grandfather sighed. "When bad things started happening in our town, most people stayed quiet. They were afraid." He tapped on the photo. "This man here, he spoke up. He lost everything. But he kept his honor."

"What about the others?" Franciscus asked.

"They stayed silent, anukas," Senelis Antanas said, his voice heavy with old regret. "And their silence... it made things worse."

Franciscus frowned, trying as best as any twelve-year-old to understand what their grandfather wanted to share. "But why didn't they say anything if they knew it was wrong?"

His grandfather turned to him. "Franciscus, remember this:'Tylėjimas—sutikimas. Silence is consent.' When we see wrong and say nothing, we become part of that wrong by agreeing with it."

"But isn't it safer to stay quiet sometimes?" Franciscus asked, thinking about the bullies at school.

His grandfather nodded slowly. "Sometimes it feels safer, yes. But safety isn't always right, Franciscus. Rarely is doing the right thing the easiest thing. There is a cost to silence. Sometimes it is higher than the cost of speaking up."

Franciscus looked up into the eyes of his grandfather. His grandfather rested his strong hand on the young boy's shoulder. "You come from a line of people who had to make hard choices. Remember, in America you have the freedom to speak. Use it wisely, boy. And use it when it matters."

The vibration from the pocket of his trousers brought him back to the present. One of the daily reminders Frank set in his phone was the terce canonical hour—a time of day set aside for prayer. If there was ever a morning he needed to pray, it was this morning. And yet, prayer was the furthest thing on his mind.

He thought of Vince—his friend, a good man trying to uncover the truth and bring about justice for those who didn't have a voice. And he thought of the monsignor, using the sanctity of the church as a cover for his evils.

Frank unclenched his fists. Looking down, he noticed the deep imprints his prayer beads had left in his palm. "Tylėjimas—sutikimas," he whispered, the Lithuanian words feeling both foreign and familiar as they left his mouth.

Instead of attempting to control his trembling hands, he used them to give him strength. First, the strength he needed to reach for the confessional door and push it open and then for the strength he would need to take each step from this day forward. Stepping out into the empty sanctuary, Frank felt a weight lift from his shoulders. For the first time in years, he stood tall, no longer lugging the burden of the complicit silence of an oath he was made to take.

He knew, stepping out into this sacred interior, what it would mean for everything he had worked for... and for everyone he loved. Nothing was off the table, and everything—and perhaps everyone—was in jeopardy.

As he walked down the aisle, each step echoing his concerns in the empty church, the realization that he was walking away from the safety of silence and into an uncertain future set in. But with each step, he felt more like the man his father had raised him to be... the man his grandfather had hoped he would become—a man of integrity, willing to pay the price for what was right.

Father Franciscus Jakubovicius pushed open the heavy church doors, stepping out into bright sunlight and bitter cold. He reached into his pocket and felt his phone. He had a call to make, a friend to stand by, and a truth to help unveil. The cost could prove to be high, but remaining silent was no longer a price he was willing to pay.

"No more," he said, walking down the stone steps to the street below. "I will not be silent. I choose the truth."

CHAPTER 55

PATTERNS

Vince carefully carried the cup of coffee out of the kitchen. He filled it higher than normal, and he didn't want to spill any of it on the papers strewn across the dining room table. The spreadsheet he created wasn't working for him, so he printed out lists of the license plates Audrey created and paired them with the DMV printouts Carmen gave him. Copies of those were compared to the criminal history list of each registered owner that Carmen had risked her job getting to him.

Vince stared. He rearranged them to see them differently. Still nothing. The more he studied them, the more he felt he was missing something—a connection, a pattern... a clue. He looked at the list of license plates he made two nights prior at the Lithuanian American Club and added them to the assortment of eight-and-a-half-by-eleven sheets of paper that covered the table.

What am I missing?

A familiar sound broke the silence of Vince's thoughts. *Dong... dong.* The grandfather clock in the hallway reminded Vince of the time and that he hadn't eaten anything since breakfast.

"Two o'clock? I don't believe it," Vince said, looking at Echo, who was lying on her warm dog bed across the hall in the living room.

Echo lifted her head, sensing Vince was speaking to her. She let out two quick barks, saying something in dog-talk that Vince still hadn't mastered.

"I hear you, girl. We'll play as soon as I'm done here. I promise."

Vince had no way of knowing if she understood his words, but he was sure she got the gist of what it meant to play—she loved to fetch sticks in the backyard and would play until Vince's arm was too tired to throw the stick.

The first sip of his fifth cup of coffee of the day was hot and strong. He chuckled to himself when it reminded him of the joke he and the guys in the department shared when they said they liked their coffee like they liked their women—hot and strong.

Vince set down the coffee to let it cool, grabbed the Rubik's Cube that was on the table, and took it to the opposite side of the table. He remembered the line his dad often shared with him and his sister: *Change the way you see things, and the things you see change.* From this angle, he focused on patterns instead of trying to read the words upside down.

He leaned across the table, surveying the mess he created. Echo barked twice again. "Girl, I promise. Just give me a minute!"

First, the clock sounds twice, and now she's barking twice, what is it with twos? Vince asked himself.

Then he saw it—the pattern he had missed by reading all the words instead of focusing on discovering a pattern. Quickly, he darted around the table to read the lists from that perspective again. He confirmed it. No doubt about it.

The next sip of his coffee never tasted so good. "Echo, Daddy did it. He figured it out. Aren't you proud of me, girl?"

Vince started for the hall closet to get his coat when his phone chimed. More annoyed than anything else, he looked at it to see who to be pissed at for breaking the ah-ha moment he wanted to enjoy throwing a stick with Echo, who had been such a good girl the past couple of weeks. He was looking forward to spending time with her as much as she wanted to be with him.

Vince stopped dead in his tracks. The name at the top of the screen read *LT Navarro*. Even though they spent a night together, Vince never got around to changing her contact to her first name. Up until this past weekend, the only time the two communicated was for professional reasons.

> Need to talk

> Urgent

> Someplace safe

Three cryptic lines of text from someone he had been waiting to hear from for days. He needed to hear that she missed him, that she enjoyed the night... what he got was a message telling him to meet her. Just like she was his boss.

Vince pushed his disappointment aside, and when he reread the text, he saw the urgency in her words. It was as if he could hear a fear in her voice. If she sent a text instead of calling, it meant it was something she needed to talk to him about in person. And with it being such an obscure message, that meant she was concerned about who might read the message if she were ordered to turn over the phone, or if it were ever subpoenaed.

This must be important.

Vince looked down at Echo who had been a good girl—patiently waiting for her master to finish what he was doing so they could go out back and play. As he had promised her.

Vince began typing on the phone's keypad while addressing his dog. "Echo, Daddy just has to reply to this message, then we'll go play."

> Understood.

> Will need a few minutes.

> Or can it wait?

Vince hit send, put on his coat, and headed out back with Echo. He picked up a large stick and told Echo to sit. Her focus on him was intense. "Go get it, girl," he yelled as he hurled it across the yard.

Vince watched Echo take off after the stick, wondering what could be so urgent that she sent him that kind of text. Carmen's reply to Vince's answer arrived sooner than Echo did with the stick in her mouth.

> It can't wait

> NOW

This shit, whatever it was, is serious. "Girl, Daddy's got to go to work. Go tinkle real quick so we can go inside and get a treat."

Echo did as asked and was rewarded with a piece of cheese from the fridge. But only after she sat and gave her paw. She looked like an angel in Vince's eyes. That gave him an idea for a safe place to meet.

While he was making her breakfast the morning after their night together, Vince told Carmen about his visit to the picturesque town on the edge of the Pine Barrens. He explained in detail the beauty of the quaint log cabin church that had its own little community library. But he couldn't recall if he told her the name of it.

> Remember the cute little church I
> told you about?

Vince waited for a reply, thinking about other clues he might have to give if she didn't remember it. He didn't have to wait long.

> YES

> I'll find it

> ETA?

With one less thing to concern himself with, Vince let out a sigh of relief. He stared at his phone for a moment, calculating the drive time in his head.

Vince hated to be late. Of all the pet peeves in the world, being late was Vince's pettiest of pet peeves. If he gave himself a cushion for any unforeseen road construction, he figured an hour at the most. But he'd rather be early than late... *much rather* be early than late. He typed *60 min* on the message thread.

Her reply was immediate:

> OK

> Bring your lists

Vince looked at the papers piled across the table. He was glad he added a cushion of time.

Vince placed his backpack filled with the lists he had compiled on the front seat and drove to the church. He looked at the digital display on the instrument cluster—he made it in fifty-four minutes. He was early. Or, in his mind, he was right on time.

The old floorboards creaked from Vince's weight as he pushed open the door of the Lakes Cathedral Church's community library building. The natural pine log interior gave a special warmth on this cold afternoon. Vince scanned the room for a quiet place where they could sit down and talk without their conversation being overheard by one of the few other people there.

How could she have gotten here before me? Vince wondered.

Carmen was sitting at a table along the log wall. She was hunched over a book, her dark hair partially covering her face. But her eyes had already seen him come in. She stood up from the table. "Hey, fancy seeing you here. How are you?" she asked quietly.

Vince instinctively stuck out his hand as if he had just run into one of his former teachers.

Carmen rolled her eyes. *Really?* She mouthed, pointing to the empty seat across from her. "Sit down so we can catch up," she added, loud enough for anyone nearby to hear, but not loud enough to draw attention to them.

"Umm, sure. Yeah, I can sit for a little while," Vince answered nervously.

Vince sat down and pointed to the book Carmen had in front of her. The paper cover jacket was worn and stained. Still, Vince could make out the title: *The Great Divorce,* by C. S. Lewis. "A book on divorce... here? Is it interesting?" he asked.

Carmen looked down at the book and laughed. "Vince, the title is deceiving. I just started to get into it when you got here. It's really not about a marriage splitting up. It's about—"

"Just starting to get into it? How long have you been here?" Vince asked at a level that he realized was too loud.

"About twenty minutes, I guess."

Vince looked down at his watch. "But—"

"Vince, the NSA is onto something we've dug up. I don't know what it is but if the NSA is looking at it, it's *big*," she said.

"What the... the NSA? Are you sure?" Vince asked.

"Oh, I'm sure, Vince. I'm as sure as *being-placed-on-administra-tive-leave-until-an-investigation-is-completed* sure. The chief called me into his office again this morning. The NSA contacted him directly from D.C. to ask him who used the department's computers to look up someone they're interested in."

"Any idea who they're interested in?"

"No, they wouldn't tell the chief. Something about national security and all that secret squirrel shit they love to throw around. But they demanded he tell them if a detective was looking at someone as a suspect, as a witness... they even demanded that he give them a list of everyone taken into custody since the beginning of the month," she explained.

"Shit..."

"Yeah, no kidding. Vince, the only thing I can think of is last week they finally identified the body they pulled from the bay the other week. This is *definitely* not public information," Carmen said, glancing around the room—just to make sure. "The victim is the son of a diplomat."

Vince took in a deep breath, hoping the increased oxygen would both help him think and calm his nerves. "Well, that makes sense. The murdered son of a diplomat would certainly draw the attention of the Feds."

"I ran the plates through the system, but every cop with a DMV computer can do that. So I don't think it was from running the plates through DMV. It had to be when I ran the CCHs on the owners the plates came back to!" Carmen exclaimed, this time her voice being the one that was too loud.

Vince reached down and grabbed his backpack from beneath the table. "Carmen, I think you might have run both the plate and the CCH on the murderer. And I think I know who it is."

"What... how did you figure it out?" Carmen asked.

"Here, let me show you." Vince fumbled through the papers until he found the list of license plates that were recorded by Audrey. "Do you see the dates and times of each one?" he asked, pointing to the column. "All these cars were regulars. They are there at least once a week, some of them twice a week," he said, running his finger down the page.

Carmen nodded.

Then zeroing in on one row. "But look at this plate. It only shows up at the church twice," Vince said, his voice pitched high with excitement. "And if you remember, the guy who confessed to the murder... the same guy who confessed a week later to being hired to kill my dad had a different sounding voice than the others. And he only showed up twice. Two times. It's the pattern I had missed all along... until just before you called."

Carmen studied the list and the pattern he showed her. "Vince, let me see the CCH printout."

The list of registered owners was now side-by-side with the criminal history printout on the table in front of them. "There it is, Vince," Carmen said, shifting the papers so Vince could read them. "Look, his last name is different from the rest."

Vince stared in shock. "I can't believe I missed it..." his voice trailing off.

"Aww, don't be so hard on yourself, Detective," Carmen said with a smile. "You were looking at all this with your steel blue eyes... what you needed was someone to see this through gray eyes."

This was now the second time in a week that Carmen used her eyes to flirt with Vince. The flirtatious way she spoke caught him off guard. "Uh, yeah. I guess... Wait a minute, did you just—"

"Vince, I promise not to take the glory if you get a medal for solving this," she joked.

"Christ, you don't miss a thing. Do you?"

"That's me. I'm the boss, Detective," she deadpanned. Carmen reached into her oversized pocketbook. "After I was told to gather my belongings from my desk, I made sure to grab these," she said, pulling out facsimile copies of photos of each person she ran through the criminal history computer database. "I thought these might come in useful."

"Wait, I saw that guy at the club last night!" Vince said, pointing to one of the photos.

"What club?" Carmen asked.

"The Lithuanian American Club on Tennessee Avenue. I ran a little surveillance there. He was outside for most of the night," Vince replied, sure of himself.

"That's where the TAC hangs out. It was freezing last night. He must have been there for a reason if he didn't go inside. Maybe waiting for someone?" Carmen posited.

Vince's' heart began to race. "Carmen, the monsignor was in the diner across the street. I saw him in there. I even called him a fucking psycho... to his face. I bet he was waiting for the monsignor."

Carmen flipped the photo over to reveal the name printed on the back. Then she slid the upside-down photo next to the list that showed the name of the person who only visited the monsignor twice—the man who confessed to one murder and the ordered hit of Michael Brown. The names matched: Tomas Etoile.

Tomas Etoile. A name that was as far from the other Lithuanian names who were members of the TAC as Lithuania is from France. Both Vince and Carmen had heard that the Russian mafia was subbing out work to insulate themselves from prosecution, but this was a first—contracting out a contract for murder.

"Vince, do you know what we've just done? What you've done?"

"To tell you the truth, I'm still processing all this," Vince replied.

Carmen reached across the table and gently, almost lovingly, grabbed his forearm. "Vince, you just solved the murder. No wonder the NSA is pissed. But you've done more than solve a murder. You connected the murderer to TAC, and we've got TAC connected to street tax collection. That's a slam dunk for a RICO case. On top of it all…" Carmen paused for effect. "We've got the monsignor connected to each piece of it. He's the kingpin, Vince!"

Vince's eyes widened. "Whoa!"

Just then the library door swung open, and a group of young and loud teenagers ran in. They were excited about whatever teenagers get excited about on their way home from school.

Carmen immediately made like she was tutoring Vince on how to take notes on a book about heaven and hell by a late writer and theologian. Vince, taking her cue, acted like he didn't understand a thing in the book Carmen abruptly picked up from the table.

The teens finally settled down into chairs and sofas at the end of the room. Carmen shifted her gaze to Vince. "We shouldn't stay here. We don't know who knows we're here, and the NSA isn't going to waste any time conducting their own investigation."

"I agree," Vince said with a repeated nod of his head. "There's supposed to be a rustic restaurant over there across the street," he said, gesturing out the window across from them. We can sit down and unwind. I won't even mind if you order yourself a drink. God knows you've earned it."

Carmen smiled, shaking her head. "Not tonight, Vince. I don't think that's a good idea."

"No, I didn't mean we were going to… Carmen, I have to ask you something."

Carmen tilted her head.

"Are we okay? I mean, is everything cool between us?"

"Of course, we are… cool. Why would you ask?"

"Well, I didn't hear from you until this afternoon. I wasn't sure if I did something or said something…"

Carmen leaned in across the table. "Vince, it was just a couple of days. And the first part of today had me getting my ass reamed by the brass. You know we need to take things slowly, right? I mean, we've both already put our careers on the line. What do you think Huertas would do if he found out?"

"Yeah, you're right. Besides, forget about Huertas; can you imagine what Bowel Movement would do with this as an internal?!"

Carmen laughed. She laughed so loud that people turned and looked at them. Once she regained her composure, she offered Vince a suggestion. "I'll tell you what. If both of us are still alive, and neither one of us is locked up, how about joining me for my birthday on Saturday?"

"Your birthday? Saturday's your birthday?"

"Yeppers. And every year, I do something special for myself. But I think this year... I think this year's birthday needs to be spent with someone. Do you know anyone available to join me Saturday morning?"

Vince's eyes lit up. "Just tell me the time and place!"

"I'll pick you up at ten. Dress casual."

"I can do that," Vince said, unable to hide his smile.

Carmen looked around the room, then looked at Vince and returned the smile that was still on his face. "Vince, we still have a huge hurdle in front of us. Maybe more like a brick wall."

"What's that?"

"We can't use any of what we have... none of it... unless we can find a way to *accidentally* discover something about this case. Everything about this is a result of Audrey recording the confessions." Carmen's smile faded. "You know as well as I do that it's all the fruit of the poisonous tree."

Vince remembered what his dad shared with him on the plane on the way home from Lithuania. He remembered how detailed Evelina was when she recounted the details of Maureen's death and his dad's agreement to work for the Russian mafia. He remembered the words spoken by the man, now identified as Tomas Etoile, who said he was hired to kill his dad.

"The fruit of the poisonous tree, yeah... sure." There was so much more on the line than finding ways to get crucial evidence introduced to a grand jury. "I'm going to work on that the rest of the week."

Carmen asked right away, "When you say you're going to work on it, you aren't saying that you're—"

"No way," Vince said, interrupting her before she could finish her sentence. "I've bent the rules, and I've definitely violated department SOPs, but I haven't broken the law. And I'm not going to break any laws now. I just have to find a way..."

"I know that, Vince. I guess I just needed to hear it," Carmen said, a smile returning to her face. "I think it's best if we leave here separately. Give me a couple of minutes to get on my way, and then you pack up and get back home."

"I'll see you on Saturday," Vince said. "And Carmen... thanks. You said *I* did this. You know that this wouldn't have happened without you. We did this. *We* solved it."

Placing the photos back in her pocketbook, Carmen stood up. "I still promise not to take the glory when you get a medal... or the blame if we both get fired," she told him before walking out the door.

CHAPTER 56

WHITE-LETTER DAY

Michael Brown's eyes grew wide with shock as a fine white powder billowed from the manila envelope marked "Personal and Confidential." Most of the powder dusted his hands and fell onto his desk, but some of it was also caught in his breath when he inhaled in surprise.

His fingers trembled reading the note as the implications hit him. In that moment, Atlantic County's District Attorney wasn't thinking about the hundreds of emails awaiting his attention after a week out of the office. All he could focus on was the powder, the cryptic note placed among a dozen or so blank pages, and the terrifying possibility that he'd just been poisoned.

His stinging eyes squinted reading the note that was covered in the powder.

Mr. Brown,

Your family's debts are not settled.

No, you can't unlearn all the facts that you've learned.
The powder speaks volumes.

Remember: what tortures you is just the beginning.

Fucking Psycho has spoken.

Breathe deep.

He didn't feel his hands drop the note, only realizing it after seeing the paper float onto the desk. He couldn't stop his body's reflex and barked out two short coughs, his throat and lungs now pissed off by what was in them. The same type of bodily reflex he couldn't control when he coughed also caused him to breathe in deeply. More of the fine powder entered his respiratory system. The cycle repeated. And it became stronger... even violent. Although he didn't detect any odor, his throat became dry, with a burning, itchy sensation that radiated into his chest.

Michael pushed himself away from his desk and, through fits of coughing, made his way to the private bathroom in his office that came with the title of County District Attorney. He turned the cold faucet on full and splashed the water over his hands, rubbing them carelessly in all directions. Right now, the powder wasn't his most pressing problem; it was panic.

The repeated coughing had him feeling lightheaded. Michael used the underside of his forearms against the sink to steady himself. Unable to take in a deep breath, he simply held it for as long as he could, a mere second, while ineffectively splashing water up to his face. Realizing the futility of it, he changed to rubbing his hands under the running water as fast as he could, then alternated wiping his face with his wet hands.

Over and over, hands then face, the process went.

Finally, he was able to slow his breath enough to concentrate on filling his cupped hands with water. He dropped his face into those hands and pushed the water out the sides. He did the same with his hair, then his neck.

With his eyesight better, he reached for the soap and lathered his hands longer than he had ever done in a bathroom before. The directions on the back of the shampoo bottle in his shower at home came to mind: Lather. Rinse. Repeat.

Once he was sure his hands were decontaminated, he went to work on his face, his neck, and his hair. He repeated this process until his custom-fitted dress shirt and pants were soaked. The puddle he was standing in was of his own doing, and he did nothing to dry it up before stepping back into his office.

Michael stumbled back to his desk, his wet clothes leaving a trail across the carpet. His eyes darted to a hinged, old-fashioned picture frame in front of the phone on his desk. Photos of his two children that filled each side of the frame were blurry. He thought of them for a moment... his mind flashing back to happier times of innocence and joy. *What kind of danger have I put them in?*

As best he could, he focused his vision on the powder-covered phone in front of the picture frame, then on the door. He needed help. And he needed it fast. But the thought of exposing anyone else to this potential toxin made his stomach churn. He would not make others join in his responsibility for whatever debt he owed.

His heart pounded in his chest. His breathing was reduced to short gasps interrupted by intense coughing. Fighting panic, Michael's mind cleared for a moment. He could not and would not risk contaminating the entire building. Michael made his way to his closed office door. With hands shaking, he pulled the white T-shaped handle on the fire alarm that was mounted on the wall there.

As the fire alarm blared through every floor of the building, Michael could hear the commotion of confused voices mixed with hurried footsteps outside his office. He wanted nothing more than to join them... to rush out into the fresh air. But he stayed put, protecting the innocent others from the threat he now carried.

Michael imagined the faces of the occupants of this multi-storied building, standing outside in the frigid winter temperatures. But at least they would be safe. They'd be uncomfortable, but they would be safe. He was wet, but at least he was inside the heated building. He looked at the thermostat in his office. *Shit! That's going to circulate this stuff throughout the building!*

Blinking his eyes down hard, trying to alleviate the stinging discomfort without rubbing them, Michael cleared his vision enough to read the digital thermostat panel on the wall. He pressed the OFF button as hard as he could. The sensation of warm air falling gently from the ceiling vents stopped immediately.

With fingers still trembling, Michael reached for his cell phone, grateful he left it in his jacket pocket hanging in the corner away from the powder. He pushed 9-1-1. His voice was hoarse as he spoke just above a whisper to the dispatcher. "This is District Attorney Michael Brown. I'm in... my office at the county building. I just pulled the fire alarm... to evacuate everyone. I received an envelope containing... an unknown powder. It's contained to the interior of my office. I've been exposed... the substance is likely toxic. I'm having... a hard time... breathing."

The dispatcher asked him to repeat what he had said. Michael's coughing clipped his words, making it difficult to understand. The alarm screaming through the building didn't help either.

"Michael Brown. District Attorney. In my office. Exposed to unknown toxin. Powder form. Contained to my office. Building being evacuated by pulled fire alarm. Send hazmat team."

The dispatcher asked him to stay on the line until help arrived. She tried her best to reassure him as he walked to the windows of his corner office. From this vantage point, he would be able to see when the first responders were arriving.

Minutes felt like hours before he saw the first police car approach with lights flashing. That was followed by fire engines and ambulances.

It could have been instinct. Or a gut feeling. Maybe even fear. Whatever it was, he couldn't pinpoint it. And it didn't matter. All he knew was that he needed to take a picture of the note... just in case. Just in case, he needed it later, and whatever agency that was going to investigate this couldn't let him see it. Just in case, it would come in handy after he retired from office—and retired from helping the Russian mafia. Just in case, Vince could make some sense of it.

While it might have seemed irrational to the Michael Brown, who walked into work this morning, it was not irrational to *this* Michael Brown, who could barely breathe and was now in fear of his life. Using the same phone that called for help, Michael snapped photos of the piece of paper from different angles. Unable to see clearly what was on the camera screen, he wanted to be sure at least one of the pictures he took would show the complete note.

"Mr. Brown, are you still there?" came the voice from his phone. "Help is there now. They'll be up to your office in just a minute. How are you doing, Mr. Brown?"

Michael looked at his office door, picturing firefighters rushing through it.

"No!" he yelled into his phone.

"Mr. Brown, you're not okay?"

"No, not that. I'm okay," Michael answered. "But whoever you sent can't come into my office. It's contaminated. Tell them not to come in. You've got to tell them not to come into my office."

"I understand, sir," replied her reassuring voice. "I will advise them to take all necessary precautions. They'll be up there to help you as soon as they can. Try to stay calm, Mr. Brown."

"I'm trying," Michael coughed out.

"I'm going to stay with you until they get into your office. I'm right here with you, Mr. Brown. You're doing fine."

In that moment, despite the fear surging through him, Michael felt a sense of relief. His eyes weren't burning as badly as they were when it first happened, and his breathing seemed to be calming down. Now, he just had to wait.

Seconds later, the fire alarm stopped. His ears immediately began ringing in the aftermath of the exposure to that horrendous noise. Michael tried shaking his head from side to side to stop the sensation, but the ringing in his ears continued. Suddenly, through that high-pitched inner sound, he heard footsteps outside his office. Then a bang at his door.

The fire department had arrived. Although their voices were muffled by the air packs that covered their faces, Michael understood what they were asking him, and he replied that he was okay. They told him it would be a few minutes before they could get him out of there; a hazmat team was mobilizing downstairs, and they'd be up shortly.

Michael told the 9-1-1 dispatcher that he felt safe enough with the firefighters there for her to disconnect the call. He then scrolled down his contacts until he came to Audrey's name. With shaking fingers, he typed out a message, paused, then hit send. He repeated the process with Vince's contact, this time attaching the photos of the note before sending it.

Michael looked back at the picture frame on his desk. He wanted so badly to hug them... to tell them in person what he'd just entrusted to text messages. But he felt he'd done all he could do. For his kids and for everyone he worked with. He protected his staff, and he'd reached out to his children one last time. One last action he thought needed to get done played with his mind and toyed with his conscience.

Whatever was going to happen next, he knew he had no control over it.

CHAPTER 57
WHITE POWDER MESSAGE

Vince's phone buzzed in his pocket, but he ignored it. The dangers of texting and driving were something he drilled into the heads of every teenager he spoke with at the high school. And even some of the parents... more than he should have had to. Once he got to the tax assessor's office, he'd check to see who wanted him.

Of all the names Carmen ran through the DMV computer, the most dangerous of them all had the least amount of information. Vince needed to learn all he could about one Tomas Etoile, and he would start with municipal property tax records. Something didn't add up, and he was determined to find out what.

An hour away, Audrey was starting her morning routine of setting up the small chapel in the school behind the church. She pulled her phone from her jeans pocket to see who was texting her. The name on the screen made her do a double take. Her father rarely texted during working hours. And she was sure he had a lot to catch up on after being away for more than a week.

She opened the message:

Audrey,

I love you

Dad

Audrey's stomach tightened. This wasn't like her father at all. First, texting her while he was working. Then, telling her that he loved her... Audrey couldn't remember the last time he said that.

She went through her frequently called contacts and called Vince's number.

Vince groaned at the sound of her ringtone. Just for fun, with a little sarcastic truth sprinkled in, Vince chose a special ringtone for his sister. "Bad to the Bone." Although he hadn't been born yet, after hearing it once on the radio, Vince knew that George Thorogood and the Destroyer's hit song from the early '80s fit his sister perfectly.

He knew if he didn't answer it, she'd keep calling him. Vince lifted his leg off the seat to retrieve it. "Yeah?" he answered, keeping his eyes on the road as the speaker feature of his phone did its thing.

"Vince!" Audrey's voice was filled with worry. "Did you get a text from Dad?"

"Huh?" Vince answered. "A text? What kind of text?"

"A strange text. From Dad. I just got one. Did you get one, too?"

"Someone sent me something just a minute ago, but I'm driving now. I couldn't check it," Vince answered, peeking at the phone's screen to see who texted him.

"Why can't you drive a car that has hands-free communication? Real cars, the ones the rest of the world is driving, even read messages to you. But you gotta drive the piece of shit Jeep."

"Hey, they don't make Jeeps like this anymore. It might be nearly as old as I am, but this thing will take me anywhere I want to go," Vince said, gently patting the brittle, ripped dashboard of his Jeep Wrangler TJ. "What's so important about this text?"

"Check it out now," Audrey insisted. "Please."

"I'll be where I'm headed in about fifteen minutes. I'll call you back..."

"No!" Audrey yelled into the phone. "Check it now. Vince. Something's wrong. I can feel it."

Vince checked his mirror, making sure no one was close behind him. He slowed his speed to increase the gap between the car in front of him. Then he did what he told dozens of drivers and soon-to-be drivers they should never do.

Vince,

I love you

Dad

Attachments are for your eyes only

"What the..." Vince let the words escape his mouth.

Audrey picked up on his confusion. "You got one, too. See, it doesn't make sense. Not from Dad."

"Yeah, I got a text from him," Vince said, looking at the road over the top of the cell phone he was pressing tight against the steering wheel. "What's going on?"

"I don't know," Audrey's voice cracked. "But something's wrong. I just know it. I can feel it."

"Audrey, maybe he's just having a moment. His first day back to work... getting all emotional thinking about what happened last week with me. Maybe he's had some kind of epiphany or something."

"No, Vince. I'm telling you. We need to—" The call waiting tone beeped.

"Hang on," he cut her off, glancing down at his screen. "It's Carmen. Let me call you right back."

Vince disconnected the call with his sister before she could protest any further. "Hey. What's up?"

Carmen's usually calm voice was not calm at all. "Vince, are you watching the news? The county building's been evacuated. They're saying something about a biological incident. Or a..."

"Or a what, Carmen?"

Carmen knew he wanted the truth. "They're saying it's not confirmed yet, but it might be some kind of a biological attack."

"Are you serious?" Vince shouted down to his phone. Taking in a deep breath, he calmed himself enough to speak in a more civil tone to the woman he cared about more than anyone else. "Thanks, Carmen. I have to get over there. Call me back, please, if you hear anything."

"Be careful driving, Vince. I promise I'll call if I hear anything."

Vince turned off at the next intersection and pulled to the side of the road. He picked up his phone and went back to his dad's message, zeroing in on the last line: *For your eyes only.*

A chill ran down his spine when he saw the note in the photos that were for his eyes only:

Mr. Brown,

Your family's debts are not settled.

No, you can't unlearn all the facts that you've learned.
The powder speaks volumes.

Remember: what tortures you is just the beginning.
Fucking Psycho has spoken.

Breathe deep.

Vince frantically called his dad's number. "Dad, pick up. Come on, Dad, be there," Vince pleaded.

Finally he heard his dad's voice, but it wasn't the voice he needed to hear. Michael's outgoing voicemail message played in Vince's ear.

Vince rubbed his forehead, squeezing it as hard as he could between his thumb on one side and his fingers on the other. He pressed so hard that when he looked into the mirror, he saw that the skin of his forehead was reddened by the pressure he put on it.

Maybe he couldn't answer because he was busy being interviewed by whatever agency was leading the investigation. *He'll answer this time,* Vince said to himself as he called his dad again.

His chest tightened when the call went to his father's voicemail for the second time.

He looked at the photo of the note once more. This time, he expanded it to make the words bigger. What had he done? How could he have put his dad in this kind of danger? The fucking psycho has spoken.

And now Vince understood with a little more clarity why Frank was so hesitant to tell him everything he knew about the monsignor.

Vince got the meaning behind the *fucking psycho* line. He had confronted him in the diner less than forty-eight hours earlier. The title Vince gave him that night made Vince feel good about himself—he confronted the worst kind of bully and put him in his place. Now, Vince was guilt-ridden seeing how this fucking psycho of a bully used his words to get even with his dad.

Vince switched the radio in his car to AM, tuned to the news station, then made a U-turn and sped toward the county building. An hour away.

The news crackled through worn speakers in the back of the Jeep that bounced down the Atlantic City Expressway as fast as its short wheelbase and wide tires would safely allow. Reporters from the major Philadelphia networks were on the way to the scene, according to the news announcer.

"At this time, we can report that the Atlantic County Criminal Justice Complex has been evacuated. Sources tell us that shortly after nine this morning, a suspicious package was opened by someone inside the building. This led to the evacuation of the building, and a large, full-scale emergency management response has been activated. This station can also confirm that the Atlantic County Biohazard Strike Force has just arrived on the scene. Stay tuned for more developments as they become available."

On any other day, Vince would be listening to any number of his favorite songs from his favorite bands through the CD player. He would always listen to at least one song from Phish before he got to wherever he was going. But not today.

Vince wanted to stay tuned but instead found his fingers turning the radio dial, scanning for a different station that could give him different information. Better information. More information.

He landed on an Atlantic City station that specialized in local news. "... in addition to the FBI's anti-terrorism task force. We can now confirm that there is at least one victim inside the Criminal Justice Complex who was unable to evacuate when the alarm sounded. The Atlantic County Bio-Hazard Strike Force is gearing up to enter the building, presumably to rescue the victim trapped inside."

Vince gripped the steering wheel with all his might. "Nooo!" he screamed, straining his vocal cords to their breaking point. After releasing his grip, he pounded his fists against the hard plastic covering of the steering wheel. He was still at least a half-hour away from the building, and each passing minute seemed like an hour.

A helicopter from one of the major Philadelphia news stations flew overhead, going in the same direction he was, down the Atlantic City Expressway. Vultures... *grobuonis,* as Evelina called them, heading out to circle their prey. He had witnessed this countless times in his career as a cop.

Their worldviews were framed by their experiences with them; Evelina saw the police as vultures while Vince had come to see the media as vultures. Neither saw them as they really were, but as they perceived them to be.

The helicopter would surely get there before Vince, and he couldn't help but feel envy knowing they'd witness the scene before he could. He switched between radio stations, hoping to hear a new development—something new to report. Instead, the talking heads repeated the same thing but rearranged their words to make the story sound fresh.

Audrey's ringtone interrupted the AM static of the radio. "Vince, they won't let anyone near Dad's office, but I made it here as close as I can get. I just heard that they're getting ready to take someone to the hospital."

"Is it Dad?" Vince asked, pleading for an answer.

"I don't know, Vince," Audrey said. "People said they heard a couple of cops talking about it."

Vince struggled to get his words out. "Audrey, you've got to find out."

There was no response from her. "Audrey... Audrey, are you there?"

"Hold on," Audrey answered, her voice faint.

Vince threw his arms up in the air. Then, realizing he was driving, grabbed a hold of the steering wheel again. Vince looked at the hands—sweat was glistening from the tops of them.

He started to wipe them on his pants when Audrey came back on the line. "Vince, I just talked to Uncle Jimmy. He said it *was* Dad!"

All the air left his lungs at once. A moment of nothingness...

Vince had to force himself to breathe in before he passed out. His vision narrowed just a sliver of the roadway in front of him. External sounds were no longer heard, just a humming sensation in his ears.

Uncle Jimmy, First Assistant District Attorney James Thomason, was Michael Brown's law school roommate and best friend. He and Michael started at the DA's Office at the same time. He might be James Thomason during the week and at press conferences, but since they were young, he has only been known as Uncle Jimmy to Vince and Audrey.

"Vince, did you hear what I said?" Audrey demanded, after not getting a response from her brother. "Vince... Vince!"

"What did he..." Vince finally answered, his words barely understandable. "What did he say?"

"He said Dad was the person inside who was exposed to some kind of poison or something. They're going to take him to the hospital as soon as they can."

"How... how did you see Uncle Jimmy?"

"He saw me on the corner where the yellow tape is and asked me how I got inside the perimeter. That's when he told me about Dad."

"Is he okay?" Vince asked, the gravity of the situation now indisputable. "Did Uncle Jimmy see him? Jesus Christ. Audrey, is he alive?"

"He said Dad's alive, but he doesn't know what kind of shape he's in. That's all he told me before he got into a car and was driven away."

The cop in Vince wanted to get to the scene. Michael Brown's son needed to be with his dad.

Seemingly stuck in a no-man's-land of confusion, Vince needed more information. "Audrey, where are they taking Dad?"

"I don't know, Vince. Uncle Jimmy didn't say."

Vince thought of the hospitals near the Criminal Justice Complex. There's the main hospital in the city with the level 1 trauma center. Another sister hospital on the mainland. The ones south of them in Cape May County or the ones to the north in Ocean County? There were too many for Vince to make an educated guess, so he went with his gut—the hospital with the level 1 trauma center. "I'm headed your way. I'm going right to the hospital."

"Which one?" Audrey asked.

"Atlantic City Central. It's gotta be that one; they're the most equipped."

"I'll meet you there!" Audrey said.

Vince accelerated to the fastest, safest speed his old Jeep would go. Yes, he was speeding, but not by much. If he was in his department-issued detective's car, an unmarked Dodge Charger, he'd be able to go at least 20 miles per hour faster. But he was stuck behind the wheel of a thirty-year-old Jeep held together by duct tape in some places.

"Why can't you drive a real car like everyone else in the world?" Just minutes earlier he scoffed at the idea. Now, Audrey's words stung in that older sister *I told you so* way.

The pressure of the seat belt's shoulder strap against his chest intensified the pressure he felt from his heart pounding with fear. Part of him wanted to drive to the church... to drive into the church office and run over the son of a bitch. Vince felt no shame or guilt fantasizing about what Augustas Paulauska might look like under the twisted wreckage of his Jeep.

A news update came on the radio. "... We're being told a state police mobile crime lab truck has just arrived here, presumably to analyze whatever suspected toxic material is inside the building. And we can now confirm that one patient, one victim of this attack on our system of justice, has just left here—en route to a hospital for what can only be presumed to be life-saving treatment. For security reasons, officials have not disclosed which hospital."

Vince's mind imagined the scene awaiting his father at Atlantic City Central. *I know which hospital!*

Up ahead, flashing red and blue lights caught his attention. They were traveling in the opposite direction on this divided expressway. As their distance closed, Vince could make out a line of state police cars followed by some kind of large box truck. Then, once close enough to see it clearly, Vince recognized the markings on it—it was the county's Office of Emergency Management logistics truck. If it wasn't painted white with red markings and orange lettering, everyone would assume it to be a rental moving truck. The emergency lights on the cab were the finishing touches that gave it away as an emergency vehicle.

But it was headed away from the city. Vince struggled to understand why it was driving away from Atlantic City, where the incident was still unfolding. Unless... unless there's another attack somewhere else in the county and they need supplies. Maybe at one of the buildings at the county seat? That would explain the state police escort.

Michael Brown's face flashed in his son's head. Whatever victims there might be at another location, the only person that mattered right now was his dad. Like a burner on a gas stove, the chatter coming from his radio turned the angst inside him to a boil. He wanted to turn it off, but he needed to know as much as he could. He couldn't bear any more details. How he craved to hear the specifics of what was going on.

The radio in the Jeep kept up with Vince's cravings. "... Yes, it does, Tim. Federal agencies, and even state agencies, have learned valuable lessons from those first ricin letters that were mailed back in 2003 and 2004. In the decades that have followed, protocols have been developed. The scene here is certainly reminiscent of the kind of responses we've seen over the decades since then."

"But, just so we're clear to our listeners... you aren't saying this is a confirmed ricin attack. You are just saying that the response is similar."

"Yes, Tim. In fact, officials here have been purposely tight-lipped and have not released any information other than what we have confirmed."

"Grobuonis!" Vince yelled into his radio.

CHAPTER 58

TRANSPORT

Vince's heart was in his throat as he left the exit ramp of the expressway. The hospital was not less than five minutes away when his phone rang. Carmen's name was on the screen. "Carmen, I'm in town. I'm almost at the hospital. Have you heard anything?"

Carmen's voice was tense. "Vince, stop. Don't go to Atlantic City Central. They didn't take him there…"

"Is he at Mainland Division?" Vince asked before Carmen could finish what she had to tell him.

"No. They've taken him to the University of Pennsylvania."

Vince slammed on the brakes, ignoring the angry horns behind him. "In Philly?" he shouted. "Why?"

"It's the only hospital in the region that can handle this kind of suspected poisoning. U of P has a special facility where they can isolate contaminated patients. And… and you know, for security reasons, they don't want everything clustered together in a tight area."

"How long ago did they fly him there?" Vince asked, imagining his dad in a sleek medivac helicopter.

"Vince, he didn't go by helicopter…" Her words ended as if she had more to say. And she did. "The safest way to get him there was in the

OEM truck. It has a contained cargo area, so there's minimal risk to the driver. A paramedic is suited up in the back with him, so he's being cared for on the trip there."

The Office of Emergency Management truck that he just saw amid the caravan of emergency vehicles headed in the opposite direction on the expressway had his dad in the back of it.

"Vince," Carmen said. "They couldn't risk contaminating the helicopter or the crew. Same thing with an ambulance. This was the safest way... for everyone."

Vince barely heard her. His father wasn't in that sleek medivac helicopter. Instead, he pictured him bouncing around in the back of a converted rental truck. Transported like nothing more than cargo.

"Vince? Are you there?"

He swallowed hard. "Yeah, I'm here. Do me a favor, call Audrey, and let her know. I'm on my way to Philly."

As he ended the call and swung his Jeep around, Vince silently cursed every decision that had led to this moment. Listening to the recorded confessions, Lithuania, the diner confrontation with the monsignor, all swirled in his mind as he pointed his vehicle toward Philadelphia, praying his old Jeep could withstand the hour-long journey without falling apart.

"I'm almost there," Vince muttered, looking down at the Delaware River from atop the Walt Whitman Bridge that connects Pennsylvania with New Jersey. The drive there took less time than he thought, and he was looking forward to beating his self-imposed ETA at the hospital.

Once off the bridge on the Philly side of the river, Vince was caught in a construction zone that brought traffic to nearly a crawl. The cold air that seeped through the door jamb that never fully closed properly brought his mind back to a cold January day in his junior year of high school. He was sitting at the kitchen table, staring at a report card. All As, except for one glaring B+ in AP Chemistry.

It was the sound of the heavy double garage door that always announced his father's arrival home from work. On this day in his life,

Vince's stomach tightened. He could already picture the disappointment in his dad's eyes.

Michael entered the kitchen holding his briefcase. "How'd you do this semester, son?"

Vince hesitated, then silently handed over the report card. He watched his father's eyes scan the page, lingering on that B+.

"Almost perfect," Michael said with a neutral tone. "Vince, you set a goal for straight As this year. And I know you meant it. What happened in chemistry?"

"I... I tried, Dad. I really did. But some of the concepts, they're just—"

His dad put his hand on Vince's shoulder. "Vince, in my line of work, 'almost' doesn't cut it. A criminal is either guilty or not guilty. There is no in-between."

Vince nodded, shame obvious in his cheeks. "I understand, Dad. I'll do better next time."

Michael's expression softened slightly. He lifted his hand from Vince's shoulder and walked to the refrigerator for a soda. "I know you will. You have a unique gift, Vince. Something very special inside of you. And I'm proud of you for that."

As his father left the room, Vince stared at the report card. He traced his finger over the B+, vowing it would be the last imperfection he'd ever present to his father.

Sitting at his kitchen table, a deeply rooted resolution became cemented in his young mind: there was no room for 'almost' in his father's world. And if he wanted to make his dad proud, there could be no room for it in his world either.

A rumbling jackhammer snapped him back to his current resolution—to make it to the hospital in time to see his dad before they isolated him. Or they took him away to an operating room. Or God forbid...

What if I almost make it there in time? What if Dad is almost okay?

"Stop it!" Vince yelled to his frightened inner child.

When the Jeep stopped again in the single lane of traffic, he blinked down hard, wondering why practicing mindfulness is so easy when nothing bad is happening, yet so difficult when things are going bad. "I can't keep thinking like this," he whispered to himself.

Vince's entire adult life had been spent chasing perfection, terrified of 'almost.' Yet, in this most imperfect vehicle, complete with imperfect doors and imperfect tires, idling on this imperfect stretch of road, Vince had a moment of clarity.

That day, sitting at his kitchen table, shaped so much of who he'd become—making his dad proud or fearing he'd disappoint him, always striving for perfection, seeing the world in absolutes. Just like his father.

Vince spoke as if a friend was sitting in the passenger's seat. "Life isn't a report card, is it? It's messy, complicated. Maybe... maybe *almost* is all we ever really have."

He laughed at the absurdity of speaking to an imaginary friend. But he continued. "I think I'm almost there in figuring out how to use the damn recordings without them being excluded as evidence. I have almost enough on the monsignor... almost ready to bring him down."

Would all of it *almost* make his dad proud?

Vince wrestled with that question as he wrested the steering wheel over potholes and thick steel plates that covered the road in front of him.

Just like this road and just like this Jeep, the world is far from perfect and is far from being absolute. Another crack in Vince's foundation was exposed, revealing the uneasy acceptance that the lines between right and wrong aren't as clear as he once saw them to be.

He looked at his watch. He was late. He ran past the time he planned to be at the hospital—his self-imposed ETA. Yet somehow, he was at peace with it.

Now finally pulling into the Emergency Department parking lot of the hospital, he saw a large police presence, including the county's Office of Emergency Management truck. Vince searched for a place to park. Seeing none, he drove his Jeep onto the curb of a loading area that was clearly marked with No Parking signs. Vince laughed as he locked the door and made his way into the hospital.

Scanning the groups of police officers who seemed to be everywhere, Vince searched for a uniform arm patch from New Jersey. The distinctive New Jersey State Police triangle patch was on a man in the hallway. "Trooper, I'm Vince Brown... Detective Vince Brown from Atlantic City. I was told my dad was brought here."

The trooper pulled out his phone and scrolled down to something on the screen. He looked Vince up and down, then nodded to himself before escorting Vince through the crowd to a conference room. The first person to recognize him was Special Agent Gwynne, the FBI agent who briefly met with him in the church hall when he and his father got home last Saturday.

"Vince . . . Brown," she said, emphasizing a pause between his first and last name. "Twice in one week. This is getting to be a pattern with your family."

"Agent . . . Gwynne. You get around, too. Don't you?" Vince shot back, hoping to match her sarcasm. "Look, I know you probably have questions for me, but can you first tell me if my dad's okay? *Please*. Anything you have on his condition."

"I don't have any medical information, Mr. Brown. But I also haven't heard anything that would indicate he is in immediate danger of dying. If that's what you're asking."

"What's that supposed to mean?" Vince demanded.

"Mr. Brown, what have you been told about your father's condition?"

Vince paced to the back of the room, stopping to stare at a portrait of a major contributor that was hung on the wall. "Nothing!" he shouted at the face in the painting. He took a deep breath. "That's why I asked you. Who do I have to ask to get some information on my dad?"

Agent Gwynne walked to Vince and placed her hand on his upper back. "Mr. Brown, we are the point of contact for the medical team that's treating your dad," her voice softened with compassion. "We will be the first to know anything. So, you'll hear it when we hear it."

"I want to see him. I need to talk to him."

"They'll let us know when it's safe to go back there. We want to talk to him, too."

Vince shrugged his shoulders to let her know he was uncomfortable with her touch. He shook his head. "How could something like this happen? What have you guys learned so far?"

"Mr. Brown, I'd love to be able to tell you. But we have certain—"

"Bullshit!" Vince cut her off. "If you'd love to be able to tell me, then you can tell me. You just choose not to." Vince's eyes swelled with tears. "There's a difference."

Agent Gwynne looked at everyone in the room looking at her for a reaction. "Can we have the room, please?"

No one in the room responded.

Raising her voice, she repeated, "I said, can we have the room? Please!"

Although no one said anything, they responded to her request by filing out of the conference room. Vince watched as she shut the door behind the last person to leave. Turning to Vince, she asked him to sit down. He declined.

"Mr. Brown, nothing I'm about to tell you is official. Do you understand that?"

Vince leaned his hands on the heavy wooden table in the center of the room. "Yes, I do. And my dad is Mr. Brown. Please call me Vince."

"Alright, Vince. Here's what I can tell you—unofficially. I don't think your dad is in any real medical danger."

"What?' Vince asked, withdrawing from the table. "What do you mean he isn't in danger? He was transported here with a state police escort. The radio said it might be some kind of ricin attack. How can that *not put him* in real medical danger?"

Agent Gwynne smiled. It was a smile held too long for Vince's comfort. "What the fuck are you trying to do? Is this one of the FBI's mindfuck 101 strategies? If it is, I'm not in the mood. Just tell me what's going on!"

"Mr. Brown... Vince. I'm not smiling to play mind games with you. I'm smiling because if that was my dad back there, I'd be thrilled to learn what's been found."

"Wh-What are you telling me?"

"Vince, the chemical analysis on the powder came back. We got it about five minutes ago. The chemical analysis showed the powder in the envelope. The powder your dad inhaled is nothing more than chalk dust. Well, chalk dust and trace amounts of the chemical they put in fire extinguishers. That's what made his eyes burn and what made him cough. It's all inert material."

Vince stood in shock. "But... but that doesn't make sense."

"It doesn't make sense unless it was intended to scare him, to coerce him maybe. It looks like whoever sent it to your dad didn't want to hurt him—at least not seriously. We think they wanted him to take it as a warning."

"A warning? What kind of warning? For what..."

"That, we don't know. There was nothing in the envelope but a bunch of blank papers. No note. Nothing."

Vince reached down to the phone in his pocket. The text his dad sent him had photos of a note attached. Vince had seen it; he knew it was real. Every fiber of his being wanted to ask Agent Gwynne about the note. *Why didn't they find it?*

Agent Gwynne kept her eyes on Vince for a response.

Vince felt something inside him telling him to keep quiet about the text from his dad. Like a soft voice whispering, he sensed a message from his gut that he couldn't ignore. He pulled his hand away from his phone. "That doesn't make any sense, does it?"

"No, Vince, it doesn't. And here's the kicker: we need to find out if it's connected to you and what you went through last week."

He fought panic. He fought the urge to run out of there. He fought the desire to come up with a lie. Instead, he agreed with her. "Yeah, that makes sense. I guess."

"Yes, it does. Vince, until we talk again... and I assure you, we will, this conversation never took place. Do you understand?"

Vince nodded. "Yeah. Sure. I understand."

Agent Gwynne opened the door to the room and invited everyone back in.

Audrey would be on her way, and it was going to be a shit show when she arrived. Vince had to get to his dad before she got there. He would find a way to get to where they were holding his dad. He had to.

"I'm going to get some fresh air. I'll be right back," Vince announced to the room.

As he turned to leave, a man in scrubs blocked the doorway. "Are there any family members here yet?"

Everyone in the room looked at Vince. "I'm his son."

"Come with me," the man said.

Vince followed the man who walked at a quick pace, traversing a maze of hallways. At the end of a hallway, the man hit a button on the wall, and a set of double doors opened in front of them. Vince was confronted with a single stretcher in a large room. The stark white lights shining down from the ceiling brightened everything in the room—including his father.

Michael Brown's eyes lit up when he saw his son. The oxygen mask covering his face hid his wide smile. The man in scrubs, who never introduced himself to anyone, told Vince he had five minutes with his father before he'd be taken back to radiology for more imaging studies.

For a moment, the only sound in the room was that of the heart monitor on the wall, reminding them both that Michael Brown was still alive—still very much alive.

"Dad... I-I don't know what to say. How are you feeling?"

Michael sat up and pulled the mask from his face. "Vince... I'm the one who doesn't know what to say. But I'll be fine. I'm staying overnight for observation, but I'll be fine. They just need to make sure whatever I inhaled hasn't settled in my lungs."

"Whatever you inhaled," Vince said curiously. "Have they told you what it was?"

With trace amounts of the dust still in his airway, Michael's laugh caused him to cough. "Yes, Vince. They told me. Chalk dust. Can you believe it? Chalk dust. Christ, I thought I was a dead man when that white powder went all over me. I didn't know what—"

Vince couldn't hold it in. "Dad!" he interjected. "What about the note? The FBI said they have no idea why the envelope was sent to you. They said there was no note inside." Vince pulled out his phone and opened his dad's text message. "What about this?"

Michael looked around. He looked past Vince, shifting his head from side to side to make sure no one was behind his son. "Vince, the note is gone. I shredded it before the hazmat guys got into my office."

"Dad, why? You... you destroyed evidence. Why would you do that?"

"Vince, look at the note again. It wasn't just for me. Read the line that says it about your family's debts. This isn't about me. It was meant for us. Or..."

Vince finished his dad's thoughts. "Or it was meant for me."

"Vince, if anyone saw that note, they'd investigate my background all the way back to when I was first elected. They'd investigate you and what you've been doing, including your kidnapping to Lithuania. I destroyed the note to protect us... to protect you."

Vince looked at the photo of the note on his phone. "I understand, Dad."

Vince read that first line of the note. "'Your family's debts aren't settled.' Dad, do you think this is about what you got yourself into with the Russian mafia and what I've—"

"Yeah, I do, Vince. It makes sense. There's a major trial coming up next month, and they're really putting the pressure on me. Vince..." He swung around with his legs hanging off the stretcher to face his son.

Vince waited for his dad to finish what he had to say. Instead, his dad lowered his head and looked at the floor beneath his hospital-sock-covered feet. "Dad, it's okay. You've already told me everything on the plane. I'm not upset anymore... I understand."

Michael raised his head and looked into his son's eyes. "No, you don't, Vince. Not everything."

"What else is there?" Vince asked.

"I've been clean for almost seven years now."

"*Clean?*"

"I mean, I haven't done anything they've asked me to do. I haven't thrown any trials or stacked any juries. I haven't given them any names of jury members they could intimidate. I haven't done any of it. Not for seven years. And they're pissed."

Vince nodded in encouragement, taking this opportunity to simply listen to his dad without interrupting.

Michael continued, "They've threatened me. And, over the years, the threats have gotten more specific... worse, you could call it. Augustas—Monsignor Augustas—has intervened on my behalf and has been able to keep them at bay. He's been able to do that until this upcoming trial."

"The huge counterfeit jewelry and precious gems case, right?" Vince asked.

Michael became silent. He tilted his head, a curious look on his face included a gentle smile.

"Dad, I told you I'd make a good detective."

Michael's gentle smile grew bigger. "You're not a good detective, Vince. You're a great detective."

Vince mirrored his dad's smile. "Kinda like a good detective is a B detective, and an excellent detective is an A detective?"

"A-plus," Michael said.

A feeling of satisfaction swelled up in Vince. He hadn't just almost made his dad proud. He had given his dad a reason to truly be proud of who he was... the person he had become from the teenage boy sitting at the kitchen table.

Michael's smile faded as he recounted what was going on. "I've been playing them, putting off their demands, for nearly seven years now. Refusing to cooperate with them. This case, though, this case is big for them. If the defendants are found guilty, it'll take down their entire operation in the city. They're serious about this one." Looking deeply into his son's eyes, "But all I have to do is delay this another month, and I'll be free."

"What do you mean, you'll be free?"

"I'll be free from them... I'm going to turn state witness. On the entire organization. If I can make it happen after next month, I'll be free of them, and I'll be free from worrying about going to prison."

"Why? Why is it so important that it happens after next month?"

"Because next month marks seven years since I did anything for them. Seven years. That's the statute of limitations for official misconduct, for conspiracy, and for bribery. Once I get past that seven-year mark, I can't be charged. But I will cooperate. I'll tell the Feds everything I know... and everything I've done."

Closing his eyes, Vince put his head into his hands. "Seven years. That's why you wanted to make sure I hadn't told anyone. You needed time. All you need is a little more time."

"Time is precious, indeed, Vince. So precious."

Vince looked behind him at the closed door. How much time did he have to get what he needed to take down the fuckin' psycho?

Vince showed his dad the note on his phone, pointing to the next-to-last line: *Fucking Psycho has spoken*. "I know this line is directed at me. I called the monsignor a fucking psycho when I ran into him at the diner the other night. But what about the rest? Dad, what is it about the powder that speaks volumes? What facts have you learned that you can't unlearn?

"Maybe that's about the facts of the case—the upcoming trial? Am I supposed to unlearn them? If this is a riddle, I can't figure it out."

"And the torture part?" Vince added. "Is this supposed to be a message to us that we're going to be tortured?"

Michael shook his head. "I don't know..." After a pause, he added, "Hey, wouldn't it be funny if they're referring to the CIA, and they're going to torture us with songs?"

"What do you mean?" Vince asked. "The CIA tortures people with songs?"

"That's the rumor. At least back in the day. Supposedly, the CIA used to play certain songs to torture people as a way to get information from them. I guess it's more of an urban legend. But you have to admit, it's pretty funny."

Vince stared at the photo of the note on his phone. He read the words to himself. Then he read them out loud to ensure that his ears heard what his eyes were seeing. "Dad! This message isn't for you. And it's not for us!"

"How can you tell, Vince?"

Speaking with confidence, Vince said, "Because this is directed solely at me! It's laser-focused, Dad. They used you to send me a message." Vince moved in to hug his dad. "Dad, I don't have time to explain it now. I've got to get going. There are some things I have to run down."

Vince released his hug and stepped back, putting his phone back in his pocket. "I love you, Dad. We're gonna get him. I promise, we're going to get him."

His dad's voice broke the silence as Vince turned to leave the room. "I'm proud of you, son."

Vince paused at the doorway, his hand on the frame. The words from the note echoed in his mind: *what tortures you is just the beginning*. He now understood exactly what that meant, and it terrified him. He pulled out his phone and called the contact in his favorites, cursing under his breath when it went straight to voicemail. "Come on, pick up..."

CHAPTER 59
PRIVATE NUMBERS

"Private number." Vince hit decline on his phone, returning to the database search on his laptop. The tax assessor's office was long closed, but somewhere in these sites was the truth about Tomas Etoile, and he needed it now.

The private number called again. Decline. And again. Decline. His finger hovered over the screen as it rang again. A voicemail notification popped up.

"Damn telemarketers," he muttered, but his gut asked him, what if it's not? He hit play.

"Vincentas, you do not answer calls. I must talk to you. Is important. I will call back. Next time, answer call."

Vince sat up straighter, his pulse quickening. The gravelly voice was unmistakable. Evelina. Impossible. His phone buzzed again. Private number.

Evelina. But how did she—

"How did you get this number?" he demanded, answering before the second ring.

"Oh, Vincentas," her smoker's laugh crackled through the line. "That is not important question. Important question is why your father breathed chalk dust today."

Vince's shoulders tensed. That information hadn't been released. "How do you—"

"Bratva is very angry, Vincentas. Very angry with Augustas. He made big mistake today, sending that envelope."

"Bratva?"

"Russian mafia, Vincentas. And they do not like attention Augustas bring to them. Not at all."

Vince imagined a scene where a mob of big Russian mafia thugs were beating the shit out of the monsignor. A slight smile came to him.

After leaving the hospital to drive back home, Vince was concerned about the things he needed to accomplish. He was expecting to get to work on some important things. On some urgent things. But one thing he was not expecting was talking with Evelina.

Evelina went on to explain to Vince that the monsignor was proud of himself for causing a major state-wide response to his letter. He believed it would humiliate Michael once it was determined the powder was nothing more than chalk dust. The monsignor sent a text to the head of the regional Russian mafia in southern Lithuania explaining everything he did with the envelope—how he filled it with chalk dust and how he wanted Michael to be afraid he was going to die. He wanted Michael's children, especially Vince, to believe their father was going to die a horrible death.

With an investigation already started on the believed kidnapping of Vince Brown, the district attorney's son, the last thing this disorganized organized crime gang wanted was more attention brought to it. In the eyes of the people he partnered with decades earlier, Monsignor Augustas Zukauskus had screwed up... but good.

"Evelina, what do you think they'll do?"

"I do not know, Vincentas. Bratva needs Augustas for laundering their money to them in Lithuania."

"So, he's like a pawn in his own game of chess?"

"No, Vincentas, not like pawn," her voice hardened. "Like bishop, perhaps. Essential piece right now. But in chess, even bishop can be sacrificed for final move."

Vince leaned forward in his chair. "And who makes that sacrifice?"

"It is player who controls game, Vincentas. Player who sees all moves before they happen."

A pause filled with the sound of a flicking lighter and a deep inhale. "But Augustas, he does not know he is piece being played. His ego makes him think he is player."

"And when he realizes he's not?"

"That's when he becomes most dangerous, Vincentas. When cornered piece realizes it is trapped, it lashes out in all directions."

"I get it," Vince said, believing he fully understood Evelina's words.

"Vincentas, you do not get everything. If Augustas believes he will be sacrificed, there is no telling what he does next. He will not accept defeat, ever. Augustas will lie and cheat and steal to win. And when he steals, he steals not material things... he will steal life from opponent. You must be very careful now, Vincentas. Promise you will be careful."

Vince tilted the phone away from his face and bounced the top of it against his cheek. *How the hell does she know so much?* He thought of how she would make a great confidential informant for some lucky detective.

"Vincentas, are you listening?"

Vince brought the phone back to his face. "Yeah, I'm listening. I'll be careful. I promise."

"That is good, Vincentas. I hope your father is doing good. Inhaling too much chalk dust is no good. Even to man in good health, breathing in chalk dust is no good."

"Evelina, I know for a fact that that information has not been released. How do you know about the chalk dust?"

"Vincentas, I thought we were past that. I am told many things, Vincentas. In my role, people tell me things. I am aware of many things.

Sometimes I see with own eyes what is happening. That is why I am calling you. This is why it is important for you to listen."

"I'm listening, Evelina."

One of Evelina's coughing fits broke the flow of conversation. It had happened so many times when he was with her in Lithuania. At least by talking to her over the phone, he wouldn't be subjected to the nasty cigarette smell that came with the coughs.

"I am sorry, Vincentas. My own breath is getting harder to be nice to me. Promise me one thing more, Vincentas... promise you will never smoke."

"That one I can guarantee!"

After regaining her breath, Evelina continued. "Vincentas, tell me about body pulled from bay. He has been identified, yes?"

"Yeah... yeah, they ID'd him. He's the son of a diplomat."

"Our Lithuanian diplomat, yes?"

More information that hadn't been released to the public. *Yep, this gal would make a great informant*, Vince thought to himself. "Okay, I'm not going to even ask this time. Yes, he's the son of the Lithuanian diplomat."

"And cause of death. What is cause and manner of death?"

"That, I don't know. I haven't heard anything. And with Carmen... I mean, Lieutenant Navarro on leave—"

"Yes, your Carmen. She is on administrative leave. But she is strong, Vincentas. She is strength for you to borrow when you need. She has risked much for you. She deserves your loyalty in return, Vincentas."

"How... I mean, come on. What do you know about us?"

"Vincentas, you do not remember when we met. You wanted answers but were not ready for answers you did not want to hear. What good is it to have answers if you do not learn from experience? Vincentas, you continue to want answers to questions you ask instead of learning what you need to know."

Evelina remained as mysterious as when she was that old homeless woman he first met outside the church in Lithuania.

"My desire for knowledge has to outpace my thirst for answers, if I remember correctly," Vince said with a laugh.

"Ah, Vincentas, you do remember. It is questions to answers that will give you knowledge to take down Augustas."

"And if I want to survive, I must learn to participate in this game. Yeah, I remember," Vince said dejectedly.

"Very good, Vincentas. You remember very good. You must listen more now."

"Go on."

A deep WHUMM-WHUMM-WHUMM... WHUMM-WHUMM-WHUMM sounded like it was getting closer to Evelina. It was the unmistakable sound of a siren. *That's funny*, Vince thought, *I didn't know they had our modern phaser siren over there*. He glanced at his watch. 8:42. That would make it 3:42 in the morning over there. "Evelina, what are you doing up so late?"

"Questions to answers, Vincentas. You still learn wrong lessons. Listen now about son of diplomat."

"I'm listening..."

"Vincentas, the body pulled from bay. You will learn that cause of death is homicide and manner of death is strangulation. The person responsible is not good what he does. He is scared now that he did murder. It was first murder for Russian mafia in United States. And Russian mafia in Atlantic City is worried he will go to police."

"Evelina, I know you don't want me to ask... but you have to tell me how you got this information."

"Russian mafia in United States talk to Bratva in Russia. Bratva ask me opinion on things. I learn when I listen, Vincentas. I hear this murder was ordered but not carried out how Bratva wanted. The man who did murder is seen by Bratva as... how do you say, stooge. He is big man, but only on outside. Inside he is small. He will not shoot gun, so he kills by strangling—with a cord. Russian mafia in United States are almost done using him. Do not be surprised if this man is next body found in bay."

Vince had nothing to do with that investigation. He wasn't even called in for additional manpower when the investigation began. He hasn't so much as seen one report on it. Yet, he felt for the young man's family. A child dying before their parent does isn't the way it's supposed to work. Vince took Evelina's advice and sought questions to his answers that might give him knowledge: *I wonder if this young man was killed to send a message to his father?*

The thought of it sent a chilling jolt up his spine. He wondered if his dad was still on that stretcher with an oxygen mask strapped to his face. He couldn't live with himself if he were to ever learn that his dad was to pay the ultimate price for his deeds. And he couldn't imagine what the father of this young man must be feeling, wondering if his son was killed to send a message to him.

"Vincentas," Evelina snapped. "Do you want to learn who this man is?"

Vince briefly pondered an awards ceremony where he would be honored for breaking the case wide open by supplying the name of the homicide suspect.

"Oh my God, yes. Yes... do you know?"

"Of course, I know, Vincentas. I am surprised you did not ask me." Her voice carried an edge of excitement. "The man's name is Tomas. Tomas Etoile."

Vince looked down at his computer. Evelina just spoke the name that was staring back at him from his laptop's screen, the cursor blinking on the county tax records database. "Evelina, I don't believe it. This is the same man who—"

"Who has been ordered to murder your father? Yes, Vincentas, I do believe it."

His chair hit the floor as he stood up. "But how—"

"Now you ask right question, Vincentas. Now you are ready to learn what must be done."

Vince was silent, his confused mind unable to form words.

"This is why it is important to listen, Vincentas. Listen to what needs to be done to stop murder of your father and to take down Augustas. It can be done at same time, Vincentas. You must trust me."

"Of course, I trust you. How can it be done at the same time?"

"Because when Augustas is taken down, everything will fall apart. Like house of cards, everything will collapse. But you must trust me, Vincentas."

Evelina then instructed Vince to upload onto his laptop's hard drive every audio file of the confessional he had—every confession to Father Frank and every confession to the monsignor from the different members of the Russian mafia, including the two confessions of Tomas Etoile.

"But Evelina, none of those confessions can be used as evidence. You don't understand how it works here. Any evidence obtained illegally can't be used for any criminal proceeding. All of the confessions were illegally recorded by Audrey. It's called the fruit of the poisonous tree doctrine."

"Oh, but Vincentas, I do understand how it works here... I mean, how it works in United States. But these recordings are not for United States courts."

"I can't do that, Evelina. That would be against the law. I'd be violating the oath I took when I became a cop. I just... I can't."

"Vincentas, I already knew you would not give them to me. And I will not ask you for them. But if they were stolen from you, then you would not be doing illegal activity."

"Is that a statement or a question?"

"It does not matter, Vincentas. We both know answer, yes? Then your mind... your conscious is clean."

"But how? I don't understand how something can be stolen if it's stored inside my computer."

"It is even better this way. You do not have to know, Vincentas. It is best if... *hack hack*... if you do not know."

Another coughing fit from Evelina seemed to come at just the wrong time. It might have been better for Evelina if he didn't know, but for Vince—he had to know. He needed to know what her plan was. He needed to make sure whatever was planned didn't violate any laws or corrupt those involved any further.

Once she caught her breath, she told Vince that there was no need to worry about what she was asking him to do. She tried her best to describe a legal term that she couldn't find the right words for.

"Evelina, are you trying to tell me I'd have an affirmative defense if this were ever investigated?"

"Yes, that is it, Vincentas. In United States, you have affirmative defense if needed to prove innocent. This gives you that, Vincentas. I found legal library on internet and made sure."

Vince chuckled, "So, you've done your homework."

"Yes, Vincentas. For you, I have done homework."

"Evelina, this is really important to me... I need to trust you. I know that now."

"It is me to thank you, Vincentas. I have not heard someone say that my whole life."

A smile came to his face. He remembered thinking he'd never talk with her again after leaving Lithuania. Now, hearing Evelina's distinct voice, an emotional trilogy of surprise, gladness, and anticipation grew inside him.

Vince reached his hand around to feel his ribs that have been healing nicely. There was barely any perceptible pain in his collarbone, and Vince moved that hand up to it and rubbed it as a reminder. The same with his sutured neck.

He had trusted her less than a week ago, and she made sure that whatever needed to get done, got done. Vince was now back home because of the trust he put in her. It wasn't without pain, but his healing reminded him that nothing worthwhile comes easily... or painlessly. "What do I have to do next, Evelina?"

She explained what he needed to do, ensuring he knew nothing more than what was needed to accomplish what she wanted... what he needed, to assert the kind of justice on Augustas that he deserved. This would offer Vince plausible deniability if, in the future, he needed it.

"Evelina, I can't help but wonder why it's taken this long for all of this to play out. It seems to me, at least, that law enforcement in Lithuania would have issued an arrest warrant by now."

"Vincentas, you still do not understand. This is not game for grobuonis to play. This is game for me. I will make sure he is cornered, like frightened fox in corner. I will make last Arabian mate move, Vincentas."

"Game? What do you mean *game*?"

"Vincentas, game is for my concern. You concern only what you need to do." More hacking could be heard, although it sounded like she moved the phone from her mouth.

"Are you okay, Evelina?"

She cleared her throat—loudly. "Yes, Vincentas, I am okay. If Lithuanian police had good evidence, they would have arrested Augustas by now. But they do not have... how do you say... concrete evidence. This is why Augustas is still free today. It is you, Vincentas, who will make evidence for Lithuanian police. Grobuonis and American police can work out details later. You will fill in all blanks they need, Vincentas. But you will not break any laws to do it."

"I understand, Evelina. At least, I think I do."

"You understand, Vincentas. That is good. Remember that understanding must come from knowledge. You must ask questions to answers, Vincentas. Then true understanding is possible. You are almost there, Vincentas. Almost there."

Wondering aloud, Vince said, "I'm not sure what questions I should ask you now."

"Ask me if I approve of relationship with lieutenant, Vincentas. This is big risk, Vincentas. For both of you. You must like her. Ask me if I approve, Vincentas."

Evelina couldn't see him shaking his head in disbelief, but Vince's head was irritably swinging side to side. "Okay, do you approve?"

"Oh, Vincentas, it is not for me to approve or not approve. If you ask me if I think your mother would approve, I would tell you "Yes," Vincentas, your mother would be happy... very happy."

Vince hadn't thought about the mother he briefly had, the mother he doesn't remember, since getting home from Lithuania. The thought that his mother would be happy for him—happy that he was with someone who made him happy, filled Vince with a sense of loving peace. He and Carmen were happy together, and they were going to be the linchpin that took down the criminal organization that had her murdered.

"Thank you, Evelina. I guess I asked the wrong question."

"No, Vincentas, you did not ask wrong question. You still search for understanding instead of finding knowledge. Vincentas, there will come time for you to show Carmen how much you care. Give her something special, Vincentas. Something special that was given to you... you can give to her. It is beautiful way of giving gift. Give it thought, Vincentas."

"I will, Evelina. Will I hear from you again? I mean, after I do what I have to do?"

"Questions to answers, Vincentas." Her voice softened. "You are learning. Almost there. Your mother would be proud. And Carmen... she will need that pride soon. Dark days may be coming, Vincentas. Keep precious things close."

The line went dead before he could respond. Vince stared at his phone, then at the necklace on the table. How could Evelina know about that?

CHAPTER 60

SOARING

"You've got to be kidding me."

Vince stared at the variety of small aircraft lined up on the tarmac beyond the window, their metal frames gleaming in the morning sun. The wooden sign at the entrance had said Southern New Jersey Municipal Airport, but he'd assumed Carmen was taking him to the Runway 27 Café he'd heard about—a cozy restaurant inside this small airport. Not... this.

"Something wrong?" Carmen's eyes sparkled, barely able to contain her excitement as she guided him past the café entrance toward a row of computer terminals.

"No, everything's fine," he lied, his stomach already starting to churn. "I just didn't realize you were such a fan of... planes."

Carmen's laughter echoed off the walls of the quiet facility. "Oh, there's a lot you don't know about me, Detective Brown." She pulled out a chair at one of the terminals and began typing. "For instance, did you know that I used part of the settlement I got from the city to get my pilot's license?

Vince's mouth went dry. "Your *pilot's* license?"

"Mmhmm." Her fingers flew across the keyboard as she checked departure and arrival weather conditions.

"You said you got a settlement from the city? When? How... I mean, for what?"

"Sexual discrimination," she replied, her eyes still on the monitor. "Made it to final interviews twice. Both times they said I 'didn't meet the requirements.'" Her smile turned sharp. "Turns out their requirement was having different equipment than I've got."

The reality of the situation was beginning to set into Vince's mind. "So, you... we... we're going flying this morning?"

Carmen looked up from the keyboard. "Thank God for your looks and that body, because, man, you don't pick up on things easily." She pushed back her chair and motioned for Vince to look at the monitor. "Every year on my birthday, I pick a new destination. Today?" She glanced up at him with a grin, pointing to an unfamiliar type of map on the monitor. "We're flying to Maryland for the best crab cakes you've ever tasted."

The small box containing her birthday necklace suddenly felt heavy in Vince's jacket pocket. He should have known Carmen's idea of "something special" wouldn't involve a quiet lunch at a local café.

His stomach reeled. "That's... that's quite a surprise," he managed, watching a tiny Cessna take off through the window.

"Just wait," Carmen said, standing up with her logbook in hand. "The real surprises are just beginning."

If she only knew how right she was about that, Vince thought, patting the necklace box and trying not to think about the complete lack of motion sickness pills in his other pocket.

An hour ago, when she picked him up from his house, Vince was thinking of the different ways he would give her the necklace. The necklace Vince asked a jeweler who specializes in gemstones to appraise yesterday. The necklace, the appraiser told him, was the most valuable he had ever seen and would need time to consult with a gemologist before giving him a dollar value.

The necklace was inside his jacket pocket, where he wished a vial of Dramamine was instead.

"C'mon, Brown, let's get the preflight done so we can meet the departure time of the flight plan I just filed."

Vince pulled up the collar of his jacket as he followed her out the door with the sign "Authorized Personnel Only" over it.

Once outside in the cold late-morning air, Vince watched how Carmen meticulously checked the aircraft. She called it a Cessna 182 Skylane. He called it a small white plane with gold and black stripes and a big wing on top. Vince arched his shoulders and put his back into the wind in an attempt to get warm.

"Isn't it too cold to fly?" Vince searched for any excuse to stay on the ground.

Carmen didn't even look up from her inspection. "Cold air's better. Smoother ride."

"Oh... because I was just thinking that maybe we should... you know. Maybe just enjoy the day here in beautiful New Jer—"

"I don't believe it!"

Carmen walked around the plane to where Vince was standing and put her hands on her hips—superwoman style. "Vince Brown is afraid of flying. Vince Brown, the cute detective all the teachers in the Atlantic City school district get all googly-eyed over when he walks into their school. Detective Vince Brown, the stud detective all the ER nurses at Atlantic City Central want to be interrogated by..."

Vince looked at her; a shocked expression he couldn't hide showed just how surprised he was to hear her say this.

"Oh, don't act like you don't know. I can't even count the number of times I've had to answer the question, 'Is he taken?' by the women in the schools and the hospital. Pa-lease," she laughed, the condensation of her breath visible in the frosty air. "And, Vince, even a couple of guys have asked," she smirked, returning to complete her preflight inspection. "Vince, you'll be fine," she yelled from behind the open engine cowling. "I'll keep her straight and level for you."

Seeing how he was out of options for ways to get out of this, Vince decided warmth would be a good idea. "Then do you mind if I get inside out of the wind while you finish checking the oil and kicking the tires?"

"I'm doing much more than that, Vince," Carmen called from behind the engine cowling. "But sure, lift the latch on the door on this side and climb in."

Vince wasn't inside the small plane for more than a couple of minutes before Carmen got in and showed him how the seat belt and headset worked. Once she started the engine, the interior started to gradually warm up.

"We can't get going until this needle is in the green," she said, pointing to a gauge in the instrument panel. Pointing to a different gauge, "Same with this needle."

"I'm going to take you mountain biking on our next date—just to get even with you for this," Vince shouted into the microphone on his headset.

"Vince," Carmen said gently. "You don't have to yell into the mic. Just talk naturally."

Vince laughed, remembering how Logan told him the same thing when they were in the helicopter. "Got it," he mumbled.

Carmen took her eyes off the gauges for a second and looked at Vince. "So... this is a date. Our first *real* date?"

He reached down and felt the box with the necklace inside. He'd planned this moment so differently—a quiet table with soft music playing. His nervousness about giving it to her was now replaced with his fear of leaving the firm ground behind.

"Yeah, our first date. And here I thought I was the one who should be taking you out on a date."

"Times have changed, Mr. Brown. Now we women can set up our dates," Carmen said before glancing over at him with the sexiest tease in her eyes. "And we can take them places they've never been. You think I earned my wings just batting these eyes?"

She paused to wait for Vince's reaction.

"Those eyes could probably earn you a commercial pilot's license," Vince muttered, then froze when he realized his headset was live.

Carmen's laugh crackled through the intercom. "Good to know they work on you too," she said with a smile, as she scanned the instrument panel with her finger, zigzagging from top to bottom. Then she nodded to him. "Let's go flyin', Vince!"

Carmen's voice changed completely when she keyed the mic. "Southern New Jersey traffic, Cessna November–Charlie–One–One–Zero–X-ray, departing runway 2-7, Southern New Jersey."

Vince blinked at the transformation. Gone was the flirty lieutenant who'd teased him about his fear of flying. In her place sat a confident pilot who clearly knew exactly what she was doing.

"Don't you have to wait for the tower to clear us?" he asked.

"No tower here." Carmen's eyes stayed focused ahead. "I need you to be quiet until we're at altitude. I'll let you know when."

She advanced the throttle, pushing Vince back into his seat. Even with the large headset covering half her head, he saw a new expression on her face—determined concentration mixed with calm confidence. For the first time in their relationship, Vince felt truly safe.

"There's 70 knots," Carmen said to no one.

Then the sudden feeling of lifting off the ground created a feeling in his stomach like he was in a fast elevator. He waited for the nausea to follow. He looked out his window down at the ground below, objects getting smaller by the second. He could see the lot where Carmen parked her new Lexus convertible—there it was, tucked into a far corner space so no one would hit it.

"Vince," Carmen said firmly. "Look straight out the front windshield. Look at the horizon and keep your head pointed in the same direction the plane is heading."

She wasn't looking at him but somehow knew what Vince was doing. He watched her concentrated control of the plane as it continued to climb—scanning the instrument panel, looking out the windshield in all directions, looking down at an iPad she had tucked to her side. She was busy. No wonder she wanted him to be quiet until she told him it was okay to talk.

Vince watched her enter some numbers into a control box in front of her. "Southern New Jersey traffic, Cessna November–Charlie–One–One–Zero–X-ray, departing the pattern to the south, climbing to seven thousand three hundred, Southern New Jersey."

She double-checked something on her iPad, then looked over at Vince. "Okay, how ya feeling?"

Vince turned to respond to her.

"Vince, look straight out the windshield. See that little cloud way out there?" she said, pointing in front of her. "Keep your eyes on the cloud. Imagine we're heading right for it."

Vince did as instructed.

"That's right. Good. Now, let's talk while you look at that cloud. I promise I won't be offended if you don't look at me."

Vince's stomach didn't develop the feeling he worried it would. There was no lightheaded feeling either. "Hey, this really works!"

"Vince, please don't yell into the mic..."

"Sorry."

Vince wiggled his butt into the seat to get more comfortable. "Am I allowed to take off my seat belt?"

"I don't recommend it."

"I just want to take off my jacket so I don't get too hot. Am I allowed?"

Carmen laughed. "Yes, Vince, you can unbuckle it to take off your jacket. There are no flight attendants up here to scold you."

After removing his jacket, Vince had a bunch of questions. His first were, why did she let go of the controls, and how is the plane still flying without her steering it?

Carmen explained the plane's autopilot and how she programmed different waypoints to get them to their destination. She pointed to the altitude indicator, telling Vince that she purposely sets it to a number that's not at a thousand or five hundred level mark. Instead of flying at seven thousand or eight thousand feet, or seven thousand five hundred feet, she set it at seven thousand three hundred and sixty feet.

"Pilots like to fly at an altitude they're comfortable with. They either fly at a specified thousand-foot level, like three thousand feet, four thousand, five thousand, and so on. Or they split those thousands in half and fly at five hundred foot intervals: three thousand five hundred, four thousand five hundred... you get the idea. I fly at altitudes that most pilots don't pick. It's safer this way, and I can keep a better eye out for other aircraft."

"Is there anything you don't plan for?" Vince asked, half-jokingly. "It's like you have a counterattack in your mind before you even start."

"It's all about planning, Detective. Thinking one step ahead," she said with a smile. "How do you think I got you to come with me today without suspecting anything?"

Vince smiled back. "Nice... nicely done."

Carmen scanned the sky in front of them, never looking at Vince for too long.

And Vince... Vince started to get more comfortable in the plane and started to scan the sky himself. "Hey, this is pretty cool up here. Look... down there. What's that we're flying over? It looks like an airport."

"That's Millville Executive Airport. Now we're going to head for the tip of Cape May and gain some altitude."

"Gain some altitude? Why do we have to gain some altitude?"

"We want to be as high as we can when we cross over a large body of water. After Cape May, all we have under us is water—the Atlantic Ocean to our left and the mouth of the Delaware Bay on our right. The higher we go, the more we increase our options of an emergency landing location if the engine fails."

Vince stared at the gauges; the RPM and oil pressure gauges caught his attention. He looked for a gas gauge, but had no idea what that might look like in a plane—he doubted it would have a gas pump symbol with an arrow pointing to the side of the plane to put the hose in.

"Umm... you said in case the engine fails? You mean the engine could quit while we're over the Delaware Bay?!"

"Well, there's always that chance. But don't you worry, Vince Brown. Your pilot did a thorough preflight inspection," Carmen said, shaking her head and rolling her eyes.

"But what if we run out of gas? I didn't see you put gas in it before we left," Vince said with a shaky voice.

"Vince, honey... I made sure it was topped off before we left. You saw me check all the gauges. There," she said, pointing to the fuel gauge, "you see the needle is all the way to full."

Vince saw the gauge she was pointing to, but even seeing the needle on the full mark did little to relieve his concern. "Couldn't you have said something like, 'In the *very unlikely event* of an engine failure'... like they do on commercial flights? That would have sounded a lot better."

"I'm sorry. I'll work on my delivery."

"That'd be appreciated."

"Want to know how to actually enjoy flying?" Carmen asked once they reached cruising altitude.

"Anything to get my mind off the engine dying," Vince muttered.

"Hold the yoke—the steering wheel—like this." She demonstrated with a gentle grip. "Now watch that instrument with the blue sky and brown ground. See how the little wings line up with the horizon?"

Vince mimicked her grip, focusing on the artificial horizon. "So if you push forward, we go down?"

"And pull back to climb. But right now, just keep us level." She watched him adjust his grip. "Perfect. Just like that."

A minute passed. "Hey, this isn't so bad," Vince said. "It almost feels like I'm actually—"

Carmen held up her hands. "That's because you are flying it."

"What? Carmen, I don't know how to—" His knuckles squeezed the yoke.

"What do you mean you don't know how? You're doing it right now. Just relax your grip." Her eyes sparkled with mischief. "Maybe I'll pour myself some coffee while you take over."

"Don't you dare!" But he was grinning now, his earlier fear forgotten.

"I'll tell you what, Pilot Brown, you keep this plane straight and level over the bay, then I'll take the controls once we get over Delaware," she said, adding a long pause. "No sense risking us getting shot down by the military because you accidentally turned into the airspace of Dover Air Force Base."

Vince felt his hands tighten their grip on the steering wheel... er, uh—yoke. "Why do you do that to me?" he asked without looking at her. He caught his breath. "I'm getting the notion my fears amuse you."

"You have no idea... you have no idea, Vince Brown," she joked. "Here, let me have the controls while you wipe the sweat from your palms."

Vince looked out his window at the shoreline of Delaware getting closer. Carmen did some inputting of numbers into some of the dials and screens and then looked down at her iPad. "Yep, right on time," she said, looking out the windshield.

"Right on time?"

"Just cross-checking our location with the flight plan I filed. Less than a half hour to go before you taste the best crab cakes in the world."

"I just thought of something. You never told me where we're going."

"You never asked."

"Yeah, well... fear can make you forget to ask important questions. Besides, I'm trying to listen more and then ask questions about the answers I get."

Carmen swung around to look at him. "Huh? That doesn't make any sense."

"Forget I even said it. It's just something I'm trying to figure out."

"*Soo...*" Carmen asked.

"So... what?" Vince asked, questioning her question. *Evelina would be proud*, he thought to himself.

"Aren't you going to ask me where we're going?"

'Oh, yeah. That. Where are we going for these awesome crab cakes?"

"It's a surprise," Carmen said, returning her focus to the clear sky in front of them.

Vince shook his head. "I should have known."

"Gotcha again, didn't I?" Carmen said with a wink.

The remainder of the flight was smooth, just like Carmen said it would be when they left.

"Sterile cockpit time," Carmen announced as they began their descent. The playful tone was gone, replaced by focused professionalism. "Only flight-related communication from here on."

Vince watched her transform again, fascinated by this side of her. Her radio exchanges with the tower sounded like a foreign language to him, yet she handled them with the same confidence she showed in the interrogation room.

The ground rushed up to meet them, and Vince was surprised that his stomach had settled. He was actually looking forward to lunch—and to giving Carmen her gift, even if his nervousness about that had replaced his fear of flying.

He was so lost in thought that he didn't sense Carmen bringing the plane to a stop in front of a large building with huge windows that went from the ground to the ceiling. "You can leave your jacket in the back. We're going in that door right there," she said, pointing to a door just to the right of the plane.

Vince reached down into his pants pocket. How he wished the box with the necklace would have fit in there. "Uh, no, that's okay. I'd rather have it with me... you know, in case we take a walk after lunch. Why don't you grab yours as well?"

"I think I will," Carmen replied, reaching behind her. "Come on, let's go eat."

The restaurant was much nicer than Vince expected—nothing like the Runway 27 Café at the airport they took off from. This was more like a fine dining place you'd find on vacation, the kind where if you don't have reservations, you're not having dinner.

"Reservations for Navarro. Party of two," Carmen told the host standing at the podium.

"She really does plan for everything," Vince said in the direction of the host, who had grabbed two menus and began walking into the dining room.

The dining room was even nicer than the entryway. Vince felt right at home—high ceilings and beautiful décor with unfiltered sunlight coming through the windows. They were seated at one of the window tables, giving them a perfect view of the planes taking off and landing.

"What do you think, Vince? It would have taken us three to four hours if we had driven here, but we made it here in less than an hour."

"Nice," Vince said, looking around the room. "I thought there'd be aviation stuff hung on the walls, you know, like the Runway 27 Café back home. I like this better."

Carmen smiled at Vince. "Me, too. Especially for our first date."

Their server arrived with water and menus. "The crab cakes are our specialty," she said. "But everything Chef Michele prepares is exceptional."

"Two crab cake platters," Carmen said without opening her menu. "Trust me on this one, Vince."

He liked this confident side of her, even when it meant surrendering control. "I trust your flying; might as well trust your taste in seafood."

After the server left, Carmen leaned forward. "So, Detective Brown, what do you think of my birthday tradition?"

"It's... not what I expected." Vince felt the weight of the necklace box in his jacket. "But then again, nothing about you is what I expected."

"Is that a good thing or a bad thing?" Her gray eyes locked onto his.

"Definitely good. You've shown me how to see things differently, Carmen. Not just today, but ever since we started..." He hesitated, unsure how to put into words what they had.

Carmen's smile softened. "Working together?"

"Yeah. That." Vince reached into his jacket. "Which is why I wanted to give you something special for your birthday."

He placed the box on the table between them. Carmen's eyes widened slightly, but her expression remained careful.

"Vince..."

"Just open it," he said quietly.

She ran her fingers along the edge of the box before opening it. Her quick intake of breath told him she recognized the necklace as something unique. "Vince, this is beautiful. I've never seen anything like it," she said, lifting it out of the box.

She lowered the reddish-colored precious gem into her open palm. "What kind of stone is it?"

"It's amber... Baltic gold is what it's called in Lithuania."

"Vince, isn't Baltic amber incredibly valuable? I've only ever heard of it... I've never seen it in person."

"Now you can say you have," Vince replied, looking into her eyes, trying to gauge her emotions.

"Vince... you didn't have to..." She stopped herself mid-sentence, lifting the necklace up in front of her face. "My mom... my mom could never afford real diamonds or anything like that. But she had an imitation stone set in a necklace—just like this. It was special."

"It was a special gift I received when I was in Lithuania. Now I want you to have it."

Carmen gently put the necklace back into the box. "It's beautiful, Vince. But I can't wear this. Not yet."

The words hit him like a physical blow. "What do you mean?"

"Vince, this isn't just a birthday gift. This is..." She hesitated as if choosing each word carefully. "This is a statement. And we're just starting to figure out where we are in this relationship." She closed the box. "I'll accept it, but I need to be sure about us before I wear something this meaningful."

"Carmen, I—"

"Vince, please understand. We work together. We're in the middle of this... investigation. And what happened between us..." She took a deep breath. "I need time to sort things out. To be certain. Please understand, Vince."

The server returned with their meals, her cheerful voice jarring against the tension. Vince barely noticed the aroma of the supposedly best crab cakes in the world.

"I understand," he said finally, though his chest felt hollow. "Take all the time you need."

Carmen reached across the table and squeezed his hand. "Thank you. For understanding. For the gift. For today."

Vince managed a smile, but as they began to eat, he couldn't help thinking that flying hadn't been the most stressful part of this date after all.

The flight back was quieter, but no less smooth than their journey there. As Carmen guided the plane through the afternoon sky, Vince watched her hands on the controls—so sure, so steady. He thought about how she approached everything with that same certainty: her career, her choices, even her emotional needs.

The empty space in his jacket pocket felt different now, lighter somehow. But watching Carmen's profile against the setting sun, Vince realized that her hesitation wasn't a rejection... it was a promise. Like the careful preflight check she'd performed that morning, Carmen needed to inspect every detail before committing to a course. And maybe that's what made her special.

She could have rushed to judgments or sought instant gratification; instead, she chose to wait until she was absolutely sure. Until everything was perfect. The way she flew her plane, the way she conducted investigations, the way she gave her heart—Carmen Navarro did nothing halfway.

CHAPTER 61

SACRED TRUST

Vince's phone buzzed just as Carmen turned onto Creek Road. The screen showed "Frank," and a new heaviness settled in his chest. Frank never called on Saturdays—he'd be preparing for evening Mass.

"Everything okay?" Carmen asked, glancing at the phone in Vince's hand.

"I should take this." Vince answered the call, "Frank?"

"Vince." Something in the priest's voice made Vince sit straighter. "I need to speak with you. Today, if possible."

"Is this about..." Vince caught himself, aware of Carmen beside him. "Yeah, of course. Where?"

"The usual place. Elissa's Coffee Shop. How soon can you get there?"

Vince looked at Carmen, her eyes fixed on the road ahead, one hand carelessly touching the spot where the necklace box rested in her purse. The awkward silence from the airport suddenly felt like an opportunity.

"Give me thirty minutes," Vince said into the phone.

"Thank you, Vince." Frank's voice softened. "And... be careful."

The call ended before Vince could ask what he meant by that.

"Everything alright?" Carmen asked again, her tone carefully neutral.

"Father Frank needs to talk with me. Says it's important." Vince studied her profile. "I know we talked about hanging out, but..."

"It's fine." Carmen's smile wasn't as convincing as Vince thought she wanted it to be. "I could use some time just to myself anyway."

They both knew what she meant by that.

The twenty-minute drive from his house to the boardwalk was filled with thoughts going in opposite directions—one set going forward and one set going backward. The forward, future thoughts were centered on Frank and why he wanted to meet with him. What was so urgent?

The backward, past thoughts were about the necklace. The contrast in who they are was as obvious as the road noise from the tires and the cold air seeping through his Jeep's doors. She drives an expensive Lexus Coupe. He drives a beat-up four-wheel drive hunk of rusted metal. He lives in a rustic, cabin-like house in the woods; she lives on the top floor of an expensive condo overlooking the bay.

She graduated from law school. And even though work has gotten in her way of sitting for the bar exam, her knowledge of the law is greater than anyone else's in the department. His knowledge consists of the sayings from the great thinkers of their time—Socrates, Pythagoras, Nietzsche... even Asimov. Were their differences too much to sustain a meaningful relationship?

What if she was only trying to be nice by accepting the necklace? What if it wasn't that she wasn't ready to wear the necklace? What if it was because she knew she was out of his league?

Up until this time in his life, Vince was so sure of himself, so confident in what he was doing with his life. Even though he felt like his job as a juvenile detective was beneath him, he still looked forward to going to work every day and using his wisdom and abilities to make a difference in the lives of others.

That time in his life brought him satisfaction and even gratitude.

But this time he was now in—this time of confusion and doubt—it only seemed to bring him angst. And now he was facing even more uncertainty with this conversation with Frank. *What is it that could be so urgent?*

The warmth inside the coffee shop was appreciated after enduring the blasts of cold air coming off the winter ocean. The only person waving his arm in the air was Frank, who motioned for Vince to come sit down.

"Vince, thank you for meeting me on such short notice."

"Frank," he replied, looking at his watch, "aren't you supposed to be serving Mass?"

"On any other Saturday, yes," he answered, looking suspiciously around the coffee shop. Then at a whisper, "But this Saturday? For reasons unknown to me, the monsignor told me to take the night off and think about where my loyalty lies."

"Your loyalty... what are you talking about?"

"Vince, he's up to something. Something nefarious. He's trying to send a message, but I can't figure out what it is. I have this sickening feeling that someone is in danger, someone who has intimidated him. I can't explain it, Vince..."

"Don't try to explain it. Just tell me what you know."

Frank held his journal tight against his chest. "You know what's in this journal, Vince. You've been a good friend, and you know most of what's in here. You... you know about me—my struggles, my doubts. All that's in here as well."

"I know it is, Frank."

"There are secrets about me that, if exposed, would bring shame to the church and what I've—"

Vince cut him off. "We've talked about this. You are who you are, not what society thinks you should be or who the church needs you to be. Imagine the people you could help who are struggling with who they are if they felt they had someone..."

Vince stopped himself from going any further. Knowing how unfair it was to force someone to reveal things about themselves before they're ready. "I'm sorry, Frank. I have no right to tell you what to do."

"There is no need to apologize, my friend. I know what your heart is trying to say."

"Do you think that's what this is all about? Is the monsignor losing his mind because of who God made you to be?"

"I don't think it's that. I think it's something much deeper. I think he's feeling pressure from somewhere. Or something... someone. He hasn't been the same since that incident with your dad. He's edgier than normal. He snaps more easily. He's..."

"He's crazier than he usually is?" Vince offered.

Frank laughed. "Yeah, that too, I guess." Then he paused. "Oh, my goodness, Vince. I have been so unkind. I haven't asked you how your dad is doing. He is doing okay, isn't he?"

"Oh, yeah, Frank. He fought like hell, but they made him stay overnight—just to be sure. But he's fine now. Still a little shaken by the whole thing."

"And they still have no idea who or why it was done," Frank offered. "What a sad world we have become."

Vince gently tapped his phone in his pocket, the photo of the note his dad sent him still saved in its photo gallery. "Umm, yeah. Nothing to go on. No leads that I know of."

The server delivered their usual. They didn't have to ask. They'd been meeting here so frequently that she knew what kind of coffee they drank and how much creamer each was satisfied with. As with every time in the past, Frank closed his eyes for a moment, then made sure to thank her and remind her that she was a beloved child of God.

Frank placed his journal on the table between them. "Vince, for years I have written what I've seen and what I've heard. I have written what he's done, and to my shame, what I have not had the courage to do. Now it includes what I've learned. It is time to share it all with you, Vince."

Nodding in agreement, Vince reached out as if his friend was going to turn over the journal.

Frank pulled it back. "You do not need this kind of burden. It is mine to carry. But I will share with you, here in this most sacred of places—a place filled with caffeine."

Frank smiled wide, and Vince followed with a big grin of his own. Lifting up his mug, Frank offered a toast. "Here's to pulling back the veil, exposing the truth, and helping who we can."

Vince met his offer, clinking mugs over a journal sitting on a small table in a coffee shop. "Cheers, my friend."

Frank didn't read from his journal. He didn't have to. The contents were etched into his memory. And his heart.

Vince had already heard most of what Frank told him, but it confirmed everything just the same: the partnered agreement with the Russian mafia to use donations as a way to launder their money from street thugs, using a type of nontraceable form of cryptocurrency to ensure not getting caught; the monsignor's personal scheme using the confessional to extort money from parishioners; the monsignor's reputation as a sexual predator against vulnerable homeless women; and the thrill the monsignor seems to get from playing real-life chess games with people's lives.

But the bulk of what Frank revealed had to do with the monsignor's personality—his extreme narcissism, his sociopathic tendencies, and his fragile ego. Frank gave example after example to explain the labels he gave the monsignor.

The monsignor's pettiness was highlighted as Frank explained the monsignor's need to have the best and the biggest of everything. The monsignor researched the biggest SUV made in America and bought this one because his searches said the Cadillac Escalade ESV was the largest SUV made in the U.S.

Frank seemed especially embarrassed to share his lack of intervening when he learned what the monsignor had done with the confessional. The monsignor didn't only have to have the biggest and best of everything; he needed to have more than any congregant. Even if it was measured in inches. As long as he had a few inches more than any congregant, he was satisfied.

The church's confessional was part of the original construction, with the booth split into two equal parts. The priest sits on his side, and the congregant sits on their side. Each side was the exact same size when the church was built. When Augustas became monsignor, he wanted to have his side of the booth bigger than the congregant's side. But he couldn't make his size bigger because of the way it was recessed into the stone wall. So he did the next best thing—he made the congregant's side smaller.

Using the ploy of it needing to be remodeled, the monsignor added wooden slats covered with new drywall on the congregant's side of the booth. The interior shrunk by two inches on each side—the thickness of the new slats and new drywall.

The smug monsignor was proud that the congregants now had less room than he did... two inches less.

"Frank, what do you want me to do with all this information?"

Frank held his mug of coffee in both hands. "I want you to have it, Vince... so it will be there if you ever need it."

"Frank, it would all be hearsay. None of it could be used in court. Or even to get an arrest warrant. You know what Audrey and I have, and even that can't be used. I'm beginning to wonder if he'll ever be brought to justice."

"Justice..." Frank said with more authority in his voice than Vince had ever heard, "Justice is what he deserves, and justice is what he'll get. I'd bet my life on it, Vince. That's how confident I am, and that's how much confidence I have in you."

Vince stood up. "That's not fair, Frank. That's not fair to put that kind of pressure on me. What the fuck am I supposed to do with all this? With the recordings, with the confessional, the orphanage..."

Vince turned, looking at the empty coffee shop. It was near closing time, and it was just he and Frank in it. "Frank, it's like holding onto a vial that contains the antidote to a major illness, but I'm not allowed to open it and administer it."

"Share the antidote, Vince. The responsibility to administer it does not fall to you and you alone. You've held the patent to this antidote; all I've done was give you an additive that makes it more powerful. Information is power only if it's acted on. You'll figure it out."

"Goddamn it! Why did all this have to happen here? Why couldn't it have happened in Lithuania where they don't have all the laws regarding evidence and what can be used and what gets thrown out?"

Frank stood up and walked to Vince's side of the table. "It's funny you should bring up Lithuania, Vince. Someone from Lithuania called the monsignor yesterday, and boy, did that call throw him off his game. As much as I am not supposed to take joy in the suffering of others, I have to admit that it brought a smile to my face. And that's why I wanted to make sure you knew what I know—all of it."

"Lithuania... the Russian mafia?"

"I don't think so. Not by the way he was talking. I think it was that Rook person who seems to know everything the monsignor has done. And is doing. From what I've heard, this Rook person has connections that make the monsignor worried."

"Wouldn't it be nice if that Rook person could bring Lithuanian justice here?" Vince said with a laugh.

Frank put his arm on Vince's shoulder. "Vince, whatever justice is going to be handed down, I want you to..." Frank's voice stopped abruptly. He opened the journal, then closed it again. "There's something else. Something I overheard yesterday when the monsignor was on the phone. He said your name, and then he..." Frank looked around the room. "No. No, I shouldn't say more until I'm certain. But promise me you'll watch your back. He's different now—more desperate. And, Vince, desperate men..." He shook his head. "Just promise me."

The intensity in Frank's eyes spoke volumes to Vince. He chose not to protest. "I promise," he said instead.

"Good." Frank's shoulders relaxed under his thick sweater, but his grip on his journal tightened. "Because I think he might know about the recordings."

Before Vince could respond, Frank shook his head. "That's all I can say right now. But if I'm right about what I suspect..." He unconsciously tapped his journal. "Remember your promise, Vince."

"I will, Frank. Look... I'm sorry for snapping at you. I've got a lot on my mind, and earlier today—" his voice trailed off.

"What is it, Vince?"

"Let's just say earlier today didn't go as I had planned," Vince replied with dejection.

"You've got the weight of the world on your shoulders, Vince. Perhaps it is I who should be apologizing. I was only thinking about myself. Dumping my garbage on you wasn't fair. I am sorry for that."

Vince threw his arms up in resignation. "Hey, I guess we're both chest deep in shit, Padre!"

Frank reeled back in laughter. "You have a way with words, Vince. A marvelous way with words."

Vince dropped a twenty-dollar bill on the table. "This one's on me; you'll get it next time."

"That's very generous of you," Frank said, pointing to the table.

"She's been putting up with us for years. She deserves it," Vince replied as he pointed Frank toward the door.

Frank grabbed his journal and headed out the door with Vince. Back into the cold January air.

"Vince, I'm going to do a little digging around when I get back to the church. The monsignor always heads out on Saturday nights. If I get the chance, I might be able to come up with something that will bring about the justice we both want."

"What *something* are you talking about?"

"Not yet..." Frank clutched his journal tighter. "Something you said made me think... Let me confirm it first."

"Frank—"

"You've carried enough of my burdens today." Frank's smile was gentle, but his eyes were troubled. "Go home, Vince. Get some rest."

As Vince watched his friend disappear into the darkness, he couldn't shake the feeling that he should have said more, done more. But what do you say to someone who's already heard all your confessions?

His phone buzzed—another message from Carmen. He'd answer it later. Right now, he needed to think about what Frank hadn't said, what was written between the lines of that journal he held so tightly.

The bitter wind off the ocean stung Vince's face. A sharp contrast to the warmth he felt sharing coffee with a kind-hearted priest... who he was lucky enough to call a friend.

CHAPTER 62

COLD DELIVERY

Vince sank deeper into his recliner, proud of himself for how he balanced the empty soup bowl on the armrest. For the first time in weeks, his mind was quiet. No conspiracy theories, no Russian mafia, no complicated feelings about necklaces or relationships. Just welcomed silence.

Echo was curled in her bed by the woodstove, her steady breathing almost hypnotic. Even his broken ribs seemed to hurt less in the dim lamplight of his modest home. His jacket hung on the hook by the door, a reminder of the cold night air just beyond the walls.

He should get up. Take the bowl to the kitchen. Check his phone. But Frank was right—he needed rest. Everything else could wait...

The sharp bark jerked him awake. Echo stood in a rigid pose at the front window, her hackles raised.

"Just deer, girl," Vince mumbled, but she barked again, more insistent this time.

The distinct pattern of amber lights caught his eye—a tow truck pulling away from the end of his long driveway. It wasn't worth investigating. He's probably at the wrong house... besides, Vince didn't have Triple-A.

He'd almost settled back into his chair when Echo's barking turned frantic.

"Alright, alright." Vince pulled himself up with a groan. He flipped on the outside lights and grabbed his jacket from the hook by the door; January nights in New Jersey demanded at least that much sense.

The outside lights revealed a familiar car in his driveway—Frank's aged Volvo.

"Frank?" Vince called through the door. No answer.

The wind whipped through the trees as he stepped outside. Maybe Frank was having car trouble. Maybe he needed a ride home. But why not come to the door?

"Frank, what are you..." The words died in his throat as he reached the driver's window.

Frank's head was tilted back against the headrest. He wasn't moving. Vince yanked at the door handle—it was unlocked. The interior light above the rearview mirror came on. Frank's face was drained of any color, his eyes fixed in a wide stare.

Vince's legs gave way. His knees buckled against the side of the driver's seat as he reached for the side of his throat to check for a pulse. His hand trembled so much that he had to withdraw it away from Frank's neck—as if touching it might confirm the terrible reality.

The deep bruised indentation around his neck made Vince's world stop spinning, amplifying the hollow feeling in his chest. Knocking the wind out of him like a punch in the gut.

Sharp, fragmented thoughts filled his mind. *This can't be Frank... not like this... not him.*

Vince jumped back, the detective in him saying, *Preserve the crime scene.*

He leaned back into the car. This wasn't just another crime scene—this was his friend. His friend's skin was cold to the touch with a mottled appearance. He had been dead for a while now.

Two hours ago... coffee, conversation. Warmth. Now an unfair contrast to his best friend's cold body.

Two hours ago.

The reality of what he was seeing brought Vince to the ground. The frozen driveway felt as cold as his best friend. Lying on the ground with his head against the cold, hard steel doorjamb, his breathing fast and heavy, tears flowed from Vince's eyes.

"Frank, no, no, no... God... No!" he screamed into the night. He reached for his phone. He'd left it inside on the counter.

The voice of the calm, confident detective who had seen too many of these scenes in his young career was gone, replaced with cries of disbelief as the dispatcher on the other end tried to get enough information to send help. Vince didn't hear the dispatcher tell him to stay on the line. He hit the red disconnect button out of habit and ran back outside.

Time seemed to have no meaning to Vince as he knelt by his friend's open car door. If the world had indeed stopped spinning, that would account for the lack of sensation of time itself—time had indeed stood still in Vince's driveway that night.

Expecting to hear sirens in the distance, Vince looked up and down the street through his tree-lined driveway. "Where in the hell are they?" he said in a panic. Vince shifted his attention back to Frank, unable to stop himself from absorbing the sick feeling of seeing the look on his face—his eyes bulging, his mouth slightly opened, forming an oh shape.

Vince had seen that look countless times on calls he responded to. Calls where loved ones were in anguish over a senseless loss. This time, he was the loved one in anguish. He wasn't sure what to do or how to do it. Through his tears, he scanned the interior of the car, looking beyond Frank's body to see if the killer left anything behind that would be a clue.

Vince knew in his heart who was responsible for this. Frank had told him the monsignor is different now, desperate. But why?

As he processed that thought, something on the front passenger seat caught his attention. It was Frank's journal. A book that held all Frank's innermost thoughts and secrets. A book that could bring shame to him and the church if its contents were made public. A book that deserved to perish along with his best friend.

Vince made a decision that would demonstrate his admiration for Frank. One last act of love for the beloved priest. The journal was a part of Frank he could still protect. It was a final favor he could do for his friend. One last rite he could perform for him.

Vince carefully reached across Frank's cold body and grabbed the journal. A journal that represented Frank's trust in Vince. He pulled himself carefully back out of the car, making sure not to disturb anything. The crime scene techs would soon be there, doing their thing. And if something seemed out of place, they would find it.

Vince shoved the journal into his jacket pocket and zipped it closed as he stood up.

Time wasn't the only sensation that Vince had lost track of. His hearing must have also been affected—he never heard the wailing sirens approaching. He had barely finished zipping his jacket pocket shut when the adrenaline coursing through his system finally slowed enough for him to think like a detective.

Those marks around Frank's neck—he'd seen them before, at crime scenes. Evelina's gravelly voice echoed in his mind: "He is big man, but only on outside. Inside he is small. He will not shoot gun, so he kills by strangling."

Tomas Etoile. The same man who killed the diplomat's son. The same man ordered to kill his father.

Vince stumbled back into his house for his phone. His hands shook as he grabbed the phone off the counter. The screen lit up with notifications:

One missed call—Frank—7:47 p.m.

One voicemail—Frank—7:47 p.m.

Why didn't I hear the call? Why wasn't I there?

Just one hour ago, while Vince was dozing in his recliner, Frank had tried to reach him. He needed him. The timestamp notification seemed to pulse on the screen like a warning.

His finger hovered over the voicemail icon, but before he could press it, bright white spotlights, backlit with red and blue lights, flooded his kitchen.

"Police! Don't move!" yelled a voice from outside his open front door.

"Police! Don't shoot!" Vince yelled back.

Police! Don't shoot was a phrase taught to police recruits in the academy. If they were ever out in public in street clothes and a police officer yelled for them to freeze, they would comply and yell back, "Police! Don't shoot." This signified that they were law enforcement to the officer giving them the command.

"What squad?" demanded the voice from the door.

"Detective Bureau, Juvenile Unit. I don't have my ID on me. I'm not carrying."

Before he knew what was happening, another cop grabbed Vince's arm that was raised above his head and took it behind his back. "Nothing personal, brother. You know what we got to do."

Vince remained silent while he was patted down, hoping that since he was only looking for a weapon, the cop patting him down would think nothing of the journal in his jacket pocket.

A simple journal never felt so heavy.

CHAPTER 63

WRONG SIDE OF THE TABLE

"Just procedure, you know that." Detective Tessa Cassidy opened one of the small property lockers outside the interview room door. A sign above the row of lockers read, "NO Cell Phones Permitted in Interview Room."

She nodded at Vince. "Chief says everything's gotta be by the book on this one."

Clutching his zipped-up jacket pocket with one hand, Vince reached into his pants pocket with the other, pulled out his phone, and slid it into the locker. Detective Cassidy turned the key to lock it, then handed the key to Vince before escorting him into Interview Room 2.

Vince looked up and forced a smile. "Freddy...I wish I could say it's good to see you."

Detective Frederick Corbett. A detective's detective and a cop's cop. One of the nicest humans Vince had ever met. Freddy mentored Vince when he first made Detective, and the two quickly hit it off. There wasn't a cop in the entire department who didn't like Freddy. And more importantly, there wasn't a cop who didn't respect him as well.

Detective Cassidy had already been assigned to the major crimes unit in the detective bureau when Vince got up there. She was always cool to Vince. Not disrespectful, just not the kind who opens up about herself.

"Well, I can say it. It's good to see you, Vince," Freddy said, gesturing to a chair across the table. The wrong side of the table. "Can I get you anything? How about a cup of coffee before we get started?"

A cup of coffee.

The words hit him like a kick to the head. Just hours ago, he'd watched Frank's hands wrapped around a ceramic mug as Frank leaned forward to confide his fears about the monsignor. Now those hands were cold and lifeless, on their way to the county morgue.

"Nah... I'm good," Vince managed. He pressed his forearm against the outline of the journal inside his jacket pocket, a constant reminder of what he had taken from the crime scene. What he'd taken to protect his friend.

"Vince, you can take off your jacket. You know we're going to be here a while."

"Oh, wow... I didn't even realize I was still wearing it," Vince said, trying his best to sound indifferent as he removed his jacket and draped it over the back of this chair. "This whole night has been a nightmare, Freddy. I still can't believe it's real."

"Unfortunately, it is real, kid. You sure you don't want some coffee? You look exhausted."

Kid. Freddy's nickname for Vince when he was showing him the ropes up here in the DB. Now he was sitting on the other side of the table—the wrong side of the table. Those harsh fluorescent lights in the ceiling above him buzzed and occasionally flickered. Up until tonight, he never realized how unsettling they could be.

"The last time I had coffee was..." Vince couldn't finish the sentence. He could still smell the coffee shop's aroma. "The last time I had a cup of coffee was earlier this afternoon with Frank. At the coffee shop on the boardwalk. Before..."

Before I failed him. Before I missed his call. Before I found him with his eyes frozen open with terror.

"Vince... Vince. You okay?" Freddy asked.

"Yeah...yeah. I was just... I guess there are some memories I'll never forget."

Detective Cassidy shifted in her seat, her pen in hand, waiting to start taking notes. "What time was that?"

Vince wanted to continue to protect his best friend. He also had to demonstrate his willingness to cooperate and appear truthful in his answers.

"I don't know exactly. Maybe four-thirty or five. I know they were getting ready to close when we left," Vince offered.

"Can you tell us what you did then?"

Vince didn't have to pretend to not know the answer. He could not remember a thing between walking out into the cold air from the coffee shop to when he was starting to doze in his recliner. The soup bowl... *I must have made soup. Right?*

"I can't," Vince said, his words shocking him. "Freddy... You're not going to believe this, but I can't remember a fucking thing until I was home in my living room."

"It's okay, Vince," Freddy said, reaching across the table for Vince's arm. "Take your time. Take all the time you need."

Vince could only shake his head in disbelief.

"Vince..." Detective Cassidy said his name in a tone he'd never heard before—a comforting tone, a tone that had a hint of compassion to it. "Sometimes it's easier just to imagine you're telling Freddy and me how you met up with a friend and shared a cup of coffee. Now, just tell us what you were talking about."

How many times had Vince used a tactic like that? Changing his tone to one of caring to get the truth out of a perp? *We're here to help you. All you need to do is tell us what happened. Tell us your side of the story so we can help you.*

Was she genuinely concerned, or was something else going on?

"That might help, Tessa. Thanks..." Vince collected his thoughts, but he had to think fast. "Frank told me he had a rare Saturday night off from giving Mass. He asked me if I wanted to meet him at the coffee shop. We try to get together once a week or so, just to shoot the shit. But the past couple of weeks... well, you know." Vince's voice trailed off, hoping he wouldn't be asked about his *kidnapping* or the incident with his dad.

"Yeah, Vince, we know," her voice continued with the caring, compassionate tone. "You've been through hell and back. I can't imagine what you've been through. Which is why I can't also imagine what you're going through now with the loss of a dear friend."

Vince looked up from the table he'd been staring at. Her eyes suggested she was being genuine. "Thanks. I appreciate that."

"You're welcome, Vince." Then, not missing a beat, "So, what did you two talk about?"

Vince didn't have the time needed to create an elaborate story, so he went with what was the easiest... and simplest. "He wanted to know how I was doing. That was the main gist of the conversation. We hadn't really talked since... since I—"

"Since you were kidnapped?" Tessa asked.

"Yeah, since I was kidnapped," Vince said, crossing his legs under the table the way a person does when they cross their fingers, hoping they didn't just open a door for more questions.

Vince looked around at the four walls that made up this interview room. Never before did they seem so close together. Never before had the ceiling seemed to be so low. The camera mounted in the corner reminded Vince that he was being watched and his answers were being recorded.

The questions continued. Not quite in rapid-fire succession but still too quick for Vince to keep track of what answers he was giving.

"Why didn't you do anything when you saw the tow truck drive away?"

"What exactly did you do when you opened the car door?"

"What parts of the body did you touch?"

"What was your relationship with Frank like?"

Vince's mind was spinning. And so was the room.

For each answer Vince gave, the detectives had at least two more follow-up questions. And his answers to those questions didn't seem to satisfy them. The two detectives often exchanged looks during his responses but never spoke to each other.

Every detective knows the best questions to ask are the ones you already know the answers to. *What did they know... or suspect? What answers were they looking for?*

The door to the interview room opened.

"How are you doing, Vince? Do you need to take a break?" It was her, the head of Internal Affairs, Lieutenant Bobbie Macher... LT Bowel Movement, herself.

Vince's heart raced. He felt himself take in a deep breath, hoping it wasn't noticed. "Oh, LT Bow— ... Macher. Umm, I'm doing okay. I just want to get this over and ... you know."

LT Bowel Movement remained stone-faced. "Yes, Vince. I think I do know. How about we take a break? We need this room for another case that just came in. Lots of interviews to conduct. Why don't you go splash some water on your face while we get another room set up?"

Vince had been around long enough to know there are times when a superior officer gives a suggestion and it should be taken as a direct order. This seemed to be one of those times.

"Sure. My legs could use a good stretch, anyway," Vince replied as he stood up, purposely avoiding eye contact with Freddy. He reached behind him, grabbing his jacket on the way out.

Although they were in a hallway off the main area of the DB, everyone upstairs knew that the bathroom walls and doors were paper-thin. Although there were updates to the building over the years, the age of the police administration building meant certain parts of it were still locked in the 1970s. The bathrooms were the best examples of a mishmash approach to remodeling.

As he stood in front of the mirror in the men's room, Vince looked at a face he had never seen before. The vibrant life in the eyes of the person looking back at him was gone. It had been replaced with sunken eyes, devoid of any emotion.

Did they see the same thing that he was looking at? Did Freddy and Detective Cassidy see the same shell of a man he once was? What about Bowel Movement? Did she see him as a weaker version of who he was? Would this be an opportunity for her to go on the offensive? And what was she doing here anyway? Was she reassigned to temporarily run the DB until Carmen returned to work?

Vince hung his head over the sink, staring at the stains left by detectives who rinse out their coffee mugs here.

After splashing water in his face, as Lieutenant Bowel Movement suggested, Vince assumed the commotion down the hall was the next case coming in that she had mentioned. But after shutting off the faucet, one of the voices became clearer. It was the voice of the boss—Chief Huertas. His voice exploded from the hallway, cutting through the thin walls. Vince let himself daydream a little, seeing the chief dressing down LT Bowel Movement made him smile for the first time all night.

"What the fuck are you doing here? You're not supposed to even be here. I want the name of the fucking idiot who reached out to you and told you about this!"

Oh, yeah, she was getting reamed out. But good!

And just that quick, Vince's fleeting moment of joy turned to worry.

"But sir... if you just let me explain," she pleaded.

"No 'but sir,' Navarro. You stay away from this investigation, you hear me? I don't want you anywhere near it. This whole thing stinks!"

"Yes, sir, but if you'll let me explain."

"Explain what? How a floater in the bay connects to a dead priest? How your boy wonder's kidnapping ties to the DA getting poisoned? How your unauthorized CCH searches got flagged by the Feds?" The chief's voice dropped lower, deadlier. "This whole thing stinks, Lieutenant. Stay away from it, or I'll have your badge. That clear enough?"

Vince reached for the door, then stopped. Any move to help Carmen now would only make things worse for both of them.

Vince didn't hear a response from Carmen, but he did hear the chief. "Good. Now, get the fuck out of here before I change my mind and have you charged right now!"

When he finally stepped into the hallway, she was already walking past. Their eyes met briefly—a mixture of warning and regret—before they moved in opposite directions. Just like their careers seemed to be going.

Back in the detective bureau, LT Bowel Movement's smug satisfaction was palpable. She gestured toward the interrogation room—not the interview room. "They'll be right in," she said as she walked out of the room. Her message was clear. Vince was no longer seen as one of them.

Vince knew these rooms well. The interview rooms had tables in them and chairs that were comfortable for the person being interviewed. But the interrogation rooms... half the size, with one comfortable chair for the detective doing the interview and a chair-desk combination for the detective taking notes. The third chair in the room is for the suspect—a hard metal chair with one of the front legs cut an inch shorter so the suspect can't get comfortable.

Vince shifted in the uncomfortable chair, his mind drifting to Carmen's face in the hallway. The way she looked at him—a mixture of concern and warning in her eyes. What had she already told them? What could she tell them without implicating herself? Without implicating him?

Vince wasn't looking forward to more questioning. But he was relieved that it was Freddy who was interviewing him. He knew the sooner he got it over with, the sooner he'd be home—out of and away from this place that just weeks ago was like a second home but now felt foreign to him.

The door opened. Not Freddy. It was Chief Huertas. His face twisted with fury. "What's the last thing I told you when you dropped your badge on my desk to take your fucked-up leave of absence?"

Vince shifted in the suspect's chair. It was doing its job—he couldn't get comfortable.

"I told you not to get dirty, didn't I?" It was a statement, not a question. "Well, here we are. Here *you are*."

Chief Huertas looked over his shoulder. "Have at 'em," he said before turning and walking out the door.

Vince's stomach dropped. Sergeant Delgado and Detective Rourke walked in. The hatchet team. Known for getting confessions by any means necessary, with a convenient habit of the interrogation room's camera recording equipment failing during their most intense interrogations.

"Yep. It sure is sad when a good cop goes dirty." Delgado took the power chair while Rourke shut the door. Vince glanced at the camera, wondering if it was already "malfunctioning."

"The scene of the murder hasn't been established," Delgado said, leaning forward. "All we know is a dead priest was found in your driveway. Still sticking with the tow truck story?"

Vince's voice was steady. "That's what happened. I called it in."

"Funny thing about that truck. No company in the city had one out tonight," Delgado shot back.

"Did you even try to look outside the city? Maybe check the whole county?"

Delgado's face reddened. "You want to play games? Fine. Let's talk about your leave of absence. Your *real reason* for taking it."

"Already covered it with Freddy."

"Yeah, Freddy. Your buddy. That's why you're in here now." Delgado rolled himself closer to Vince. "Time for the truth. Who would want Father Frank dead?"

The realization that everything Vince had worked for was in jeopardy if he didn't sound convincing. "That's the question I keep asking myself. And I keep coming back to... what if Frank wasn't the target? What if this was a mistake?"

"A mistake?" Delgado leaned forward.

"You didn't know him like I did. Frank spent more time with the homeless than he did in the church. Always in the worst neighborhoods, never worried about his own safety. I told him it would get him hurt someday." Vince's voice was strong, emphasizing the truth. "He wouldn't even tell me specifics about his outreach work; said the homeless deserved their privacy, their dignity."

The questioning sharpened, with each answer eliciting two more questions. Vince recognized this technique—he'd used it himself. Keep them talking, keep them nervous. Wait for the slip.

Then Rourke passed a note to Delgado, and Delgado's tone changed. "When was the last time you spoke with Lieutenant Navarro?"

Vince's jacket lay face down beside him, Frank's journal hidden against the floor. Carmen's perfume still lingered from their hallway encounter. They weren't just building a murder case. They were constructing a conspiracy.

"Your phone's been blowing up, Vince. We can hear the vibration through the locker door. Someone really wants to talk to you. Who do you think that is?"

"No idea. It could be anyone."

"Or it could be someone. One person. Who would that be?"

"I told you, I have no idea. It's not like my phone is in my hand so I can look at it."

As soon as he said it, he knew he had screwed up. They set him up for this one. He walked right into it. "Alright, Vince, let's put it in your hand. Can we go get it for you?"

Think, Vince. Think... "I'm not in the mood to talk to anyone."

"Who said you have to talk to anyone? Why don't we just check to see who's been trying to get a hold of you?"

"Not interested."

Delgado turned around again to Rourke. It looked choreographed—Rourke pulled out a form from his binder and gave it to Delgado. "Well, we are, Vince. We're really interested in who's been calling you. What if it's the person who killed your friend? What if he wants to tell you something?"

"I doubt it."

Delgado pushed to form in front of Vince. "You know what this is. All we need is your signature on this consent to search authorization, and we can go get your phone and look at it together."

Vince reached down and felt the lump the key to the property locker made in his pants pocket. "I don't think so. We all done here?"

"What's wrong, Vince? Something to hide? Someone you don't want us to know about? A message you don't want us to hear?"

The longer they kept him there, the better their chance of getting a search warrant affidavit completed and then getting it signed by a judge.

They left him no choice. "Let's do this right," Vince said. "I don't consent to any searches. I refuse to answer any more questions. I want my lawyer. Are we done?"

Any one of those statements triggers an immediate stop to search anything or continue asking questions. Delgado stayed silent, as if searching for something that could counter the way Vince just ended the interview. And Vince wasn't done.

One final slam dunk as an exclamation mark on this. "Am I free to leave?"

If the answer was "Yes," there was nothing Delgado or Rourke could do to prevent him from walking out the door.

If the answer was "No", they would need probable cause to believe he committed a crime. Everyone in the room knew that threshold wasn't close to being met.

Before Delgado or Rourke could answer, the interrogation door opened. It was Bowel Movement. Her smile forced and fake. "Break time. Vince, you want coffee?"

More stalling. They were probably typing up the affidavit right now. Vince stood, grabbing his jacket. "I'm good. I'm going home."

"Vince, no cars are available to take you back home. Why don't you wait in the lobby until a car frees up?"

More stalling.

"Nope. I'll walk home. I think the fresh air will do me good."

"Vince, that's a two-hour walk."

"Like I said, fresh air will do me good." He retrieved his phone from the locker, feeling every eye in the detective bureau on him. The thin blue line had vanished, replaced with suspicious stares and whispered theories.

Freddy gestured toward the elevators, but Vince took the stairs that were right behind them. No last words, no goodbyes. Just the sound of his footsteps bouncing off the concrete walls of the stairwell, a harsh reminder of what used to be his second home.

January's cold air slapped him in the face. The illuminated cross of Rytis Eparchy pierced the darkness two blocks ahead. Vince's hands curled into fists. He ducked down an alley but couldn't escape the church's reflection in the puddles at his feet. Empty liquor bottles lined the curb, their labels familiar as old scars—a reminder of a time he'd rather forget but couldn't afford to. Mini vodka bottles glinted in the weak streetlight, looking just as innocent as they had years ago.

He reached into his pocket. He needed to clear his phone—wipe it clean. Delete his phone call history and every message he sent or received. In the shadow of the alley, Vince's finger frantically hit the delete button on everything. He looked up often, checking the area—making sure he wasn't being followed. He continued mindlessly deleting everything, remembering the question from Delgado: *When was the last time you spoke with Lieutenant Navarro?*

Finally done deleting everything, Vince used his phone to call for an Uber ride home. He gave the pickup location of a nearby homeless shelter.

He kicked a mini vodka bottle aside, listening to it skitter across the pavement. There was a time when just one was what he needed to get him through the day. Tonight, he just needed to make it home before they got the warrant signed. And before the ghosts of his past caught up with him.

CHAPTER 64

SANCTUM'S EDGE

Sleep didn't happen. Not that Vince tried very hard. Every time he closed his eyes, he saw Frank's face in that car. Now, stumbling through the 10:30 Mass crowd milling around the back of Rytis Eparchy, exhaustion and rage fought for control of his body.

The homeless regulars clustered near the back doors, seeking warmth from the cold, damp morning. Frank's people. The ones he'd called "the forgotten children of God."

"Just move," Vince mumbled to himself as he shouldered through them. None of the compassion Frank had taught him survived the night. "For Christ's sake, can't you all just..."

An old woman wrapped in a stale, smelly wool scarf blocked his path, her face hidden beneath the worn fabric. She reached for his sleeve, but Vince jerked away. "Not now!"

The woman stumbled back, steadying herself against the wall. There was something in her eyes... but Vince didn't have the time to engage with even the sorriest of the forgotten. He was already pushing past her, his focus locked on the altar ahead where the monsignor's voice carried through the nave.

"...and let us pray for our beloved Father Frank, taken from us so tragically..."

Vince stopped in the center aisle, arms crossed over his chest. Parishioners turned. Whispers rippled through the pews like waves in the back bay. Some blessed themselves; others simply stared.

The monsignor's voice stammered as he looked up from his notes. For just a moment, something flashed behind those practiced eyes—fear, maybe. Or recognition.

"Vince." The monsignor's smile was pure performance. "This is hardly the time—"

"It's exactly the time." Vince started forward, each step vibrating against the marble floor. "You think you'll get away with it. I know everything now."

"My brothers and sisters," the monsignor addressed the congregation, his voice steady but his hands gripping the pulpit. "Our friend Vince is clearly distraught over Father Frank's passing. Perhaps we should—"

"Tell them." Vince's voice carried to the rafters high above. "Tell them how you use their confessions to extort them. How you work with the Russian mafia to launder money from this church."

Gasps echoed through the sanctuary.

"Vincent, please." The monsignor's smile tightened. "You're not well. Let's step into the north transept and—"

"Like Frank stepped into your confessional?" Vince was halfway up the aisle now. An usher stood up. Then quickly sat back down seeing the rage in his eyes. "Did he know about the recordings? Did he know about the orphanage in the Sakiai District?"

Vince turned to either side of the aisle, addressing the congregation. "This man changed his last name to avoid being arrested in Lithuania. He only entered the seminary to hide from the authorities there."

Vince was just a few feet from the base of the pulpit now, unable to contain the rage in his voice. "These people have a right to know the fucking psycho monster you really are!"

"Should someone call the police?" a voice called from the congregation.

Vince's laugh was harsh, the sound of it bounced off the stained glass windows. "They're already involved. They just don't know what they're looking for yet. But I do."

The monsignor raised his hands, a gesture of peace that looked more like surrender. "My friends, please continue with your prayers while I help our troubled—"

"You helped enough people, Augustas." Vince used the monsignor's first name like a weapon. "Frank figured it out, didn't he? That's why you had him killed. That's why you sent Etoile."

The monsignor's expression changed. Just for a moment, but long enough for the front row to be able see something dark in his face.

"Why Frank?" Vince's voice broke. "Of all people... why him?"

The monsignor pressed his hands together in a sign of prayer to the congregation, then stepped off the chancel toward the north transept. Vince was right behind him. "You won't get away with it... I won't let you!"

As the exchange between the two men continued, a call was made from someone in the congregation. "Nine-one-one, what is your emergency?"

"Threats in Mass at Rytis Eparchy of the Sea Church. Two men. One man talks of ... murder."

"Can you describe the men?"

"One is monsignor... Hurry."

"Are there any weapons? Hello? Hello, are you still there?"

When they reached the back of the transept, the monsignor turned to face Vince. "Vincentas, I can no longer allow you to violate the sanctity of this sacred place. I know you are hurting, my son—"

Vince started to breathe heavily. He took a boxer's stance, made a fist, and cocked it tight against the side of his chest. "I told you once before, don't ever call me your son."

A man's voice yelled from the middle of the church. "Vince!"

Vince turned in the direction of the voice. He couldn't make out the face, but there was no mistaking the uniform—it was Atlantic City PD.

"Vince, it's Burns. Come over here. Don't make a bad thing worse."

Vince brought his eyes back on the monsignor. "Burnsy, stay out of this. This is between me and this piece of shit."

"I can't, Vince. I'm here on business. I was right around the corner. Please. Don't make this worse for either of us."

Joey Burns. He and Vince bunked together at the academy. Joey helped Vince study for the final written test and saved his ass more than once during inspections. He also saved him, literally, through the department's employee assistance program—getting him into treatment when others wanted to give up on him.

"You don't understand, Burnsy."

"Vince, it's not worth it. Come over here so we can talk this out."

Vince wanted so badly to rip the monsignor's head off, to beat the living crap out of him. But if he did that, Joey Burns would have to do what Joey Burns took an oath to do—to serve and protect the citizens of Atlantic City. Vince couldn't do that to him.

"You're lucky he walked in when he did," Vince said to the monsignor, looking deep into his eyes.

Vince left the monsignor where he was and met Burnsy just to the side of the altar. Vince didn't recognize his new partner, who was told to stay with Vince while Burnsy spoke with the monsignor.

Vince looked over his shoulder. He didn't know how many people were in church for that service, but he knew how many people were staring at him. All of them.

Standing naked in front of strangers in a dream is one thing. Standing in front of a church congregation who had come together to collectively grieve a loss made Vince feel more vulnerable than he thought was possible.

He didn't know where to look. In order to look away from the parishioners in the pews, he had to face the altar. The altar at this church made him feel more shameful than looking back at the people who were now grieving, confused... and probably scared. All because of him.

The best worst choice for Vince was to look down at the floor until his academy roommate returned from speaking with the monsignor. Frank would be disgusted by his behavior.

Frank... Father Frank. How lucky Vince was to have been able to call this gentle soul his friend.

"Vince..." Burnsy's voice interrupted his thoughts for the second time in less than five minutes. "The monsignor said he doesn't want to press charges."

"That's a relief... I guess."

"But it comes with a price," Burnsy continued.

"Of course it does."

"He won't press charges as long as you are trespassed from the property. You can't come back here, Vince."

Vince looked over at the confessional booth along the side wall. "Not a problem."

"Good. You know we have to make this formal. Let's go."

Burnsy led Vince to the monsignor. "Go ahead, Father."

"You are no longer welcome on this property," the monsignor said with a smirk that Vince wanted to wipe off his face with a solid right hook. "You may not return here. If you do, you will be arrested."

As they escorted him out of the church, back up the same aisle he entered, Vince turned one last time, looking over his shoulder at the altar. Monsignor Augustas—a smug, evil grin. Vince felt every eye on him.

But one set of eyes was different, not as judgmental, maybe... but shame and rage had blinded him to everything except his own pain. He wouldn't remember those eyes until later, when everything would change.

Outside, the raw January rain cut through his clothes, but Vince barely felt it. Behind him stood the church where he'd been baptized, where he'd served as an altar boy, where he and Frank had shared so many conversations after Mass. Now he was officially an outsider—banned by the man who'd killed his best friend, removed by his own department, watched by faces that used to smile and welcome him.

Hearing Burnsy's squad car pull away, Vince thought about all he had lost. He'd lost his friend, probably his badge, and now his dignity. All he had left was a dead priest's journal and a drive home to a house with a memory-stained driveway. The driveway where, just hours ago, he'd found Frank. The same driveway he'd have to face again and again until something broke inside him or something finally made sense.

CHAPTER 65
PUDDLES AND REFLECTIONS

Vince's tires crunched on the wet gravel as he pulled into his driveway. He turned off the engine but didn't move, watching rain streak down the windshield, distorting what had been, up until yesterday, a welcome feeling of being home.

Echo's barking penetrated the din of the rain bouncing off the Jeep's canvas top. She'd recognize the sound of his Jeep in every type of weather. The longer Vince sat there, the more excited her barks became, then increasingly urgent as he remained still in the driver's seat.

"I'm sorry, girl," he whispered into the emptiness that surrounded him. "Just... give me a minute."

But Echo's desperate cries continued, each one sounding like another accusation. She had been alone too long already—last night during his interrogation at the station and now through his disaster at the church. Her unconditional love was more than he could face right now. He'd feel like a fraud if he were to experience her loyalty and trust now... when he had failed both so completely.

The rain intensified, sounding like scattered gunfire drumming off the soft top of the Jeep. A small trickle made its way down the inside door jamb that hadn't shut tight in years. Vince sighed, remembering when he left the house without his jacket, not interested in any type of warmth or protection from the weather.

His clothes were still damp from the church and clung to his skin as he stepped out into the frigid downpour. "Not yet," he called toward the house, his voice raw. Instead of heading for the door, he walked to the spot where he found Frank's car. A car that his best friend fought like hell in while he dozed in his recliner.

Inside, the journal waited on the counter, finally safe after hiding it from the investigators in his jacket the night before. Soon he'd have to read it. He had to know what it was that cost his friend his life. But first, he needed to face this spot, this moment, this reality.

The rain collected in depressions across his driveway, each puddle a warped mirror showing fragments of clouds, trees, and his own broken reflection. How appropriate that so much of what he saw when he looked at his reflection in the puddles was distorted, just like all the things he once thought to be true. Especially righteousness, justice, and truth.

Each puddle was like a piece of a truth he couldn't quite piece together. The tow trucks that were in his driveway the night before carved deep ruts with their large tires. Vince couldn't distinguish which set was from the one that delivered Frank's car from the police wrecker that towed it away.

Murky water had now collected in the ruts. Evidence of a story written with sharp, dirty rocks.

He could smooth them over. He could rake fresh stone across these scars until his driveway looked normal again. But wouldn't that make him just like everyone else—covering up ugly truths to make things look more acceptable? The monsignor would love that, wouldn't he? Everyone pretending nothing had happened here.

No. Frank deserved better than smoothed-over evidence.

Echo's cries at the window grew to pleading whimpers. Vince barely heard them while he traced one of the ruts with his shoe, watching dirty water seep into his footprint. How many times had Frank's car sat in this exact spot while the two of them shared stories inside?

The puddles deepened as the downpour intensified, ripples warping everything they reflected. Like his memory of last night—crystal clear in some moments, yet so frighteningly blurry in others. The tow truck pulling away. The door handle so cold in his grip. Frank's eyes...

Vince's legs finally gave out. Wet gravel soaked through his pants as jagged gravel dug into his knees. He looked up to see Echo pressing herself against the window, her worried whimpers barely discernible through the pounding rain. He couldn't hide out here forever, he couldn't keep staring at these wounds in his driveway hoping they'd somehow make sense.

The journal was inside. It toyed with him, teased him to open it to see what it revealed. Enough so that it convinced Vince that maybe inside it, in Frank's own words, he'd find the answers that these mud-filled puddles couldn't give him.

Once in the house, Echo pressed against his legs as he stripped off his soaked shirt. The journal, still on the kitchen counter where he left it before heading for the church, its leather binding tempting him. Inside were Frank's private thoughts. His secrets. His confessions.

"What would you do, girl?" Vince asked Echo, scratching behind her ears. She leaned into his touch, forgiving him for making her wait. If only forgiveness was that simple for what he was about to do.

The journal's pages had dried stiff, wrinkled from last night's moisture. Vince's hands started and stopped, then started again as he opened it, like a thief unsure of himself, waiting for the right moment—the way Frank would have described Judas. But Frank had tried to tell him something last night. He left Vince a voicemail he never got a chance to listen to. Instead, it was deleted in a mindless, frenzied cleanse of his phone after he left the police station. What if somewhere in these pages was the same message?

A photograph dropped from between the pages. It was Frank standing next to Vince at his one-year sobriety celebration. Frank's neat Catholic-school handwriting on the back: "The strongest man I know. The best friend I've ever had."

Vince didn't recall this photo being taken, but he couldn't mistake the setting—on the boardwalk in front of their favorite coffee shop. Frank's face was so vibrant and full of life, his smile wide and, oh, so natural. His eyes... pride beaming out of them into the face of whoever snapped this picture.

The contrast between the Frank in this photo and the image of him from last night, now permanently etched in his mind, was too much. Vince's breath became shallow and labored as the walls of the kitchen began to close in around him. The air in the room that had been so easy to breathe in became thick, almost nonexistent. It wasn't just breathing air in. Vince had to push hard to exhale as well.

The walls closed in like the inside of a car at night, like the confines where Frank had spent his final moments. Vince couldn't breathe, couldn't think, couldn't...

The only escape was the front door. Vince ran. He raced shirtless out the door and into the freezing rain. Ignoring the cold, he focused on his breathing. At least out here no walls were caving in on him.

Is this what one feels like?

His hands started to tingle, another sensation he'd dismissed when Audrey described her attacks. "Just breathe through it," he'd told her. As if it were that simple.

Through the years, especially more recently, Audrey had tried to explain to Vince what her panic attacks felt like. Always in a dismissive tone, he would tell her if they started, all she needed to do was become mindful of her surroundings, focus on her breath, and they would go away. She would be fine. *You're so dramatic, Audrey. We get it; you need the attention!*

As the seconds turned to minutes, Vince's breathing became easier. Maybe it was the shock of the cold air or the cold water. Maybe it was just time that gave him a chance to focus on his breathing. He also focused on words that came out of his mouth that lacked compassion and empathy.

It wasn't about sucking it up or simply being strong. More shame poured into Vince's already shame-filled system. The shame from the way he treated Audrey numbed him, flooding his system and adding to the puddles at his feet.

Yet even this amount of shame could not stop him. He made his way up the steps and through his front door. Standing over the counter, water dripping off his chiseled naked torso, he continued to flip through the journal.

Vince's heart sank as he turned to the last entry dated the day before—the day Frank was murdered: "I failed him. All these years of listening to confessions and offering guidance, and I can't even tell my best friend the truth. That his strength inspired me when my own faith wavered. That his sobriety helped me believe in redemption again. I fear Augustas knows what I've discovered, and I fear what's coming. If anything happens to me, I pray Vince stays strong. The drink isn't the answer; it never was. But God help me, I understand the temptation now more than ever."

The words disappeared as Vince slammed the journal shut. Frank had been worried about him until the very end. Had been protecting him while carrying his own doubts. And how had Vince repaid that faith? By sleeping through his friend's final call. By disrupting his congregation. By standing in the rain feeling sorry for himself.

He couldn't do this anymore. He couldn't bear the weight of Frank's private struggles on top of everything else. The journal seemed to have a pulse now, like a heart beating outside the human chest. He should have left it sealed. He should have preserved Frank's privacy the way he'd intended when he took it from the car.

But now he couldn't unsee those words, and he couldn't unknow Frank's doubts. He couldn't erase that photograph or the message or the last journal entry that showed how much faith Frank had in him. Faith he'd just betrayed by reading these pages.

Another choice he couldn't take back. Another betrayal to add to his growing list.

The shame of his panic attack, of finally understanding what Audrey had tried to tell him all these years, settled into his bones alongside his grief. He needed something to wash away both the shame and the loss. Something stronger than rain.

Echo whined softly, pushing her head under his hand. But for the first time since he got sober, this type of comfort wasn't enough. He needed something stronger. Something like a fresh promise from an old friend. Something to dull the edges of this knife twisting in his chest where his beating heart reminded him... just for today.

The bar on Pacific Avenue would be open by now.

CHAPTER 66

FIVE MINUTES

The neon Budweiser sign in Murphy's Slam Dunk Bar window reflected a dim red glow across the wet sidewalk. Guys in the patrol division refer to this shithole as Murphy's Slam *Drunk* Bar—a reference to the number of intoxicated patrons regularly stumbling out the door.

The guys in the traffic unit call it the same name, but for a different reason—if you need a DUI arrest, all you have to do is drive past Murphy's three times a shift. In one of those three passes, you'll get a drunk getting into his car. They call it *batting three hundred* and joke that those stops will get you inducted into the DUI Hall of Fame.

Vince had walked past this dive a thousand times, each time counting days, then months, then finally years of sobriety. This afternoon, he was counting reasons to go inside.

Frank's dead. Reason One.

I failed him. Reason Two.

I can't pray anymore. Reason Three.

Everything I believed was a lie. Reason Four.

On his way there, Vince convinced himself he'd use the "three strikes and you're out" metaphor. He told himself that if he could come up with three reasons, he'd go inside. Just to see what might happen. And that if there were more than three reasons, then whatever happened really wasn't his responsibility. It would be fate. And that was all the justification he would need.

Oh, the lies we tell ourselves when the pain is too much to bear.

The familiar smell hit him as soon as he opened the door—stale beer, urine, and broken promises. Three people huddled at the bar looked up, then quickly away. Day drinkers. He used to be good at that too.

"What's your poison?" the bartender asked. Vince laughed at the accuracy of the word and took a stool at the end of the bar.

"Four shots of Jack." The voice his ears processed was strange, like a recording of someone he used to know. "Line 'em up."

The bartender's eyes flickered—recognition, maybe, or just his professional assessment of another man about to fall. Bottles clinked as he pulled a fifth of Old Number 7 Sour Mash off the shelf, each sound an echo of another step down a path Vince thought he'd left behind forever.

Four shots.

One shot for his dad. One shot for Audrey. One for Carmen. And the last one... for Frank.

The first shot glass hit the sticky surface of the stained wooden bar. Then the second. The third... And the fourth—Frank's.

Vince inhaled deeply, hoping to savor a hint of the aroma of the amber liquid that was his first best friend before he met Frank. In the dim light of this slam-drunk bar, Vince began the mental gymnastics required to believe *this time* it would keep its promises.

Like the way his hands started and stopped before finally opening the journal, Vince's hand shook as he reached for the shot closest to him. How many times had Frank steadied that same hand? How many meetings had they attended together? The shot glass felt warm against his palm, familiar as an old friend's handshake.

"Just for today," he whispered, twisting the daily meditation into permission rather than restraint.

His arm tensed to lift the glass, his muscles remembering a motion they hadn't forgotten in all these years.

"First one is always hardest."

The hacking smoker's cough. The gravelly voice with that distinct accent. The stale cigarette smell that had given him migraines. Vince's hand froze in mid-air. The shot glass floating above the bar top like a cheap magic trick. Except this time, the amateur magician had just been exposed.

"Evelina?" He turned, shocked to find her standing there. The woman wearing the wool scarf from church... But how? She had now pulled it down to reveal that weathered face he had spent days with in Lithuania. "What are you... how are you even here?"

She coughed again, a sound that carried memories of long conversations they shared not that long ago. "Or maybe," she continued as if he hadn't spoken, "is hardest because right thing to do is hard."

"You followed me from the church!" It wasn't a question. He should have recognized her eyes earlier, should have known despite the disguise. His detective instincts really were shot to hell.

"Is not important how I am here, Vincentas. Is only important that I am."

"To do what? Watch me throw away years of sobriety?" He dropped the shot glass down on the bar top. "You want a show, is that what you want?"

"Vincentas, you still ask too many questions... wrong questions. Questions that do not lead you anywhere."

"More of this shit," Vince muttered to himself.

"You mean, more of this sudas, Vincentas," Evelina replied.

Vince shrugged his shoulder. "What the hell is that supposed to mean?"

"Sudas is shit in Lithuanian." If she thought her smile would penetrate the wall he had put up, she was wrong.

"Look, I appreciate what you're trying to do... but it's too late. I'm already committed to my date here—my date with these four fine ladies," Vince said, pointing to the shot glasses.

"I am not here to interrupt date, Vincentas. I am here to give you information. Important information. Information that, if it is given after first drink, will be too late."

Vince looked down at the quartet of temptation lined up in front of him. "What information do you have that could even possibly help me now?"

"Not here," she said, looking over at one of the other patrons nodding off on his stool. She nodded toward a corner booth.

Vince scanned the darkened room. A corner booth—the top of the back of a head barely visible above the seatback. "Who's that?"

"Yes, Vincentas. Your detective sense is still good. It would not be good after first drink. There is someone else here... Someone who believes in you, as Father Frank did. Come, now," she said, gently touching the back of Vince's shoulder.

The mention of Frank's name should have driven him straight back to the shots. But something stirred inside him...

Instead, Vince found himself following Evelina through the bar's dim light, her cigarette odor a familiar guide. As they approached the booth, the figure seated there turned.

Carmen.

Just when he thought his shame tank was completely full, more potent—the most potent shame he could have ever imagined—poured in. It couldn't be measured in shots, pints, or fifths. This shame poured into him by the liter and by the full handle.

The way it used to...

His first instinct was to run. Back to the bar. Back to the familiar comfort of his old friend, Jack. But Carmen's eyes held no judgment, only concern. The same look in Frank's eyes the last time they enjoyed coffee together. Yesterday.

"Five minutes, Vincentas. Only five minutes, and then you can make decision that is best for you. Okay?" Evelina said, sliding into the booth. "If you still want to drink, drinks will wait. They always do." Another cough. "Trust me, Vincentas. Like you did in Lithuania."

"I was different in Lithuania," Vince said, as he slid into the booth next to her. "I wasn't filled with so much…"

"So much shame, Vincentas?" Evelina said softly.

Vince looked at her. Once again in awe of her mind reading ability. *How can a woman like this possess so much mystical wisdom?*

"But shame is like vodka—it only has the power we give it."

Carmen reached across the table, not quite touching his hand. "We can help, Vince. But you have to trust us."

Vince's eyes drifted back to the bar, to those four shots begging for his attention. Waiting. Patient. Faithful… Everything he wasn't feeling right now.

"Trust?" He laughed, shaking his head. "I trusted Frank, and now he's dead. I trusted the monsignor, and he's a fraud. I trusted myself and look where that got me."

"Will you trust this, Vincentas?" Evelina asked, pulling something from her bag. "You gave to me in Lithuania, remember? It was extra one you brought. You said you could not solve."

Vince stared at the Rubik's Cube, its colors a jumbled mess like his life. "What's your point?"

"Sometimes solution is not in focusing at one side only." She turned the cube, showing its chaos of colors. "Sometimes we need different eyes to see pattern."

"I don't need riddles right now," Vince said, starting to rise. "I need—"

"You need to listen," Carmen cut in. "Because what she's about to tell you will change everything."

The certainty in Carmen's voice froze him. Not quite sitting, not quite standing. He looked between the two women—Carmen's determined face, Evelina's knowing smile. Something had passed between them, some shared understanding he couldn't grasp.

"Five minutes," he said finally, sinking back into the booth. "Then those shots and I have a date to keep."

Evelina's smile widened. "Five minutes, Vincentas... it is said five minutes is all Rook needs."

CHAPTER 67

THE FINAL PLAYER

"I think it will work, Vince." Carmen's fingers traced the edge of her coffee mug.

"What will work?"

"Evelina's plan," Carmen said. "The one she told me about while we were waiting for you."

"Waiting for—" Vince's detective instincts finally kicked in. "You two planned this?"

"This was not in plan, Vincentas. Plan was changed because of how you acted in church. I had to make new plan. Calling police was not part of plan, but I had to stop you."

"Wait. What?" Vince threw himself against the seatback. "It was you? You're the one who called..."

"Vince," Carmen said, reaching for his arm, but he pulled it away. "There was a good reason. Let her finish."

"I don't fucking believe this."

"Believe it, Vincentas. It is true. If I did not stop you from telling every person in church what you knew, plan would be ruined. Board would be knocked over with your words. Pieces would fall to ground. Final result would be draw, not checkmate."

"A fucking game. Is that all this is to you?"

Carmen spoke up before Evelina could respond. "Vince, she called to save you from yourself. Yes, from the way she explained it, it is a game, her game. But just listen to how she plans on ending it. Vince, I know it will work. If you give it a chance."

Vince looked over at the bar. The shots were just where he left them. He looked back at Carmen. "Because of her, I was banned from my former church... by my former department. And you want me to give her a chance?"

"Yes, Vince, I do."

Vince looked over at Evelina. She was focused on the cube. He watched her hands working the Rubik's Cube, her weathered fingers moving with surprising grace. Each turn revealed new patterns, new possibilities.

"See here, Vincentas? When you focus only one side..." She showed him the solid blue face he'd managed before. "You miss pattern forming on other sides." She made a series of quick turns. "Sometimes solution requires seeing whole picture."

Vince's eyes grew wide. "How did you do that? How did you solve it that quickly?"

"Vincentas. You forget what I told you. You look at cube and ask, 'How do I solve this?'" She held the completed cube up in her palm, studying it herself. "You must look at completed cube and ask, 'How did this get solved?' It is question to answer, Vincentas. You must not forget again."

Vince reached his hand out for the cube. Evelina acknowledged his silent request and placed it in his hand.

"Okay, you got my attention. But I won't agree to listen to anything until you tell me how you did this."

"Watch videos on internet, Vincentas. Many videos show technique to solve cube. Once technique is learned, practice. But first, Vincentas must be willing to accept help from people who know what to do. Experts on internet share secrets to solve cube. You must let go of pride, Vincentas."

Vince stared at the cube, every side a different color, and all the sides were completed. The cube that had frustrated him for years was just solved right in front of his eyes.

"I think I understand, Evelina." He then turned to Carmen. "I-I understand."

"Vincentas, you must also stop seeing only one side of cube. Like life, cube has different sides. No longer focus on just one. Yes?"

Vince looked back at the bar top. He had only been focused on one side of things since Frank's murder. He had focused all his energy on just one side when there were many other sides he didn't even consider. Sides he refused to see because he was too absorbed in guilt. Too focused on anger. He couldn't see any other side simply because he wasn't looking.

Vince motioned for the bartender. "Barkeep! Those shots are for the three men over there," he said, pointing to the men at the bar. "The fourth shot is my gift to you. Can I get a cup of coffee? And a refill for my..."

He was unsure what to call Carmen. Who was she in his life?

He didn't have to wait long for an answer. "For his girlfriend," Carmen said with a bright smile.

"Vincentas, Carmen is good for you. This part was not planned. I am happy for you." Evelina looked across the table at Carmen. "I told Carmen I am happy for her. She knows how important her role is in plan."

"Her role?"

"Yes, Vincentas. Carmen has role. She is from law school, yes? Plan needs legal advice that is good."

"Legal advice?"

Carmen let out a soft chuckle. "Okay, so I haven't sat for the bar yet, but you said it yourself, you don't know anyone with more legal knowledge than me."

"Sure, but why do we need legal advice?" He looked back and forth at them. "I mean, I'm sure we're all gonna need it after this is over, but why now?"

"The plan is good, Vince," Carmen said. "It's going to take some work, but it'll be effective."

Evelina laid it out, each point like another turn of the cube. Vince listened, his frown deepening.

"It'll never work," he said finally. "Too many moving parts. Too many people who'd have to cooperate. The monsignor's too protected, too connected."

"Like cube seems impossible at first?" Evelina asked.

"This isn't a puzzle, Evelina. This is –"

"Is exactly like puzzle. Must see all sides. Must know which piece to move first."

"And you think you can coordinate all that? Make all those pieces move together?"

Evelina shifted in the booth. "Like cube, Vincentas, game has many sides. Monsignor sees only his side. Police see only theirs. But Rook... Rook sees all sides."

"The Rook." Vince set down the cube. "How do you expect to work around someone that powerful?"

Evelina's weathered face cracked into a smile. "Who says we work around?"

"Everyone knows about the Rook. Dad mentioned him. Frank wrote about him in his journal. This mysterious guy who can make things happen on both sides of the law. Who has connections everywhere." Vince shook his head. "The Rook's not going to let your plan work."

"Ah, Vincentas..." Evelina picked up the cube again, turning it slowly. "In chess, what piece moves from corner to corner, changing whole game?"

"The Rook, but—" An understanding dawned. He stared at the old woman across from him, seeing her—really seeing her—for the first time. The network of connections. The influence in Lithuania. The way doors opened wherever she went.

Carmen squeezed his hand. "I had the same reaction when she told me."

"Impossible," Vince whispered. "Everyone thinks the Rook is…"

"Is what, Vincentas? Strong man? Important man?" Evelina's eyes sparkled. "Perhaps most powerful pieces not always what they seem. Perhaps little old woman who smell like cigarettes can move across board without being noticed. Can see all sides because no one thinks to hide them from her."

Vince sat back, memories realigning themselves. "The diplomat's son—you made sure I learned about his murder. And Frank's journal… you knew I'd read it. Every time we needed information, it just seemed to appear…" He shook his head in wonder. "You've been orchestrating this whole thing from the beginning."

"Pieces that must move certain way to win game." Evelina set down the solved cube. "Now you understand why plan will work? Because Rook has been moving pieces long before you saw board."

Vince looked at Carmen. She smiled. Then nodded.

Before either of them could say anything, Evelina spoke up. "Why here, Vincentas?" Evelina's eyes swept the grimy bar. "Many nice places in Atlantic City. Why choose this… sudas?"

Vince's laugh was hollow. "That's exactly why. Because it's shit." He gestured at their surroundings. "When I was drinking, I figured if I was going to be a drunk, I should drink where drunks belong. Nice places were for people who deserved them."

"And now?" Carmen asked softly. "Why choose here today?"

"Old habits." Vince stared at the amber liquid in untouched shots, remembering. "Last time I was here, Burnsy found me stumbling to my car. Probably saved my life. Definitely saved me from a DUI arrest." He shook his head. "Dragged me straight to treatment. Didn't give me a choice."

"Like we not give you choice today?" Evelina's smile was gentle.

"I always thought it was simple," Vince said. "You're either drunk or you're sober. A good cop or a bad one. A victim or a perp. But…"

"But life has many sides." Carmen reached for his hand. "Like that cube. Like being in recovery. Maybe it's not about being perfect. Maybe it's about accepting help when you need it."

Vince's gaze was fixed on nothing. Nothing but nothingness in his eyes. Except for tears that filled those eyes and ran down his cheeks.

"Vince, what if it's about living in that space between certainties?" Carmen asked, squeezing his hand.

"Just for today," Vince whispered.

Carmen glanced at her watch. "Speaking of today, Vince Brown, there's a meeting starting in forty minutes at the Mays Landing rec center. And we are going with you."

"We?"

"Vincentas, do you think Rook lets important pieces move alone?" Evelina was already standing, adjusting her scarf. "We go together, yes?"

The bartender noticed them standing up to leave. "Everything okay?"

"No," Vince said honestly. "But maybe that's okay too."

He followed Carmen and Evelina toward the door, then paused. The four shot glasses still sat on the bar, untouched, catching the dim light. Four perfect circles of amber temptation.

"Leave them," Carmen said softly. "I doubt that you want them."

"Like puzzle solution on internet," Evelina added. "Is about choosing different path, yes?"

Vince nodded, thinking of Frank's last journal entry. About understanding temptation. About staying strong.

Outside, the rain had finally stopped. Carmen's car waited in the lot, but Evelina headed for her own vehicle.

"You're really coming?" Vince asked. "Both of you?"

"Rook sees all sides, remember?" Evelina's eyes crinkled above her scarf. "Including this one."

"Besides," Carmen said, taking his hand, "I hear these meetings always have decent coffee."

Vince squeezed her hand, feeling the solved Rubik's Cube in his pocket. One step at a time. One side leading to another.

Just for today.

PART 4

CHAPTER 68
DIGITAL MOVES

Vince's laptop screen threw a blue glow across Carmen's dining room table, the cursor blinking in his empty inbox. He refreshed it again, wondering if he was doing the right thing by following Evelina's vague instructions.

"Stop checking it every thirty seconds," Carmen said, setting two mugs of coffee on the table. "You'll know when it comes."

"Yeah?" Vince reached for his mug. "How exactly will I know?"

"Because Evelina said you would." Carmen settled into the chair beside him, close enough that their shoulders touched. "You trust her now, remember?"

"I trust that she's the Rook." Vince took a sip of coffee and tasted the memory of Murphy's Bar. Just two days ago, he'd nearly thrown away everything.

Vince looked back at his computer. If watching a pot on the stove doesn't make water boil faster, then why stare at a laptop screen? He couldn't find an answer that made sense. Yet, he kept staring. "But this plan... there are so many ways it could go wrong."

"Like what?" Carmen's tone was the same one she uses in interrogations—gentle but persistent.

"Oh, I dunno…" Vince started. "Like the fact that we're counting on hackers we've never met. Or that we're assuming Lithuanian authorities will actually do something with the evidence. Or that—"

A quiet chime from his laptop cut him off.

New message from Microsoft Service Updates.

"Speaking of hackers…" Carmen leaned forward. "Remember what Evelina said—just open the attachment. Nothing else."

Vince's cursor hovered over the file. The email looked legitimate, complete with Microsoft's logo and correct formatting. If he hadn't known better, he would have assumed it was a routine terms of service update.

"Once I do this," he said, taking a deep breath, "there's no going back."

"Vince, there's been no going back since Frank was killed," she said, reaching for his hand under the table.

Frank. His journal still fresh in Vince's mind. Still there, as if pressing against his chest inside his jacket pocket. "You're right." He clicked the attachment. A progress bar appeared as the file began downloading. "Now what?"

"Now we wait." Carmen pulled a legal pad from her bag. "And while we wait, we start planning. The department can't know I'm involved—not after Huertas put me on leave. But I can help you build the framework."

"Framework for what?"

"For when this evidence lands in the right hands." She uncapped her pen. "I may be banned from the department's computers, but I know how this kind of investigation needs to be structured. Every 'i' that needs to be dotted, every 't' that needs to be crossed."

They worked side by side in a relaxed silence, broken only by the scratch of Carmen's pen and the occasional ping from Vince's phone. Text messages from Audrey asking about Frank's funeral arrangements. A missed call from his dad.

"You should probably call your dad," Carmen said after the third notification.

"Yeah." Vince stared at his phone. "But what do I tell him? 'Hey Dad, remember that Lithuanian woman who helped save my life? Turns out she's an international power player who's about to help us take down the monsignor, a murderer... and the Russian mafia using illegal confessional recordings?'"

"How about just 'I'm okay' for now?" Carmen's smile was reassuring. "He's probably worried."

Vince nodded, but before he could make the call, his laptop chimed again. The screen flickered, then went black. "Carmen..." His heart raced. "Is this supposed to happen?"

The screen came back to life, but now a small icon pulsed in the corner. It was a chess piece—a rook.

"I'd say that's our signal." Carmen turned to a fresh page in her legal pad. "Now comes the hard part. We need to map out exactly how this evidence is to be handled once it surfaces. I'm sure Lithuania has the same kind of chain of custody requirements. And then, there are the jurisdictional issues, international law..."

"You've been thinking about this."

"Let's just say I've had time since Huertas benched me." She tapped her pen against the paper. "I may not be able to make the calls or run the operation, but I can make damn sure whoever does has a blueprint to follow."

"How will you know?"

"I called a friend at the FBI and gave him a tip. He was shocked that I knew anything about the case."

"What case?"

"The son of the Lithuanian diplomat. They've been working on it around the clock with HSI but haven't had a solid lead."

"So you—"

"Until I called... He promised to sit on it until the FBI was contacted by Lithuanian agencies. Dan said a tip coming from someone near where the murder occurred that corroborates whatever Lithuanian law enforcement tells them will make this a slam-dunk case."

"Vince, I'm sorry. I shouldn't have used that…"

"That's in my past now." Vince laughed. "My very recent past. But at least you didn't say, slam-drunk case!'"

Carmen's laugh joined Vince's as they embraced each other. Vince looked softly into Carmen's eyes. "So, who's Dan?

Carmen's laugh became louder. "Vince Brown, do I sense a hint of jealousy?"

Was his question too obvious? It just came out. It was like his mouth went into gear before his brain did. Then his mouth continued without the consent of his brain. "Umm… Uh. No… I mean, I-I was just—"

"You are so cute, you know that? And your insecurities make you absolutely adorable."

"No, no… I was wondering, that's all."

"Yeah, right," she said smiling, reaching down for her mug of coffee. "Well, since you've been completely honest, especially with yourself, I guess you can handle the truth from me."

Vince's heart raced. Was Dan a former lover? Even worse, a current lover?!

"Dan Perez. He's the assistant director for the FBI's National Security Branch."

"That's pretty high up in the FBI, isn't it? How do you know him?"

"I got the DB under me as soon as I made lieutenant. One of the first classes the department sent me to was an anti-terrorist class down in Quantico. Dan was the instructor. At the end of the class, that Friday, he asked me if I wanted to go to dinner with him. And…"

Vince's heart raced faster. *Please don't tell me…*

Carmen continued. "I went. But only because I wasn't driving back until Saturday morning. So, we had dinner, and he started to hit on me. I—"

"How good-looking is he?"

"Would you stop and let me finish?"

Vince wasn't sure he wanted to know how it finished.

"At the end of the night, he gave me his business card and said if I ever needed anything, he'd be glad to help. We've stayed in touch since then."

"What about what happened between dinner and the end of the night?" His mouth was still outpacing his brain.

"Mainly me dancing..."

"Dancing?!"

Carmen smiled a mischievous grin. "Yeah, dancing around his advances, dancing around his innuendos, and dancing around his stupid jokes."

"Oh, that kind of dancing." Vince did nothing to hide the sense of relief in his voice.

"You are really something, you know that?"

"So... how good-looking is he?"

Carmen moved her arms from his shoulders to the sides of his face. "He's no Vince Brown, I can tell you that," she said as she kissed him gently on the cheek. "Now that the insecure Vince is gone, can we get back to work?"

Vince thought of Frank's last journal entry about having faith in him. About staying strong. He looked at the rook icon pulsing on his screen. "The department's loss is my gain. I can't imagine anyone else planning this but you."

"Good." Carmen sketched out a timeline. "Because we've got about twenty-four hours before all hell breaks loose, and we need to make every minute count."

"Do you really think she has those kinds of connections with social media propagandists?" Vince asked.

"I can't think of any reasons not to... she's connected with everyone else in Lithuania and Russia."

Vince looked down at his watch. "Christ, if it goes as viral as she says it will, Augustas will be safer behind bars than walking the street."

"Or in his confessional."

The rook icon seemed to pulse faster, as if acknowledging the count-down had begun. Vince watched Carmen work, her legal training evident in every precise note she made.

Maybe that's what being a team is really about—recognizing that sometimes being sidelined from one role lets you excel in another. A role you were meant to fulfill.

CHAPTER 69

THE ROOK'S CHAMBER

The small room at the Tides End Motel smelled of stale cigarettes and real-life nightmares. Evelina sat cross-legged on the bed, her laptop balanced on her knees while her weathered fingers moved across the keyboard with practiced precision. On the nightstand, next to packs of her cigarettes, a small magnetic chessboard was set up mid-game—the pieces frozen in an Arabian mate configuration she'd been perfecting for decades.

Three screens glowed in the dim light offered by the bed lamp with a broken shade hanging off. Her laptop was on her knees, her phone on the nightstand, and a tablet propped against a pillow. Each device represented a different piece moving across her board: the hackers in Lithuania, the social media propagandists in Russia, and the authorities who didn't yet know their role in her endgame.

A coughing fit seized her, and she reached for the glass of water beside her bed. The doctors in Vilnius had been clear—six months, at most. But they didn't understand that time had always been her enemy, even before the diagnosis. Time had taken the innocence from her, had let Augustas build his empire of lies... had allowed evil men to hide behind sacred walls.

She'd spent nearly thirty years building this network. Three decades of being underestimated and overlooked... dismissed as just another street person who'd lost her way. But being invisible had its advantages. No one noticed the homeless woman who could speak five languages, who remembered every conversation, who collected secrets like others collected coins.

Her phone chimed. Confirmation from the hackers. The recordings were in their possession. She reached for her tablet, typing instructions to the social media team in Russia. Then to her laptop, where a draft email to Lithuanian authorities waited. Each message had to be as precisely timed as each recipient was carefully chosen.

She glanced at the worn photo taped to the corner of her laptop screen—herself in her apostolnik, the black veil she received as a young novice. She was so bright-eyed, standing outside the orphanage in Sakiai. Before Augustas. Before everything changed. The abbess of the Refuge of Divine Mercy had been the only one who saw past her facade, who recognized the mind behind the quiet servant's demeanor. "You're playing chess while everyone else is playing checkers," Reverend Mother had once told her.

Only one piece remained. She opened her messaging app, finding the thread marked simply "A."

Time grows short, monsinjoras. Game enters final phase.

She hit send, imagining Augustas's reaction when he read it. Would he see the threat? Or would his ego not allow him to recognize it? She remembered him at the orphanage, so sure of his power, so certain of his control. He never noticed how she watched him, how she remembered... how she planned.

The phone chimed again. A response from the hackers—they needed more specific instructions about timing. Through the smoke of her exhale, Evelina smiled as she saw the time. In a matter of hours, every piece would be in position. Unless...

Her eyes drifted to the chessboard. The knight stood ready to support the rook's final attack. But knights were unpredictable pieces, prone to unexpected moves. And Vince Brown had become nothing if not unpredictable.

Time passed in the small, dirty motel room. She reached for another cigarette, letting the familiar ritual calm her thoughts. The boy was so much like his father—strong, determined, righteous. But he didn't understand that some games required sacrifice. Some victories demanded payment in advance.

She drew in a deep inhale and opened her bottom drawer, pulling out a small wooden box. Inside lay a tarnished key on a frayed ribbon—the key to the orphanage's records room. The last physical link to where it all began. Soon it would be evidence, along with everything else she'd collected over the decades.

Another coughing fit struck, harder this time. She pressed a handkerchief to her mouth, trying to steady her breathing. When she pulled it away, spots of red stained the white fabric. *Not yet*, she thought. *Just a little longer*.

The notification of another message interrupted her concern. Lithuanian authorities acknowledging receipt of her information. Everything was in motion now. Soon, very soon, she would face Augustas across a very different kind of confessional. And this time, Augustas would be the one begging for absolution.

Her weathered fingers tapped the top of the rook on her chessboard, keeping time to a song in her head that only she knew. Thirty years of patience. Thirty years of moving pieces into position. She would not let anyone—not Vince, not Carmen, not even her own failing health—deny her this moment.

Check, she thought, hitting send on the final message. *Your move, Augustas*.

She closed her laptop, picked up the chessboard, and placed it carefully in her bag. The pieces didn't rattle—each one secured in its place, just as each player in her real-world game was positioned exactly where she needed them. Soon everything would change. Very soon... checkmate.

But tonight belonged to memory, to preparation, to the quiet satisfaction of knowing that every move, every sacrifice, every year of waiting had led to this moment. She touched the photo one last time.

"Watch now, Evelina," she whispered in Lithuanian. "Watch how the game ends."

CHAPTER 70
TIME AND TRUST

Vince's phone vibrated against Carmen's coffee table, dancing across the stack of legal papers they'd spent the morning organizing. The caller ID showed "private number." Only one person ever called him from a private number.

"Evelina?"

"Time to move final pieces, Vincentas." Her raspy voice was more urgent than usual. "Your father must make calls now."

Vince looked over at Carmen, who was scribbling more notes on her legal pad. Catching the change in Vince's posture, she put down her pen. He put the phone on speaker.

"What calls?" Even as he asked, he sensed something in her tone was different.

"To FBI, to Justice Department. He is district attorney. They will listen to him. He must arrange for me to be there to take Augustas."

"Be there?" Vince exchanged looks with Carmen. "Evelina, that's not possible. The FBI won't—"

"Is not question of possible." A wet cough interrupted the flow of her words. "Is required. Is nonnegotiable. I am Rook. Without me, game does not end."

"My dad can't make those calls," Vince said. "Not now. Not until next month. it's only a week… until the statute of limitations—"

"Statute of limitations?" Carmen whispered. "On what?"

"Seven years," Vince explained quickly. "It's been almost seven years since he last worked or did anything for the Russian mob. Once that time passes, he can't be charged."

Carmen's eyes grew wide. She shook her head and mouthed, "Really?!"

"I was gonna tell you," Vince whispered. "I was going to explain everything after—"

"After what? After we were all indicted?"

Vince brought his finger to his mouth. "Shh. Not now." His boyish smile did not do its job.

"Vince Brown, we are going to talk about this as soon as this call is over."

He nodded and turned back to the phone. "Evelina, you have to understand—"

"No, Vincentas. It is you who must understand. Thirty years I have waited. Thirty years I have moved pieces into position. I did not come to America to watch from shadows. I came to see his face when Augustas falls. I am here to knock him off his square."

"We can find another way," Carmen offered. "Maybe after the arrest—"

"There will be no arrest." Evelina's words fell like chess pieces knocked off a board. "Not unless I am there."

Vince's knuckles squeezed around the phone. "What do you mean?"

"Is simple, Vincentas. I am there to see Augustas… to take him, or I warn him. I give him time to disappear."

"Evelina, you wouldn't." As soon as he said it, Vince remembered her words in Murphy's Bar about sacrifice, about the price of victory.

"Try me, Vincentas."

Carmen stood up, pacing the small living room. "Everything Vince has worked for—the evidence, Frank's murder, all of it... you'd throw it away?"

The speaker in Vince's phone was silent.

"Evelina, did you hear me?" Carmen wasn't joking.

"You think this is game to me?" Evelina's voice snapped. "This is my life's work. My revenge. My justice." Another cough, deeper this time. "Vincentas, your father has connections. Has influence. Make him use them."

"I won't risk his freedom," Vince said. "Not even for this."

"Then you risk everything, Vincentas. Everything Carmen just spoke. I will call Augustas myself. Tell him what comes. By time authorities move, he will be gone."

The sound of Carmen's phone ringing broke the tension. She looked at the screen. "Vince, I have to take this!" she said excitedly, walking into the hallway.

Vince closed his eyes, remembering Frank's face in the car. Remembering the pain in his father's voice when he finally told Vince about his dealings with the Russian mafia.

"You're still playing games," he said quietly. "After everything... Frank's death, the recordings, my father's full disclosure of what he's been forced to do... you're still moving pieces around your board."

"Not game, Vincentas. Is chess match. In chess, every piece has purpose. Every move has consequence." Her voice softened slightly. "You are knight in this game. Strong piece, Vincentas, but you think only of next move. Rook thinks of endgame."

Vince couldn't quite hear what Carmen was saying in the hall, but her voice suggested that whatever it was, it wasn't good news.

"Vincentas, you pay attention to Evelina, yes?"

Carmen came back into the room. The look on her face...

"Vincentas. Vincentas, you hear Evelina?"

Carmen shook her head, motioning to Vince to tell Evelina to wait a minute.

"Evelina, I'm here. But there's a problem here, something personal." He was counting on her to buy that line. "Just give me a minute."

Carmen touched Vince's shoulder. "It was Dan... Dan Perez. He kept this word—told me he'd call me if anything developed." She closed her eyes. "If he had anything to tell me."

"Well?"

"The FBI doesn't have the lead on this one. Because it was a diplomat's son, HSI is the lead agency. FBI will be there in support only."

"HSI? Homeland Security?"

"Yep, direct order from the Justice Department. HSI is going to be running the show..."

Vince finished her thought, "If there is one."

Vince suddenly felt the weight of his phone in his hand again. "Evelina! Are you still there?"

"I am here, Vincentas. Are you... Is Carmen okay?

"Yeah. Yeah, we're good," Vince lied. "You were saying something about a game."

"It is not game, Vincentas. It is chess match with time running out."

"How long?" he asked finally.

"Vincentas, stop asking questions to gain only information. Ask questions to answers so you gain understanding. This is not threat as you think of threat... this is chess clock close to zero. Time remaining for your move is suppertime. Do not let clock run out, Vincentas. Make your move by suppertime. I will call you. Okay?"

The line went dead. Vince stared at the phone, then at Carmen. "She's really willing to blow this whole thing up."

He looked up to see understanding in her eyes, maybe even a grudging respect for Evelina's position. Carmen nodded slowly. "Because she knows she's right, Vince. She's earned this moment." She picked up her legal pad. "And maybe she's not the only one still playing games."

"What do you mean?"

"I mean, maybe it's time to stop thinking like a cop and start thinking like... I don't know."

"Like your boyfriend?" Vince joked, an obvious reference to how she identified herself to the bartender at Murphy's the other day.

"As long as that boyfriend knows how to play chess," she replied playfully.

Vince shared a smile before Carmen quickly changed her demeanor and tapped her pen against the pad. "There has to be another way... we need to find a way to give a dying woman her final move without sacrificing your father in the process." She smiled grimly.

"We're missing something. I can feel it," Vince said with resignation. "But I don't know where to start looking."

Carmen dropped her pen and pad on the table, brought her hands up, and rubbed both sides of the back of her head. She pressed deeper, moving her hands down to the back of her neck. She slid her hands down to each shoulder and crossed her arms across her chest to hug herself. Carmen glanced up at Vince, her neck open above her hands that were still crossed in front of her.

Vince looked at her bare neck, at the way her low-cut top showed off the area below both collarbones. Like a blank canvas that needed something to be hung there. He imagined what the necklace would look like there, the brilliant amber suspended from a thin, white gold chain.

The necklace she said she couldn't wear... she wouldn't wear until she was sure. The necklace Evelina shoved in his pocket before he was dumped out of the van in front of the U.S. embassy in Vilnius. The necklace he learned about only because the HSI agent told him he'd taken all of Vince's possessions when he woke up in the hospital there.

The necklace.

"The necklace!" Vince blurted out, startling Carmen.

"What necklace?"

"The necklace Evelina gave me in Lithuania. The necklace I gave you."

"Vince... I thought we weren't going to talk about this. I can't—"

"No, no, no. I'm not talking about you wearing it. I'm talking about how I found out about it."

"I'm listening."

Vince took out his wallet and dumped its contents on the table, frantically searching through credit cards, bits of torn paper, and business cards. "The HSI agent. In the hospital. Before I left, he said my kidnapping was a priority investigation." He touched his throat where the scar had formed. "He gave me his card and told me to call him if I remembered anything about the kidnapping, or if anything happened back here that might help the case."

He separated everything, moving the wallet's contents around like a dealer would wash a deck of cards in a casino. "C'mon, c'mon. It's gotta be in here."

Carmen looked on. There was nothing she could do but watch as Vince searched for a business card among a mix of stuff she wouldn't think of keeping.

Finally. Stuck to the back of his library card. "Yes!" Vince said confidently.

He held it up and showed it to Carmen:

Terrance Coleman
Senior Special Agent
Homeland Security Investigations
Eastern European Branch

Vince started for the balcony door, then paused, resting his hand on the handle. The last time he'd seen Frank alive, they'd sat in that coffee shop talking about truth, about doing the right thing even when it hurt. And his father... the weight of secrets had nearly destroyed him. Maybe the real price of justice is not what it costs to tell the truth, but what it costs to keep hiding it.

"I know what I have to do," he said, more to himself than Carmen. He stepped onto the balcony, Coleman's card in his hand, ready to trade his freedom for something bigger than himself.

"Agent Coleman, it's Vince Brown... I'm surprised that you answered. The time difference is what, seven hours?"

"I answered because I'm not in Lithuania. I'm in ya'll's neck of the woods workin' a major case."

The conversation started with Vince saying, "Listen to everything I have to say before you respond."

Agent Coleman was shocked when Vince shared what he knew about the case he was working on—specifics about the case. This got Agent Coleman's attention.

"I not only know about it, I'm ... I'm kind of involved in it. And I'm going give you the suspect... at the very least, the suspect's co-conspirator."

"I'm listening."

With certainty, Vince said, "I need a favor. And if you come through for me, you'll not only get the suspect in the diplomat's son's murder, but you get a full statement from me about the open case in Lithuania. Your case that's still open... my kidnapping."

"You're telling me... Wait, your kidnapping? I knew something was off about that. I felt it, man!"

"You get info, intel, and evidence on a minimum of two cases—major cases. And the intel I'm talking about... you'll be taking down a big chunk of the Russian mafia."

"Alright, Vince. What do ya need?"

Vince hung up with Agent Coleman after getting his word that he'd do what Vince had asked. Vince's new plan was now set in motion.

Vince rubbed his hands together, getting warm after coming in off the balcony. Carmen hadn't moved. Now she looked at him, waiting for an explanation. "What was that all about?"

"We got it. We got our in with HSI." Vince looked at the business card. "I never thought he'd go for it."

"Go for what?"

"Letting Evelina be there. And... you're not going to believe this. Letting her take him down."

"What the hell did you have to promise him, a kidney?"

Vince turned away from her. For the first time since he got back from Lithuania, he was naming himself as a fraud. "I promised him a complete statement about my kidnapping... actually, how I got into Lithuania and then staged my kidnapping."

"You're giving him a full statement? About everything?"

"Yep. Everything."

Carmen put her hands on his shoulders and turned him around to face her. The concern on her face was deep. "Vince, if you do that, you'll implicate yourself in at least one federal crime."

"I have to do it, Car... I have to do it for my dad. And for Frank."

Carmen's damp eyes showed just how concerned she was.

"Besides," Vince went on, "by the time they charge me, you will have passed your bar exam, and you can represent me!"

Their emotional embrace was held in silence. Neither had anything else to say.

Carmen looked down at the coffee table where Vince left the Rubik's Cube he had completed just before Evelina's phone call. He'd gotten up early and spent hours watching online videos on techniques to solve it.

"Except, Vince, call Evelina... now."

CHAPTER 71

CHECKMATE

The unmarked Gulfstream touched down at Atlantic City International just as the sun was setting behind the FAA Tech Center. To anyone watching, it was just another government plane using the facility. They wouldn't have noticed the Lithuanian diplomatic credentials or the small delegation of justice officials who deplaned first, led by a stern-faced prosecutor from Vilnius.

Agent Coleman met them at the bottom of the stairs. "Welcome to Atlantic City, gentlemen. Transport's waiting."

Twenty minutes later, their convoy of black SUVs pulled into the old bus depot on Arctic Avenue. The building's windows were boarded up, but inside, the FBI's SWAT team had already set up their command post, checking weapons and reviewing floor plans of Rytis Eparchy.

Coleman watched them work, remembering Vince's voice on the phone: *Listen to everything I have to say before you respond.*

"Quite the operation you've put together," Dan Perez said, joining Coleman near a table set up in the front. As assistant director of the FBI's National Security Branch, he technically outranked Coleman, but this was HSI's show. "Is your new marshal ready?"

"Should be here any minute." Coleman checked his watch. "Along with your... observer."

Perez smiled. "Lieutenant Navarro's involvement is strictly unofficial. A professional courtesy, just like Brown's deputy marshal status."

"Speaking of which..."

The veins in the chief's neck bulged when he spotted Carmen standing near the tactical gear, Vince beside her with a U.S. Marshal's shield clipped to his belt. Lieutenant Macher's step back was pure reflex, her usual smugness replaced by confusion.

"What the hell are they doing here?" Huertas demanded.

Carmen met his glare without flinching. "Following the evidence, Chief. Just like we've been trying to do all along."

"Evidence that was obtained illegally," Macher cut in. "Through unauthorized computer access and—"

"Through an international investigation involving multiple federal agencies," Coleman interrupted. "Lieutenant Navarro and Special U.S. Deputy Marshal Brown are here at the request of those agencies." He turned to Huertas. "Your department will receive full credit for its cooperation, of course."

Vince caught Carmen's slight smile out of the corner of his eye. Vindication didn't need grand gestures, sometimes a simple nod from federal authorities was enough.

The briefing was quick and precise. FBI SWAT would secure the perimeter. HSI would make the arrest. Lithuanian authorities would serve their warrant. Everything was held in the balance by one elderly woman who would spring the trap that had taken her thirty years to set.

"Endgame enters confessional at seventeen-thirty hours," Coleman concluded. "Any questions?"

Perez spoke up with a concerned voice. "What's the contingency if he recognizes her?"

"He won't." Vince's voice was steady, as he scanned the room to see if she had arrived yet. "He's never seen her face. The Rook has only ever been words on a screen to him."

"And that's what makes this perfect," Coleman said. "If this goes according' to plan, it'll be his own arrogance that's gonna take him down."

Time was nearing for the final moves of a game three decades in the making.

"You want me to wear what?" Evelina held up the Kevlar vest as if it might bite her. "Is not necessary."

"Standard protocol, ma'am." The SWAT team leader looked to Coleman for help.

"At least wear the wire," Coleman said, his voice firm but gentle. "Give us ears inside."

A slight smile came to her face. "Ah, you want to record confession?" She took the small microphone, turning it in her hands. "Like Augustas did for past year. Using confessions to hurt people, to take from them." She tucked the wire into her collar with surprising precision. "Yes, is fitting. Let him taste his own medicine."

"And the emergency signal?" Coleman asked.

"If something goes wrong, I will say 'checkmate.' Simple. Now go. Is time for old woman to pray." She turned away from them, ending the discussion.

The stone clock etched above the doors struck five o'clock precisely as Evelina entered the church, her magnetic chess set tucked into her bag, the cold wire itching her skin. A few parishioners were gathered in the church, some lighting candles, others kneeling in prayer. None of them noticed the old woman in her familiar scarf as she took a seat in the back pew.

Augustas appeared right on schedule, making his way to the confessional. Even his walk betrayed his arrogance—the way he adjusted his collar, the slight tilt of his head. His side of the booth... two inches wider than the penitent's side. Such a small thing to take pride in, Evelina thought, watching him disappear behind the ornate door.

She waited, letting the first two people in line take their turns. Her eyes drifted to the crucifix above the altar. *Watch now*, she thought in her native Lithuanian. *Watch how his own sins become his undoing.*

Outside, the FBI's SWAT teams moved silently into position. No visible radios, no hand signals, just practiced precision. The church's thick stone walls provided both concealment and cover for the agents.

At 5:25 Evelina stood, her joints making noises that announced her movement. She touched the small microphone, remembering all those who had sat in that confessional, unknowingly speaking their secrets into Augustas's recordings. Now it was his turn to speak into a hidden microphone. Her hand moved to the chess set in her bag, feeling the magnetic pieces shift slightly.

One more confession before the endgame.

The confessional's small door slid open with a squeak of polished wood. Evelina could see Augustas's profile through the latticed screen—the same proud tilt of his chin she remembered from thirty years ago.

"In the name of the Father, and of the Son..." His voice carried that familiar note of superiority, even in prayer.

"Before confession begins," Evelina said, her accent thicker than usual, "I have something to show you." She lifted the magnetic chessboard from her bag, positioning it so the light from his side caught the pieces. "You recognize this setup?"

Through the screen, she saw his head tilt even more. "Chess? You come to confession to play chess?"

Augustas started to close the small door.

"Not to play. To end game." She leaned the board slightly, making the shadows of the pieces stretch toward him. "See how rook and knight work together? Rook cuts off escape routes while knight..." She pointed to the board. "Knight delivers final attack."

"I don't understand." His voice filled with irritation. "If you've come to waste my time—"

"Skilled player would recognize Arabian mate." Evelina's voice hardened. "But you never were as clever as you thought. Were you, Augustas? Augustas Paulauska?"

His deep breath was loud enough to carry through the screen. And through the wire she was wearing. "Who are you?"

"I have message for you. From Rook."

"The Rook?" The superiority in his voice returned, hiding his unease. "Why would the Rook send an old woman as messenger?"

"Because Rook knows you never look closely at those beneath you. Even now, you make people like me sit in booth two inches smaller, so proud of such small victory." She coughed loudly. "Rook waits in parking lot. Wants to meet you face-to-face."

"The Rook..." Pride swelled in his voice. "Finally, after all these years, the Rook recognizes my influence." He sat straighter. "Tell me, does the Rook know how I've expanded our reach here? How I've built an empire that even Bratva respects?"

"Rook waits in parking lot," Evelina said.

"Of course. Where else would someone of the Rook's... status... wait for someone like me?" He chuckled. "I suppose it's time I showed the Rook exactly who runs things in Atlantic City."

"Oh yes," Evelina said softly. "Rook wants talk about everything." She touched the white rook piece on her board. "Time to make final move, Augustas."

She lifted her chessboard one last time, studying the pieces in their final formation. Outside, she knew Coleman and the FBI SWAT teams were shifting into position, closing off every escape route, just as her rook had done on the board. Thirty years of patience now condensed into these last few moments.

Time to deliver checkmate.

The monsignor's private entrance opened into the parking area behind the church. Augustas stepped out, adjusting his collar in the cold air. His eyes swept the lot, seeking any sign of the legendary Rook. Nothing but shadows and a few parishioners' cars.

"Where?" he started to call out just as floodlights rapidly lit up the lot in harsh white light.

"FBI! Don't move!"

The SWAT team emerged from their positions, weapons trained on the target. Augustas stumbled backward toward the door. But Evelina made sure it had already clicked shut behind him. His shoulders hit the cold stone wall as Coleman stepped up, badge raised in his hand.

Augustas barely flinched at the guns trained on him. His laugh echoed off the stone walls. "You dare to point weapons at a man of God? On consecrated ground?" He spread his arms wide. "This is *my* church. You have no power here."

"Monsignor Augustas Paulauska," Coleman's voice boomed across the lot. "You are under arrest."

"Arrest?" He spat the word. "Do you people know who I am? Who I'm connected to?" His eyes swept over the agents with contempt. "One phone call and your careers are over. All of you."

"This is not a U.S. arrest." A heavily accented voice cut in. Two men in suits approached him, holding up credentials. "We are with Valstybės Saugumo Departamentas, Augustas. VSD. Surely you have not forgotten about the Lithuanian State Security Department?"

VSD. Their reputation preceded them.

"Lithuania?" Another laugh, sharper this time. "I have not been in Lithuania since my transfer here nearly thirty years ago. That place has no reach here. I know judges in three states. I have politicians' private cell numbers in my phone. Your badges mean nothing."

"We have a warrant for your arrest and immediate extradition."

"No. You cannot. You cannot arrest a priest on church property."

"We can and we will." The Lithuanian prosecutor held up a document. "For conspiracy to defraud the country by working with Russian mafia in Sakiai District. Your co-conspirator, Monsignor Dominykas Klastūnas, has just been arrested there.

The color only drained from his face when the prosecutor mentioned Dominykas. Then his arrogance cracked, revealing the coward beneath. "Money laundering? Tax evasion? That's—"

"That's how we took down Capone, *Monsignor*." Agent Coleman's smile was just below the level of an evil grin. "And ya friend, Tomas Etoile... He's in our Philly office right now, giving a full confession.

Somethin' scared him enough to walk in and tell what he knows and what he did. Someone got to him."

"Etoile? He's a lunatic!" Augustas protested.

Coleman was unfazed by his objection. "So, there's gonna be more warrants from these fine gentlemen for at least two additional counts of conspiracy to commit murder."

"Wait!" Augustas's voice cracked. "I can help you. Please, I beg of you. I have information... about the Russian mafia, about government corruption. I know things about a spy that goes by the name the Rook who—"

"About me?" Evelina emerged from the line of government officials, the magnetic chessboard still in her hands. She walked slowly toward him, the ocean breeze causing her worn scarf to flutter against the sides of her face.

"No way. The Rook... a woman? That is disgusting!" His senses narrowed, studying her face. "Wait. Those eyes. I know those eyes."

"Yes, look closer, Augustas. Remember young nun at church in Sakiai? The one who lost at chess?" Her voice carried three decades of pain. "The one who watched you destroy many lives before church sent you here to hide your crimes?"

His face dropped with recognition. "Sister Evelina?"

"That naive girl died in your private chamber, Augustas. Along with so many others who suffered your 'punishments' after losing your chess games." She held up the board so he could see the final position. "A stronger woman resurrected. A new kind of woman. A woman who has learned to play better. Has become master chess player. Has learned to plan. I have planned this for long time, Augustas."

"Wait," he sputtered, turning to Coleman. "This is Lithuanian jurisdiction. You have no authority here!"

Agent Coleman looked over at Dan Perez, who was standing next to him. "Ya wanna let your girl take this one?"

"Sure. Lieutenant Navarro..."

"Actually, Augustas, we do have authority," Carmen said as she stepped around Perez. "The Doctrine of Dual Sovereignty allows foreign authorities to pursue their investigations on U.S. soil when diplomatic relations and international security are involved. The murder of a diplomat's son opened that door."

"But—"

"And once that door was opened," she continued, "everything else came pouring through. The abuse in Sakiai. The money laundering... maybe you never heard of the International Anti-Money Laundering Act?" She continued. "The exploitation of the confessional. And most recently, the murder of Father Frank, who still had dual citizenship as a Lithuanian citizen when he was killed. So, yeah, the jurisdictional authority is right in your face."

"No. That's impossible."

"Not impossible. Inevitable." Evelina said as she held up the board so he could see the final position. "Like Arabian mate, yes? All pieces in place, all exits blocked. But you do not have intelligence to recognize it." She lifted the white rook piece. "*Check...*"

"The recordings," Evelina added, smiling as Augustas looked up to the sky. "Yes, perfect timing." The sound of helicopter rotors cut through the night as news crews circled overhead. "Your shame goes viral in Lithuania, even now. Every confession recorded, every secret sold, every life destroyed—all playing on news and social media."

She knocked over his king with her rook. "*...mate.*"

"You can't do this to me," Augustas pleaded as Coleman put him in cuffs. His eyes became wide and wet. "The prisons in Lithuania... the Russian mafia... they'll kill me! I beg of you. You cannot send me to prison in Lithuania."

Augustas took inventory of the compassionless faces watching him sob, away from the perceived safety of his confessional. "Unthinkable things happen there... What can I do?"

"Ah, you have question, Augustas. Question to answers that are now known by everyone. If only you thought of question before you chose wrong side in game." Evelina tucked the chessboard into her bag. "Time to face what you've earned, Augustas."

Evelina's smile was thirty years in the making. "Dabar tu verki kaip ta kalė, kokia esi!"

Coleman laughed. "So true, ma'am. So true."

Vince spoke for everyone who heard it by asking Coleman what she said.

Coleman's smile was only half of Evelina's, but his voice was just as firm as he translated for the international collection of law enforcement agents surrounding Augustas. "She said, 'Now you're crying like the bitch you are.'"

A harsh truth shared by a dying woman in the frigid air of a church parking lot.

Coleman looked at Vince. "Go ahead, make it official."

Vince pulled an index card given to him by Coleman at the briefing. "I am Specially Deputized U.S. Marshall Vincent Brown..."

Fear pulled whatever bit of color was left on his face as Augustas had no choice but to listen to what Vince had to say.

"You have the right to remain silent. Anything you say can and will be used against you in a court of law. You have the right to speak with an attorney and have an attorney present during questioning. If you cannot afford an attorney, one will be provided for you at government expense. Do you understand these rights that I've read to you?"

"Vincentas... Vince. Why? I am the monsignor. How could you betray the church like this? Do you have any idea what they are going to do to me?"

Vince reached down and tapped the phone in his pocket, remembering the message from his dad. The text with the note his dad frantically attached. The note he deleted fearing his own department would confiscate the phone.

"Remember, what tortures you is just the beginning... I'll take that as a 'Yes,' you fucking psycho." Vince handed the card to Coleman, then stood with Carmen and watched as his former monsignor was led away.

Carmen squeezed his hand. "Thirty years," she whispered. "Was it worth the wait?"

"Ask her." Vince nodded toward Evelina, who stood watching the Lithuanian authorities secure their prisoner. Her face showed neither triumph nor joy—only the quiet satisfaction of a master chess player who had finally completed a long, complex game.

Evelina took Vince's hand and turned it palm up. "You have earned this, Vincentas. You have done good. Have avenged death of friend.... Have brought justice for your mother."

She pulled her hand away, leaving a token of their friendship in Vince's half-opened fist. A small chess piece—the king that she had just knocked over.

Then coughing slightly. "New Philadelphia," she asked. "Is across river, yes?"

"About an hour away," Carmen answered. "Why?"

"Is where many Lithuanians first settled in America." Evelina looked up at the church spires one last time. "Have always wanted to go there. Nice place for old Rook to rest. Whether from Russian mafia or from tired lungs... America will be good place to die. Final moves in land of liberty and opportunity for Rook, yes?"

Evelina smiled as she walked slowly toward a waiting federal vehicle that would take her to where she had always wanted to go.

Reporters, who had gotten several anonymous tips, gathered on the other side of the yellow police tape, the lights from their cameras casting shadows into the parking lot.

Vince looked down and laughed.

"What is it?" Carmen asked.

Barely visible among the shadows lay an empty mini bottle of Jack Daniels, probably thrown out the window of a passing car sometime earlier in the week. Vince kicked it, sending it spinning across the cold pavement. He laughed again at the perfect metaphor it represented— how his life was once spinning out of control. But like the empty bottle that had stopped spinning, so had his life. It was no longer spinning out of control.

Now it was ready to be refilled. Filled with questions to answers that will give him the wisdom to see the world differently.

As the lights from the news cameras accentuated the unique color of Carmen's eyes, Vince smiled... not just to see the world differently but to see life differently. Just for today.

"Liberty and opportunity... I hope you find it, Evelina."

CHAPTER 72
SHADES OF GRAY

The winter sunlight filtered through Rytis Eparchy of the Sea's stained-glass windows, creating prisms of color across the changes that had taken place. Sunday School paintings of childhood wonder now brightened the alcove where the confessional once stood. The front pews, usually reserved for prominent parishioners, were filled with Frank's people—the homeless, the forgotten, the ones he'd called "the real Church."

In the weeks since his arrest and the seizure of his assets and all his accounts frozen, the gaudy furnishings purchased with Augustas's extortion money had all been removed. The church was transformed back to its humble, modest beginnings when it was built more than 100 years earlier.

Vince adjusted his stance at the pulpit, wiggling his sockless toes inside his dress shoes. Some habits do indeed die hard.

His eyes found his father in the crowd—Michael Brown's first week of retirement was evident in his relaxed posture. Next to him sat Audrey, her painter's hands folded in her lap. They'd both warned him that he'd better wear socks this morning, just like they did on Christmas Eve that felt like a lifetime ago.

Vince shifted again to soften the ray of sunlight in his eyes.

Looking out from a slightly different angle, there she was—Carmen. Sitting across from Audrey, still bundled up from just walking in from the bitter February cold. Her reassuring presence a gift. She wanted to be there just as much as he needed her to be there.

"Frank..." Vince began, then stopped. He took in a deep breath and let it out slowly. "*Father* Frank used to say that genius and virtue are more often found clothed in gray than in brilliant bright colors." He smiled at the memory. "I didn't understand what he meant back then. I saw everything in black and white... life was either right or wrong, good or evil, legal or illegal. There was no room for gray. Or any shade of it."

Vince looked up from his notes, scanning the faces in the pews. He brought his attention to Carmen. He looked for the one sign he had been hoping for in their growing relationship. The sign that would tell Vince she was sure of this. But the only jewelry he saw her wearing were earrings and her mother's ring that she was so fond of. It was not to be. Not yet for her. Not today.

Vince cleared his throat. "But Frank knew better," he continued. "He understood that sometimes our deepest moral convictions can blind us to what's right. That justice isn't always found in law books, and truth isn't always spoken in sacred places."

He looked at the transformed alcove where the confessional had stood, now filled with children's artwork about who they believe God is. "This church is changing, becoming what Frank always believed it should be—a place where children's laughter replaces whispered secrets."

He looked over and smiled at Deacon Deloris, who had been assigned as the interim deacon. "Where a woman can lead us in prayer... where no one is relegated to the back pews because of who they are or what they lack."

His eyes found familiar faces among Frank's homeless congregation. "Frank used to quote Epictetus: 'Difficulties reveal the depths of a person's character.' But I think Frank revealed the depths of all our characters—by showing us who we could be when we stopped judging and started loving."

Vince touched the small chess piece in his pocket—the fallen king Evelina had given him. "An old Lithuanian saying tells us that old love never rusts. Frank's love for this community will never rust... it will never fade. It lives on in the changes we see here, in the choices we make, in the gray areas we learn to navigate. And embrace."

He thought of his resignation letter, still fresh on Chief Huertas's desk. Vince spotted him and the rest of the brass when he walked up to the pulpit. They were sitting in the farthest pew, closest to the door. "Sometimes those gray areas lead us to places we could have never imagined. I'd like to think that Frank hoped one of those places was the land of forgiveness."

Vince looked toward the back of the church, looking each one of them in the eyes. Including Macher. "Frank once shared with me the power of forgiveness. He said forgiveness doesn't mean we've condoned the actions of another. It simply means that we no longer allow those actions to control our happiness."

He brought his attention back to his loved ones. To Carmen studying for the bar exam. To Audrey, who was now leading art classes, teaching kids to see beauty in unexpected places. To his father, finally free of decades-old debt.

"Although it can be fleeting, Frank reminded all of us that happiness is a wonderful gift we can share with others without it costing us a dime. And speaking of currency... Maybe the highest reward for our labor isn't what we get from it," Vince said softly, "but what we become by it. Frank helped me, and all of us, become curious about how we can see the world in all its complex shades. That we can accept the idea... no... that we can embrace the idea that doing what's right sometimes means letting go of what we thought was true."

The tears in his eyes came without warning. He paused to wipe them away, to compose himself, to finish reading what he had written for his best friend. A best friend whose cremated remains sat on a small table in front of his photo on the other side of the chancel.

Vince glanced over at the modest pine box that contained more than his friend's remains. It also held the cremated remains of his secrets and his dreams. Vince made sure of it. His last act of love? Ensuring that not just the pages but the leather cover was also reduced to ashes after he 'donated' it to the crematorium.

"I'd like to think that Frank's legacy will include a living truth. How useless it is to hold on to our sense of morals so tightly that it stops us from doing what is right."

"So we honor Frank not just by mourning what we've lost, but by living what he taught us. By remembering that every day offers us a choice between what's easy and what's right. Between judgment and love."

Vince turned his notes over. He was given a gift today, being asked to give Frank's eulogy. *Gifts...* he remembered Frank's words. "May we all remember this when we remember Frank: The best gift we can give to those who love us, those who have invested themselves in our life, is a better version of ourselves."

The morning light had shifted slightly, sending new patterns across the church floor. Vince thought of new possibilities, of minds opening. His eyes found Carmen again, now slipping off her winter coat. There, against the soft gray of her sweater, the Baltic amber caught the light—its deep honey color glowing with an inner warmth. Their eyes met, and in that moment, he understood what Frank had always known: sometimes the most profound truths aren't spoken in sacred places, but in silent promises that kindle hope.

The church bells rang out, and Vince thought of the only other church he'd ever been in—that quaint log cabin church where he met the organist.

Deacon Deloris encouraged everyone to stand and sing together the closing hymn. Hymn number 408, "Be Still My Soul."

EPILOGUE

PRESS RELEASE
FOR IMMEDIATE RELEASE

MAUREEN'S LEGACY HOUSE OPENS DOORS TO SERVE JERSEY SHORE AREA FAMILIES

ATLANTIC CITY, NJ – Its board of directors proudly announces the grand opening of Maureen's Legacy House, a nonprofit comprehensive family support center located in the newly renovated former school building of Rytis Eparchy of the Sea Church.

The nonprofit facility, founded by former decorated police detective Vincent Brown and Carmen Navarro-Brown, Esq., offers vital services, including domestic violence intervention, adoption support, and temporary shelter for families in crisis along the Jersey Shore.

"Every family deserves a chance to heal and grow," said Navarro-Brown, who specializes in family law and serves as the organization's president. "This facility represents more than just services—it represents hope and new beginnings."

The center's first floor provides safe housing for domestic violence survivors and their children, working in partnership with law enforcement agencies along the Jersey Shore. The facility offers comprehensive legal support while courts process restraining orders and custody arrangements.

The second floor houses administrative offices and the center's innovative adoption search program. "We named it Maureen's Legacy to honor my mother, a woman I never met. She understood that family connections matter," explained Brown, the organization's founder and CEO. "Whether those connections are born of blood or choice, every child who wants it deserves the right to know where they come from and where they're going."

Future plans include career training programs and educational scholarships for homeless and food-insecure youth, developed in partnership with federal agencies.

The renovation was made possible through the generous donation of the building by Rytis Eparchy of the Sea Church and contributions from community members from all walks of life. The program itself is being funded by an anonymous foreign endowment that will allow it to run well into the future.

"This project was one of redemption," Mr. Brown said. "Twenty months ago, this building was part of a church disgraced by corruption and greed. It has been rehabilitated into something that gives hope to those who are suffering. In a very real way, it represents all of us, showing that we are all worthy and deserving of redemption—of being the best versions of ourselves."

The public is invited to meet the staff and tour the facility at an open house this Saturday, from noon until 5 p.m. The date holds special significance for the founders—it marks their first wedding anniversary.

"This project represents everything we believe in," the Browns shared. "That justice and compassion can work together, that everyone deserves a second chance, and that love can transform lives."

Media inquiries should be directed to Public Information Officer Audrey Brown.

A NOTE FROM THE AUTHOR

Dear Reader,

Now that the final words of *Moral Fractures* have been written, I want to take a moment to connect with you directly and share a bit about the journey that brought this story to life.

The seed of this novel was planted during a visit from a dear friend with whom I served at our church. We were talking about some religious stuff, and the topic of privileged conversations between clergy and laypeople came up.

After she left, I sat in the family room and did some channel surfing until one of my favorite movies, *There's Something About Mary*, appeared in the lineup. Yes, even as an ordained minister, I enjoy this type of humor. If you've seen the movie, you'll recall Mary's elderly friend who listens to her neighbor's phone conversations using a portable radio receiver. Mary, while listening to some of the conversations, said it wasn't right to hear what other people were saying.

Voilà! The two came together in my mind and the idea of *Moral Fractures* was born. During the initial outline of the book, I had a different working title... "The Confessional." However, as the characters developed, it became obvious the book was much more about them than the confessional that sparked the idea. While Vince's development is apparent throughout the book, we also see the development of the other characters. So, with everyone's morals cracking or having already been cracked, the title became *Moral Fractures*.

A little personal background so you know where this is heading: I was raised in a conservative household. My brother and I learned early that our dad did not see the world through progressive eyes. He was so conservative that when our church brought in a woman deacon (in the 1970s), he found another church to attend—a church that was more in line with his idea of "Christian values."

That conservative upbringing probably had something to do with me becoming a cop. And as a cop, you're taught that there are two kinds of people—good guys and bad guys. Twenty-five years of that thinking isn't easy to change. But luckily, the seminary that accepted me was progressive, and the walls that contained my conservative view of the world crumbled under the knowledge and wisdom that was shared there. One of my favorite topics was ethics.

Now that you know a little about me, let me share more about the development of this book. (My wife would have heard this as me saying, "I told you that to tell you this.")

Creating the characters was both a joy and a challenge. Vince's initial struggle to understand the difference between doing things right (following the rules) and doing the right thing mirrors my own journey into seeing the world in shades of gray instead of strictly black or white.

That journey was set in motion in high school when a Catholic priest challenged me to look at the world differently. It went against my conservative upbringing, but it was the first domino to fall. Father Frank's character—his honesty and genuine humility—reflects who he was and the influence this priest had on my young mind. Father Frank is half of the ingredient to a question attributed to the author of Ecclesiastes, King Solomon: "Why do the righteous perish while the wicked flourish?"

Audrey is a mixture of many students I had the honor to work with while I was a school resource officer. Their hearts were in the right place, yet the hormones in their teenage bodies wreaked havoc on their decisions. And often, they didn't understand why what they had done was wrong. But, like Audrey, they wanted the best possible outcomes for their loved ones when it was all said and done.

As far as Vince's dad, Michael, I think we all know a male figure from a previous generation who believed in not showing emotion. For me, it was my dad. Although my brother and I never doubted he loved us, neither of us ever heard him say it. The first time I told my dad I loved him was just before the funeral director closed the lid on his casket. Michael's character was the most difficult for me because it brought back so many memories and emotions.

Carmen—In all my years as a cop, I had just one female supervisor. Women have fought hard to be seen as equals in the field of law enforcement. They had to fight harder to rise through the ranks. I wanted to honor those who have dared to make it in a male-dominated field and give a name to those who have succeeded.

What about Evelina? Every good mystery seems to have an interesting spy. Every cop has informants, and every detective needs reliable informants to make cases... and make them stick. Evelina represents the best and worst of how informants can act, as well as being a critical means to take down the arrogant and malevolent antagonist.

And that's Augustas. Have you ever worked for a boss who was a real jerk? Have you ever known someone who had the hardest heart and cheated their way through life? Augustas is the other ingredient to King Solomon's question, "Why do the righteous perish while the wicked flourish?"

My writing coach suggested the chess theme between Evelina and Augustas. Her identity as the Rook was established before I researched the Arabian mate move, which uses the rook (with the help of the knight) to checkmate the opponent. It was pure luck.

And speaking of research: For every hour of writing, I spent two hours researching. While I'm sure I may have missed some things, I wanted the details to be as authentic as possible. I have never been to Lithuania, but now I feel like I could be dropped in Vilnius and feel right at home!

Why Lithuania? I hear you. I also wanted the organized crime aspect to be as authentic as possible. The Italian mob was too obvious and has been done, and done, and done. The Russian mafia is more mysterious because less is known about it. The Vilnius Brigade was a real criminal organization operating in Lithuania, and their ties to the Russian mafia fit perfectly into the plot.

This book would not exist without the support of many people. Beginning with my wife. Elissa not only encouraged me to start this project, but she also listened to me as I struggled at times (lots of times) in creating the manuscript that eventually became this book. Elissa's patience and suggestions are the reason this book was written.

My gratitude extends to my editor, Ita, who took the raw material I gave her and helped mold it into a novel. A note of thanks goes out to my proofreader, Doris, who cleaned up what I missed. I am appreciative of a special group of people in the Twelve Week Book Community who inspire and encourage me to be the best writer possible.

The first to see the manuscript were my beta readers. They offered suggestions that made this book better. Without their commitment, *Moral Fractures* would not be the book that it is. They include: Eileen, Lianne, Bill, Neha, Rich, Steve, Larry, and Michele. The phrase "Thank you" seems inadequate.

And most importantly, you—the reader—who chose to spend precious hours of your life immersed in the world of Vince Brown. I am indeed grateful for you and your interest in the character arc of Vince "Vincentas" Brown.

If Vince's story resonated with you, I would be incredibly grateful if you'd consider leaving a review on your preferred platform. Your thoughts not only help other readers discover this book but also provide invaluable feedback that helps me grow as a writer.

Thank you for accompanying Vince on his journey through the time he needed to become the best version of himself. Your willingness to invest your time in these pages means more than I can express.

With gratitude,
Rusty
March 2025
P.S. I never wear socks... not even in church.

ALSO BY RUSTY WILLIAMS

Finding Gratitude in H.O.P.E.
(2023)
"This book seems like a conversation with an old friend."

—

Cranial Constipation: Proven Ways to Let Go of Sh!tty Thoughts and Cr@ppy Ideas
(2023)
"A serious subject wrapped in humor."

—

G-Pa Has Stinky Feet
(2023)
"Delightful children's book."

—

What We Learned from Fostering Dogs: One Family's Journal of Pee, Poop, Heartache, and Unconditional Love
(2022)
"I laughed, I cried, I rejoiced!"

—

Tender Truths: Caring for the Dying (contributing chapter author)
(2022)
"A treasure trove of practical information for those facing another's death."

—

The Living Eulogy Journal: A Year of Sharing Gratitude and Becoming Happier
(2021)
"This book changes the very paradigm for embracing gratitude as a daily practice."

—

Doubt on Trial: An Agnostic Minister's Case for Questioning the Bible
(2021)
"*Doubt on Trial* is a must-read!"

—

Doubt on Trial: Jury Notes – Journaling Your Thoughts During Doubt's Testimony
(2021)
"Thought-provoking, interesting perspective on reading the Bible."

—

To learn more about other books by the author, follow this link:
RustyWilliams-Author.com

ABOUT THE AUTHOR

It's been said that an author shares much of his or her own life story in their books. So, most of what you need to know about me has already been revealed.

However, if you really want to know, here's my abbreviated CV.

I was ordained into the Christian ministry in 2008. I hold a Master of Divinity degree in Pastoral Counseling and a Doctor of Ministry degree in Church Development. I served a small community church as a youth minister until I was diagnosed with a spinal cord tumor in 2009. I now devote my time to writing and healing my mind and body through the practices of self-hypnosis and mindfulness.

People have said my entire adult life has been spent in service to others. Before starting a 25-year career as a police officer (where I retired as a detective), I entered a paramedic training program right out of high school and was, at that time, the youngest paramedic to be certified in the state. During my tenure in both professions, I was an instructor and board member for state organizations and presented workshops around the country. I am also a clinical hypnotist, working with people to help them overcome challenges in their lives. I formerly produced and hosted a national weekly radio show on mindfulness and hypnosis.

But most importantly, I consider myself the luckiest guy in the world: In addition to being a grandfather, I'm the father of two amazing men, a father-in-law to their wonderful wives, and the husband of a beautiful woman—Elissa. Because of my disability, gravity and I have a love-hate relationship. My children and Elissa have picked me up when vn—both literally and figuratively—more times than I can ...m forever grateful they are in my life.

...ia and I love spending time with our pets and enjoying the possibilities waiting around every corner of this journey called life.

I'd love to connect on social media; I post regularly on Facebook and offer weekly sermonettes on Sundays. Find me there as *Rusty Williams, Author*.

If all this isn't enough, I encourage you to visit my website: Rusty-Williams-Author.com